PRIVATE MIDNIGHT

ALSO BY THE SAME AUTHOR

Zanesville

PRIVATE MIDNIGHT

Kris Saknussemm

THE OVERLOOK PRESS
New York

This edition first published in the United States in 2009 by
The Overlook Press, Peter Mayer Publishers, Inc.
New York

NEW YORK:
141 Wooster Street
New York, NY 10012

Cataloging-in-Publication Data is available from the Library of Congress

Book design and type formatting by Bernard Schleifer
Manufactured in the United States of America
ISBN 978-1-59020-176-3
FIRST EDITION
1 3 5 7 9 10 8 6 4 2

For Ann Kovack
> *for the dark to see by*

For Evil Steve
> *for the inner soundtrack*

And with deepest appreciation to Phil Abrams,
Lyric Powers, Paul Nunns and Nel Staite
> *No one could have better collaborators*

ACKNOWLEDGMENTS

Portions of this book appeared originally in sometimes different formats in *The Hudson Review*, *The Southwest Review*, *Thieves Jargon* and *The South Carolina Review*. A recording of the chapter known as "The Memory Wound" received First Prize in the 10 Minute Play category of *The Missouri Review's* first Audio Competition.

The author is grateful to the editors of these publications for their support.

To approach the stranger is to invite the unexpected, release a new force.

—T.S. ELIOT

El Miedo

caught myself saying, "I want to be the first to know about anything that's not above board," and El Miedo said, *You would. That'd be just like you. You pussy.*

I heard a mention of "prior convictions" . . . and I didn't think suspended sentence or time off for good behavior, I thought about my convictions. I'd had infractions. I'd had warnings. I'd been written up. But convictions. . . . Had I ever had any of those? Really?

Even when I had the shakes I hadn't been as shaky as I'd been at the grand jury that morning. Coming back to the Precinct, it just got worse. The whole welter of phrases and faces. Arraignments. Bail postings. Extradition orders. Interstate flight.

I was trying to get up to speed on the Whitney case when the Captain fronted me for a chat. He called our prep briefing sessions "chalk talks," as if we were back in high school. He'd come up through Alcoholic Beverage Control and COMP-STAT—terrifically appropriate training for someone heading a major case squad like Robbery-Homicide. He looked, dressed and tried to talk like Larry King, and could recite every section of the California Penal Code. He was waffling on to me about some "regulation," when I got hand-delivered the final divorce agreement from Polly's lawyer. Their office, on her instructions no doubt, was always sending the stuff to work, so in case anyone in the station house just might've happened by some mad chance not to have heard, they'd get the picture.

And what a pretty typical picture it was. Especially for a cop. It felt like cold paper to me, but coming not long after my partner on the job had requested a transfer, it didn't make me feel so hot. Bruce Wyburn, who'd worked with me less than a year, had given me the heave-ho. A guy named Bruce, for God sakes. I signed on the dotted line and tried to focus. But I couldn't. The song had crept into my mind again. The tune. Her voice.

It was one of those obscure jazz weepers—with the kind of sentimental lyrics you hear when you're weaving out of a fern bar—the melody something a spare change saxophone would do in a tiled tunnel by a bus stop . . . always wavering and wandering, getting away from you . . . then slipping an evening-cool hand back into your pocket when you were well past. That's what it sounded like. The past. Lost secret moments that hurt you to recall and yet you longed to regain—and believed you could recapture . . . like an escaped felon . . . but only while the song lasted. As if, just beyond the bars of the music, she . . . whoever she was . . . was waiting beneath a streetlight for you. Time had changed its mind . . . summer was back for a refill and the precious sorrow was about to begin again. *"Wayward Heart . . . always leads me in danger . . . of staring fondly at strangers . . ."*

It was nothing that some goat hair and dynamite couldn't fix, but I'd taken the pledge. Not even El Miedo could scare me back in the gutter again. That made it line ball which I hated more . . . the emptiness of the weekend or . . .

. . . also referred to as . . . *perdida del alma* . . .
Susto is an illness attributed to a frightening
event that causes the soul to leave the body.
Individuals with susto also experience significant strains in key social roles. Symptoms may
appear any time from days to years after the
fright is experienced. It is believed in extreme
cases, susto may result in death . . . Ritual heal-
ings are focused on calling the soul back to the
body and cleansing the person to restore bodily
and spiritual balance.

—*Diagnostic and Statistical Manual
of Mental Disorders (DSM-IV-TR)*

THE
DARK
WAY
HOME

1

I T WAS WHAT MY MOTHER WOULD'VE CALLED A "BIG floppy" day. As in hot—brutally hot for only early May. I called it ball-sweating, and out of the scorching blue, in struts Jack McInnes. I might not have recognized him if it hadn't been for the Brut 33. Can't say what it was exactly that was different, but something. Hadn't seen him in just on a year and then he stunk into my cubicle as if I was expecting him. As if. I was getting ready to go meet Padgett to take a statement in the Whitney case. As soon as I realized that it was in fact Cracker Jack, I tried to look even busier. But I was on my guard from the get-go. Jack had this unearthly ability to start shit—to get you in over your head before you even knew it. He laid a business card down on my blotter and walked out. Not one word. I was relieved. At first. The smell of the Brut was enough to deal with. It brought back the whole dark tangle from before.

Once upon a crime we worked Vice together over in Wetworld, the street name for the Warfield district—partners in an op to take down Freddy Valdez. I'd been seconded because I speak decent Spanish. Things were cooking along

OK until Jack got a little too cozy with Raven, Valdez's favorite whore at the Jaguar House. She tipped him off to a score he could skim and wound up with a police caliber bullet in her left breast on a ruptured waterbed with red satin sheets soaked in even redder blood. A wad of hundred dollar bills that smelled suspiciously like those bags of stale peanuts they sell at the racetrack found its way into my pocket. Exactly $10,000 when I counted it over a bottle of Vat 69 behind the Chicken Shack.

The guy who set up the deal was known as the Mongoose. Whether he had a personal beef with Valdez I don't know. But he got greedy. Then Raven got her thong in a knot about Freddy dissing her somehow. McInnes caught a whiff of opportunity and cut me in before I had a chance to say no, gracias. As my oldest and pretty much only friend, Jimmie One-Leg, had once told me, "McInnes is what you could become, if you're not careful." We were shooting eight ball at Jimmie's club at the time, and I remember I almost gouged a strip in the putting green.

How much old Cracker pocketed I never asked, and whether he pulled the trigger or the Mongoose, I didn't want to know. The 10 G was my take for keeping quiet and not asking questions. The first serious felony I'd ever been party to. I'd like to think my last.

Of course Valdez was no fool. News was out on the street by the time I finished throwing up in a little park near my house. My wife Polly was just as quick, but she didn't ask any questions. Sweet Polly Purebred never did.

Two days later, the Mongoose was found with his forehead blown off, his own wiped down Colt Cobra beside him. The next day McInnes and I were sitting in a bar at Frontera and 6th waiting to meet a snitch when a Columbian in an aluminum gray suit walks in. I figured this was it. Out of towner hired to do the deed. I half wanted to let him. Then he spilled. Valdez's fat frijole heart had attacked him when he was doing the nasty with some new black chick. His contract on us wasn't going to be paid and there was actually a bit of celebration amongst the Latino Brothers about his demise. The op was a bust but we were in the clear for the moment in Wetworld, and as far as we knew, no one on the Force was the wiser. McInnes ordered a double. I vomited my guts out on the way home. The next week I went back to Robbery-Homicide and never said another word to Jack. Didn't want to see him again, and hadn't until he came in with the card. I should've thrown it out, but you can't turn your back on a guy like that. Old friends like Jack make you paranoid, if you're smart. I slipped the card into my pocket and hurried to meet Chris.

We were going to interview a fresh widow—a special breed I always enjoyed. It was usually a snap to get a squirm of submission out of them. If there was anything that wasn't kosher, they'd be working the grief show hard. And if there was any real change on the table, the squirm could be particularly satisfying, with an almost guarantee of some titty getting flashed.

Her late husband was Deems Whitney, a real estate tycoon found dead in his burned up Mercedes at a lookout on La Playa, the day after he'd fairly publicly changed his will. The new wife was still under warranty, sixteen years younger, with a nice set. The dead man's three grown kids, who thought they stood to inherit at least two mil each, not including a pleasure palace near the Gardens, smelled last week's fish.

Chris Padgett, my new partner, was 32 and still moist behind the ears. I called him Cub—as in Cub Scout. He hated that. At 49, I was doing the uncle / brother thing, teaching him the ropes. This was only our third case together.

On the surface, Whitney appeared to have committed an extravagant see-you-later. The lover's lane turnout in question commanded a good view of the harbor despite a lot of development nearby, some of which he'd played a key role in. As the event had occurred early in the morning, it wasn't surprising that the RP was a lone dog walker. According to his testimony, there was no one else around. Whitney was last seen dowsing his Mercedes saloon inside and out with gasoline. Then he slipped inside. The vehicle erupted in flames and then partially exploded. There was no evidence of any car bomb and the Forensics investigation indicated Whitney himself had lit the fire with a cigarette lighter. The thing that made it doubly hard to process was that the remains of his badly charred corpse showed that he had been chained inside the car, which going with the Forensics theory, meant that before setting the interior alight, he'd secured himself in such a way as to make exiting the car impossible. The full fuel tank had been fed with soaked wadding to try to make it blow—which it had. It wasn't any kind of suicide like I'd ever seen, and I'd seen them all, from a 12-gauge in the mouth to guys who got clever with shoelaces. DNA from the barbecue indicated similarities to Whitney—although not a direct match. Another incongruity. But with that kind of weenie roast, who knows. To my instincts, the whole thing reeked. Greed, rage, accelerants. We couldn't put anyone else at the scene and the dog walker's story checked out. Nevertheless, I found it hard to accept that a millionaire businessman with a trophy wife and no record of depression or mental illness would do himself in that way.

Then there was the revised will. He'd been remarried for five months. Why hadn't he changed it earlier if he'd wanted to be so generous? And why such an aggressive prenup? Things didn't tally. Given the significant financial motive, the new flesh was the prime candidate for further inquiry. Maybe the Forensics boys were right and Whitney had just cracked. But it didn't hurt to look a little deeper. I told the Cub Scout to take her back to the station. He told me to fuck off. I think Chris actually liked me. He was good at pretending anyway. The curvy Mrs. Whitney would lawyer up faster than she could reveal more cleavage, but as long as I kept the paperwork in order, I figured he'd slam dunk it whichever way it panned out—and he'd have learned something about looking beyond the obvious. I pulled out the card McInnes had left. It gave me the feeling—like El Miedo was awake and watching—like something was going to go down. What can I say? I'm superstitious. Always have been. You'd have been too, in my shoes.

The marriage with Polly was my second time at bat. Since leaving her and the house in Vanilla Land, I hadn't had a drink, and the only action I'd gotten was one night back in Wetworld with a butterface hooker called Echo (because she repeated every damn thing you said). Muzzle velocity was slow but I hit the target and she saluted the cannon. Still, that part of town was filled with unexploded ordnance. I couldn't face it before sundown, but I could feel El Miedo coming on. I had to do something. I found myself examining the card. It had an unexpected texture to it, slippery and sticky all at once, with just a street address on it—4 Eyrie Street, an address I recognized as being in Cliffhaven. The numbers and lettering were made of scarves—colorful silk scarves neatly curved and arranged. My first thought was that it was some high class hooker. McInnes had no doubt heard about me and Polly. Probably about Wyburn too. Maybe he was trying to do me a favor. Then again, maybe he was just trying to do me. I couldn't get a steady fix on the vibe. But I needed more female trouble like I needed another kidney stone or a subpoena. I decided to head over to the Long Room and shoot pool with Jimmie—see if he'd gone to the doctor like I'd been telling him. That old gimp could make me worry like a mother hen. Instead I found myself driving over to Cliffhaven.

The district used to have some high brow mansions, but during the War the big places got divided up or turned into rooming houses for drunks and servicemen. Now a lot of them had been chopped up into apartments or bulldozed to make way for newer high rises. In some cases, the history had just been plowed under, leaving gaping pits and vacant lots waiting for someone with enough dough, like the late Mr. Whitney, to erect another cement and glass monster.

The neighborhood had been built on a granite and sandstone escarpment, riddled with smugglers' caves it was said. Half sat up on a bluff. The rest was a nest of dwellings constructed around tunnels and cellars bored into the rocks and serviced by steep narrow stairs. Down below was a landfill spit, formerly home to Zagame's, a gangster-owned seafood restaurant that had been torched a couple of months before. The fire had swept across the car lot into Funland, one of the last great derelict seaside amusement parks, a place that was so melancholy it always cheered me up. The park had been struggling before the blaze and had been shut down tight ever since. I pulled up at the Cyclone fence and gazed at the wreck of the Scenic Railway with the huge seahorse made of plywood, and rows of shattered light bulbs. You got the feeling that if you kept watching, you could see those broken bulbs fall down into the water one by one. I took another look at the card and got a shock. The lettering seemed to have changed colors—and the stock seemed to be a heavier weight. It was little unnerving. The address was the same though. 4 Eyrie Street.

I sat in my car down by the closed up gates to Funland, savoring the residual odor of some green enchilada I'd eaten at the wheel while waiting to bust the chops of a fence over on Republic. It was peaceful watching the trash drift between the shuttered ticket booths. Padgett phoned in with a report on the widow. He was a diligent Cub Scout, I had to give him that. Wasn't his fault that his life had been such a straight drive, although sometimes he had just a little too much bounce in his stride. Like a guy striding down the fairway, and not ducking and weaving on streets of whores and dealers—spittle and grime—and things no one in their right mind would want to know about. He'd learn.

A freighter passed by in the distance—probably full of electronic gear I couldn't afford anymore. I tried to remember how I'd spent the ten grand McInnes had divvied me in for, but all I could bring to mind was a mammoth stainless steel barbecue that Polly had nicknamed the Beast. Just before I left her to the lawn nazis, I found there were mice living in it. My cell rang again. Her lawyer's secretary. The cunt. Dragging me through the dirt. I looked back down at the card again.

Jack's normal style would've been something more along the lines of "Get Horizontal at the Vertical Smile." This had an unpredictable level of class to it. But it was a hooker, I was pretty sure. It was trouble I was certain.

All the smells and feels of Wetworld came back. Sailors and cradle robbers—the girls appearing like hastily planted flowers. Runaways from Spokane . . . rebel daughters from some Main Street in the Midwest. Strippers past their use-by-date trying to hide their wrinkles.

Then out of the blue neon one summer night, there'd suddenly be this lap dance mirage. A new twilight-blonde mink with jackknife legs and marzipan boots—eyes like bits of bashed-in mirror. I slipped the peculiar card in my pocket and turned on the ignition, feeling like I'd been asleep for a hundred years.

Still, some things never change. Mondays are such damn lonely days.

2.

NUMBER 4 EYRIE STREET WAS AS DIFFERENT FROM THE Jaguar House as you could get and as close to a castle as you'd find in Cliffhaven. A cream colored villa packed in against the stone steps connecting the park at the top of the bluff to one antique streetlight down at the bottom on the ribbon of asphalt between burnt-out Zagame's and Funland. It was a solid seven figure address. I felt my Buick's tires compress against the curb and switched off my cell. I had an intuition that whatever lay inside—wherever the situation was, I wouldn't want to be taking a call smack dab in the middle of it.

There was a tall iron gate with a dragon medallion on it guarding the driveway, but it was locked without an intercom box. When I crossed the street to access the stone stairway, I saw a sliver of lawn and a clean bed of geraniums under the front bay window. I seemed to remember a poem from high school by T.S. Eliot about a madman shaking a geranium. I hated school like poison. Which is maybe why I didn't learn to hate poison enough.

I got to the narrow stack of sandstone steps—maybe two-thirds of the way to the top, with no houses below to block the view, but a demolished and partially leveled site for one on the first cross-path up from the streetlight. Above and behind I could see the scaffolding bones of some construction project, although it was hard to judge the proposed size of the building at this stage. I should've turned around and gone home. But I kept seeing the scarves that formed the address on the card. Who has just an address on a card unless it's something bent? Or very gracefully curved. I'm not the kind of guy who gets scared by some tricky card.

I opened the stiff little gate to the garden and spat out a wad of gum into the geraniums. I reached into my coat pocket for another stick as I strode up the steps—and was surprised to find a Camel. I must've not worn that coat for a while. I used to smoke like a coal plant until I quit cold. And don't think El Miedo made that easy.

The porch was swept as clean as a rich old lady's kitchen floor, and for an instant I imagined that some wealthy white-haired woman lived there. Maybe she had some private security needs. McInnes had always done freelance stuff—most of it legit, for him. He'd heavied whiplash fakes for a PI company, done personal protection, debt collection. I could handle that. I started to relax and reached in my pocket for the Camel. Then the front door opened and I saw her for the first time— but it was really more like seeing for the first time. I didn't even know I'd put the cigarette, my first in months, into my mouth. Her eyes moved on me like a pit boss.

"You can't smoke in the house," she said, and lit me up.

I dropped the cig and ground it under my heel on the welcome mat that read **Hello Goodbye** in bristle letters.

She let me pass and I caught a hint of her perfume. I couldn't place it and I've had women tell me I know a lot about perfume. But it had the expensive hint of entrapment. She closed the door behind us and we were standing in a Victorian-era entryway, gaudy and austere all at once. There was a black bamboo umbrella holder in the corner with a white parasol poking out and a rose globe with filigreed brass overhead. Polished wooden steps with a red Persian patterned runner climbed to a landing and then zigzagged out of sight. At the base was one of those Sweetheart stair elevators set into a wrought iron frame with mythological faces peering out. To the right, through French glass doors was a sitting room inhabited by a pink satin sofa with mahogany paw feet, a leather library chair and a fireplace topped by a marble mantel. On view was an original looking 18th century or so clock. Beside it was a sex toy. I figured my first assessment was dead on the money. It was starting to look like I knew where I was after all. Of course the moment I thought that, I recalled how much danger that kind of relaxation had gotten me into before. There's something about being a cop. You can't relax. Something is bound to break out right in front of you. Or behind you.

"Why are you late?" she asked, plucking out a long beige cigarette from an enameled case and inserting it in a gold holder.

I'd somehow gotten hold of her lighter and was put in the awkward position of igniting the tip of her cigarette before I gave it back. She slipped into the sitting room, then into the library chair. I heard more than saw her slap the uncomfortable looking sofa, although I couldn't work out how she'd reached over that far. It reminded me of the way you'd summon a dog.

She wasn't beautiful in any conventional way. Early 40s, maybe late 30s. Five foot eight or thereabouts . . . brunette to auburn shoulder length hair. It was hard to tell the eye color. Somewhere in the brown to hazel range. I got the feeling that she had a full sensual body but it was impossible to be sure because she was covered up in a pricey velveteen lounge suit the color of ashes of rose. Made me want to do a pat down. She wore no foundation make-up. Just mascara and Seville leather tinted lipstick. Her face, or my impression of it anyway, seemed to arrive intermittently, as if broadcast from some distance.

I tried to avoid looking at the Chinese balls on the mantel, shiny silver on a length of beaded tassel. They seemed to demean the richly decorated clock.

"I know what you're thinking," she said with her teeth clamped on the holder.

I dropped the long beige cigarette from my lips, hastily retrieving it, before it burned the Turkish rug. When had I accepted one of hers? I tossed the smoke in the grille of the fireplace.

"Then you know I'm thinking that I'm not late. I'm just here," I said. Women always think they know what you're thinking—that they know you because you're a man. Then they complain when you don't "share." Shit.

"Oh, really?" she laughed, and blew a smoke ring that circled my head like a noose. "Where would you like to be? Back in the valley with the shitkickers—and what do you call them —mojados? You're the mongrel product of two misdirected machismo cultures, amigo."

"How do you know that?" I asked.

How trumps why in my book every time. Did you get good look at the assailant? Can you pick him out of a line-up? Will you go all to pieces on the stand?

But damn McInnes. I kept trying to think what I'd told him about my past.

"You're an open book," she shrugged and went over and manipulated the window blind. The sun was still hot and ripe, like a blood orange. That freighter I'd seen before was still going past, unless it was one just like it. I suddenly felt very tired. She walked back to the library chair and sat down again.

"You're tired," she said.

"Yeah," I nodded. "I'm tired of . . ." I was going to say having my chain pulled, but when I thought about it . . . allegations, alimony, AA . . . being single again . . . yeah, I was tired of . . .

"Everything," she answered, and her voice changed. Soothing . . . like calamine lotion or aloe vera. "You want something you don't know how to ask for. That's why you're here. You've come looking for something beyond anything you could expect—or imagine."

I wanted to say something sarcastic, but I couldn't help thinking she was damn right.

"What about you?"

"You may call me Genevieve," she said and pressed down on the arm of her chair, which released a brass ashtray. She crushed out the butt. "And I'm going to call you Sunny."

"S-sonny? As in little boy . . . ?"

She pointed out the window at the tortured ball that was setting the windows on fire like lights at an accident. "S-U-N-N-Y."

My mother had called me that—before Dad died. It was weird.

"M-my name's Ritter," I grumbled.

"B-birch Ritter," she mimicked, becoming hard again. "What did kids call you? Bitch? Shitter? Switch Hitter?"

"Yeah . . ." I chuckled. "Couple of kids did make that mistake. Once."

Birch had been my grandfather's name. The kids' nickname that hurt the most was actually "Cheese Grater" on account of my acne, which set in early and checked out late.

"But you learned 'em didn't you?" she nodded, the orange-red glow filling the room but not quite reaching her face. "What do you weigh? 230-240? With hands like meat slabs."

"I w-was a wrestler in school," I said—not sure why. You can't blame a guy for being big. I hadn't eaten myself there. I was born that way. At least I had a good head of hair.

"A way for you to be intimate and violent with other boys without calling attention," she said.

I let that pass. When it comes to looks, I have all the sex appeal of a bar code. The acne scars didn't help, but all that oil had dried up at last, just like my self-esteem when I was a young buck. As a grown man what women liked about me was my size, the sheer don't-mess-with-me bulk. Didn't always work—but that's what fists and 9 mm's are for. Yes, I'd had a few biffs on the chin and my jaw and nose broken more than once. But I never ended up in the ICU on a respirator. Other men had.

"You chose police work because of the violence. The same reason you joined the Army before that. You thrive on violence, Sunny. But only if it's approved. Like wrestling. You need an arena, a badge. Sanction."

The sunlight was starting to make me hot and itchy. Where was this broad headed?

"And you were attracted by the gear, the equipment. The uniforms. The weapons. You like the power, but you *adore* the objects and implements. You appreciate textures. Steel. Vinyl. Rubber. Velvet."

"Is that why you think I'm here?" I asked. "You some whips and chains gal?"

"Sunny, you're already so chained up, I doubt you'd notice any others," she answered softly. "You're here, as I told you, because you want to see life through a new window."

"Well," I shrugged. "I'm not liking the view from here."

She stood up and unzipped the lounge suit, which fell away onto the floor, where I saw she was barefoot. Why hadn't I noticed that before?

She was stark naked underneath. Heavy well-formed breasts with unusually large nipples, but a narrower waist than I'd have thought. Punishingly narrow. And skin that seemed much too clear and tight for a woman her age. Didn't seem right.

"I still don't like the view," I gulped and tried to get up off the sofa. Talk about a well-trimmed lawn.

"Then you must be blinded," she smiled.

That does it, I thought. Door time.

"Not permanently," she laughed, and then from under the chair she pulled out a yellow scarf made of raw silk with a delicate fringe on the ends. It was like the scarves on the card, the invitation that had lured me there.

"Sure," I snorted. "You tie that around my head and then what? I end up with a knife at my jugular?"

"Is that what you'd like, Sunny?"

"Stop calling me that."

El Miedo was starting to close in. A claustrophobic amputated feeling.

"I can do something you can't imagine. You're trying but you can't. I could send you out that door right now, and it would drive you wild. Not knowing."

I managed to rise.

"I could send you away, Sunny. But that really would be cruel. Worse than any whip—or branding iron."

The mention of a branding iron got me. Why was the sun so fierce? It was like an alarm that wouldn't stop blaring.

"Do you know what the scarf smells like?" she whispered, snaking out her arms and passing the fabric slowly between her legs.

"Jesus," I breathed.

"He left earlier. But he's coming back."

I tried to grin. "So, you're just going to blindfold me. And then I'll tell you . . . what I . . ."

"You don't need to say anything. And you don't listen well enough yet to hear me."

"I don't get it then," I shrugged, and realized I was sitting back down on the sofa.

"That's why you want to stay. Why you will stay."

Her voice worked like cortisone on an achy joint.

"Do I take off my clothes?"

She solemnly shook her head. "Another time perhaps. I already know exactly how you look. You think I'm naked, but it's really the other way around."

I felt my heart beating hard under the pistol in the shoulder holster beneath my coat.

"You can keep hold of your gun," she said. "All you have to do is sit here with the blindfold on until the sun's gone down."

"I'm not sure that's ever going to happen," I said, trying to get comfortable.

"Oh," she trilled. "Even I can't stop the sun from setting."

That struck me as the oddest thing she'd said yet. "All right," I agreed. "No tricks."

She gave out a hiss of breath and stepped toward me with the scarf stretched between both hands. I wanted to reach out and pull her down to me. For us to roll on the Turkish carpet with all that sunset bleeding off the walls. Instead I let her bind the scarf around my head. The touch of her hands on my worn face was like morphine. Coming up to my high school prom, I'd overheard the hot pompom slut Bridget Clovis say to her friend, "That guy looks like he's been kissed by a wasp's nest!" I can still hear the way they laughed.

Suddenly my eyes were sealed in a yellow fog that then went totally black when the knot was tied. This woman, who called herself Genevieve, stood before me. Voluptuously nude. Scented. Then I heard the clicking of those silver balls that had been sitting on the mantel, and her footsteps pad softly out of the room. I got this wavy feeling, as if I was walking out after her, even though I remained seated. As if I was slipping out of that fancy room into someplace else altogether.

3

I FELT LIKE I WAS IN A HOLDING CELL, ONLY IT WAS INSIDE my own head. There was something a little spooky about this babe, normal rich witch sitting room and all. That made it more somehow.

I don't know how long I sat there waiting for something to happen. Waiting for her to come back. Or for some boyfriend or pimp to split my head open. All I was aware of at first was the scent of the scarf and the thudding of my heart. Gradually my pulse steadied and turned into the ticking of the clock. An insistent but reassuring sound. I kept trying to picture how the light was changing on the walls. Whether that freighter had finally passed.

I saw the trash skittering in Funland. McInnes' face in a cloud of Brut. I heard that song of Stacy's, playing on my mind like the smell of jasmine when you're trying to sleep. It seemed long ago and hearts away, and yet still deep inside.

I was never going to be free of her. Or Polly. I saw her folding my underwear. The patience of that woman. All my nights of rocket fuel and Trojans. It made me sick to think that maybe she hadn't put up with me out of weakness or fear of being on her own—but out of love. With the blindfold on, I could actually look at it up close. Over the years, I've beaten people stupid—in garbage can lanes behind topless joints—in jail cells, toilet stalls and the back seats of cars. Some scumbags would rather burst open all over you than tell the truth. I thought of all the times I'd come home to Polly with the odor of the streets on me. Not because it was my job. Because I went looking. That was my truth. Because I was restless and empty and couldn't look her in the eyes. I dropped the dime on myself every time I went home.

The moistness of the silk wasn't evidence I wanted to process. I wanted to rip the thing off my head. But I couldn't. There was something about this Genevieve. Conversing with her was like looking down the sights of an assault rifle while getting a Geisha footrub. It was clear she talked a good game, but something in my gut told me she played one too. How serious could it be? I was just sitting there with a scarf over my eyes.

Eventually, out of the darkness came another face. All that darkness . . . a lot of faces. This was one I hadn't thought of in a long time—or maybe I had just gotten the hang of not thinking about him finally. Frank Lockett.

We'd known each other since grade school. His older brother Jake had been kind a hero of mine—worked for my Dad. Dad had taught him the building trade and was one day going to make him a partner. They were what you might call "close." A very special relationship as it turned out. But they got into a fight just before my Dad died. Jake skipped town, never to be heard from again. He had a problem mixing Black Beauties and red wine. I suspect he came to a bad end. Frank grew up with me and we stayed buds.

In a kind of jigsaw way, he was why I'd become a flatfoot (I've always loved that term—makes me think of Cagney). While I was always trying to win trophies and have girls want me, Frank didn't care what anyone else thought. Other guys like me were lucky to cop a feel let alone fiddle the bean—but he pulled chicks without even trying. He lived his own life and did the hard yards taking care of his drunk old man after his mother died.

He was as thin as a tailpipe, but tough. Knew everything there was to know about cars. He was restoring a '32 roadster and a '39 coupe, and he put a lot of love into those hunks of metal—always debating whether to cad plate certain bolts or buff grind them. I was curious about where he got the money for his habit. I sensed it involved something illegal. I was right.

One afternoon he let me in on his secret. He paid for his love of old cars by stealing new ones. He'd started off joyriding—like sneaking inside other bodies. He collected the bits and pieces he found in the cars he borrowed. Stuffed animals, fuzzy dice, photos—whatever he came across he built into this altar hidden in his closet. I remembered my awe and anxiety looking at it. It seemed like something I shouldn't have been allowed to see. But people have always made a habit of showing me things I don't want to see. It started back when I was still wetting the bed.

The trouble was his old man was on the serious skids and they needed money just to get by, let alone afford a hot rod jones, so Frank turned his private ritual into an enterprise. He worked out a deal with a chop shop in Tijuana. Pretty soon he got addicted to that too. You know how it goes—it started with a little but the little wouldn't do it, so the little got more and more.

One Friday, he stopped me by the lockers and said it was time for a "road trip." There was something else I had to see. Naturally, I was scared. I was a shoo-in for the State Finals in wrestling. I had a B+ average. I looked like a good shot for a scholarship and a chance to get out of our drag race valley town for good. But I was curious then just like I am now. A sucker, if you want to call it that—always a sucker for the dark low ride. Besides, he'd trusted me with a look inside his deepest hiding place.

We drove his street car, a 1968 supercharged Plymouth Duster down to San Diego, where he did most of his "shopping." He'd done a scout mission two days before and had his target in sight—a BMW in for emission control at a big chrome boneyard by the railroad tracks. I waited by the Cyclone fence, keeping watch. He cut the lock and was into the car and back out the gate before the Doberman or the night guard even knew. He'd learned his trade well. Then we parked his car across town and drove across the border in the Beemer . . . me scared as a girl.

We went straight to this warehouse garage on the east side. Stifling hot even before sunrise, with soccer posters on the walls and statues of saints beside Tecate beer cans . . . coverall legs thrusting out from under bumpers in grease pits, engine blocks hanging from chains . . . paint nozzles jetting and all these somber and sometimes face-masked Mexicans cutting and stripping steel and attaching license plates.

Frank got me involved, haggling with a burly cat with a Zapata moustache in Spanish instead of gringo inglés. Truth was his Spanish was better than mine. We ended up with a tight roll of American cash and a powder blue Maverick with an Arizona tag to go back over the border. But we didn't go back. We bought a bottle of tequila and headed south with the sun coming up.

"Is that what you wanted me to see?" I said when we finally stopped for a leak.

"Hell no," he said, looking at me blankly. "That was just business."

So we drove on. It was starting to get really hot. I was praying the car wouldn't break down, or we wouldn't get nailed by the Federales. We just drove. Stopped off at this gecko scurrying cantina for pepper soup and beers. Slept a little in the car with the windows down. Then back on the road. I kept waiting to find out what he wanted me to see.

About two miles south of the turn-off for the beach, we hit an unpaved road leading into the hills toward a hot springs. Frank got me to drive. A mile later, he said suddenly, "It's right behind you. Stop the car and then look up real slow, man. It's in your rearview mirror."

So I looked up. It was the first time I'd ever seen a glimpse of El Miedo in the presence of someone else. This time it took the form of a long red-brown tunnel of dust behind us. I knew on one level that it was just the backfly from our tires, but it had taken on the shape of a living thing . . . dust drifting in the glare . . . seeking. A minute later it had vanished completely, as if we'd never driven down the road. As if we weren't really there at all.

"Did you get it?" he asked.

"Sí," I said, not knowing if he could even begin to imagine what I'd really seen—what it meant to me. Maybe he did. I was friends with him for a reason. That's something I've learned a hundred times and all the hard way since—everyone you know you know for a reason. So, you better find out what it is.

Frank told me we were going to Mazatlán, and we drove all the way there in that powderpuff Maverick, drinking tequila and listening to mariachi on the radio. It was like some heat shimmer illusion. Rattletrap chicken buses. Adobe alleys choked with burros and goats. I can't remember if we slept in the car overnight or not—but we arrived at dusk on the beach with the lights of fishing boats bobbing out beyond where the waves were breaking. Frank bought a cigar-sized joint off a boy without a shirt on and perfect white teeth. The dope was dark pungent green with black hairs in it, laced with local opium. We ate tortillas with spicy fish and beans cooked off a stone stove by a full-blooded Indian woman. Then he led me up through a mudbrick arcade where a marimba band was playing, to this old hotel painted seashell pink . . . a white satellite dish mounted on the tiled roof and little paper lanterns swaying on the balconies.

We were greeted at the door by a silver-haired don dressed in a Monte Carlo suit and a Panama hat, and offered rum and cokes with thick lemon wedges on a verandah upstairs overlooking the sea. Slowly, the girls appeared, like night-blooming flowers. Frank chose this obsidian-eyed Aztec. I was left in a quandary, nervous and blazed. My mother and stepfather didn't know where I was and would've died twice over if they did. I'd put everything I'd worked for at risk. But I was having a great time. And that's when things got wiggy. One by one the other girls filed out, and I thought for a second I'd done something wrong or offended them. Then she appeared and I knew instantly it was the real lady of the house. Our host.

She was dressed in a matador's traje des luces, the suit of lights, with a flamenco dancer's hat. She approached me like a cat, her shadow sweeping across the prickled arms of the cacti in their ceramic planters. She tossed her hat down at my feet. I stooped to pick it up, and when I rose to look into her face, I saw it was a mask of fiesta make-up—heavy, lurid. Her long dark hair was streaked with white—she was older than the old man who'd let us in.

In her mouth was a rose with thorns as sharp as the spurs on a fighting rooster. She wore polished leather shoes and had a length of braided cowhide hitched to her waist with a scarlet ribbon. She clapped her hands and a dwarfish little hombre in a white suit brought in a tray with a bottle of mescal and two glasses. She motioned for me to sit down at a wrought-iron table. She took the rose from her mouth and plopped it down. Then she poured two shots. We drank in silence, me trying to listen to the waves and not look her in the face. Meanwhile she kept her eyes on me. I could feel it—both of them burning through that mask of make-up. I wondered if Frank knew this was happening. Something else he'd wanted me to see. A set-up?

After we'd had two shots . . . the last faint plinks of the marimba band fading out in the street . . . the old gentleman brought in an antique wind-up Victrola with an elephant-ear speaker trumpet, and cranked it up. Tango music. Scratchy and melodramatic. The woman stood and flipped the rose into her mouth and snapped her fingers. I'd never even slow danced at high school parties. The old man came back to wind up the machine again. The music played on. Our shadows stalked across the tiles.

She didn't care that I had bad acne. She had lines and troughs. How the rose got in my mouth I don't know. Then she kissed me, and I felt the sharp barb of one of the thorns puncture my skin, the bittersweet iron taste of blood coming after the mescal. Alone in a glazed pot on the tiles was one particularly bulbous cactus. She pointed to it, and then made a rude gesture and laughed. The old man was standing in the doorway. He saw it all. I knew then she intended for a lot more to happen than a dance. I hadn't chosen one of the girls, I'd been chosen by her.

She led me down a paneled hallway into a plastered chamber lit by a wall of candles like you'd find in a Catholic church. Across from it was a mahogany bed with lions carved in the posts and an enormous wicker bird-cage on a three-legged stand. Inside the cage was a lime green parrot. It seemed to be staring right at me, accusingly.

It was like being with some ghost come back to prey upon a young man. The candles became blades of fire, and through the window I could hear the tango music. We seemed to swim through animal heads . . . pinwheels spinning in a parade of burning matadors—and then I exploded like a piñata—gored and released at the exhausted same moment.

It was only the third time I'd had sex. If that's what it was. Then we lay there, watching the wax drip on the parquet floor, and she ran her old hands through my hair and whispered dark, crazy things to me in Spanish, although it sounded like the pages of some leather-bound book turning in the breeze out on the verandah. Then I about jumped out of my skin when I felt this creature leap up onto the bed and claw me. It was a Chihuahua with a beaded Indian collar that said PICO. I tried to toss it off the bed, but the old woman slapped my face and cradled the dog to her saggy breast. Suddenly, the entire scene that had passed between us came back to me, clear and horrifying. She laughed and chucked me a lace comforter that had fallen on the floor. Then she said in knife-sharp English, "Go sleep out on the balcony. I've finished with you."

I felt my fists clench, I'll tell you. She just laughed as if there was a joke I didn't see. Confused and ashamed, I grabbed my clothes to storm out, when my eye caught the parrot cage. I went over to slam it against the wall—but all that happened was the green bird tipped off its perch and fell on the bottom of the cage. It was stuffed. The old woman roared with laughter.

The next morning I woke up groggy and cold on the beach below, fish nets drying on a rope beside me. Frank came and found me about an hour later and we went for café con leche in a little place around the corner. Then we started on the long road home. We never said a word about that night the whole way back to San Diego. And nothing was the same after that.

Two weeks later Frank died in a stolen car outside National City. He'd been spotted by police. He got chased and rolled over an embankment into a concrete retaining wall. He'd always lived a toda madre. Me, I went on to fail two courses and lose my Semi-Final match. State University, medals, ribbons—everything I'd hoped for dematerialized—just like that cloud of dust. El Miedo haunting me, looking for another form to take.

Sitting there blindfolded, in Cliffhaven, more than 30 years later, I saw it distinctly. My old life had ended with that trip. What grew instead was a garden of failure and luminous broken things. A fixation on crime and a fear of it. Anger and lust that couldn't tell each other apart—and a doomed sense that it didn't matter anyway. The candles would burn, the waves would break and the cloud of dust would disappear behind you no matter what. And then find another way to get to you.

I took off the blindfold and Genevieve was standing there, fully dressed. I suspected she'd been close, watching me for quite a while, just like that parrot. Only she was so very real. I rose, as stiff as I'd felt that morning on the beach. At least the sun had set. The lights of the harbor shone through the window.

"I knew you would be a good pupil, Sunny," she said. "Despite appearances, you have a real imagination."

"I won't be back," I said brusquely.

"You can't return Sunny," she replied. "If you never really leave. And you won't really be leaving now . . . because your need is too strong. Somewhere back in your little boy hard-as-nails cop head, where you're really frightened and alone, you know that what you're chasing can't be found unless you face yourself. I'm going to help you do that. No matter how much it hurts or frightens you."

"Why me?"

"I like the look of your dark," she said. "It calls to me."

I noticed that there was music playing in some other part of the house. Tango music. It was just a coincidence I figured, but it still upset me. Just like the silk pajamas she was wearing, that reminded me of a matador's suit. She turned on her heel and swept down the hall to wherever it was she'd gone before. The tango music wafted after me across the patch of lawn.

The street was vacant and my footsteps echoed on the steep pavement. I seemed to see the night like infrared heat images— but by the time I got to my apartment I thought I'd wake up, go to work and everything would be back to normal, even the emptiness.

The trouble was I reached into my coat pocket. I had my keys in hand already, but my right hand dove into the pocket without me even thinking . . . and pulled out . . . a little dog collar that had the word PICO spelled in white beads.

Ten minutes later I was shaking out in front of the Liquor

Mart. Antabuse or not, I drank with both hands. I tried as hard as hell to chuck the collar in a trashcan, but I couldn't damn well do it. I dumped the pack of Camels I bought instead. I knew if I didn't have the collar when I woke up, I'd have something worse than El Miedo to be afraid of.

4

ALL NIGHT I WAS SICK AND SWEATING. BUT THERE'S something strangely therapeutic about staring into a toilet bowl, and I should know—I've done a lot of it. I felt like I'd been ground through the hamburger and broken glass of a lot of years. Things I hadn't thought of in a long time came back to me with unusual clarity. Simple, foolish things. Like back in first grade . . . when we'd lie outside on hot days during our Quiet Time. Frank, me—five or six of us, boys and girls. We never did anything blatantly childish like pointing out the animal shapes in the clouds, unless there was a really flagrant ostrich or fish—a dragon or a whale. We just lay very close, the warm pale grass worn to soft dirt beneath us. Sometimes Sims O'Driscoll would lie about how his father had beaten him up the night before. We'd listen and nod, and go back to studying the sky. Nobody knew where to find us. For a little while, no one even thought to look, all of us lying out in the open in what might've been a small field.

What I wouldn't have given to be back in that field, even for a moment. I was sure as shit glad I'd hung on to the collar.

It was still there when I went to examine it over black coffee. The tango music and the matador looking pj's could've been just a coincidence. The dog collar was something else. Something to hang onto. Sort of anyway.

I had a twenty minute hot shower and then went for eggs and smoke-link sausages at Cheezy's. I needed to refuel and my stomach seemed inclined to let me get away with it. Over the feedbag, I checked my voicemail from the night before. Four messages. Cub Padgett, being a good Scout, wondering if I was OK, and a guy named Brewster, an informant whose cover had been blown back when he was helping out me and Jack. I'd sent him off to Salt Lake City. He was just reporting in. Said he'd gone straight. They always say that. I texted him BOL and deleted the number.

It was Cracker Jack who'd wised me to the text message lingo. All his snitches and contacts, from bookies to love dolls, had code names. DV8. G9. TIAD. FYEO. And they all communicated in this dyslexic kindergarten finger-speak. Jack's favorite text response when one of the under citizens would reach out for some advice was IANAL, *I am not a lawyer*.

It was a good thing he clued me in because my card had been passed through those circles too.

BM&Y, I think it's pretty moronic, but it had come in handy with Polly, BC she had no head for the stuff and that made things a little safer if she ever had a peek at my phone and I hadn't scrubbed a message. I think she always figured every signal that ever came through had the smell of crotchless panties to it, or was about some line of toot for a pigeon. She couldn't understand that a lot of the calls and texts I got off-duty were from people who needed my help. Not the kind of uniformed help you can ask for openly. Real help. Like Terry, one of our old dispatch supervisors, who'd get walloped every time her ex-hubbie went off his meds. A lot of victims can't go through legit channels for a lot of reasons, and in my line you end up owing and being owed a lot of favors. That's just how it is. "Why can't you be friendly with normal people?" Pol always asked me. I never had an answer for her. I couldn't say if it was the cop work or something inside me. When the feverbeast was loose inside me and the ravenous need for anonymous sex came on, I always forgave her the distrust. I deserved it.

The third message was some telemarketing survey. The fourth message was just someone listening. Private number. Could've been anyone, but you know who I thought it was.

I bought a *Sentinel* and did a quick scan of the crime reports. The news had leaked about the new wife's windfall as a result of the "Mercedes Inferno" and there was a file photo of a pre-scorched Whitney. He looked like The Racketeer in that old game Lie Detector, only decked out in a Pal Zileri suit. It made me think of Padgett.

Chris was young and extremely good looking. A whiskey brown welterweight Most Likely to Succeed from the strip mall side of town. He'd been raised an only child by a large-and-in-charge mother when his skirt-chasing pop ran off to Reno with some gold lamé mutton dressed up as lamb. Now he looked like a lifeguard with his eyes on the prize. He never walked into a room when women didn't turn their heads. And yet men couldn't hate him because he was so damn likable. I'd heard locker room rumors that he'd picked up the name "Coke Can," but being more of a grower than a shower myself, I couldn't vouch—I try to keep a low profile around naked men. But it wouldn't have surprised me if he was big in the pants. He had all the luck.

It would've been nice to be to do some buddy things with him outside the job. Go to Big Dog and have a rootbeer float—I knew he was as sober as a nun—I respected that. Maybe the go-karts. I'd always had this dream of having a son and taking him to the go-karts. But I was embarrassed about hanging with him off the clock. His future was too bright to chaw the rag with the likes of me on his own time. Funny thing is, I think he thought I was too good for him.

His new wife Tabbie was a Gucci do-gooder. She was cur-
rently working as a Public Defender, but she was a Yale grad-
uate who'd done her law degree at Boalt. She looked like a
vegan version of Jennifer Aniston and she wore too much
White Linen perfume. Her father just happened to be
Humphrey P. Moran, the District Attorney, who had well-
known schemes for a much bigger political career. (His handle
on the Force was "Humphrey Dumpty," on account of him
being short, bald and far too well-tailored for an elected official.) I think the Botox mother's people manufactured thumb
tacks or something back in Illinois. The box score? Chris the
Cub had married well and his future looked rosy to golden, but
from what I'd seen, he was stand-up in every way.

Still, while I was flattered with being given the charge of
taking him under my wing, I wasn't so doddery that I didn't see
there might've been a hidden agenda. There almost always is. I
had a few question marks against me, the odd reprimand—and
one very formal review. My record was clear officially, but you
can't do this job as long as I had without making enemies
behind both kinds of bars—and on the bench. He could've
been assigned as my partner to keep an eye on me. I tried to
put the private mystery of the day before out of my mind and
headed to the boiler room.

Another day in the telephone jungle. More like the inside
of a cuckoo clock rigged with testosterone and C4. You've seen
the sorts of offices on TV and in the movies. That's one thing
they get right—at least where the places are crappy. Everything
new fangled and high tech was somewhere else in the system.
Ours was an old building with an old building smell of ceiling
tiles that needed replacing, stained boxes of Chinese food remnants and photocopier ink. Then there was the human odor of
plastic combs left too long in back pockets. Mennen's. Milk of
magnesia. At first glance, it was more like the News Room of
a failing city paper than what you'd think a den of detectives
should be—until you noticed Hatcher's Table of Relative

Stopping Power tacked up, or the poster that said **Read them their rights. Know your responsibilities.** You'd see a notice board and roster sheets, then on another wall, wanted posters of interstate and Federal criminals at large—and the time and place of the next professional development training seminar "Effective Management of Physical Force," to be followed by what would be a much more popular one entitled "Electronic Surveillance Technology Update."

The waiting area looked like something you'd find in a barrio medical clinic except for the framed photograph of our glorious Governor, and, I'm pleased to say, a larger portrait of Darko, the bomb squad's star German Shepherd, our mascot and patron saint.

One thing you wouldn't find is any doughnuts. You may think cops and doughnuts go together like doctors and nurses, but not in our house. We were committed to the bearclaw and the cinnamon bun—from Nelly's two doors down. Even the beat boys working out of the engine room on the ground floor had taken the oath. Dunkin' Doughnuts only for coffee. We were loyal to Nelly's to a man—and we were mostly men. Only three gals of consequence would be seen in our clubhouse. One looked like a bull mastiff and kept the gears turning at reception. One was a pint-sized crème brunette named Colby with more plenty stand-tall than her partner Strothers knew what to deal with—and the sharpest PMT tongue you've ever heard. The third was a n00b nicknamed Phat, a former Pennsylvania State Trooper with a rear end that always looked like it was in a four-wheel slide. The word was she was impressive in the field and had both attitude and the right attitude to get by. "None of you are gettin' within six inches of this bubble butt." I liked her style, almost as much as her ass.

I logged in to find Chris already on deck—looking like he'd had a roll in the hay with his wife before a close shave and a healthy fruit and fiber breakfast. He gave me the usual "Buenos días," and then pointed to another envelope from

Polly's lawyer. "El regalo es para usted."

That was his special gimmick with me—always trying out his spic. It sort of pissed me off, but it was his way of trying to buddy up. He thought I knew it because I came from a melon patch. It was true I'd grown up between the wetback shacks, Okie tractor sheds, and holy roller radio trailers out in the valley. My first clear memory was a train of Southern Pacific Golden Pig flatcars chaining through a field of rapeseed. But the real reason I'd picked up the lingo was because my mother was half Hispanic, a very light-skinned well spoken lady, and she made me and my sis Serena learn it. It was about my only skill outside the job, but it often came in handy. And it was a way to fool around with Chris. I called him a bolillo.

After the briefing session, it was clear he'd taken my lecture to heart on not letting the opinions of the lab boys speak louder than gut intuitions. He was fired up about the Whitney-cide being a cleverly staged murder, but the wife had an airtight alibi for the time of both the husband's disappearance and his death. Now his gut was saying there was someone else involved, and given the nature of the crime, he figured it had to be a male. I wasn't sure I was ready to follow his lead so soon, but I couldn't say squat since I was the one who'd wound him up. Besides, I was grateful for anything to take my mind off the fragrance of that scarf and the thought of the dog collar. I couldn't work out how she'd pulled that off. Magic.

The Cub Scout pulled out a half-page of notes. If we were going to pursue it, there were two strong possibles: the widow's ex-boyfriend, who ran a trucking business on the west side, and her brother, a guy named Spencer, who was of all things a "chocolatier," the head technologist at Dilley's. I didn't even know Dilley's Chocolates still existed. Hadn't seen a box in years, but then I despised chocolate. All the women I'd been close to loved it—worshipped it—talked about it like it was sex. We agreed to divide and conquer. "I'll take the trucker," Chris volunteered. He didn't know how much I hated chocolate.

The Dilley's factory was on the other side of the harbor. The day was hot so I decided I'd skirt the traffic and take a ferry. I hadn't been out on the water for a while and the view of the city I thought might bring some clarity regarding both the current case and Genevieve—and I needed to clear my head of her big time. All of the commuters were already in town, so the passengers were mostly tourists, old people, a school field trip, and a couple of oddball loners. If it weren't for my size, people would probably say the same about me. I was just start-ing to wish I'd brought my camera to snap a few pics of the abandoned Grain Terminal when the entertainment started.

Some city arts administrator had gotten the brilliant idea to hire young people and street performers to put on "shows" on the ferries. So now, instead of a little quiet in between cell calls, I was inflicted with a nutty open air song and dance act. These kids were all dressed up as hobo clowns. They kept popping off their crumpled porkpie hats, singing this ninny song, *"Living in the Hobo Jungle . . . you never know who you'll meet . . . living in the Hobo Jungle . . . there's never enough to eat . . . But we get by! But we get by!"*

Edwards, the desk jockey on duty at the station house, rang twice for the stupidest reasons, but what really irritated me was one of the hobo clown kids. He kept sidling up to me, even when I made it clear, in case he hadn't noticed, that I had 30 years, half a foot and 75 pounds on him. I even buzzed him and let him see the roscoe. No muss, no fuss. I wondered if he was high. Then, at one point, when he was up against me, I noticed something.

He had a tattoo on his forearm. At first I thought it was just a cartoon picture of an old man swinging a hatchet. Then I realized who the old man was. It was a caricature of Gandhi. Mahatma F'ing Gandhi. He had the sort of enraged expression on his face that Elmer Fudd would get when Bugs would get the drop on him, waving a tomahawk over his head. The thought of peaceful Gandhi finding his inner Elmer Fudd cracked me up. It almost made up for that damn song and the kid's schiz behavior. The ferry arrived on the other side and the clowns started passing their hats. I didn't make a contribution and got off quick.

Another call on the cell. I thought it might be her. I knew she had my number. She had my number all right. It was Harris at central booking. What a pansy.

The terminal on the other side gave immediate clues as to why civic officials felt the need for distracting entertainment en route. There weren't enough garbage cans. Not nearly enough. In fact, the only one in sight was overflowing with rancid fish and chip remains and Styrofoam coffee cups—probably writhing with bacteria. A couple of seedy men loitered in overcoats they didn't need on such a warm day and enough graffiti covered the walls to make a single woman nervous at night. It put me in a bad mood, coming after that kid.

I was going two blocks up, past the old lighthouse and gunnery memorial. There was a tavern on the corner and I seemed to remember a morning in there years before, putting out a private fire with five or six cold beers while I watched my pager vibrate off the bar like a wounded insect. I saw a guy in the window that I made for one of ours raising a glass as I walked by. That's why I never went back. Good troughs for day-play don't advertise whose snouts are in. You have to get your feet wet to find out who's in residence. I half felt like ducking in and giving him some words of wisdom, but he might've tried to buy me a round—and I might've taken him up on it.

The hill puff was good. Got the ferry ride out of my head . . . and the garbage can . . . and helped me concentrate on the questions I wanted to ask Spencer. I knew I was getting close when I saw a bunch of Central Americans wearing white dust jackets and hairnets. They were on a cigarette break, leaning against the wall of a turd-brown building with a new Lexus parked in the one reserved spot out the front. There was the stomach curdling smell of chocolate in the air. Reminded me of the old Susie Homemaker Oven my sister got for Christmas. I hit the intercom at the main door and got let into a reception area. The "technologist" came down a flight of carpeted stairs about a minute later, dressed in a white coat and hairnet just like the working stiffs. I was pleased to note a cardboard sign over the steel doors that led to the factory floor that read REMEMBER TO WASH YOUR HANDS AND PUT ON NEW GLOVES. They were, after all, making a kind of food. From all the merchandising around the place, you'd have thought they made toys. There were teddy bears and stuffed love hearts everywhere.

Spencer seemed PO'd but not worried. He led me into a conference room with a whiteboard and a table covered in candy boxes. Through the open door I could see into another room occupied by a disturbingly large foil Easter Bunny with a demonic smile. Enough to scare the shit of out of any kid. What were they thinking?

"I thought you guys had gone out of business," I said to break the ice.

He still had his hairnet on and gave me a technologist's frown.

"Dilley's dates back to 1919. We're an institution, and we do OK as a premium gift item, and bulk stuff for special occasions."

"Like Easter," I said, nodding at the demented bunny.

"Christmas, Valentine's. We've just had a pretty good Mother's Day. It's either flowers or chocolates. Did you get your mother something?"

"My mother's dead," I answered.

"I'm sorry to hear that," he said.

"She choked on a Crème d'Orange. You still make those?"

She hadn't really. She died of a heart attack while watching an old movie. Or you could say she died of a broken heart. Take your pick.

"Some people just can't get enough Dilley's," he smirked,

and then added in marketing-speak, "The brand has great customer equity in certain demographics, but our image is in need of freshening. I'm working on getting a new range of product right. It's a question of balancing tradition with managing change."

"Always is," I replied. "Tell me about your sister, Susan Traynor." I decided not to make any smart-ass remark about her knockers. I do have some decency. Occasionally.

More importantly, I saw straight up that this guy wasn't the kind to shackle a man in a new Mercedes and set it on fire. Not even the hairnet could make me think that, and fifteen minutes of more pointed chit-chat didn't convince me otherwise. He openly admitted that his sister stood to inherit a lot, but I got the impression he didn't care. He had a new line of product to get right and the way he talked made me think he had a hefty stake in the business and a long-standing policy of minding his not hers. I drew a line through his name in my mind, but still tried to heavy him about being available for further questioning. He didn't seem to have a problem with that. In fact, he got chatty.

"Tell me," he asked with a glint in his eyes. "What do you think of the name Obsexions?"

"I think it's a little rich for candy," I replied. "Unless the shapes are mighty interesting."

He frowned. Must've been his own idea.

"White Delight? Succulent Suggestions?"

"Makes me think of classified ads at the back of the paper. Service to local motels. What can I say? I'm a cop. And I don't like chocolate. I hate it—with a passion."

"You're lying! Chocolate *is* passion," he insisted.

"That can be your new ad line," I sniggered. "But I get stomach cramps. Then I start thumbing through romance novels. It's not a pretty sight for a guy my size."

He seemed put out. "What about a box of assorted creams?"

I didn't have the heart to tell him that phrase conjured up a picture in my mind that wouldn't have sat too neatly in one of his plastic trays. But he didn't give up. On the way out the door, he insisted I take a couple of sample boxes. The one on top was a line called Fixations, little igloo-shaped dollops "dripped in a minty dark chocolate with scrumptious vanilla centers." The picture on the lid showed an open box on what looked like a hotel bed, with a pair of long female legs in sheer black stockings stretching into view.

"Women *adore* chocolate," he said.

"I've heard that," I said. "Diamonds and big dicks too."

He ignored the sarcasm and smiled like he was bestowing upon me the secret to life.

"There's nothing more sensual than hand feeding a special woman an elegant chocolate."

I was somehow able not to laugh at this, which given the lab coat and hairnet wasn't easy. Made me think there was a little less technology to him than I'd first assumed.

"Thanks," I said, on the way out. "Maybe I'll get lucky."

I left with images of Genevieve preying on my mind. Her eyes. Her voice. What went on in that house.

The hobo clowns were thankfully not onboard for the ride back and I managed to resist the growing urge to do a drive-by in Cliffhaven. Back at the Precinct, Padgett had more news to report than I'd come up with. The ex-boyfriend had a rap sheet. Four assaults. Two were just boys-will-be-assholes, but one was a DV incident from three years before that had put his first wife in the hospital with a broken collarbone and led to a TRO. Not having much faith in court ordered niceties after her emergency room vacation, she fled out of state with their kid. The other was a notch up from that—an ADW charge that had the odor of a moonlighting loan shark gig that a radio car had just happened to interrupt. That effort won him a deuce at Drake, but a very sharp Jewish defense attorney turned that into a bullet at the Men's Center, and then pulled some more strings to get him community service. Still, a report card at least gave us something to work with on the possible murder theory—and we needed to dig up something fast because the Boss was taking the lab boys' verdict of suicide. He didn't want us wasting department time on hunches that went against the physical evidence. That was fair enough. And frankly, I was starting to hope he was right and it would just go away. I couldn't stop thinking about the lady with the scarves. That was the case I was eager to solve.

Still, the thing about Whitney is that evidence is always damaged in some way unless it's faked, and when you've spent years working with it—and damaged some or faked it yourself, you don't trust a chemical readout over your own read of a situation. Why wasn't the DNA a perfect match? Was it really Whitney who'd gone up in flames? If it wasn't him, who was it?

Chris and I went into a huddle and I agreed he should be the primary. I made it sound like I was trying to boost his confidence. But any chance of playing hooky got blown out of the water when a call came in from our neighbors at the Two-Four—about a guy found in a lake of blood behind the depot, apparently having hacked his own unit off. Of course they wanted me to have a look.

You see why people in my line turn to the bottle or the pipe? When the numbness shows any signs of wearing off, you just medicate more. But of course, it's harder to medicate your relationships—like with wives. I'd come around to thanking God that Polly and I hadn't had any kids. For a long time I'd really wanted 'em. Hoped I could do a better job than was done with me—which wouldn't have been hard. But I had slow swimmers, and after she lost the baby boy years back, we both closed up that way. Then when we started trying again, I think I let her down for real. A little matter of a .25 caliber handbag wound. Sometimes I found myself wishing I'd just oozed out on Frontera Street and been done with it. It might've been better for Polly. *"My love is just for the night . . . always wrong . . . never right . . ."* Better for me too.

Given the traffic, I got to the depot just on Happy Hour at the High Five Bar, and the regulars came out to welcome me with their Roi Tans and pickled olives. An ME was on site, an old drinking buddy named Lance Harrigan. When he pulled back the plastic sheet, it was like a punchbowl of sangria poured over a naked groin—everything taken off with a razor. I noticed Lance had a small suitcase with him.

"I was just on my way to the depot," he said. "Coroner's Convention up the coast. This was a DIY job."

Lance was exactly my age—his birthday two days before mine. Both of us Leos. But he looked much younger since he'd cut out the hooch. Like a cross between the actor William Macy and a basset hound. "You're the expert," I said, taking an olive from one of the rummies to be polite.

It felt good being near a bar, even a chafa one like that. When I was drowning, I always liked to think I was a snifter of Edith Piaf kind of guy. But it wasn't true. These were my people. Men of all colors who didn't get the breaks, they just got broken. They missed their train and ended up at the depot. Smelling the Red Hots and Wild Irish Rose breath reminded me again how easy it would be to slide into the eddy of their lives. One day I'd be at the counter talking curve balls with them over a beer and a shot—the next I'd be lined up for the veteran's breakfast at the Chat 'n' Chew—whiling away the night in a wifebeater in the lobby of the Zebulon Pike Hotel. From there, it would just be one stumblebum step down to warming the pavement on 1st and Montana and sharing a bottle of Thunderbird with Hobo Nickels and El Presidente, wondering about a cot at the Salvation Army and who was going to get the DT's first. That's what can happen to men like me. They lose their women and weed trimmers, or leave them behind—and they slip right off the radar of respectability and enter the Lost World of the last fandango. I've seen it happen many times before. I've smelled it happen.

"He'd apparently had a couple and then stepped out qui-etly into the alley," Lance said, breaking that missed train of thought.

"That seems a bit suss," I replied.

"Maybe that's why you're here," he shrugged. "I just call 'em like I see 'em and I have the Coast Starlight to catch."

"Any ID?"

"Mervyn Stoakes. The beat cop over there has more details. Guy worked for the City."

"Well, then we know why someone would want to do this," I snorted.

"Ixnay," Lance shook his head.

"You thinking drugs?"

"We'll do the tests. There's a good chance—because he also tried to eat the evidence."

"Pardon me?" I said—and you can imagine how many times I've ever said that.

"It's the most extreme example of repudiation I've seen."

"Repudiation," I echoed. "Of what?"

"His masculinity, of course."

"Oh, right," I said. "Well, we'll run this Merlin Stoakes through the system."

"Mervyn," he said under his breath. "God, what's hap-pened to you, Birch?"

I let my shoulders droop. "A few too many mangled bod-ies I guess. A few too many strange nights and definitely too many strangers."

"Don't bullshit a bullshitter," Lance barked, and then low-ered his voice. "It was that Briannon cupcake—and the damn shooting. I told you then you should pursue the counseling program."

"Appreciate your concern. I didn't know my groin or my head was of public interest," I replied, spitting out the pickled olive I'd been rolling around on my tongue.

I'd once snuck a peek at my debrief evaluation after that little episode. Apparently I have a tendency to something called "magical thinking." Fucking weasel of a union shrink. Made me sound like some fairy godmother. I had no intention of repeating that humiliation. After all, there were so many new kinds to try.

"Birch," he said. "Get some help. I know someone who consults to the Force. Someone good. I could set up an appointment? Don't be a big girl's blouse. There's no shame in it. As to this case, consider it a suicide with extenuating circumstances. I'd at least recommend checking the guy out."

"Thanks Lance," I told him. "But we tend to do that in my division."

He patted my shoulder and headed to catch his train— probably wishing he was going out with his new tall drink wife. I knew he meant well, and I liked him. He always said my choice of car showed "individual style." But I'd been doing this job a long time and I wasn't about to sit down with another "trained listener" to work through an Anxiety and Depression Inventory. *Tick the boxes that apply . . . Do you have frightening fantasies or daydreams . . . fears that something terrible is about to happen . . . ?*

I'm one of the guys who get called in when terrible things do happen and I had my own copy of the *Diagnostic and Statistical Manual of Mental Disorders*, a.k.a. *DSM*, which I took perverse enjoyment fanning through. I didn't need someone with a gilt-framed diploma to hip me to the price paid for taking my pay check. I could look it up for myself. And I wasn't about to do a Meryvn Stoakes, no matter how messed up I got. Poor guy. And to think that he tried to eat it.

Ah, well. Mine was just the street level carnage—I thought of the other stuff Lance had to face every day. Banks of stainless steel sinks and bleached white cutting boards . . . that fine cloud when the cooler door opens . . . metal trays with bodies wrapped in heavy clear plastic. X-rays revealing what a hollow point did to an occipital lobe or a xyphoid process. I knew he was just looking out for me. But still, what I needed wasn't a counselor. I needed—something to look forward to. I needed a woman. Or hope in the shape of a woman.

The shooting incident Lance was referring to was a little too well known (and talked about). I'd gotten plugged by a girl half my age near my privates. Good police work, huh? I wasn't careful enough, for reasons you can probably guess. Believe me, I wasn't proud of it. But that didn't detract from the fact that ever since I'd stepped out of uniform I'd been an investigator who closed cases. If I was a damn street musician, I'd have been given my own ferry boat to work. As it was, I had high blood pressure and a mint condition heartache. I was a two-time loser at divorce, living in a change-your-shirt apartment and peeking under sheets in front of a terminal lounge, wondering why a public servant had slit his Johnson off and then mistaken it for a Dilley's Chocolate. I made some calls back to the Precinct and then went cross town to the Long Room and shot pool with Jimmie One Leg. I let him win, as I always did. Afterward we smoked primo Cubans. His late wife had come from Miami and knew the right wrong people.

Old Jimmie was grass stem thin, wasted and trembling a lot of the time, and yet still mainlined with that unexplainable Old World joy of living, even if his life was crap. I never believed a thing he said and yet I loved to hear him talk. There was something deeply fatherly about him, despite his pint size—and yet motherly too. You just naturally poured out your troubles to him, even though he so obviously had plenty of his own. I'd have trusted him with my very soul but not my wallet. Still, I looked up to him. As small as he was compared to me—and missing a limb—I looked up.

Once when I was so sick and shaky I didn't think I could make my shift, I stopped into the Long Room just on sunup. He'd spent the night on one of the tables. It was right after Camille died and I don't think he could face going back to their hotel. He was rickety and flustered—but he hobbled around and made me an omelet on the Long Room hot plate—just a simple omelet with some shavings of spring onion he found in the back. It was Heaven.

He looked a little jaundiced and palsied now—kept scratching himself. It worried me. He'd worried me for a while. He looked thinner every time I saw him.

"Hey Jimmie," I joked as I was leaving. "You think I'm crazy?"

"Course Rit," he tried to smile.

"What if I said I was really going crazy-crazy?"

"Then I'd say you was in love. Or, in your case, maybe you're just finally finding yourself. Just watch your back," he added, his Adam's apple bobbing. "No man has to like what he finds."

"And you, you old wop, go in and see the damn doctor and have those tests you've been talking about!"

"Tomorrow, Rit. I promise."

He'd been saying that for about as long as I had. We both talked a lot about tomorrow. That's what too many yesterdays will do to you. Too many last lost nights.

5.

EL MIEDO. TASTE OF METAL AND THE SMELL OF sheetrock when a hammer's been slammed through it, making a hole that looks like some animal head. Sometimes it came just as voice, soft and cloying. Sometimes heaving with breath. Every so often I'd get a glimpse of the shadow, like a cockroach skittering out of sight. And other times, good and terrible times, it would seem to sit right down with me, slipping inside and hitting my intestines like the first blood warm rush of bonded bourbon. With any luck, you don't know what the hell I'm talking about and never will. Good for you.

It was still dark when I straggled out of bed in the morning to find the empty box of Dilley's Chocolates. I thought I'd left both boxes in the car, but the physical evidence indicated I'd brought one in—and eaten every last piece. Just the thought of it made me feel like upchuck in a bag—but the chocolate itself made me feel worse than the alcohol the night before. At first I was constipated, then I had an explosive bout of diarrhea that still left me cramped. I tried munching on a bowl of Bran

Flakes and slivers of a leopard-skin banana, which along with a mug of instant coffee that tasted like bong water, had the effect of cleaning me out well and truly. I couldn't remember anything from the night before other than coming home and flicking on the TV. It was like El Miedo had taken a new form since my little adventure at Eyrie Street. Maybe I did need to see a therapist. Or another kind of therapist. When I'd first moved into the apartment I'd run a tight ship. Looking around at the mess now, it was obvious things were falling apart.

If you've ever lived alone, maybe you know what I mean. It's not just the pile of laundry or jacking off on the toilet when other normal people are snuggled on a couch canoodling to a horror movie. It's the real horror of seeing your face reflected in the oily water of a frying pan that's been sitting in the sink for days, remnants of stir fry noodles looking more like dead worms than any kind of food—although I guess there are a of lot things out there that feast on worms. In fact, I'd met more than my share of them.

But maybe such squalor is only a "guy thing." I was start-ing to look like a guy thing all right. And I felt like I'd had a razor bath in sea salt and lighter fluid. I fucking hated being alone. But it beat getting cozy with El Miedo over twenty quick ones and cleaning my old back-up service revolver for the umpteenth time.

I decided to grab a newspaper and nibble on some raisin toast at Cheezy's. They had clean lavatories in case of another emergency, and the bustle of the morning crowd always cheered me up a little. I limped in and out of the shower and tried to find something decent to wear. It was starting to get desperate clotheswise—and you know what they say about clothes. How else you gonna hide the man? By the time I hit the street, the hum of the traffic had risen. Maybe it was just the sorry condition I was in, but I felt like I could hear the traf-fic in people's heads. That's never good.

When I got to Cheezy's, I slipped into a booth near the rest-

rooms with an early morning edition. There was no more fol-
low-up on the Whitney case, but *The Sentinel* had a half-page
on the Stoakes story with a photo of the jake legs out in front
of the High Five. I was scanning through the rest of the paper,
listening to the crash of the silverware as the Nicaraguan bus-
boys dumped the tubs under the counter, when I caught a snip-
pet of the tune on the radio in the background. "Maneater" by
Hall and Oates. The song flushed out a dream I'd had during
my uneasy sleep. I don't think I would've remembered it otherwise, but it came back as clear as anything when my toast
arrived.

I'd run into this girl I'd known in high school at a bar.
Naomi Sparks, an alternate cheerleader I'd made out with once
in my car and had never spoken to since—after she called me
Mayonnaise Face. She was alone, both of us freshly separated.
We had a couple of drinks, then it turned into Saturday and we
were going for a picnic on the beach. I stopped by her house,
which was unusually messy for a woman—like the inside of
her handbag. She went into her bedroom and changed into a
two-piece. She asked me if I thought it made her look fat.
Naturally I said no. I didn't care that it made her look fat, but
there was something about her that didn't sit right.

We got into my car and headed towards the beach. Then
she blurted out, "Do you mind if we swing by the hospital? A
friend's in there and he's really depressed."

Yeah, I thought. I do mind. A hospital was the last place I
wanted to go. Then she told me we were going to visit Les
Frame and I felt my stomach turn.

Les had been her boyfriend in high school, always driving
to the coast to surf. He later went pro and made a bit of money
in Hawaii. But he got busted for drugs and came back to Cal
with his tail between his legs and opened a surf and beachwear
shop in the city.

He looked traumatized and pale, staring up at us from this
gruesome metal bed in a private room. He called Naomi

"Bubs" and started recounting in a high cracked voice what had happened to him. He'd been surfing up the Coast Highway early in the morning and had been attacked by a shark. All he remembered was hitting it on the snout as it pulled him down—trying to gouge its eyes.

While he was saying all this, my eyes were drawn to a television on an adjustable metal arm stretched out across the room. Some cooking show was on and an anonymous female hand was dusting a raw pink chicken breast with flour. Les looked spaced out—his tan faded to a color that looked a little too much like the chicken. The room went silent except for the sound of the breast sizzling in a shot of white wine—and then he burst into tears and babbled, "You wanna see it?   You wanna see it?" He ripped back the sheet to reveal a mass of bandages where his groin should've been. Fingers sprinkled something that looked like parsley on the TV chicken that now seemed to take up the entire room.

We left Les sobbing, and drove down to the beach. There were old men scouring the sand with metal detectors. After a while we ended up kissing. Then I ran my hand along Naomi's thigh and over her bikini—and I got the shock of my life when I saw the imprint. She was getting an erection.

I didn't know what to make of the dream. To be honest, I usually don't remember my dreams, and most of the time they're about a case—something I should've seen earlier. That's the thing with the job and what can drive you nuts. Everything's important. An ash tray—a shoe lying in a street. You don't get to say what matters. Not at the time. Later you can—if you can remember when later is. More often than not later comes in a dream.

That's the way it was with Briannon, the lovely little tramp who shot me. She had a laugh like Stevie Nicks on nitrous oxide and a slow burn gotta-get-there bed moan like an ambulance in Friday night rush hour. I shouldn't have had to shatter her jaw before limping out into the street with peo-

ple staring at me. At that part of me. In that part of town. I
should've seen the whole thing coming. And the damnest
thing is I think I did. I actually wanted it in some way. Just not
the staggering out of the bar and falling down on the sidewalk
part. Polly was on to me—and so was Briannon. She knew it
wasn't her I had in my mind when I had her. She was a crutch
I was using to prop up something gold and gone. So she shot
that truth out of me. But she still couldn't get that song out of
my head. *"Only regrets will endure . . . there's still no cure . . .
for a Wayward Heart . . ."*

I tried to pull myself together and drove to the Precinct. I
drive an old Buick Electra. It's a classic—from an era when
there was optimism to spare in America. It puts a smile on my
dial. Your mileage might vary, but the roomy back seat has
come in handy as a place to transact business of many kinds.

Despite my diligence, the hive was alive already, with an
eager beaver sales rep from Surefire checking on field performance reports, extra security beefed up for a high profile line-up
in Ms. Colby's latest case (with poor Stutter Strothers flopping
around behind her like a prick in a shirt sleeve), reminders
about the Captain's upcoming birthday and word of a demonstration of new embedded face identification technology. I
thought I just might get in before Cub Padgett, but he was
there, looking more boyish and dashing than ever. Made me
feel like an old bloodhound trying to keep up with one of those
sniffer beagles.

After the pep talk-duty roster biz, he jumped into back-
grounding Susan Traynor's ex-boyfriend. The charbroiled real
estate man may have had more chips in his stack, but the wife's
ex squeeze still had a substantial operation of his own to protect, and a truck fleet means big overheads. Meanwhile there
were phone lugs to be pulled. Had they been in contact in
recent times? Just by phone, or had there been motel meetings?
If it was a conspiracy, there had to be a plan—and that meant
a communications trail.

I started checking into Traynor's personal affairs, but to be honest I was starting to lose the juice. Maybe it really was suicide, and she should just be left alone to be rich and stacked. I had other butterflies to chase and I was thinking my net wasn't big enough. Still I tried to focus. Couldn't throw away all the professional disciplines because of a silk scarf—or a hypnotic voice.

If Traynor had any real wampum of her own though, any conspiracy theory would really start to wobble. Of course, there was always the chance that someone had a gripe with Whitney independent of family connections. I felt to be righteous, I should at least have a look at his books as well as the terms of the will. Were there any codicils? And the relevant insurance policies. Was anyone suing him? Any threats or hassles? Most likely we were just chasing our tails, but sometimes that's what an old dog needs to do. It helped take my mind off McInnes and more importantly, the Eyrie Street enchantress and the Jamaican handkerchief routine she'd pulled with my mind.

Over the course of the morning, in spite of the muscle spasms and the nerve-wracking fluid feeling I had in my chest and abdomen, I made some progress. I visited Whitney's office and his lawyer's. Then I worked the phone lines and paid a solo call on the widow. Can't blame a buck for trying.

She did have money of her own as it turned out. Not a fortune maybe, but her bank balance sure would've put pluck in my pecker. It certainly helped prop up her version of the story. Her only insight into a possible explanation was that Mr. Whitney "hadn't been acting like himself" for a few weeks—which naturally wasn't all that helpful. Other than that he'd gone sour on her sexually and seemed a little "body conscious," she didn't have anything specific.

She'd done well out of an earlier divorce, which appeared to have been no more acrimonious than usual—plus the ex-husband was alive and remarried. She had a relatively thriving business of her own booking temp office staff. The more I sniffed around, the less the conniving bimbo she seemed and the more her aggrieved and confused act seemed on the level. Why Mr. Whitney, who'd been so admiring of her physical assets, had gone cool on her was the question. I'd have been more than happy to bang her silly, but maybe he'd found another field to plow.

His past was checkered to say the least. It was more a question of who didn't want him dead. He had a list of trust account queries from the Real Estate Board that overflowed the file and had been invasively audited by the IRS three years before. Of still greater significance was the fact that even without a probate lawyer's opinion, it appeared that the terms of the will didn't cover all the dealings he had in progress by quite a long shot. He owned properties in the names of other companies and had shares in companies that were tangled in a canny, and I suspected not entirely textbook way. I'm sure the IRS would've agreed and most of the knotwork looked like it had been arranged after the audit. Two major developments were in the pipeline, one in Cliffhaven, and he'd been making more than just inquiries regarding the Funland site. That piqued my interest. Could've been coincidence of course, but as I said, I'm kind of superstitious. The sure thing upshot was there were indications of a considerable amount of business activity that he'd deliberately tried to keep free of the disposition of the will. So I could make him for fraud and embezzlement—he definitely had the odor of advantage by deception. Just not suicide by arson.

For his part, the Cubster concluded that Traynor's ex-stickman was equally skilled at questionable business practices albeit on a smaller scale. He used a silent partner to get around the problems of his criminal record, while providing the real technical smarts of running the operation. It seemed to be working out for him just grand. Far from being in hock to the finance companies with a morass of liens and penalty interest rates to confront, the balance sheet looked downright robust, and their principal bank manager spoke in glowing terms. Maybe he was a pollero or a smoke runner. I'd certainly have liked to fine-tooth his manifests. It prickled me majorly that a guy of his lack of character could be staring down the barrel of an early retirement while I was wearing a five-year-old suit that didn't fit and driving the Thunderbolt Grease Slapper purchased from Otto the Auto King. I loved that car—but not that much. Still, you can't fault people for getting rich in America, especially in tough times. Chris headed out to dig up some dirt on any love interest that still existed between the Big Wheel and the widow. The sand was running out on our murder theory. I needed something else to keep my head straight. My thoughts were starting to run away from me—and that was always a sign that El Miedo was laying for me.

After a can of soda and four aspirins, I was starting to feel a little less woozy when I got a call from Wardell, the fat black dude who was partners with Jimmie in the Long Room. Jimmie had been rushed to the hospital. Somehow I wasn't surprised. Just stunned. It totally blew whatever cool I'd recouped.

Wardell's East Texas accent swelled with emotion. Definitely a deep fried kind of guy. But he never missed a bridge shot, and that was saying something—given that you couldn't imagine how he'd keep one foot on the floor. He was bit of a dim bulb but he had a good heart. And it made the bad news sound even worse.

Jimmie had a tumor in the pancreas. The gnarly old fool had finally hauled himself off in pain to the doc that morning like he'd promised, and an urgent CAT scan had instantly told them what he might've been suspecting for a long time. The growth was large and situated in a way that compromised major blood vessels and blocked the bile duct. They were doing emergency surgery to insert a stent and resolve the bile problem. Then there'd be more scans and blood tests, but the fear with a cancer that large was that there were already secondaries in the liver. Jimmie always said he was 62, but he'd been 62 for a few too many Christmases. I had a bad feeling about his chances. It was clear Wardell did too.

"Which hospital's he in?" I asked. "I'll go right over."

"St. Pat's," Wardell sighed. "But they doin' the proceeedshure this afffernoon. Maybe he be out and woke up in the evenin'."

"I'll swing by after work," I said. "You hang tough like he'd want you to. He's a fighter. You know that."

"Ah knowww!" Wardell sobbed, which made me almost choke up too.

Dell and I had this thing where we'd riff on old Flip Wilson routines. He'd do a Geraldine joke and I'd do Reverend Leroy, pastor of "The Church of What's Happenin' Now." If you're too young to remember Flip Wilson, sorry. He was a funny man. Now to hear Wardell crying. God. He was as soft as one of Nelly's buttercreams inside, although he could a punch a hole in a brick wall if he'd had enough to drink. I hung up and said as much of a prayer as I could stomach for Jimmie.

I knew that one-legged little palooka had a place at the Stanton Hotel but I'd never been there. He seemed to live his whole life, or what was left of it, in the gloom of his old pool hall. It was like Kelly's Barbershop, with the crank-up chairs and jars full of combs soaking in blue barbecide. The Long Room still had brass spittoons and smelled of cigars and pastrami, the way that Kelly's had smelled of Lucky Tiger Hair Tonic and sun-faded *Argosy* magazines.

Kelly's closed last year when Strapper had his aneurism. It got turned into a health food deli selling smoothies, salads and designer sandwiches. The Long Room would go the same way when Wardell cashed out. Maybe it was better for Jimmie to go before the pool hall did. "Never ask a one-legged guy the story," he used to quip. "When he's ready to tell you, he'll only lie about it anyway." I always liked Jimmie's lies. One of the few people I can say that about.

I went out to buy a hot dog slathered in fried onions but I ended up over at the Fresh Start Deli where Kelly's had been. I thought some rabbit food wouldn't hurt me, especially the disturbing way I was feeling. I settled for a Reuben Wrap and a Zinger Tea. Glancing around, it was impossible to imagine Strapper and Huxley and the other chin-waggers in the bright new feminized surrounds. I felt less out of place than I expected and left considerably less nostalgic for the chipped linoleum and sweaty Naugahyde.

When I got back to my desk, the land line was ringing and there were messages stacked up. I thought it might be Wardell with more news about Jimmie—and then I had a notion that it was McInnes, wondering how my visit to Eyrie Street had gone. I could feel Jack lurking in the background—just like El Miedo. Instead it was Lance Harrigan. He was back from his conference and had made an appointment with the shrink for me for the next week, same day.

"Why, thanks, Lance," I grassed.

He was undeterred. My appearance and demeanor must've worried him.

At least I wrote down the name, address and appointment time, and then sealed it up in an envelope. Lance was an old soldier and had spent several years in the close company of Jack Daniels. But now, he'd beaten the bottle. He had a sexy second wife and was well on track to heading the Coroner's office. I could do worse than taking a leaf out of his book. I hung up the phone and slipped the envelope into my drawer as Becker from the Two-Four dropped off the background file on Mervyn Stoakes.

When I'd seen him lying in the alley drenched in his own blood, I hadn't taken much note of his face. Staring at an earlier pic of him from the City Directory, I saw that despite his size—and he would've gone 6'2" and 240 pounds—there was a meagerness in his face. A "something's missing look," with eyes as cold as a brass monkey. Reminded me a little too much of my reflection in the dirty sink water.

At the time of his unorthodox surgery, he'd been a 44-year-old divorced resident of Foam (a rather unfortunately-named district because the only foam on its excuse for a beach was phosphate residue leeching from the old holding tanks). He worked in the Planning department overseeing developments, subdivisions and building permits, which was a good wicket to be on for taking bribes. Someone who knew the game could quietly skim some thick cream, providing they didn't get too greedy. I still wasn't convinced he'd done such a perverse deed to himself. Not without drugs, and the tox scan had come back negative.

Padgett was giving testimony in the first case we'd worked. I hit the phone and made notes, tying up what loose ends that I could, and then decided to shoot over to the Records Department at City Hall and see what I could find out about the projects Stoakes had been working on. I wanted to walk. I told myself it was because of the sultry spring weather and because I still felt a little iffy. The truth was I was getting heavy flashes of Genevieve. Her body. Her feet. That voice. What in hell was her game?

I'd left the house on Eyrie Street in a state of fear. I hadn't wanted to think of it openly at the time—it only overcame me when I found the dog collar in my pocket. I felt like I'd been selected for some black bag job and hadn't been briefed. Now I could smell the scarf again, as if the scent was on my hands, coming out of my pores. I'd only known one woman to have that kind of effect on me. This Genevieve was disturbing my peace for real.

In the Records section of the Planning Department, I interviewed three of Stoakes' fellow employees. All three of them had gotten wind of what had happened to him despite the media supposedly keeping his name out. You could see the revulsion on their faces.

Had he been acting oddly or out of character in any way

before the incident? Two of them shrugged and said that he kept to himself so much it was hard to say. The woman in the group got a little uncomfortable at this question. I bored harder. "Confidentially," she whispered, with a lactose intolerant expression, she thought he'd started "seeing someone" and that maybe it was "an affair he wanted to keep quiet."

"Why do you think that?" I asked. He was divorced, but maybe the new mujer wasn't. I could tell his co-worker hadn't made up her mind what she'd seen. It turned out that it was just some lingerie. She'd been shopping on her lunch break over at Kettleton's, one of the older department stores that the big chains and boutiques of the new BayFair Center were trying to drive out of business, and she'd seen Stoakes buying a watermelon shade camisole.

"So, you saw him purchasing a naughty nightie, and you figured he was up to no good?" I smiled. Can't a poor guy do something nice for a lady without raising eyebrows? No wonder men don't like shopping for those kinds of dainties.

"It . . . was a . . . large size," the woman said, after much hemming and hawing.

I shrugged. Stoakes wasn't little by anyone's standards. Maybe he liked his jellyroll big. I didn't see why buying a camisole was an example of acting strange—but then I'd never met him.

"And . . ." she added. "He was upset when he saw me."

I shrugged this off too. Men feel shy being amongst a bunch of bras and panties. I know. They get turned on and don't want to show it. They don't know what to look for exactly and usually get it wrong—it's either too raunchy or too baby doll. Plus, they're worried someone's going to think they're perverts. On the other hand, given Lance's professional opinion of what he'd done, maybe his female counterpart was on to something.

"Did he end up buying it?"

"I—I don't know. He got so agitated I left. He didn't come back that afternoon."

That did seem a little queer—as in suggestive. Possibly queer in the other sense too, but I didn't want to get side-tracked. I thanked her for her help and shifted my attention to his files. Thirty-five minutes later I hit pay dirt.

If Stoakes had been engaging in extracurricular activities, he'd also been busy on the job. In the last two months he'd considered more applications for development projects and granted more outright permits than anyone else on the payroll. The majority were based in Cliffhaven. The pits and vacant lots I spoke of? They didn't look like they'd be empty much longer.

That was all interesting enough, but if it hadn't been for the crash course I'd done into the complex skein of Deems Whitney's business ventures, I wouldn't have picked up on one detail. The only significant project that, uncharacteristically, Stoakes had not approved a planning permit for in the last few weeks was a Cliffhaven development instigated by a company I suspected Whitney to have recently invested in called Salmaxis. That name had popped up in Whitney's records and now it popped up again. What was of particular note was that the paperwork approving the permit had been started and then put on hold with the file note, "Pending further review." I borrowed one of the computer screens to do a company search on Salmaxis. They had UK connections but the West Coast outfit had been registered only six months before by a woman named Denita Kent, another name from Whitney's list of associates and/or enemies. Whitney wasn't listed as one of the directors but he had a bevy of holding companies that he could've used to invest in Salmaxis. ShoreGens was one such company I recalled from the morning, and sure enough, they featured prominently on the Salmaxis share register, although it looked like this had become official only in the last month. ShoreGens, when I turned over a few more rocks, was a venture capital biz that had its official address listed as none other than 4 Eyrie Street—the Managing Director, Genevieve Wyvern.

I heard in my head that satisfying clack—like when a mousetrap goes off behind the refrigerator at 3 AM.

It was too much to process there in front of a bunch of clerks. Not only were the two investigations I was working related, they connected back somehow, in some way, to Genevieve. If they were suicide, that still didn't make her connection less any screwy. And it instantly raised a question about McInnes. What did he know about all this, and how had he come by the info? The idea that he'd also sat on the pink couch at Eyrie Street—and had maybe done a lot more—that made me sicker than the chocolate had.

Of course, I could take the bull by the horns, or rather the cow by the teats, and confront Genevieve openly. She was now a person of interest in two suspicious deaths. Part of two parallel and potentially interrelated investigations. She could pull her sleight-of-hand on Birch Ritter, the civilian, but giving false information to a peace officer was another deal altogether. I liked those odds much better and left the Records section with a dip in my hip and a glide in my stride. I'd just swing by for a knock and talk. I might have to reach out to McInnes, but not yet. I needed to gather a bit more intel on my own first.

I don't know whether it was the rush I got over the link that had suddenly emerged between the two deaths—or whether the Reuben Wrap wasn't sitting well with my recovering chocolate stomach—but on the way back to the station house I got nature's call. I'm talking Code 3. Fortunately I was close to the Civic Center, and I knew they had nice clean restrooms in the rear of the lobby by the Ticketron office. I made a beeline there and was relieved to find the echoing john empty. I checked the messages on the cell while I sat there listening to the muffled strains of Billy Joel singing *"Don't go changing to try to please me . . . I love you just the way you are . . ."*

I have to admit I was there longer than I expected. The hits just kept on coming, so to speak—on the piped-in music as well as the pipe out. I was at last getting around to thinking it was safe to reach for the toilet paper when I heard that old Helen Reddy feminist call to arms from the 1970's: "*I am woman, hear me roar . . . in numbers too big to ignore . . .*"

I had to laugh, and that almost made me roar some more. Years and years ago that song came on and I remarked to a buddy, whose name I've forgotten, that I was surprised at the call for unisex toilets in the lyric. He looked at me like I was loco, and I said, "You know, the line where she says, *until I meet my brother in the can.*"

I thought he was going to have kittens. I wasn't sure he was ever going to stop laughing, but when he did he said, "The line is *until I make my brother understand.*"

Finally, when I'd regained control, I heard other voices. It sounded like an older woman and a little boy. I could hear them stressing outside the door to the restroom. It made me sad to hear them, because I knew how big a deal going into the Men's Room had been for me at that little kid stage. They nattered on a bit longer and then she must've hustled him into the Women's Room. I heard a door whoosh and their voices faded away.

I finished up, washed long and hard and had a look at myself in the mirror. I remember as a teenager staring at my face, examining each and every acne peak and crater, then turning out the lights—as if I could change my face by changing the mirror. Now I couldn't have picked myself out of a line-up. I looked pale and pasty, like some kind of illness or change in chemistry was at work. No wonder Lance had been adamant about me seeing a shrink—although it looked like I needed a doctor more than a psychologist. Then I glanced over and noticed the Tampax vending machine. What in hell was a Tampax machine doing in the Men's Room? That's typical city administration, I thought. They couldn't put enough trashcans in tourist hubs and then they whack a white mouse dispenser in the tomcat's toilet.

Then I got one of those famous sinking feelings. There were no distinctive white porcelain receptacles. No long silver trough with water gently running down. ¡Por Dios!, I thought. I'm in the Ladies'! The kid and the old woman are in the Men's! It was an honest mistake, but I had to bolt out of there. And just when I did—I ran straight into a woman in a Ticketron uniform. My face went bright red and I gobbled down some air, which made me look and sound even more foolish when I blathered, "Sorry. Police. We heard there was an intruder."

She backed out the door faster than I shot through—with the granny and the tyke out in the lobby to see the whole thing. The only sensible thing I did was not dash for the exit.

6

FELT MORE FLUISH TWINGES WHEN I GOT BACK TO THE
Precinct, but I had to do a background check on
Genevieve Wyvern. This was the part of the investigation that really got me where I lived. I ran the name through
the DMV, voter registration and business licensing—then
NCIC, CORI and all the usual other databases—plus a good
quick Google. Trumped up profiles turn up either too much
detail or not enough. Hers was the bare minimum—like a web-
site designed overnight to bolster a fake company. I tried to
detect the handiwork of the Feds, but people who go into the
WSP don't become company directors—or invite unknown
men into their houses. Underworld-arranged backgrounds
have their own special footprint. This was something else. I
couldn't fix the feel. Just more mystery.

I was due at the firing range to meet the small arms practice requirement, and I was glad of it. As jittery as I felt at
first, blasting away at the silhouette targets and doing the
reaction course steadied me. I liked drilling and always looked
forward to it. I liked the impact of the weapons in my hands,

traveling up my arms. I liked the smell of burnt brass and nitrocellulose in a confined space—and for some reason, I liked wearing the hearing protectors. Plus targets don't shoot back. By the time I got back in the Electra, I was a little better. It was just on 5 PM and I wanted to have a shower and change my clothes if I was going to pay a surprise visit to Eyrie Street. I could claim official business and anyone at the Precinct could ring me on my cell.

I shaved and showered and tried to find some fresh clothes that fit. It was hard not to think about the dog collar . . . hearing her voice again . . . *"You can't return Sunny. If you never really leave . . ."* I don't know how she pulled Sunny out, but maybe I could teach her some tricks too.

I tried to focus on my questions. My previous encounter with Ms. Genevieve had been a little too ex parte. I aimed to even things up this time. Get her on the back foot. What did she know about Stoakes and Whitney? Had she met them—intimately? What was the nature of her involvement and what was the nature of the proposed Salmaxis development? From the dimensions at Records, it appeared to include the premium site below her residence but was centered on what had formerly been the main parking lot of Funland. The consortium that controlled the amusement park had gone belly-up a while ago, and Zagame's was owned by the gangster tribe of the same name. More title searches and company checks were in order. Either way, I wanted to hear her theory on why two men she was doing some kind of business with had apparently killed themselves within days of each other in such savage, unexplained ways.

I'd broken into a sweat by the time I finished dressing and was half-considering another shower. My nipples ached with the friction of a shirt. I thought of Jimmie, and what must've gone through his mind when they told him about the scan. He'd been under the knife while I was poring over Stoakes' file.

I wondered if I should call the hospital. Not being family, they probably wouldn't tell me anything. I went to pick up the phone and saw the dog collar lying on the table. I put the receiver down. It was better that I swing by in person later. He'd probably still be under the anesthetic and I didn't want to get any important news over the phone. Besides, I had to get to Eyrie Street. There was good reason now. As well as bad.

Driving over to Cliffhaven, there was a song on one of the Mex stations, "Yo Qiero Mojar Contigo." I turned back to Melody Lane to catch Nat King Cole doing "Walking My Baby Back Home." That was much more my speed. Cool West Coast jazz from the '50's, Tin Pan Alley and one hit wonders from the '70's, like "My Baby Loves Lovin'."

I thought about other things Genevieve had said before. I couldn't stop thinking about the things she'd said. She was right about my fixation on equipment. Stun guns, pepper spray, telescopic steel batons. I'd always had a thing for stuff— and textures. Stuck in the limbo of traffic, moments from the past started to connect in my mind.

Growing up in the Colorado River irrigated valley, there was always a lot of produce around—in the fields, on the sides of the road, and in our house. We had all the usual bright plastic Pop-O-Matic stuff of the time—the kind of games and toys that carry Choke Hazard warnings now—and the fake Pillsbury Doughboy food. But there was a lot of real food with real smells around. Valencias, radishes, cantaloupe, broccoli and zucchini.

I couldn't remember the first house very well, but the one I really grew up in was in a subdivision that had appeared almost overnight beside a cauliflower field and a row of orchards. Dad built the house himself—and put double the normal insulation in. He built a lot of houses in the area, and then started traveling 100 miles a day or more with guys like Jake "knocking together" other places in other towns.

We had a big walnut tree in the back yard and Dad made

me and Serena a tree fort in it. There was nothing he couldn't do with his hands. Big white Arkie hands. His family had come west the hard way. There were old photos I'd seen of jalopies and canvas tents. They'd burned corn in the stoves because it was cheaper than coal—and when he was just a kid he'd picked figs and prunes. He listened to cracker music from Bakersfield on the radio, but there was nothing redneck about him.

I remembered the mysteries of his tool shed . . . his rock maple miter box . . . and the smell of the walnut dust on him when he came down from the tree, having finished our secret refuge. "Everybody needs a place to hide away," he said.

His tools were the balance to the spices in my mother's kitchen—and the underwear and clothing she hung on the washing line to dry. Nobody used a drier then. The smell of the fabrics—the miraculous design of a brassiere—the scent of wood shavings and ripe tomatoes—my father's spirit level—or his steel tape measure with the shiny yellow tongue. I felt and smelled them all again. Sheetrock and flour for biscuits. Sheetrock. Washing powder, linseed oil. Ten penny nails and black currants. My father's tool belt and my mother's girdles . . .

I wondered if Genevieve would be home. Or alone. She might have another client with her. Was that what I was? Jesus, I hadn't put it that way to myself before. I about rear-ended a guy on Molson and had to pull over to get steady. Over the years I'd walked into bars and meat-packing plants to meet men I knew were armed and "dangerous," but now here I was panicked about meeting a woman in a harbor view house. And a dame with great tits at that.

I detoured by La Playa where Whitney's body had been found cremated inside the smoking shell of his Mercedes. Pretty soon—probably as early as the next morning—there'd be pressure from above to sign off on the Stoakes matter as death due to self-inflicted injury. I was going to have to move fast to connect the dots to Whitney's death, or the whole thing could blow away like dust in the rearview mirror. I went to start the car again and noticed the tip of the other box of Dilley's Chocolate poking out under the seat. The name on the cover said Compulsions, and the image was a close-up of a woman's mouth about to engulf a piece of chocolate in the shape of a man. I laid the box on the passenger seat and swung back into traffic.

I parked over on a street called Rockview, which was lined on both sides with flowering fruit trees. I stowed the box of chocolates under my arm and walked around the corner to Eyrie and then up the hill and down the stone stairs. If she was home, I didn't want to give her any more opportunity than necessary to spot me before I got to the door.

I half-expected some sort of manservant or bodyguard to open the door. But when I pressed the buzzer, which I noticed this time, in the different light, appeared to be a tiny flying dragon, the door opened almost immediately—and there she was—dressed in a white lab coat of all things, with high-heeled black pumps. At least, I sensed it was her.

The woman I'd met before had had a grind house savvy with a heady dose of Sherry-Netherland class—like a bell of Poire William with a thumbscrew in it. She looked different now. Her hair was strawberry roan for one thing, but that could've been just a wig, or a dye job. Her face had changed too, although I couldn't say exactly how, other than the Fearless Fly glasses. In my mind, she'd become irresistible—and this woman was. But was she the same woman? Suddenly all my rehearsed questions about Stoakes and Whitney flew right out of my head like birds. Damn her.

"You're early," she said without expression.

"Is that good or bad?" I asked, trying to get casual and official all at once. Maybe another session was in progress. Maybe the guy had a thing about lady scientists.

"It's good for me," she answered. "Time will tell whether it's good for you."

I didn't have a quick comeback so I let it go. She let me in the front hallway, which was just as it had been the day before, except the white parasol had been replaced by one the color of a Dilley's Fixation. Maybe the parasols changed every day at 4 Eyrie Street. It reminded me of the box in my hand. She saw it and said, "Pour moi?"

"Yeah," I shrugged, with a God-ate-my-homework feeling of a kid faced with his teacher.

"I adore chocolate. And from a big tough man like you! You're a closet romantic. That's another reason I've pinned my hopes on you."

I squinted. "I don't like things being pinned on me."

She looked at me with stony eyes behind those intellectual glasses. Her irises didn't appear to be either brown or green now. More amber. But the lines around her mouth softened, which made me focus on her full bow lips. She could've been the model for the lid of the Compulsions.

"You're already making progress, Sunny. Don't be afraid. I won't make the obstacle course any harder than you can handle. At least, I don't think so."

I was about to start in on my questions when I looked to my right, into the parlor / sitting room where I'd been blindfolded before. The whole room other than the fireplace and the mantel was different. Before I knew it, she'd swept me inside, and although the room had been at least partially visible from the foyer, it was like stepping into some other kind of dimension.

The walls had been painted a stark hospital white and the crystal light fixture had been replaced by single naked bulb. The Turkish rug was gone. The blinds were hard metallic silver and fully closed. The library chair and the pink sofa were nowhere to be seen. Instead the room was crowded with rat cages, expensive laboratory ones—and filled with rats. A series of interconnecting wires linked them to a console on the mantelpiece. At the center of the console was some type of scientific clock. It had only one hand and a face that was segmented by colored bands: blue, red and black. There was a stack of black anodized boxes with needle arm gauges. All of the rats in the clear cages were lab specimens, mostly pure white. The key exception was an ugly and very large sewer rat. It was isolated in a wire cage, but despite its street-drain appearance, it was methodically rotating on one of those spinning exercise wheels. I didn't think you could teach a gutter rat to do that.

The only lab rodents that seemed anxious were the ones in the cage closest to an aquarium on the floor. There was no water inside the tank, but there was a cat, a well-groomed Persian that didn't look at all happy to be so confined. The roof of the tank had perforations to allow the animal to breathe, but I noticed a tube slipped in through the top—and following the tube backward, I saw that it disappeared into a hole in the wall. I didn't like the look of that for some reason. I liked the look of the larger steel cage that stood beside it even less. This structure was big enough to hold a human, if crouched or squatting. Facing all this was a chair that might've been at home in an early 20th century gynecologist's office. I liked this not at all. Behind the chair was a black leather stool on wheels and a stack of more electrical gear, some of it blinking. She let me take in the new contents and décor before swishing in front of me in her lab coat which was now unbuttoned. Underneath she wore only a finely netted push-up bra and see-through knickers the color of delphiniums. I tried to recapture my questions, the official police tone that was going to put her on the back foot. As if.

I got even more confused when another female swept into the room behind me. She was petite, maybe 20 years old. Rich dark hair fell in ringlets down to her shoulders. She was naked with a skin tone the color of olive oil in a lightly simmering pan. The idea that a babe that hot could be standing next to me without a stitch—without me slipping her a couple of C-Notes! I didn't even feel Genevieve slip the collar around my neck, and only realized she'd done so, when I heard the catch lock.

"Don't worry about this collar. At least not yet," she said. "You know all about collars, don't you, Sunny? That's a term you use in your line of work."

I flashed back to the Chihuahua buckle at home and reached up to rip the restraint off—when she casually produced from a pocket in her lab coat a remote control, which gave me a very bad feeling. It was only a little bigger than the enameled cigarette case she'd carried before, with several buttons embedded in its surface and an antenna that she extracted from one edge.

"Wait," she soothed. "Sophia wants to undress you."

I felt the girl's hands on my skin, the combined fragrances of the women fevering my head.

When Sophia had finished undressing me, she laid my clothes on the floor at my feet. Then she reached down to massage between my legs. It felt so good I didn't see when she reached over and picked something up from the floor at her feet . . . a little foil ring, connected by a wire to one of the boxes on the mantel. Before I knew it, she'd propelled it skillfully into a very awkward position. A raucous buzzer sounded and I just about jumped out of my skin. The door of the largest cage opened, and to my chagrin, Sophia went over and ducked inside. Genevieve depressed one of the controls and the door clanged shut behind the girl. Suddenly I realized I was standing there naked before two smoking females . . . the lab rats' noses twitching, the Persian looking stressed inside the tank, and that street rat still working away on its wire wheel. Sophia squatted on her haunches in the big enclosure.

"Now Sunny," Genevieve began, and her voice sounded like another kind of cage door closing. "As you may have guessed, around your neck is a shock collar."

She pointed with the antenna of the remote to the old medical chair.

7.

I SAT DOWN AND SHE REMOVED THE LAB COAT TO GIVE ME a good look at her curves, the expensive underwear and smooth black shoes. The shoes and the glasses seemed like lingerie too.

"We're about to conduct a simple but deeply important experiment," she said. "Any lapse in your concentration will result in the administration of a shock. The problem is that your collar is set for maximum voltage. Even a man of your body mass will find the pain excruciating. Your hair will have a static, fried texture. Your eyeballs will throb. Your heart will jolt—and it's said that subjects exposed to this high an electrical charge often bite off their tongues. At best, there will be a taste of burnt metal in your mouth, which will linger well after you've stopped seeing stars and caught your breath. The muscle spasms may persist longer."

I couldn't accept what I was hearing, even though she said it so matter-of-factly. I felt like a trap door had opened underneath me and I'd fallen right out of anything I understood.

"You're going to read to me, Sunny, from a book I'm going to give you. You must read every word, clearly and meaningfully. As we express ourselves, so do we listen. This is the first thing you need to learn to step through the barriers that surround you—that have become you. If you mispronounce a word or stumble on a sentence, you'll be given a shock. If I press this button, you'll scream like the most delicate schoolgirl—and probably even cry. Then you'll buck and shudder in that chair like a ridiculous marionette."

I think I bucked and shuddered right then. She smiled sweetly and malignly all at once.

"The good news is that while you're reading, Sophia is going to kneel between your legs and put her pretty mango wet mouth to work. If you remain still and appreciatively open to her, she will satisfy you more deeply and expertly than you've ever experienced. You're free to enjoy this artful privilege as completely as you can, but you must remain attentive to your reading. It's my pleasure in hearing your voice massage each word that you must be concerned about. The slightest slip of your tongue while Sophia graces you with hers—and you taste the fire. Understand?"

I stared stupidly back at her, unable to comprehend what I was hearing—hearing it as if from another place in time. Or mind.

"Now, there's another element to this experiment," she continued. "That little foil ring Sophia has attached? It's also an electrical device. A sensitive, precise way of assessing the fullness of your arousal. Of measuring it. The device is connected to this switch relay over here." She pointed to the mantel.

"As you read, water will fill the tank in which the cat has been placed. The greater your arousal, the slower the water will enter the tank. The other conclusion is obvious."

"The cat could drown," I said, feeling my stomach rumble. Nothing El Miedo had ever thrown me could compare to this scene that had taken hold of me.

Genevieve's eyes brightened.

"Do you know about the case of Wagner and Brahms?

Wagner accused Brahms of being a serial cat killer for the pur-
poses of learning how to translate the death wails of cats into
music for the violin. An historian has now officially cleared
Brahms. A pity really. I think Wagner's view of him was more
interesting."

"You're going to kill a cat! That's—"

"I'm not going to kill the cat, Sunny. *You* may. But don't
make it sound so dramatic. You've never been a big animal
lover—going to back your childhood in the valley. Don't you
remember? You now have a chance to save a cat simply by
responding like a virile male to a beautiful and much younger
woman. Is that too hard? No, I see some things are certainly
not hard enough. But you may yet rise to my occasion.

"However. Life is a precarious balance. Should you discover
some masculine enthusiasm—giving you the benefit of our
hope—as soon as you demonstrate sufficient stimulation to cut
off the water to the cat's tank, you'll trigger random charges of
electricity to the rat cages. There's always a price for performance and pleasure, just as there is for failure and humiliation."

"My God, you're . . ."

"Shh, Sunny. It's very difficult when you have this power at
your fingertips not to use it. And lest you shrivel further, let me
say that you won't be alone in the hot seat. Sophia will also be
wired. The charges for her are much smaller, but they will be
all over. Her devices will be monitored by the clock on the
mantel, which has a feedback connection to your sensor. The
longer it takes her to encourage you, the more the pain will
increase for her. So you see, she has great incentive to entice
you to achievement."

"What happens if I . . . ?" But my voice didn't sound like
mine. It didn't sound like El Miedo. It sounded like an echo
bouncing off a wall I'd somehow walked right through.

"Another significant aspect of the expected male demonstration. If you should sow your oats before the clock hand
reaches the blue area, then the waterflow will flood the cat's

tank. All of the rats will be electrocuted and Sophia will receive the maximum charge from all the pain points. You won't receive an electrical shock—only the shock of seeing the consequences of your inadequacy. If, on the other hand, you respond properly, maintain an acceptable degree of firmness and reach a climax after the clock hand has entered the red area, then only the rats in the left cage will be terminated. The cat will survive, and Sophia will have endured but a variation on the usual discomfort women experience in trying to please unworthy men. You, of course, will then be free to go. Just as you're free to go right now."

"Yeah, right. I make one move and you zap me!"

"No," she answered, shaking her head. "You're here by choice, not chance. If you ask, I'll remove the collar and you may leave. But you'll never be able to come back for a private consultation.

"Oh, Sunny, don't be resentful . . . your problem is that you feel so vulnerable now. Only you can't admit to yourself that that's exactly what you wanted. The idea that you were no less vulnerable two hours ago doesn't occur to you. When you come to understand the kind of collar you were wearing then, you'll be started on the true unbinding."

I stared at the rodents, the cat, the girl, the wires, the clock. "What will happen if there's a volcano but no eruption?"

She pursed her lips and replied, "When the clock hand reaches the black marker, you're free to go. If you haven't delivered your payload, but have maintained your angle of attack, the cat will survive. Sophia will suffer though. And all the lab specimens will be exposed to the charge you would've gotten. Life is a matter of balance, sacrifice and shared distress."

"What are the time increments on the clock?" I asked, sweat breaking out on my forehead and back, making me stick to the chair.

"Time is a curved Riemannian four-dimensional space,"

she answered. "Concentrate on the things that are familiar to you: what's between your legs, the mixed fear and enjoyment of pain, and the sound of your own voice."

She held the remote control out in front of her. My cell phone started ringing in my jacket on the floor. She laughed. "Would you like to answer that?"

"No," I scowled.

"Then answer me," she said softly and undid her bra with her other hand. She whipped me across the cheek with it, which stirred more of her scent through the air. "Are you going to read to me? Or is this farewell to the surprises and the possibilities?"

"I'll . . . read."

Genevieve leaned in close to me, her breasts brushing my skin. If I'd have been fast enough, I could've broken her lovely neck. Instead she prodded me with the antenna of the remote control. Raising it and circling each of my nipples. The metal felt cold against my flushed skin.

"Very good, Sunny," she whispered in my ear—more a fragrance I could hear than a voice. "I'll give you one concession. The first time you falter, one of the specimens here will take your punishment for you. Like this."

She pressed one of the buttons on the remote. A lone hooded rat hopped and hit the roof of its cage, falling back down in a puff of smoke, its fur singed, legs raised.

I swallowed down a glob of phlegm. My throat was so tight my tongue felt like glue. She eased behind me and hit the button to open Sophia's cage.

"Grovel!" Genevieve commanded, and the girl did exactly that, shimmying across the floor to the older woman's feet like an animal—what kind I wouldn't want to say. Then Sophia began attaching patches to her body, each one linked to a length of wire. Two went on her nipples. One between her legs. Others on her arms and abdomen. And a final one, Genevieve inserted between the cheeks, which even from where I sat smelled like musk and womanly perspiration. Then a face harness and choke collar was secured, and Sophia submissively slipped to the floor between my legs. Genevieve moved behind me and passed around my shoulder a book—a red hardbound textbook entitled *Mammalian Sexual Behavior*. She'd employed an unused fluoro pink studded condom as a bookmark, opening to a chapter titled "Sexual Exhaustion and Recovery in the Male Rat." I felt my vocal chords atrophy.

"Read to me, Sunny," she said. "Let your mind exist only for the words before your eyes. Give them your total devotion and your body will be free to behave like a body. This is your first chance to make love to me. Perplexed and even terrified as you are . . . release yourself."

The clock began to throb more than tick. I heard the sound of water begin to enter the aquarium, the whine of the cat, the awful creaking of the wheel in the sewer rat's cage. And I felt the warm, wet breath of Sophia . . . what I'd dreamed of so often in my loneliness in the last months. I sensed her appetite to please me in every cell of my body. I took one glance at the cat in the trickling tank and knew that if I looked again I'd regret it. I began to read . . .

"Twelve male rats were left with receptive females and allowed to copulate and ejaculate. Sexually active males were selected on the basis of their mating performance in three or four prim . . . preliminary tests with receptive females."

A sharp brightness flared in one of the cages when I swallowed the word "preliminary." There was an acrid smell, but I read on.

"Males were housed individually and were maintained in the experimental room in which the light-dark cycle was controlled by an electric clock. Drinking water and Purina chow were available ad libitum."

I hesitated on the Latin words, just long enough to hear the clock again. Like another animal in the room. I felt Sophia wince and a sympathetic tremor of electricity ran through me.

I was still soft and withdrawn. Slippery and gratified, but afraid. The collar around my neck seemed to tighten. I could feel the carotid pressure and the slow ache seeping through Sophia without a word spoken. The words were for me. The current hummed. The wheel of the sewer rat squeaked. The cat's paws were growing used to the rising water. My voice droned on . . .

"The apparatus included special observation cages and a recording device. The rear half of the top was surmounted by a cylindrical release can in which a receptive female was placed."

I heard the cat shaking the water from its fur. Sophia growled with a surge of electric anguish. I read on, trying to do to the dead scientific words what she was trying to do to me.

"Three observation cages were fastened to a rack in such a position that they could be watched simultaneously by an observer . . ."

Something happened then. All of the details of the room began to dissolve. The collars and the electrical current. The creatures and the cages. It was as if a door had opened to a secret world that had always been there, close by, only I'd never known about it.

"At the observer's side were three counterweights control-ling the trap floors . . ."

I felt the rush of blood and the cat's tank stopped filling with water. Each word I encountered from that point seemed engraved. The sentences began to radiate before my eyes and I read them like holy inscriptions revealed in a vision. I couldn't hear the water, the clock or the electrical flashes anymore—only Sophia's encouraging breathing. I was on the verge of exploding—not like that hooded rat—when another buzzer sounded. Deafening. Final.

"Congratulations, Sunny," Genevieve said—and the reality of the room, if reality it was, came flooding back. The clock hand was stopped in the depth of the black area.

"Your curiosity hasn't killed the cat. In fact, an exotic pussy is free to live another day. Unfortunately, you weren't quite able to let yourself go. Your tumescence is proof of your capability, but your partner in this experiment was longing for your fulfillment."

The spell broken, the cages and animals returned. "So . . . what happens . . . ?"

"You'll be released, as soon as the consequences have been made clear to you."

There was a crackling of current. The bare bulb overhead dimmed for a second. Instantly the cages full of the surviving rats lit up—the creatures leaping and jerking. Those that didn't burst open outright simply collapsed in tufts of smoke. My whole body was rigid in the chair, too startled to move. Where my mind was I couldn't say.

"Now, Sunny. You're going to see Sophia dance. She knelt down and pleasured you. Now she's going to wriggle on the floor like a maggot. Have you ever seen someone have a grand mal seizure? Oh, of course you have. Your sister for instance."

"P-please . . ." I stammered, rage and disgust racing through me like a current.

"Very good!" Genevieve praised. "That's a word you haven't used nearly enough in life. But it won't do now. Didn't your sister's death result from a seizure? She fell and broke her neck didn't she? While you and your friends looked on."

"You don't—understand!" I cried. "You weren't there!"

"You were feeling naked and ashamed, and yet perversely excited, as you are now—knowing you could do something to help her but not knowing what. It was not a sexual failure you faced then—or now. It was a failure of love. Of care. Prepare Sophia."

My head spun. How had she known anything about my sister Serena—and what had happened that afternoon? She couldn't have known.

"Give me the juice," I yelled. "That's what you want. Fry me!"

My cell phone rang again from my coat pocket on the floor. The contrast to the scene in the room was ludicrous. I let it ring through to the voicemail. Then I stood up and wrenched off the foil ring. I was going to peel off the neck collar too and then beat some sense and decency—

But to my horror, even more than my exasperation, Genevieve bent down to the grilled cage that held the dump rat. She opened the door and summoned the vermin into her hands, nestling the filthy thing to nurse at her bosom like a much loved pet.

"I'm proud of you, Sunny," she said, stroking the mottled fur. "You've proven yourself in more ways than one—my affection for you grows. You've left some of your mammalian performance anxiety behind and can now advance. Get dressed and take your prize home."

I wanted to hit something—like her. But that line threw me. "You mean . . . ?"

She cackled. "I meant the cat."

My face went red and I started wrestling my clothes on. Sophia waited on her knees at Genevieve's command. When I had my underwear and pants on, I yanked the shock collar from my neck as I should've done right at the start, and flung it on the chair that still bore my sweat marks. Then I stuffed my arms in my shirt and snatched the rest up in my hands.

"Save the cat, Sunny," Genevieve said. "Notice that I didn't say *take* the cat?"

My eyes considered the electrocuted lab rats and I crossed to the tank to release the sopping Persian. "I never want to see you again," I said.

"Really?" she laughed and pressed a button on the remote control. The shock collar leapt out of the chair and hit the clock. "Some collars are more easily removed than others. I'll expect you at 4 PM on the dot on Friday. That's the time your mother used to expect you home from school. Be prompt. And bring me another present—but nothing like a box of chocolates. It must be something personal, from your past. As befits our budding intimacy."

I lurched out the door with the wet cat and my shoes. I was almost to the stone stairs when I heard Sophia yowl like a banshee. Just as my cell phone rang again.

8

I DIDN'T WANT ANYONE TO SEE ME RUNNING—AND I couldn't anyway with the cat. But I sure as hell wanted to. The air was muggy and the cherry and plum trees along Rockview gave off a heady scent as the sun hemorrhaged over the derricks across the harbor. I hadn't been in Genevieve's parlor as long as I thought—not by the clock in my car anyway (for some reason I'd left my watch in the apartment, which was so not like me). How I drove home, I'm not sure. It was all I could do to get my socks and shoes on in the street after stuffing the cat in the car. The soaked thing quivered in the back seat, happy to be safe from the tank. The last call had been from Padgett, keeping me in the loop. ¡Dios!

Genevieve was right about me and animals. We'd had a bulldog when I was growing up named Winston. It tried to dig its way under the back fence and somehow tangled an intestine and died not long after Dad went off the construction scaffolding and smashed his head in. El Miedo laughed about it. I never wanted another pet after that.

"You'll have to be the man in the family now," my mother said after the service. The insurance company behaved surprisingly honorably and paid out the full policy on Accidental Death. And not too long after that Rod started sniffing around. A year later they were married and he was on top of her every night (except when there was a Rotary meeting).

I thought of Sophia's howl.

The whole scene came back to me. Dreamlike, druglike, but so real. Too real. A nightmare executed like theater. Anything I'd hoped to learn about the Stoakes and Whitney investigations had been struck out of my mind in a bolt of electricity. I felt so jangly I could barely drive, and I'd never been so grateful to see the big sign for The Rumpus Room that marked the edge of my neighborhood. Ladies Baked Bean and Jell-O Wrestling—$$ Prizes.

The cat didn't want to get out of the car and scratched my hand when I tried to grab it. Mrs. Ramona, the older widow from across the hall, saw me struggling and remarked that it was nice I'd gotten a pet. I didn't want to prattle with her in the condition I was in. And I always felt guilty when I saw her now. I knew she was sort of sweet on me. When I'd first moved in, she invited me over for some of the best red tamales I'd ever had. The next visit she talked me into teaching her how to play Texas Hold 'Em, and it was kind of fun at first. She said she wanted to pick it up so she could meet people. Pretty soon it wasn't hard to work out what kind of people she meant. She liked repeating the words *Flop*, *Turn* and *River* after me, but when the Tia Maria came out and the attention shifted from how she was playing her hand to what she was trying to play with in her other hand, I had to fold. She was one of those sad, soft cow-faced older women who'd have been pure bitch in heat when she was younger. And very maybe still was. Very maybe. But I couldn't deal. I hadn't been back and I never left a note in her mailbox. I knew she was pissed at me. Or just hurt, which was worse. Now I felt bad every time I ran into her, but I couldn't worry about that just then.

My whole body seemed wired still. I bear-hugged the cat

and lumbered through my door. Inside, I made sure all the windows were shut and let the animal get its bearings. I had to work to get mine too. I thought at first I was in the wrong apartment, but the PICO collar on the table and the empty box of chocolate proved otherwise.

Other than the police scanner and the *Diagnostic and Statistical Manual of Mental Disorders*, there was all the ambience of a roach motel. Trash had stacked up, and dishes too, even though I hardly ever cooked. Mostly eggs and stir-fries. Clothes were piled on the floor. The medicine cabinet mirror yawned, with dried shaving cream and crusted hairs glued to the sink like sprayed ants. Polly had kept our house so neat, except for one little patch of tile near the shower. I always marveled at the sight of her footprints in the talcum powder there. The cat seemed as appalled as I was. There couldn't have been any place more different than Eyrie Street.

My new chum was a female all right, quite beautiful now that her fur was starting to dry. I tried to think what I should call her, then my eyes fell on the collar again. It occurred to me that it was about the right size for her. Punched into the last hole, it fit. She didn't want to be stroked though. Probably hungry—and just as washed out as I was. I splashed some water in my eyes and didn't recognize myself. My skin was soft and clean. My razorburn had cooled.

The Koreans had no pet supplies whatsoever and were unfriendly even for them. I hustled down to the 7-11, where the Indian man behind the counter scowled at me. They had cat stuff anyway. I bought one can of jellied pilchards and another one of something called "Seafood Platter," along with a sack of litter and some dry food. The counter guy wouldn't let me have an empty box though. Asshole.

On the way back I noticed that the weather was changing fast. The sun had streaked out in a mass of gunmetal cloud and the Duke of Earl was sidling back to his burrow. I called him the Duke, and he seemed to like that, but his real name was

Landon Moore. He gave me a smile and a holler when he spotted me. He looked like what Scatman Carothers would've looked like if he'd spent a couple of years living in a lice-ridden sleeping bag—and I think he might have been a candidate for a diagnosis of Grave's Disease, because his eyes were beginning to bulge. He was always cheerful though, like some mad monk. He'd been a promising singer somewhere back in time, and was always happy to show you a faded newsclipping of him in his 20's posed with John Davidson and Leslie Uggams. Whether through drugs, bad luck, some mental disorder—or all of the above—he'd found his way into a long-term engagement in the bushes of Peralta Park. Two years back he'd come forward to identify a prime suspect in a rape and murder case I'd worked, and I'd been trying to look out for him ever since. Urged him out of the park to a sheltered doorway and abandoned shop front around the corner from my apartment when I moved. It was safer there, and when I couldn't keep an eye on him, I had the beat boys make sure he was left alone. For some reason, with really busted up people like him—wounded souls who remade the world so they could survive in it—I felt at home enough to help them as best I could.

Besides, he remained proud and self-sufficient in spite of his circumstances. He wouldn't take any outright assistance, just spare change for singing. Billed himself as the "Human Jukebox" and loved it when you challenged him with requests for songs. I was still feeling pretty damn frazzled but I hit him up for "It's Not for Me to Say." His face lit up, and he carried it off as good as Johnny Mathis. Damn fine pipes for a dude who slept on concrete. A twist of the dial and he might've been a big star. But life ain't fair. I read somewhere the strongest erections come during sleep. I laid a tenner on him and hurried home.

I reached the front of the whitewashed and mold speckled cinderblocks of my apartment building when the first dime-sized drops started striking the pavement. Then I remembered

I hadn't gotten myself anything to eat. I'd have to call out for a delivery. My whole body felt like a rejected organ—my mind still fidgeting and popping with images of the cages and the sparks. And I kept imagining I still had that blasted collar on.

The phone was ringing as I fumbled with the door key—I'd forgotten to put on the answering machine. Then I dropped one of the bags, which split open and kitty litter spilled in the hall. By the time I got inside, the phone had stopped. I went out and swept up the litter, but the call got me thinking about who'd rung earlier on my cell and if I'd missed any other calls. I had. One had come from a private line—Number Withheld. Maybe it was her. Although it could've been McInnes. Hell, it could've been anyone. One was from Polly's shyster. She was griping about me paying for her tickets to *Wicked*. Christ, how petty. The other was the Long Room. Suddenly I remembered Jimmie. I'd said I was going to go by St. Pat's to visit him.

Pico, my new playmate, didn't want to have anything to do with me. She'd taken up a defensive position under my bed and seemed inclined to give me another taste of her claws rather than come out. I ripped open a can of jellied pilchards. As soon as she got a whiff of the stinking fish goop, she was there, sidling up against my leg in a way that reminded me uncomfortably of the way Genevieve had touched me . . . and the feel of Sophia. I wondered how that poor girl had gotten into the clutches of Eyrie Street. What was she, some kind of love slave? A chattel? I couldn't think about it. I had to go see Jimmie. He'd be conscious now, scared, and lying in a ward with strangers all hooked up to bleeping machines.

I rummaged through the junk in the apartment trying to find something to use as a litter box. In the closet I pulled out an old carton. Photos, postcards and my first citation. There was a kewpie doll from Funland—and my old transistor radio I used to listen to ball games at night on, trying to drown out the noise of Rod porking my mother. The man was a machine.

The photos were creased Army pics from Germany. Me

and this girl named Johanna sharing a bratwurst in front of the university in Heidelberg. She probably had five kids by now. Then there were others of Ft. Sill and Ft. Ord, where I'd done my Basic . . . long shuttered now and being sold off for housing lots. They brought back all the hours spent shining boots, the ordeal of shaved heads and ice-cold toilets—huffing double time in the damp chill of dawn. So long ago. So many thoughts.

They made me think of the yellow scarf and what it had seemed to reveal—even though I knew it had been just stuff in my head. Except the dog collar. All the things piled somewhere in some dark, waiting to be found again.

One day at Ft. Ord we were out on the rifle range, squeezing off rounds into the targets embedded in the side of the hill. Suddenly, without any warning, this guy we nicknamed Trigger started firing in the air. It was one of those days when the blue sky seems to be moving very fast behind still white clouds that are so low you think you can hit them with a stone. Trigger started plinking away. He pointed his gun into the glare of the sun and the bullets seemed to whack into the shining air, tearing off bits of cloud. For every crack of the rifle, a seagull fell into the sand. Sergeant Perada later congratulated him on his shooting. Then he ordered Trigger to bury each of the gulls in a grave that was deep enough for him to stand in. The MP's came for him one night. We never saw him again.

Down at the very bottom of the box, wrapped in tissue, I found the last wrestling trophy I'd ever received. I pulled it out. A wooden base with a golden pillar rising out of it, and on top two identical male figures grappling with each other. I set it down on the kitchen table and tore off the top of the box. Then I lined it with newspaper and dumped in a layer of litter, which made my throat constrict. I filled a dish with water and set everything down on the floor. I didn't think the cat would ever want to see water again. But, hell. Cats are survivors. The phone rang again. It was Wardell.

"Aw, Rit," he moaned. "You home."

"I'm just heading over there now . . ." I started to say, and then I heard him hyperventilating. He may have only been as sharp as a bowling ball but he was loyal to the core. I knew instantly what he was going to say.

All I could do was stand there, listening to Pico consume her food, trying to make sense of his words. He kept saying "Complications"—and the way he said it was complicated. But it didn't change the meaning. Jimmie, damn his old ass—had died on the table. They'd gone in with keyhole surgery to insert a stent in the bile duct, then found there was a swelling—a mixture of retained fluid and internal bleeding. They had to cut him all the way open. He lost blood pressure and when they acted to bring it up, he went into arrest. Maybe a clot had broken free and rushed to his lungs or heart, they weren't sure. He was in no shape for major surgery, and the tumor was pronounced, with secondaries advancing in the liver. No wonder he'd looked so thin, with jaundice setting in.

I felt numb hearing Wardell pour his guts out on the other end of the line, but I let him go until he was empty. He went back a long way with Jimmie—before Jimmie had met his "last wife," a puffy old Florida beauty queen who drank martinis for breakfast. She looked like Peggy Lee but she had connections, which is how Jimmie got his cigars. After she passed away, Wardell had looked after Jimmie like a wife. He may have even known the truth of how Jimmie lost his leg.

I always suspected it had to with horseracing. One day a couple of summers back I'd spotted through his thin cotton shirt, two telltale burn marks on his shoulders—the kind that old-time jockeys would get before a weigh-in when they'd spend so long in the steam room, they'd pass out and burn their backs. I figured some time back in ancient history Jimmie might've taken a fall in the stretch.

Wardell felt guilty for not having pushed him into going to see a doctor ages ago, but I reminded him that no one could get that little squib firecracker to do anything he didn't want to.

Jimmie had lived his life on his own terms and maybe a quick end wasn't so bad, given what lay ahead. Wardell sniffled but agreed. I asked about a service, and the big guy said that Jimmie had left strict instructions when he went in for the stent. He'd obviously had the hunch. He'd asked to be cremated quick and Wardell had pulled some strings with his cousin over at Greenlawn to have the job done in the morning. A small service would be held at the Long Room the next afternoon. That was Jimmie—he'd put off going to the doc for two years, but he'd want a funeral arranged at the drop of a hat.

"His note say he want you to spread 'em, Rit. Out onna harbor near Fairy Point."

I'd been holding up pretty well until then. Being asked to spread Jimmie's ashes got me a little choked up though, even in the weirded out state I was in—and that got Wardell choked up again too. I told him I'd be by for the service and then take the ashes out on the ferry. Whatever Jimmie wanted.

"An' Rit . . . he left somepen for you. Bless his sweet soul, he did."

I smiled and started crying all at once, stifling it down so Wardell wouldn't hear and get to blubbering himself again. I can't remember when the last time was I'd really let go with some tears. I figured old Jimmie had left me some Cubans.

After I hung up the phone I sat at the table staring at the wrestling trophy for about 200 years. The raindrops flicking against the windowpane sounded like the plastic pennants rattling over Otto the Auto King's lot. I raised one of the windows enough to let in some fresh air. Some of the city grit had been calmed by the moisture and there was an edge of ozone and blossoms. Made me think of Eyrie Street. Almost everything made me think of Eyrie Street now. I couldn't even stay sad about Jimmie. I wondered where in hell that was going to lead.

The idea that Genevieve was some high tone hooker didn't play. What she was playing with was my head, and the damn thing was I sensed some pattern to the game. For a lug, I've always had sort of a sense, like my mother had—for queer stuff. I don't mean gay queer stuff—I mean bizarre stuff that a lot of men like me don't like to think about—and never talk about. Like the kind of things that happen in dreams, only you're walking around. El Miedo stuff. But what had just happened on Eyrie Street wasn't like any kind of dream or even nightmare I'd ever had. It was like looking into a window—then realizing it was actually a mirror. Only something was missing. Someone you expected to see wasn't there.

I couldn't make her out at all and that just got me more curious. Why had she chosen me? A cop in the pocket? Maybe. But she had the moxie to take bigger scalps than mine. It was like an undercover assignment where everything's last minute need-to-know. Play in the dark so you'll keep it real.

The first night I'd thought she was using drugs or hypnosis on me somehow. With the rats and Sophia, I was certain I'd been straight. Too clear. I had some connection with her—on a level I hadn't been aware of before. Gave me the heebies.

So far, I'd only seen her as a civilian. No money had changed hands. If she had any idea what I was interested in from an official point of view, no one else did. Now I wasn't sure I wanted anyone else to find out, least of all Chris. Even if there hadn't been any link between Whitney and Stoakes—and I don't know why, but I didn't believe that anymore—Genevieve had an unnatural influence over men. A means of coercion—or collusion with some part of them that lay below their awareness. I could feel it working in me. Her. Transmitting on some unassigned frequency. A black new angle started to form in my mind. Maybe those two guys, who may or may not have even known each other, had been compelled to kill themselves for reasons they didn't understand—and maybe by means they couldn't understand. I wished I could get drunk. I ordered in Vietnamese instead and tuned in the familiar realm of the scanner.

Some guys need to keep up with the stock market or the

sports news. I like listening to the city—what the mood is. 415. Man with a gun. No outstandings. Just checking in. I listened until the food arrived. Then while I slurped coriander noodles, I watched Rico Salazar's press conference before the upcoming fight with the big Nigerian on the tube. His opponent looked like he was on fast forward in the clips. 19-0 with 10 TKO's and three other men knocked so cold you could've chilled beer with them. Poor Rico seemed both frail and flabby by comparison—all the aggressive style and voraciousness of his earlier career gone.

I felt as full and as lonely as an impound lot and turned to a rerun of *Barnaby Jones*. Then I threw some old blankets down for Pico and threw myself in bed. I figured I'd sleep like the dead. But I had dream after dream that I couldn't quite remember. Except for Stacy singing that song . . . *"Wayward Heart . . ."*

I woke up and went and sat on the toilet. I sit down to pee at night because I can't stand turning on the light and I don't want to miss the bowl. I figured it was the coriander flipping me out. It was still outside, and foreboding, like when you've heard someone chamber a round just behind you. My body was humid and tense.

Back to the cot. There were more dreams—about experiments and tortured animals—erotic scenes. I woke up again, my skin bathed in sweat. I heard a low rumble like the sound of luggage being wheeled on pavement—and a whip of lightning tore through the sky overhead—just like the crank that had doomed those rodents in the cage on Eyrie Street.

Just then something licked my ear—rough but warm. I flinched—and a motorish purr began softly right beside my face as the night itself seemed to drizzle down, the memory of Genevieve's scent invading the room as it had my head.

9

BY THE TIME I WOKE UP I WAS RUNNING LATE. THE storm had cleared the air but not my mind or the inside of my apartment. All my joints were tender and the water pressure in the shower was actually painful. I figured I was coming down with a monster flu. I just hoped it wasn't something more serious. Pico panicked when she heard the splashing. When I got on the scales I noticed that I'd lost 10 pounds since the last time I'd weighed myself, although I couldn't remember when that was.

Of course I couldn't find anything to wear. Polly had always joked me about my Thanksgiving suit, but this wasn't funny. Racing stripe underwear and piles of old shirts that looked like second hand Don Ho. The newer stuff either looked faggy or really didn't fit. I must've shed the flab when I gave up the booze. I'd have to schedule in some shopping. Chris the Cub Scout always looked so neat and fashionable.

I do have OK eyes though, milky blue like my father's but shaped like my mother's. My face seemed to have less of that clenched fist look and my beard was light enough not to need a shave. Even the old pockmarks seemed smoother. I'd have a good healthy dinner that night and hop in the tub and listen to Chet Baker, and maybe I could stave off whatever bug I'd picked up—or whatever I may have been dosed with that first night at Eyrie Street.

I zipped around closing up the windows and putting out some dry food for Pico, then I was off like a bride's nightgown. We had to sort out the Whitney investigation and I had to make a decision on the Stoakes case. And I had to be sharp, especially if I was going to be out at Jimmie's service in the afternoon. It struck me again that he was gone. Before it had been too painful to deal with—especially after the "experiment." Now it was like missing a limb.

That made me grin—and then I was bawling my eyes out behind the wheel. It was partly about Jimmie—and it was partly because I suddenly missed Polly—she'd have made sure I didn't look like a stewbum when I went out the door. I wanted to call her, but I knew I couldn't. That would be total defeat. I was just so tired and lonely. I kept hearing the one thing Genevieve had said that gave me hope. *"This is your first chance to make love to me."* I made it to the station house without thinking of anything else.

Chris was already in, looking like a cross between Johnny Depp and Brad Pitt. It annoyed me how handsome he was, how sure of himself. After his usual español pleasantries, he hit me between the eyes the minute I got back from telling the Captain about Jimmie and the service I had to go to in the afternoon. (I also took the liberty of giving the Boss a heads-up on us going limp on any murder charge with Whitney. It was suicide. We'd had it right the first time. I had to get some breathing room to have more to do with Genevieve—whatever way that turned out. Tanking the case was the way to do it. And who knows—maybe the truth.)

"I want you to come to lunch with us on Sunday, Rit. We're going to that new seafood place in BayFair. The Lobster Trap."

"Who's us?" I wanted to know. He'd said it kind of awkwardly and Chris didn't do much that was awkward. I caught a hint of pity.

"Me and the girl. And her folks," he grinned, Colgate-white.

He always called his wife "the girl." She could've been on the partnership track at any firm in town, not messing around with slimeballs and jail fodder. As D.A, her father was officially her boss adversary, so she obviously had some little girl issues. And her liposucked mother chaired the Ballet Company board. I thought shucking some oysters with that team might be an education—or a punishment.

"Why me?" I wondered. It worried me that he was worried about me.

"I want them to meet my partner," he answered—and almost convinced me. You'd have to have shaken down a lot of people—and animals too—to have seen it. But I did.

"Worried about me?" I queried, and what I meant was, embarrassed.

"Yeah," he replied. "A little. But I really thought it would be fun."

"I don't know if I have anything to wear to a fancy place like that," I said.

He stalled. "Maybe you should think about how you spend your paycheck and get yourself some clothes that fit."

That cut. First Lance and now Chris. And come to think of it, the Indian guy at the 7-11 had made some crack too. I'd filtered it out because I was focused on the cat.

"That sounds good," I tried to recover. Maybe I was in a deeper nosedive than I'd thought.

"Great. We're on for one o'clock."

"Llegaré a tiempo," I replied and his eyes lit up like a silent burglar alarm.

"Bueno, por lo menos te podemos prometer que sin ti no vamos a empezar el partido."

I clapped at that, and he rose and bowed like a bullfighter.

"And the best news of all . . ." he smiled, sitting back down. "Ole Humph is footin' the bill. I just don't want to be the only one at the table not to recognize things on the menu. I made a slip the other night—and the mother-in-law gave me a look like a cattle prod."

"I understand," I mumbled . . . instantly back in that chair on Eyrie Street with the sound of the wheel turning and the water flowing . . . Sophia's warm wet mouth . . .

If he hadn't lobbed a file on my desk, I would've phased out right there.

It was from the Two-Four, the close-out paperwork on Stoakes. Just as I'd predicted, they were definitely pushing to have the case sealed up as suicide, and with no extenuating circumstances as in the Whitney matter—at least not that they knew about. In the state I was in, I couldn't see any reason to cough up any more info and stir the pot. Better to sign off. Maybe a man who takes his own life so violently deserves to rest in peace. Besides, going against the grain meant taking Lance's opinion head-on, and with the possible exception of Chris, he was my ace boon coon now that Jimmie was gone. Plus, no one else had the dimmest idea of any connection between Stoakes' and Whitney's business affairs—and I wasn't sure there really was one. I'd dug up a few things, but that was a long way from evidence and a very long way from proof—of anything. Whitney was in real estate. Stoakes dished out or denied permits—that was the only association, and nobody would take any notice. The connecting rod was Genevieve. But I had only hunches and suppositions and none of it I felt good sharing with anyone, certainly not Chris. I may have been a bit jealous of the guy but I had no intention of doing anything to damage his career—or put him in the way of something so far out of his comfort zone.

If I was going to go after her, I'd need something a lot more probative than I had, and I wasn't sure I wanted to hunt that hard. No—that was the one thing I was sure about. I wanted to know *much* more about her, but not for the sake of the badge and any investigation. For me. She could've also been that Denita Kent woman whose name had poked up in Whitney's affairs. She might've had a chain of aliases and Interpol warnings running around the globe. Something in her brought to mind duct tape and bandage scissors—and a lynx stole in Gstaad. What kind of con was she running? And what the hell did it have to do with me? That's what I wanted to know. Didn't I?

Maybe that was my big problem—I always wanted to know stuff I didn't want to know about.

The way I was coming around to seeing it, or to justify it in my mind—two men who may or may not have had any personal feelings about each other, or even any knowledge, had killed themselves in especially forceful ways. If Genevieve was implicated in their deaths, it wasn't in the kind of way that was going to be easy to investigate, let alone prosecute. It wasn't easy to even talk about, and I sure wasn't going to open my mouth and try to fill everyone in. Not after my lesson in mammalian sexuality. She was rich and beautiful—and she had some special power. That's what made her formidable—and more desirable than any woman I'd ever met. She said she was going to open a window for me. From what I could tell so far, the view was something I had to see. Because I had a sense that the window wouldn't be just for looking out. It was a way of getting out. Where I'd be when I jumped, I didn't have a clue.

In any case, I thought confirming Stoakes' suicide was a good play. It went a long way to shutting down the Whitney incident on the same grounds. Our job was investigating crimes, not psychological phenomena. All I had to do was keep my trap shut about the real amount of money I thought Whitney had stashed—and bear in mind it was only a surmise not substantiated by expert evaluation—and probably wouldn't come as that big a surprise anyway. I figured there was a good chance the Mercedes fumes could blow away too. His kids could fight the will in court if they wanted to, and if some of the other investment trails started to unravel, so be it. In one view it gave even more motive for suicide. People's minds start to come apart the more they try to hide things.

The only real problem I saw flittering in the background was McInnes. I had no doubt he'd been to Eyrie Street. One way or another he'd seen what the scarf revealed and he may have undergone his own "experiment." Why he'd suckered me into Genevieve's web was still unknown. The worst I felt I faced in protecting her was a question of competence—and after what she'd put me through I thought I could weather that. At the very outside, if a whole lot more information came to light in unwanted ways, it would be an obstruction charge. But then Chris would get some on his sleeve too, and given his father-in-law, that didn't seem likely. I suddenly felt like I was in a very strong position to bail out on any further investigation, and I signed off on Stoakes.

"Hey Rit, whatta ya think?" a voice needled.

I realized someone had been talking around me and then at me and I hadn't been paying attention. Padgett was still there, but we'd been joined by Montague and Haslett, two other defectives in our house.

Monty's tagline was "Ice cream has no bones." Said it all the time no matter what the situation. He was a whisker shy of my age. We called him Head and Shoulders on account of his dandruff, which he seemed to shrug off easier than he could brush off. He was a P-whipped Presbyterian father of two Campfire Girls and a Pop Warner benchwarmer rightly known as the Burrito. Why anyone would let their kid get so fat I have no idea. I'd only seen Monty blazed once, belting out a U2 track at a karaoke night. But he was OK.

Haslett was in his late 30's and a chronic sufferer of Personality Deficit Disorder. He was what my mother would've called "un cuchichero." Although he shared my "better let them bleed out than plead out" philosophy, I wouldn't have trusted him with my back in a buffet line let alone a CIP. Someone once told me he kept a nose hair trimmer in his locker. Either way, he had an unpleasantly thin head and a compressed body that reminded me of a flounder. There was a deadbolt on his private life, but he always made out he was a player.

He was speculating again about Quisp and Quake, two patrol cops who used to work out of our Precinct. Quisp was small and smart, Quake was big and not so smart. But they'd gotten along. In fact they'd gotten friendly enough for a rumor to have started. I was pretty sure Haslett had started that rumor—the same way I made him for the one behind the bilgewater about me "misappropriating" some confiscated bud. I scribbled a note on my legal pad to Chris . . . *One day his fingerprints are going to end up in the wrong place at the right time.*

"Si yo fuera tú, haría eso."

I nodded. White Boy was getting some game.

"So, whatta ya think?" Haslett badgered. "That why they got split up?"

"Gee, Ron, I don't know," I said. "We've been kinda busy."

"Yeah, you don't look like yourself," he replied, turning his flounder head. "Too much *work*. Or maybe you picked up some tasty new virus."

"Thanks very much." The fact that he knew I could've bitch slapped his flounder head in always made me feel better.

"Listen to this one," he smirked. "This 'pinkie' goes to the doctor, right? Finds out he's got AIDS. So the doc writes out a script for him. Two cans of pork and beans, three cans of refried beans, a pound of bran, two pounds of mixed nuts, three pounds of prunes and five boxes of Ex Lax. The pillow biter says 'Doctor, is all this really going to make me well?' and the doc says 'Probably not, but it'll sure as hell teach you what your asshole's for!'"

"I think you've missed your calling, Ron," I replied. "You should be working one of the ferries—as a clown."

Two months ago, I'd seen Kovak, the little cop they called Quisp, front three bikers in full break-action frenzy and not back down. He just talked to them. It was artful street policing at its most courageous and disciplined best. I'm certain he wasn't even thinking of his Glock. He *knew* he didn't need it—and those hogmen knew it too. So what if Kovak traveled on the other bus, he was on my team in the alleys.

Haslett, thick as he was, got the scent of disapproval and slunk off to gossip about me at the other end of the floor. "Un chico antipático," Chris confirmed—to which I added, "You damn skippy."

But I didn't care about Mr. Flounder. One day the higher-ups would notice that he spent too much time lurking around the water cooler. What I cared about was softening up the Cub for a finish on Whitney. He was like a dachshund ready to race down any rabbit hole. I had to start boarding up those holes. I'd gone cold on the chase for both personal and legit reasons, and now I wanted him to wave goodbye with me—like a good partner should. I told him about Jimmie's service and started rehashing the reasons why the Whitney deal wasn't worth any more of our time. I felt like I was on pretty solid ground, at least on that score. But as chance would have it, another case came in to give us something else to really think about.

The Laotian owner of an all-night store in Wetworld had been found shot in the back of the head. The wife who'd called it in said they'd fallen behind in their protection payments to the Ghost Tigers. Padgett had apprenticed on the Asian Squad and was hot to trot. We took his car over to the scene and the time alone together helped me set him straight on Whitney. I told him I'd changed my mind about my intuition of foul play. It was a heavy way to 86 yourself, but the evidence wasn't pointing to anyone but Whitney. Maybe he'd been given a bad medical diagnosis no one knew about. Maybe he just lost the plot. I kept softening the suspicions, repeating the points that were sure. All I wanted was to change homicide to suicide in Chris' mind—just as it had been before I got a bee in my bonnet about the new will.

I think I laid it down pretty simple, but in the middle of my spiel I had to take an awkward call on the cell. Every time it rang, I thought it might be her. No dice. This patrol cop called Brandenberg was in a pickle. He'd screwed the pooch on the first case Chris and I'd worked together and Chris knew it. But Brandy couldn't afford a rap on the knuckles from Infernal Affairs and he was reaching out to me. Thing was, I owed him. He'd done an after school favor. About six months back there'd been this old showgirl in trouble. Felicity DuMarr. That was her real name, I swear to God. I'd never done the dance with her, but I liked her. She'd run afoul of a blade-happy Shylock who was chummy with the Brucatos and needed some no questions asked protection. Me, I hit you and no matter how big you are, you notice it. Brandy could tap a downtown building on the nameplate and the elevators would stop running. He was the man for the job and had stepped up to the plate when I couldn't. Now at full count he wanted a walk. I pretended to blow him off, and then texted him straight ILU. I figured he'd pick up the sticks. I could put in a good word on the QT, or at least not point the finger. As long as Chris stayed clean on it, I thought things would be cool.

By the time we got to Wetworld, we'd agreed that while I was at Jimmie's service, he'd speak to the Assistant D.A. and put the nail in the coffin. All going well, we'd have the Whitney affair off our desks forever in 24 hours.

Jensen, the attending uniform, didn't give me a nod— which I took as a snub. I'd worked a case with him four blocks over at the Shark Fin Inn not that long ago. We did a cursory canvass of the neighborhood, but based on the wife's statement, Chris had already formed the view that the Ghost Tigers were responsible and was straining at the leash. He'd forgotten all about the call from Brandy and Whitney's self-imposed exit was a done deal. Sometimes his attention span reminded me of a house fly. But that worked for me. Just dandy.

In our town, the bikers had the amphetamine and Ecstasy markets stitched up. The late Freddy Valdez's Latino network vied with a couple of black gangs to take the remains of the heroin and crack business away from the old-timers who were in disarray after the Zagame and Brucato war (in which the heads of both families had been snuffed). Herb, Ice and the new synthetic known as Liquid Crystal were hotly contested markets. That left the Asians with holes to slip through, but they needed working capital and that meant extortion, nunchaku massages and every so often a plain old bullet. One from a .38 revolver it looked like in this case.

The only problem with this theory was my instincts again. The liver temp indicated the body had been dead a few hours—so the wife had sat on her hands before picking up the phone. What was even more suggestive to me was that although I'd been out of touch with the night-to-night pulse of Wetworld, now having checked out the actual address of the store, it struck me that if I owned the place I'd have been paying off the Latino Brothers. This was their real estate, Freddy or no. They had a vested interest in keeping the Ghost Tigers blocked up in Chinatown. That may have only been a few streets away, but that was like another world in this part of town. So many other worlds in a city.

I could see it was possible that the Tigers had gotten ambitious and had targeted the Laotians because they were Asian. But gang killings outside ranks are always about sending signals and I couldn't see the Tigers trying to send that kind of signal when they had their own network to shore up and more prosperous people to shake down without triggering a turf war. If they felt strong enough to cross Frontera Street and wanted to throw down a gauntlet, drugs and real money would've been at stake, not some Beef Jerky store owner, who even our sloppy canvass revealed was respected for the long hours he put in. As to the Latinos, they never shot people in the back of the head. If the cause had been delinquent payment of suck money, there would have been a warning and any lethal retribution would've been signature.

The real gangs, as in organized crime, actually are organized. Even the old crimesters like the Zagames and Brucatos had always taken pride in the order they maintained. If the recent Dons had gotten greedy and strangled the shipping and driven the transport industry off the road, newer players like Valdez had become a little smarter. Freddy would've cut your heart out himself if you'd insulted him, but like every sensible businessman he valued stability—and if you treated him and his con safos, he'd have gone a lot further than most bank managers to keep people like the Laotians paying their way. Whether it was Domino Luis or Jorge Pacheco who was calling the shots now, I was willing to bet that a look into the crime stats for that block would've shown that no retailer had had any trouble in recent times except for a random robbery by some tecato with the meter running out or a slobbering tweaker, in which case the culprit would've been found and probably disemboweled or blowtorched before the police took any action. The Latinos were ruthless but they had a business plan and 90% of the mayhem they got up to was with their own people. No, I was sure there was something fishy about the wife's story, but I wasn't about to pipe up with all the other things I had on my mind. Not least that I might be losing my mind.

Chris and I scarfed won ton soup at the Golden Orchid and I agreed that he could handle the investigation however he wanted to, then I shoved off for the Long Room early on foot. I had in mind to do some shopping for a few new threads if I was going to be dining at Humphrey Dumpty's table over the weekend.

I didn't have any luck. The new styles made me look like a

nancy boy. I got depressed. I really needed to find a few cool things—and not just for work and the sake of Padgett's clan. I wanted to impress Lady Genevieve. I knew that would be damn hard to do, but I'd definitely trimmed down of late. I just needed to find the right fashion. Instead I found myself cruising past the boutiques on Republic, thinking of getting something for her. Lance Harrigan rang on the cell. I told him I'd call back.

I'd never been good at buying stuff for either of my wives. Sweet Polly Purebred was built for comfort, Joan for speed. Pol was a size 16, made a nice meatloaf and started giggling after a glass of Zinfandel. Joan was a carrot-top spitfire, who sprayed on her clothes and mixed a mean Tom Collins. But neither one was into lingerie. Now I felt an urge to pick out something really sexy. But if I went lace, I knew Genevieve would be latex. If I chose lace, she'd be barbed wire. She was such a mix of carnations and case-hardened steel it made my head spin.

And it wasn't just that I was horny for her . . . I wanted her . . . to respect me. Yeah, that was it. I don't know—maybe something else. That was hard enough to swallow by itself. I was just so curious—and she knew it.

I tried to think what it was I was truly hoping for, and I guess it came down to a woman I could actually trust. Not that I would. That really would be insane. But it would've been nice to have the damn chance. The fact that she seemed so much like the last person anyone could or should trust somehow gave me a sick kind of optimism. If you knew all the things I'd seen, maybe you'd understand.

A sign in some financial adviser's window said UNDERSTAND YOUR OPTIONS. That's what we all want to think we're rich in I realized. Doors to choose, windows to look out of. Things to look forward to. Someone to believe in—and who believes in us.

Another cell call. Not her. A ratbag lawyer named Satir. Said he had some mud on a judge that could be swayed.

Wondered if I was interested. I told him I wasn't. Just hearing his voice made me want to wash my hands. But you have to listen to the streets. That's the job. I bagged and tagged the info and stuck it away in my mind where nobody else would find it. That's what Cracker Jack would've done.

Before the blue line, when he was a pup, he'd worked as a runner for Vig Abrams, a big time old school bookie who it was said never wrote anything down. Jack had obviously listened to His Master's Voice because he never kept a single name or number in his phone. Everything was in his head.

I was feeling more of the queasy twinges when I looked up and saw that I was in front of Nutwell's Toys. There was a man in the window—with veins and arteries showing—and his guts. His heart. It startled me. It was just one of those Visible Man educational toys—but it was life-size for God sakes—and holding up a little sign: **Win Me For Your School!**

My skeleton and internal organs are housed in a transparent body wall sculpted to show my muscular details and major blood vessels. A removable breast plate gives you easy access to my internal organs.

Christ almighty. Whatever happened to normal shelf-size models of Captain Action and Johnny Unitas? Getting high on plastic cement and "the enamel with the sprayed on look." Internal organs deserve some privacy.

Speaking of which, the won ton soup had run straight through me. I had to take an urgent leak so I cut through the Cannery Building, a big undercover market where Greeks and Italians yell at you to buy appetizing stuff like tripe. I came in through the Delicatessen end, full of booths of swarthy faces peeking out behind huge netted salamis. The restrooms were in the Fish section and I got to confirm, that yes, Ron Haslett's head, indeed his whole body really did bear a strong resemblance to a flounder. This cheered me up—but when I bumbled into the restroom, I found a man with stunted arms standing at the urinal. He was like "Sealo," the circus freak whose hands grew directly from his shoulders. My Aunt Di had given me a book about Sealo for a birthday once. He was actually amazingly dexterous, able to shave and sign his name. He could even zip up his pants by using a stick with a hook on the end. I was puzzled about how the guy at the urinal managed to unzip himself, but I couldn't handle standing next to him. I went in one of the stalls. There's nothing wrong with a little privacy.

The disabled toilet next to me was occupied. I could hear the guy making sounds. I started to wonder in what way was he disabled? With those noises he was making—he sounded like something that belonged in the water. Then he said in this guttural voice, "Got any paper?"

I imagined for a second he meant newspaper. Maybe he was going to soak it to keep himself moist. Then a hand appeared. He had a fused finger—so the hand looked more like some kind of swimmeret. Believe me, that's not the kind of thing you want to see sneaking up under a stall. I stuffed a couple of two-ply squares underneath the partition and got the hell out. As my hobo clown friends told me, you never know who you'll meet.

I made a call to the Boss about Brandy and spread as much goodwill as I thought the market would bear. Then I hit the nickel hard and got to the Long Room right on the button for the service. Wardell had gone formal, ditching his Fat Albert sweatshirt and stuffing himself into a suit that made him look like a home plate umpire. Even more surprising, he'd splashed out with cold cuts, a brand new bag of Wonder Bread, plus a mop bucket brimming with ice and bottled Bud. Nothing but the best for the Long Room's own.

He'd been busy on the phone too. Milwaukee Mike and Grabowski from the Avenue Bar were playing rotation, Stojanovich, the night clerk at the Stanton—and of course Stutter, Pig Dog and Gershwin the Orangutan, the redheaded bouncer from the Boardwalk. Jimmie's ashes had just arrived and were sitting proudly in one of the old spittoons under the leadlight on the tournament table. Wardell had cleaned and wire-brushed the spittoon, apparently deciding the crematorium's standard urn was not up to standard (those more expensive, beyond the budget).

I was miffed when Grabowski had to ask Stutter who I was (which took him a good thirty seconds to explain). The photographs lifted the mood. Wardell's sister LeRine had gone into Jimmie's rooms at the Stanton and selected a bunch of photos of him and his wife Camille and arranged them along with some fistfuls of flowers on a couple of the tables. Jimmie and his honey were smiling and smooching in the snapshots, swilling martinis, playing cards and trying to dance. For a guy with only one leg, Jimmie had been surprisingly agile. LeRine was a waitress at the coffee shop in the lobby of the Stanton, but she had a smoky voice, and sang along to some Sinatra. "You Make Me Feel So Young" and "I've Got You Under My Skin."

Soon after, the corned beef came out and the mustard started squirting, and I knew I'd want to drink the whole bucket of beer so I took the Dell aside and told him I was heading off. Poor guy, whatever was left of Jimmie, that's what he wanted to keep. But as fat as he was, he'd have paddled across the harbor himself, with the ashes over his head if that's what it would've taken to fulfill Jimmie's last request. I was glad to save him the trip. He loved corn beef. I hefted the spittoon, which could've held five one-legged men, when he pulled out an envelope.

"Jimmie . . . wanted you to have this."

"T-hanks," I stammered, a little disappointed because I was hoping for some Cubans. Jimmie must've run out. I stowed the envelope in my pocket, thinking it was more photos.

"You look affer him," Wardell admonished. "An' yo own damnself. You look like we be spreadin' you soon."

I tried to smile at this parting shot. Pig Dog and Gershwin were talking about the actor Wally Cox's ashes that had been left in the keeping of Marlon Brando—how it was rumored that

Brando's ashes had been mixed in with Cox's when he died.

"They were both faggots," Pig Dog insisted. "Brando was still in love with him."

"An odd couple, that's for sure," Gershwin nodded.

"That's what *that* show was about too," Pig Dog said, opening a Bud. "Tony Randall and Jack Klugman. Two queens, man."

No one had paid me much mind, which sort of ticked me off—and now the beer was starting to flow. I caught a cab to the ferry terminal thinking that Jimmie would've been pleased by the gathering. He'd at least gone out with some dignity. Dignity was a little harder for me to come by. First the cabbie made some yuck-yuck about the spittoon and then I had to sit on the ferry holding it between my legs. Fortunately there weren't that many people on board—and the hobo clowns weren't in sight. On the shoreline, where Jimmie had maybe gone fishing once, or lost his virginity for all I knew—a titan crane thrust out from the pier and vapor from the refinery hung in the air. The view back toward the city was nice though. I said, "So long you old guinea. Hope you find your missing leg," and spread the ashes as evenly as I could.

I'd worked a case around the Point years back—two different arms floated in wrapped in kelp. One was from a boy, the other a woman. Both cases never closed. Looking now at the cuttlefish shells and pieces of broken Styrofoam, I wondered again about the people connected to those limbs, and let the last of Jimmie blow away onto the water. That's what we become in the end. Ashtray sand and driftwood. Pieces of boats and booze bottles. Unsolved summer nights.

Made me think of Stoakes and Whitney again—how all suicides are unsolved murders in a sense. I suddenly had a devastating desire to see her . . . be with her. Genevieve. Holding hands. It was psycho. Or pathetic.

But at least it was honest. Frighteningly honest.

SWEETHEART, THEY'RE SUSPECTING THINGS

1

I sat out on the shore of Fairy Point, with its marooned inner tubes and Happy Meal packs, longer than I wanted to. When the cell wasn't haranguing me, my mind started to wander. A military jet flew over. It reminded me how often we used to see them pass overhead when I was a kid. We had sonic booms all the time in those days—when the windows would almost break and Emily Akin, whose breath smelled like celery, would run out and lift her skirt to catch all the birds she expected to fall. Civil Defense was a big deal.

Once at school, they made us play this game. The teachers put on white smocks and hardhats, the fire department came, and a man with suede elbow patches explained air raids. He told us *teamwork is the key to survival*. He made me a doctor and Pam Cook, a nurse—the other kids became casualties. They wore signs that said things like *Head Injury* and *Third Degree Burns*. We were supposed to sort them out and line them up according to the nature of the damage. Adam Tarkington, the tractor man's son, couldn't stop laughing. He closed his eyes and kept running into people saying "I'm blind!

I can't see!" Miss Kavanaugh, who was later fired for not wearing underwear, twisted her ankle when he collided with her. No one else was hurt, at least not that you could see—not unless you'd grown up with them.

I saw the signs hanging around their necks. But when I read the words *Internal Bleeding* or *Radiation Poisoning,* all I could see was Jamie Hogebom, whose ears got red when we kidded him about his crew cut or accused him of farting. I wanted to say I know you, all of you. You're Gareth Owens, the masturbator. I saw you crying alone in the schoolyard once when the chain nets on the basketball hoops were ringing in the wind. And you, Tina—your real father's in Soledad for killing that man he got into a fight with at the Five Spot. They found the body in the power plant turbine on the Díaz Canal. I wanted to tell them it was going to be all right. Everything. But I couldn't touch them. If I reached out for Jamie, he would've thought I was a sissy. If I tried to take Tina's hand, she would've said I had cooties. I tried hard to look like I remembered what I'd been told, but it was difficult to concentrate. On the other side of the backstop, Mr Estevez was using a knitting yarn cone as a megaphone. He kept saying *No pushing. Come on now, find that shelter.*

All these years later—all the nights of handguns and handjobs since, and I still hadn't found shelter. At last the ferry returned, arriving ceremoniously it seemed, like a second chance. I had business with a bath, Chet Baker, a mouth load of vitamins and a bowl of steamed vegetables. I was just silly enough to think about getting into fighting shape for Genevieve. She wasn't like any woman—or person that I'd met. She was like one of those prize Arabian mares who can eat the back furlong. I hadn't even gotten in the saddle, let alone to the gate—but I wanted to. With all my being.

I dug into a newspaper flapping around on the top deck and found out that the stuffed bison in the lobby of the Frontier Bank building had been discovered to have a 40-

pound wasp nest inside it. The local crime news had gone quiet—and that was the best news I could get. I flipped through the sports pages. The odds were running hard against Salazar in the Saturday bout with the Nigerian. I turned to the dirty personals in the back.

Angelcake, a beautiful pre-op transsexual, specializes in Fantasy Fulfillment. Experience the Love Torture of the Bitch Goddess, Molina. Mother Superior teaches lessons in disgrace. Limits respected.

That was comforting, I thought. You want to have your limits respected while you're being disgraced. I couldn't decide if it made me feel sick or made me feel relieved—to be reminded what people were getting up to in plastic palm hotels named after Presidents and those seamy side entrance labyrinths down where the streetlights turn a blind eye.

Naturally, there was an on-going battle with the newspaper for running these types of ads—the fundamentalists and puritans were always raising a stink. Responding to that kind of pressure, I'd once been in on the bust of a prominent brothel owner called The Panda. We raided his Mercado Street club on a Friday afternoon. We found the then-head of Police Infernal Affairs being ridden like a pony by a chick with a blue Mohawk. In the next room, the soon-to-be former chairman of the investment company (a born again!), who managed the pension fund for city employees, was frolicking with two underage Filipinas in a manner that would've raised the eyebrows of even a Finn. Of course the intelligence we were working with was just fine. Me and the raid team were only pawns in a power struggle between the Commissioner's office and City Hall. Two high profile local execs and a mayoral minder, all family men, also got caught with their pants down.

It's the J. Edgar Hoover story time and again. The director of the Children's Charity gets nailed for child porn. Firebrand Reverend Mathers, who feeds his collection bowls by railing against the sodomites, is found in a red garter belt, blue around

the gills from amyl nitrate. If you want to find real moral corruption, look at the sermonizers and policy makers. Why do
the limousines have tinted windows and the churches stained
glass? Stained is right.

I didn't know where this put me with Genevieve. There was
something sordid about it, I admit. I probably wouldn't have
been involved otherwise. But if it was prostitution or therapy—
or the beginning of blackmail (and there's often a link between
those three), why hadn't any mention of money been made?
And police favors? I was willing to make a start on that without her asking, and without me even knowing how big a favor
would spread the jam. No, everything that had happened so far
seemed consensual—as in "con" and "sensual." If I wanted
more, and I confess I wanted a lot more—it was my risk, my
ride. My dream.

Reading the personals did, however, remind me again of
McInnes, jiggling in the background, like one of those Creepy
Crawlers I cooked up with Mattel Plastigoop when I was a kid.
It was time to get out in front of that unknown, so I called him
on my cell from the ferry deck. The open air of the harbor
made it easier. I needed to know if anything I was doing—or
not doing—was going to come back and bite me. I got his
voicemail. I left a message for him to call or text me ASAP. I
thought maybe a little prick of urgency would work to my
advantage. It was strangely bolstering to hear his old voice on
the message bank. If he hadn't seemed himself the other day in
appearance, his voice message reassured me. It was the same
one he used to have.

When I got back to the city, I checked in, completed some
paperwork and made some more calls. Monty needed to
remind me that ice cream has no bones and for me to have a
listen to a 911 tape. The incident presented as a B&E gone bad,
but he didn't buy it. I think old Head and Shoulders kind of
liked me. And he hated Haslett. I agreed with him about the
background noise and said it was worth getting analyzed. I left

a message on Padgett's voicemail and some file notes on his desk. Then I got in my car. I wanted to go by Eyrie Street. Just to have a look. Then came the worry that I might be observed—if she thought I was spying . . .

It raised again the thorny question of how she'd been spying on me. How had she known I was coming? How had she found out about my sister—and what else did she know? I drove over to the gates of Funland. I could just see the roof of her house from there. It was something at least. Like the shreds of paper on the other side of the fence, a hint of what used to be—what might give rise to something new. And I heard that old song that Stacy would sing . . . *"Wayward Heart . . . why do dreams never die . . . is that why we cry?"*

The amusement park may have been closed down in the wake of the Zagame fire—arguably it should've been closed down long before—but it was all still there—only a couple of the parking lot fronted buildings had been hit. Watching the bags and drink cups stray—it occurred to me that I could stray too. I was after all a police officer. Still.

The loss of weight helped me slip through the diamond-link fence and I felt that old crossing-the-boundary buzz I'd known as a kid. I'd only been inside Funland when there were hundreds of people milling about. Now there were just empty sacks and inquisitive gulls . . . stopped-still, collapsing rides. It made me think of opening the Visible Man's chest and reaching in to touch the internal organs.

I came to the arcade of Whacky Mirrors. They'd all been shattered by vandals and the distortions they put forth were even more extreme than in days of old. In some I was huge and lumpen, or emaciated and tugged—like some kind of quicksilver taffy. I wondered if any of them told any kind of truth. That's the question, when things start to slide. Have you become truly ugly, or are you just looking in a damaged mirror?

Most of the rides like The Spider and the Tilt-a-Whirl had been at least partially dismantled. The same way I felt. Graffiti had been sprayed over the ticket booths and main toilet block—the Merry-Go-Round animals sold-off or stolen, the one survivor, a unicorn with a broken horn. In what used to be the Oceanside Dance Hall, bird spatters crusted the torn-up floorboards and pieces of the spinning ball lay like shards of a dead star. The whole place was eerie and decrepit, and I could just imagine how unsettling it would be at night. Not entirely uninhabited either, which added to the edge. Down under the Mad Mouse and the Scenic Railway tracks, it looked like some vagrants had taken shelter. I noticed a couple of cardboard lean-tos—sheet metal sections and harvested plywood. My cell rang twice but I let it go.

I decided to skip the Midway and the stretch of the park that contained the old food emporium and the Swing-a-Ling rides. But I didn't want to run the gauntlet of those warped mirrors again, so I detoured through the Shooting Gallery. All of the tin ducks had been pinched, and only one of the clowns whose heads used to rotate remained. Someone had stuck a bottle in its jaws, which looked disrespectful and lewd. I pulled it out and heaved it against a wall. That's what we really need. Not amusement parks—places where you pay to smash things.

Remarkably, the Skill Tester hadn't had a rock thrown through it. It was once a Plexiglas booth that you stood in front of, operating two handles that worked a claw, fishing for prizes. I remembered being there once with Briannon and a group of young Samoan boys were trying to pick up these red stuffed devils (like something Dilley's Chocolates would give away for Valentine's). I was thinking that my Dad had had a pair of boxer shorts with little devils like that on them—when Briannon said, "I'd like to see a bigger one—where those kids are down in the box and a devil's working the claws, trying to grab 'em." It struck us both funny. A big pile of entangled kids, wriggling to get out of the way of the descending claws.

Now the kids were gone and a couple of Hello Kittys wallowed amongst a bunch of flattened cans and cigarette packs.

Maybe Briannon's wish had come true. I felt a little wistful then, thinking about her. We'd had some fun, even if it was squalid. But she was just a dime bag version of Stacy. She had the racket but not the game. It wasn't her fault. It wasn't mine either. Her dream was to save enough money and move beyond the methadone clinic, out to the suburbs somewhere. What could I tell her? She looked the part, sometimes. In those Bearpaw boots. But whenever she said something funny, I knew my glass was half empty and it was almost closing time. At least I bought her a burial plot at Greenlawn—and don't think the word didn't get out on that.

She OD'd a week after she shot me, and from the size of the speedball, she meant to do it. You can't plug a cop, even one you've been screwing, and just walk. She could see the claws coming for her. We were both using each other. But I was using her more—because she was only a warm ghost—a way of regaining the past with Stacy, the snowflake blonde I'd hooked up with when Polly was pregnant. Stacy looked into my eyes one summer night after I'd been pulling OT, her expression all switchblade and lipstick, and that was it. I was gone. It didn't last long. But it lasted too long for me to forget. And I'd never been able to lay her to rest.

I turned to go—and then I saw the Foto Booth. It had rude images scrawled over the faded faces of the sample photos. The curtain had been ripped but it still hung in place. I figured the camera would've been removed or foraged ages ago. I sat down on the shelf seat, just like those ones in department store dressing rooms, and stared into the black hole with the red circle, trying to pose for the lens that wasn't there.

It was a very peculiar thing. Very. I *knew* there was no camera in there—but I heard the sound of the shutter. I would've sworn in court. I'd been so mired in thoughts about the past and the neglected atmosphere of the park, I hadn't looked down at the little slot where the photos are supposed to come out. When I did, I saw that there was a strip wedged in place. The simple explanation was that someone had left it there. It had just been forgotten. Whoever it was had gotten distracted—or they were stoned. I couldn't bring myself to look at them. Yet I couldn't leave them there and not know either. So I swiped the little sheet of pics and slipped it in my pocket, feeling the envelope from Jimmie. I remembered I'd better get the spittoon back.

I got up to go drive back to the Long Room, and ran smack dab into a big blue shape.

When we recovered our balance I lost mine again. He had Coke bottle thick glasses tied with rubber bands around his head, which sported a burr haircut I suspected he'd given himself using one of the trick mirrors. Above his glasses was a head-lamp on a strap, the kind that people who do caving or work in mines wear. His pants were flophouse rayon, and made me feel better about my own. He had on a worn blue jacket that said *Security* and in big yellow letters **FUN**, but he was carrying a kid's plastic walkie-talkie. Hanging from an improvised loop in his belt was a small but very red fire extinguisher.

"Contact with intruder," he huffed into the toy walkie-talkie.

"I'm sorry," I started.

"Roger that," he said emphatically, as if in response to some instruction.

He looked to be about 40, pipe cleaner legs under a fast food paunch. Medium height.

"I didn't mean to startle you," I said.

"Roger that," he called again into the walkie-talkie, squeezing the fake squelch button.

I wondered if he'd been a guard there once and couldn't accept the change in situation.

"Who are you talking to?" I tried.

"Command," he snapped, holding the plastic device up closer to his ear. "Are you authorized?" His eyes mooned behind the glasses.

I flashed my police shield, and to my surprise, he authoritatively displayed his own credentials—an old ACCESS TO FUN pass that used to let you go on all the rides.

"Roger that," he barked at the handset and then jammed the device in his jacket pocket. "You've been granted a Day Pass. Not good for night. Night is not good."

"Thanks," I answered, eager to begin shuffling away. You never know with these kinds. They can seem innocent at first, like the Duke—and then come out of a bag on you. He looked and smelled like one of the residents of the sheet metal huts across the Midway. But that headlamp would've cost a pretty penny. I swiveled to make my break—only to my further surprise, he grabbed my hand, which is something very few dudes do to a guy my size. Then he extracted from his other pocket a little ink stamp and selected a red plastic token from several on a silver ring he held up close to his face.

"B is for Buffalo," he announced, examining an orange token. "And for Bonus. Rides and a burger. D is for Dragon and for Day. Day ends at Dark."

He stamped my hand with a poofy little red dragon. Just then my cell phone beeped in my pocket. A text message. My security friend took that as a sign or got a message of his own, because he brandished his toy walkie-talkie again.

"Roger that," he confirmed and walked briskly away.

I guess Command wanted him to resume patrol. I smudged the dragon when I tried to wipe it off, so that it looked like my hand was bleeding. Just another one of those screw-loose people a mild climate and a bankrupt medical system allows to roam freely. At least he had a gig. Self-appointed guardian of a forsaken carnival—protector of FUN. I pulled myself through the fence and drove a flock of insolent gulls and California blankets skyward.

Back at my car I checked the cell phone. There were two voicemails. One from the squad secretary regarding a case number. The other from PERS, the state retirement system, about an accounting error in my favor. Naturally, there would be an adjustment. The text was from McInnes. *Cab du Neant Sat 10 PM.*

That surprised me more than anything else the whole day. I'd been to the Cabaret du Neant once—to bust a pillhead art dealer called Peter Pan for the bathtub murder of his Guatemalan houseboy. I had no idea why McInnes would choose to meet there. While it had once had some pretensions to musical and atmospheric quality, from what I remembered it had declined terminally into a tragic female impersonator's club and a creepoid bar where transsexuals and predatory midnighters rubbed flesh with Liquid Crystal addicts (what us cops call gargoyles). At least we weren't likely to be recognized by anyone without an outstanding warrant.

I went home to feed Pico and have my rendezvous with Chet Baker, but I kept seeing those images from the corridor of mirrors. Then I remembered I'd forgotten to return the spittoon. I couldn't handle it being in the apartment and I didn't want to leave it in the car in case I got broken in to. I drove over to the Long Room through fender bender traffic. The place was closed. I guess after the party everyone flagged and Wardell didn't have the heart to stay open. I used the key Jimmie had given me and let myself in. It seemed more desolate than Funland.

When I finally got back to my place, I took off my coat and found Jimmie's envelope. I slit it open expecting photos to fall out. It was money—and a note in his crabbed handwriting *... Look after yourself, Detective. Use your head but follow your heart and don't forget your gut ... or you'll end up without a leg to stand on. Ha ha! Your dead friend, Jimmie Forever.* I counted out the dough. Exactly 10 large. The second time in my life I'd received that exact amount in an envelope. However he came by it, I hoped I was more deserving this time. There'd always been something of the old Murphy man about Jimmie. It was as warm and generous as one of his goofy grins. And the way I was starting to feel, I figured I might need it.

Coping with opening the envelope made me want to look at the pictures from the Foto Booth. The top shot was blank, the second one chowdery, the third a little clearer. The bottom shot showed traces of a woman of indeterminate age staring vacantly—or fearfully—I couldn't tell. But I got the impression she wasn't right in the head. Maybe someone like "Roger That" would be associated with. She wore a man's sport coat, like something she'd found in a clothes bin. Nice eyes. I slipped the strip of photos onto the fridge door under a faded vinyl Funland magnet.

2.

AFTER I FED PICO I REMEMBERED THAT I DIDN'T HAVE anything for my dinner and hadn't eaten since the won tons with Padgett. I knew I should check in to see what was happening with the investigation of the store owner's murd, but I couldn't bring myself to call him. I felt cramped. Both stretched and compressed. Fluidy. And my mind kept flitting . . . back to the richly appointed interior of Eyrie Street . . . to my fantasies about what lay in hiding in the other parts of the house. Forbidden rooms. Private worlds. Gave me the flicker of El Miedo.

I decided to walk over to a Lebanese place called The Cedars. It was early for dinner but I figured I could grab some take-out and reheat it at home. Maybe El Miedo could be held at bay. My reflection wavered across the glass of the TV screen. I damn sure needed to adjust my horizontal hold.

Beyond paying another visit to Cliffhaven, I couldn't think of anything that I wanted or hoped for anymore. You can't blame a guy with a past like mine. I wondered if Genevieve had drugged me—certain that in some way at least, she had. But how? It felt both like I'd been poisoned—and awakened.

I seemed to alternatingly float and crawl down the pavement, words and pictures from the advertising messages streaming by like colored noise. *Consolidate your debt. Increase your bustline. Microsurgical Reverse Vasectomies . . . Cruelty Free Meat . . .*

I didn't even remember ordering my food at The Cedars, but coming back I could smell it was lemon chicken. I took 10th Street and passed Shenanigans, a bar where I'd spent hours in the past, months maybe. Merle the Pearl, Juicy Fruit, Latigo, Slippery Will Carothers and Star Fontaine, this gim-cracked stripper who had no qualms about taking her dentures out at the bar—they were all still there, mechanically drinking like toy dipping birds in the Blue Curaçao gloom. They might not have even noticed that I'd been gone several months. Dooner was probably on dialysis now, or six feet under. And Betty's Always Ready, a dissipated brunette who worked at a boob job place (she gave me a silicon implant once that I used as a paperweight)—she died of breast cancer just before I went on the wagon and Polly pulled the pin on our marriage. Guido gave us one on the house. Then the circle closed and the hole she'd left sealed over.

I'd come in and order two double brandies, one neat, one on the rocks. Half the time I wouldn't even be listening to the others. I'd slide out of my body . . . oozing like albumen into the past. Juicy Fruit would be swilling gimlets, Merle would be on the beer until he got on the Beam and onto the floor. Will would be pounding Johnny Walker Blacks, standing there as if his tie was nailed to the bar, all of us knowing that his middle management job had been axed half a year before and he hadn't had the stones to tell his wife about the pink slip. As if she did-n't know. We were like children playing peek-a-boo, thinking no one could see us if we closed our eyes. But still I missed them. Not the booze, I missed their broken company. I didn't think I'd paid much attention to it in the old days, but I had.

On the wall above the garnish station I could see the clock

with the maraschino cherries, olives, onions and lemon slices—
and the three swizzle stick hands. According to that clock . . .
It's Happy Hour! Yeah. Today is Happy Hour. I shuffled home
to my Persian roommate, thinking back to Joan, a lifetime ago.
Bee stings up top, but a caboose on the loose.

A chica shimmied past already wearing a July-short skirt
and it wasn't even June. A Rapid Response car shot the yellow
light—a 459 in progress. So many sirens and singles bars . . .
memories of Briannon . . . and Stacy before. All that was left
was a Kotex container that smelled of sinsemilla, a cinnamon
toothpick and a song that stuck in my head. *"Only memories
survive . . . surprised I'm alive . . . with this Wayward Heart."*
There was even less with Bri. Just gun shot residue and regret.

"You're going to be OK," the ER white who'd removed the
slug said. When I asked my own doc later about what the other
boys in blue called "shot term manhood loss," he said "You'll
come good. Just give yourself time to heal." I remembered
wondering how many Happy Hours that would take. Even
with swizzle sticks for arms, you can't put time back in the
clock, and when the real wound is yourself, healing's got to be
a kind of dying, doesn't it?

Polly I found too hard to hold in mind. It was too near in
time. Too raw. I had a feeling she was seeing this shipping
agent that her friend Melissa had introduced us to. Tall. Dark.

Back in the apartment, the scanner was pretty quiet. The
television news, on the other hand, was one crisis after another. *Earthquake in Java triggers tsunami. Israel launches
another attack. Greenhouse gas emissions up.* I shut it off, ran
a bath and put on Chet. "You don't know what love is, until
you learn the meaning of the blues . . ." I could've been back
in Shenanigan's.

Then, while Chet was crooning and the suds were bursting
around my ears, I must've dozed out. That's where things get
even hazier, crazier. I could've sworn I woke up and climbed
out of the bath, but left the water in. I don't know why I did,

maybe I was thinking I'd have another soak later. The Chet Baker CD was long over. Art Pepper too. It seemed surprisingly quiet outside. I put on my robe and made some chamomile tea, thinking that in days gone by I'd have had a Scotch. My skin felt very tender, swollen and elastic at the same time, and my eyesight was blurred. I found it hard to focus on the mirror. My JT seemed sucked up into my body, not lolling loose as it usually did when I took a bath. Then I tried to remember the last time I'd had a bath. I always took showers.

I went to the fridge to see if I'd put away the remains of the lemon chicken. I couldn't find the take-away container anywhere. But I noticed the little strip of pictures from Funland stuck to the Westinghouse door. Before, the top two frames had been empty or so grainy you couldn't see anyone. Now the figure was quite apparent in the second one, at least not as fuzzy as I remembered in the third and almost completely in focus in the final square. She looked now like a woman I recalled seeing in Shenanigans. A reflection in the bottle-lined mirror behind the bar. I made the tea and turned on the TV again. It was all those late night ads. Lustrous haired women in skimpy outfits staring back with glossy lips and eyes. "I'm Simone. Call me now . . . for a chat . . ."

Superimposed numbers started trailing in. For a hoot I turned down the sound, picked up the phone and dialed. It rang and rang—the chatlines are on fire I thought and was just about to give up when a woman answered. But it wasn't Simone or Cheetah asking for a credit card number. It was Polly. I recognized her voice instantly. I must've called the number by instinct. She sounded out of breath and annoyed. I was so surprised and embarrassed I dropped the phone. She hung up. I flicked the channel, hoping she didn't have caller recognition now. There was a Johnny Weissmuller Tarzan movie on. *Tarzan and the Mermaids.*

I don't know how long I tried to watch, I felt so skuzzy I had to haul myself to bed. I lay there listening to my heartbeat until things started to break apart in my head. *Then I was in some kind of city park. Palm trees, Japanese-style gardens. There were sculptures all around. One was a primitive piece carved out of driftwood. A male nude. When I got closer I saw that his John Thomas was the head of a duck decoy. The narrow pathways were lined with rosebushes. I stalked down them carrying a spear. It was a large spear but surprisingly light. I was expecting trouble but there was no one around. On basalt and sandstone pillars were finely wrought pieces of silver. They were so complex I couldn't look at them. Then from the opposite end of the park a funeral party emerged, led by a woman talking loudly. The sculpture park had turned into a crowded cemetery. There were so many marble angels their wings touched.*

Above the graves, on an embankment overlooking the iron fence that surrounded the cemetery, a billboard advertised a new Dilley's Chocolate in the shape of oysters. The pallbearers were women. The coffin they carried looked like an ice chest. Inside was a child. People clutched wreaths woven in the shape of babies—dolls made of ivy. The loud woman led the service because the mother of the dead child was too distraught to attend. I tried to mingle with the crowd, mostly women, but the spear drew attention. Some of the women asked how I knew the mother. I slipped away, trying to get out. On a bench I found a small carved coffin. Inside the coffin was a smaller coffin, and a smaller coffin inside that—like Chinese boxes or those Russian dolls. One by one I opened them. Finally I got down to the tiniest coffin of all. Inside was a miniature orange plastic buffalo.

I woke up naked in the empty bathtub at 5:30 AM. Muscle spasms, hot flashes then rushing cold. A mass of gelatinous fuzz had dried to a crust on my upper body, but between my legs and under my buttocks it remained slick and gooey, with that smell of brine shrimp and pantyhose that I associated with Polly when she got home late from work on a hot day. I wondered if I'd had a wet dream—or some kind of hemorrhage. But what kind? It wasn't like any bodily fluid I was familiar with, and I thought I was an expert.

I tried to stand. I had to grab a hold of the sink and then the door. Pico was snuggled in bed where I should've been. The light in the kitchen was on. Still no sign of the missing Lebanese. Even in the old blackout days there'd always been something to take hold of. Now I couldn't be sure of what I'd just dreamed and what I'd actually done. Or what had been done to me.

My bones felt lighter. My face was leaner and softer—and younger looking I thought. The acne scars had cleared. I got on the scales. My feet seemed to take up less space—a notion that so stirred me up I had to race to the closet to see if my shoes still fit. They were all a size or more too big for me. It was high. I went back to the bath to investigate.

The unnatural gel had hardened into a pearly scum. I wished I had a chest plate like the Visible Man so I could reach in and feel if my internal organs were still there. I went to have a leak and was disturbed even further to find my boy was smaller. It'd looked little when I straggled out of the tub, but I'd figured it had gotten scared from being in the bath for so long. Now it actually *felt* smaller in my hands. What was happening didn't make any damn sense. People don't shrink, get younger . . . change shape . . . because of a bath . . . or even a drug. I stepped into the shower while a pot of very strong coffee brewed. I had to wake up.

Hot lather and needles from the showerhead streaming down brought both relief and a wildfire of sensitivity to my skin so that I had to turn up the cold. Scrubbing was out of the question—I was forced to let the weird film rinse off with just the pressure of the flow. Any way you looked at it something major was wrong—with my body or my mind. Or both. The gunk in the bath, the dreams, the not being sure of where I'd slept—it appeared I'd never made it to the bed. I had to get a grip. But onto what? Even El Miedo seemed familiar relative to this.

Finding anything to wear was another serious challenge. Nothing fit. My underwear was no longer serviceable, the waistbands all stretchy. I tore through piles and drawers—and down in the back of the closet I found a bra and g-string. Mauve. Like something from Victoria's Secret. I'd never brought a woman back to the apartment. It had to have been something I'd bought for Briannon and stashed away. I wondered how Polly had never found it. Maybe she had. What would it be like to find something as intimate as lingerie in the bottom of your husband's drawer, knowing only that it wasn't for you?

I tried to remember where and when I'd made the purchase, but it was lost in a haze of booze. I'd been so spaced I'd squirreled the things away and forgotten about them. I held up the delicate pieces against my body and realized I was losing body hair. Not only did my skin feel smoother, the flesh of my chest and legs was more visible.

I knotted some old pants tight enough to not fall to my knees and put on a wrinkled cotton shirt Polly and I'd bought on a trip to Phoenix—stuffed wads of newspapers in my shoes. I looked like I was working undercover at some soup kitchen, but it was the best I could do. I had to get out of that apartment. Let them make jokes at the Precinct. I wondered what Genevieve would say when she saw me. Or if she knew.

I went straight to work, picking up a buttercream from Nelly's—but it looked so grossly fattening when I got it out of the bag, I only took a couple of bites. For once I was in before Chris. I was braced for banter and put-downs from the likes of Haslett and Montague, not to mention the Boss. Instead I got whispers from Has Been and worried stares from Monty. That worried me all the more. I tried to look busy shuffling papers. Then I got the notion of calling McInnes. Maybe some casual work-related shooting the breeze would open a door to what in hell was going on—or at least clue me in on why he'd chosen the Cabaret du Neant as the meet for Saturday night. I got his voicemail message on the cell again, so I decided to ring him on the land-line. When I called the Three-One-Two, the station house that he worked out of, I got an earnest young pup named Rodriguez—and a big shock.

McInnes had resigned the day before. The word was his pension was under review for such a sudden departure. I figured the union rep would make a noise about that—but what would Jack do? You don't just quit a job like this. It's a life. Not much of a life, but not something you throw away either. It was too much of a coincidence, coming on the heels of my problems, but I didn't have a chance to dwell on it because Padgett arrived, looking downright dapper. I shuddered to think what I looked like to him, and when he got a good look, he shuddered too.

"You going to tell me about it?" he asked when he'd gotten settled in across the desk. "What's the diagnosis?"

That term threw me. He was just responding to my appearance. If he knew what was going on in my mind . . .

"Rit, you look like hell. Actually, *you* look a little better today. But your clothes—you working the bins? Something's up, Dog. Yesterday I said to myself he's either using or there's some medical condition. Which is it?"

"I'm just going through some changes," I said, and my voice sounded so different to me and my answer so lame I had to look away. The way he said, "using," made it sound like he'd listened to some of the rumors about me. Maybe he really was babysitting. Maybe my paranoia was something I still could trust.

The official word came in on the Whitney case. Suicide. Matter closed, the DNA discrepancy notwithstanding. It was a big relief. I was still dealing with the news about McInnes. Of course once the Whitney update blew over, I could tell

Padgett would want another bite of the cherry. I was beginning to think maybe the medical angle was my best bet. He'd given me the out. If I looked even half as fucked up as I felt, maybe I should take some time off. See my doctor—see a specialist. I was owed the time, and now with the money from Jimmie I had some extra cushion. But I knew that not having the job to go to would only send me whirling down into the dungeons or fantasy rooms I imagined that lay hidden in Eyrie Street—or some nightmare hall of mirrors inside my head straight into the cold, cold arms of El Miedo. What would I do if I didn't have this chump dump to come to each day? I started to panic. Who was I without the job? I could end up like Slippery Will.

But how much longer could I bluff my colleagues? I wasn't able to concentrate for even a few minutes at a time. The only thing that was clear in my mind was her. My need for her—the hold she had on me, and the potential she held out. Four o'clock seemed like an eternity away. Her words kept echoing in my mind . . . *That's the time your mother used to expect you . . .*

Lance Harrigan rang. He prodded me again about the visit to the therapist. I tried to blow him off even as I reached for the envelope in my drawer where I'd written down the details. Ordinarily, an appointment with a psychologist was the last thing I would've wanted anyone to know about. But I could see now that having one on my record could be played to advantage. It wouldn't help my career any, but I wasn't sure I'd have much of a career left. And what would the cop chop matter if I scored with Genevieve—she was rich.

Nah, check that—that was stupid. That really was insane. I made up my mind I would go. Sometimes you just need to talk to strangers. Those have always been the people I know best.

When I got off the phone, Padgett started in on me again.

"Go home, Rit," he said. "I think maybe your pal Jimmie's

deal has gotten to you. I'll cover for you. You're not well. You need a break."

Boy, did I. "Keep me posted on the Laotian thing."

He nodded, somewhat sadly I could tell. I ducked out before I had to speak to anyone else. Even in the wild white-knuckle days I'd never skipped out on work officially. I was sneaky—I was often sick as a dog—but I had some honor. Now it felt like I'd cut my own nuts off. But I didn't know what else to do. Sooner or later we'd be called out to something heavy and if I wasn't in the game, someone like Chris would get hurt. That wasn't going to happen. Not because of my personal shadowplay.

But I couldn't go home. So I drove around for an hour, lost in my own city. Then of course I ended up in Cliffhaven. For the life of me, I couldn't stop thinking about her. I knew she was trouble. Maybe even evil, if you want to use that word. Something I couldn't understand anyway. But she was all I had. As pervy and twisted as the deal with the rats and Sophia had been, I had to admit it turned me on. I mean it actually scared me and made me feel like I'd fallen through a manhole in reality, but it charged me too—in ways way beyond electricity. I'd never known anything to do with sex that had so much show business to it—so much planning—so much stuff I couldn't believe—and yet had to believe because it was happening to me. Because I'd become part of the show.

Now the biggest, maddest bit of stage magic I wanted to believe in was that it all actually meant something—that in some way beyond my dumb bum straight line thinking—she cared for me—enough at least to be doing what she said. Trying to help me. Maybe she saw in me something I'd missed. Call me a sucker. But a lifetime of dealing with some serious shit had taught me a few things about people and the games they run. How well that applied to her—well, that was the whole point of this new game—the new dark

ride I'd found myself on, not even knowing when I'd bought
my ticket. How could I call myself a tough guy and not ante
up?

I assumed an observational position, pretending I was
on a stake-out. My having driven around aimlessly might've
been a good thing. From years on the job I can verify that
it's much easier to shadow someone when they know where
they're going than someone flittering around at random. It
was possible that she, along with McInnes, might've had me
in their sights for a long time. She had to have a way of
finding out things about me. And she couldn't just have
been bugging my phone, although I'd been tempted to call
my old bud Nat Bandler, who was a TSCM consultant, and
have him give my place a good sweep. Something told me
that wouldn't help though. Hers was a much more subtle
kind of wiretap. It was the M.O. I couldn't work. Who was
she really? She couldn't have been around for long. The city
was laced with webs. She'd have triggered a vibration
before this if she'd been in town. One way or another, our
paths would've crossed. And now? Through any two points
in space there is only one line, I remembered that from
school. Like a laser sighting to reveal the path of a sniper
shot.

Nothing seemed to be happening at the house. It was like
one of those enchanted kingdoms under a spell. No figures
passing in front of the windows. The iron gate closed. Nothing.
Until . . . I saw a figure coming up from the path around the
seawall that made me sit bolt upright. Even at a distance I recognized him. It was that kid with the tattoo from the ferry
boat. He climbed the stone stairs and waltzed through the garden gate and up to the front door like he'd been there before.
More than twice.

The door opened and a giant African stepped out onto the
porch. My eyes were out on stalks. I forgot about how off I
felt, all I could do was stare, trying to take in every nuance.

The African had on a tribal patterned shirt—but black pressed pants that had a uniform look to them. I couldn't decide if he seemed more like a lover or a servant. Or both. I'd found it hard to believe a woman like Genevieve wouldn't have had some muscle around. Maybe he'd been on tap and waiting to be poured both times I'd been in the house. I was glad to be in the know now. I had to work out a strategy—as useless as that might be in her presence. If I could just understand what it was I was expecting. Wanting. Because I knew it was more than sex. Although that would've been a damn fine start.

The boy got ushered in, which didn't surprise me. He'd come for a reason, not a chat on the porch. I'd gotten all the counter-surveillance I could stand and I drove off. I hadn't been on the Antabuse for several days and I needed a bit of Dutch courage. I hit a place around the spit called Romeo's Bar & Grill, an upmarket new joint where no one knew me, and ordered some Vitamin Beam with the gusto only a recidivist can understand. That was followed by a tapas plate of salt and pepper calamari. A bit hoity-toity, but that was what appealed. That old Four Tops song "Working My Back to You" played while I made some notes on a cocktail napkin. Over the years I'd have written an encyclopedia on cocktail napkins—a Bible of private midnights. This was a new page— a whole new chapter.

Genevieve was the first woman I'd ever feared—and I wrote off her voodoo aphrodisiac effect to that. She might've been involved in the deaths of at least two men—maybe more. She might've been involved with seriously mind-altering drugs. For all I knew, she could've had psychic powers for real. She was certainly adept at over-the-line sex practices. But she had something to teach me. Something to give. And that made me want to risk all I had. However taboo. How much more did I have to lose—truly?

The head of the Gang Unit rang. Asked me if Padgett was on track with the Laotian shooting. I knew he was feeling me out. I tried to play it cool but gave Chris a thumbs up. Maybe my instincts were screwed up too. Either way, I wasn't going to piss on my partner.

I drove back to my apartment. I was sweating bullets about what to bring her. Then I saw the wrestling trophy. At 3:40 I left for Cliffhaven. Again.

3

LONG AGO I ARRIVED AT THE DOOR OF A FLEA-RUG apartment down near the old shipping yard about a suspected baby murder. A young junkie couple had reportedly slipped over the line and done something ugly. When I broke down that door and barged inside, I left everything I assumed about normal, human behavior behind. What they'd done to that baby doesn't bear repeating.

I felt like I stepped across another kind of line just arriving at the door of Eyrie Street this time. At first I didn't recognize the woman who let me into the house. She had a bouffant hairdo and was dressed in a floral pleated dress with a starched white apron wrapped around her waist—just like my mother long ago. It was uncanny.

The same henna dyed hair, which always seemed artificial to me because she had such lovely dark hair all her own . . . skin the color of hazelnut cream. I sure didn't get mine from her. Her father had come from Puebla where his family ran an anise seed farm. Banditos, so the story went, drove them off their land, and they fled to America . . . some to El Paso and Albuquerque, others to California. Mom grew up on a strawberry farm in Coyote, her mother a tough white widow who gave birth to her at age 40. She'd moved south and studied to be a dental nurse before meeting my Dad and becoming a housewife. Most of the time she seemed like a typical white bread mother of the era, but she taught me and Serena Spanish, and every so often, in between the Swanson TV dinners and the Salisbury steak, she'd make bean tacos and barbecued chicken backs with salsa.

I tried to shake off my shock as Genevieve led me into the front room. It had been entirely redecorated and seemed bigger than on either of my two previous visits—very much like our old family living room, except for the fireplace. Ours had been made of clinker brick and had fake logs that you pressed a button to light up. Dad had been very proud of that.

On the mantel this time was a plaster bust of John F. Kennedy and a miniature mechanical robot that I recognized as The Great Garloo—"the bright green battery operated monster that picks things up here and puts them down there." She must've got it on eBay. The detail of the scene was phenomenal. What wasn't this woman capable of?

I presented her with my high school wrestling trophy—and found myself unable to say anything other than, "This is from my past." Jesus, the whole room was something from my past. She put it up on the mantel next to The Great Garloo.

She had an ironing board set up, like my mother used to have—with the same daisy cover and Sunbeam steam iron. There was a corduroy sofa much like ours—and a butcher block coffee table. And a big brown Zenith TV in the corner *exactly* like ours. An old ad for Cap'n Crunch was on—the cereal that stayed sweet and crunchy and didn't get soggy in milk. The Cap'n was having a swordfight with Jean LaFoot, the barefoot pirate. Then Mr. Ed the Talking Horse came on. She gestured for me to sit down on the sofa. In the background I heard the Robert Goulet record my mother used to sing to. I couldn't sit still.

"You forgot your lunch box," she said in a motherly voice—and I almost fell off the sofa because she handed me my old *Gomer Pyle, U.S.M.C* lunchbox. It wasn't simply a replica—it was *my* old one. The wax paper I wrapped my sandwiches in—carrot sticks in Glad cellophane, Orange Hostess Cupcakes or a Scooter Pie . . . the scents came rushing up out of the old metal, not just out of my head.

I'd given up that lunchbox and asked for a *Man from U.N.C.L.E.* one with Napoleon Solo on the side holding a pistol with a long silencer. Some kids had razzed me because they'd heard that Jim Nabors, the star of *Gomer Pyle*, was a fag. It was better to be a secret agent than a dumb Marine anyway. Later, when the rumors started that Nabors and Rock Hudson were a queer couple, I'd thrown out the lunchbox. It was rusting away in some landfill a hundred miles away. I couldn't have been holding it in my hand. I kept my mouth shut and stared back at the television, as I always used to do when I didn't want to look at my mother.

Wallace called from the Two-Four. Then Hartley, the wet-nosed n00bie prosecutor wanting to know if Padgett was good to testify in the Grimes case. I shut off the cell.

A rerun of *The Rifleman* starring Chuck Connors was coming on—Chuck Connors as homesteader Lucas McCain, booming away with his Winchester rifle with the large trigger ring. The same Chuck who played Jason McCord, the disgraced Calvary captain in *Branded*, who had his saber broken in half when he was dishonorably discharged. I remembered the theme song . . . *Branded . . . scorned as the one who ran . . . what do you do when you're branded . . . and you know you're a man?*

Kids in school came up with a variation. *Stranded . . . stranded on the toilet bowl . . . what do you do when you're stranded . . . and you don't have a roll?*

Genevieve got up silently and turned the channel to a Doris Day movie called *Move Over Darling*. Mom had always adored Doris Day, especially Doris Day and Rock Hudson movies. She wanted to trade her beautiful chocolate colored filbert shaped eyes for perky blue ones. She sang that song "Que Sera, Sera" from the movie *The Man Who Knew Too Much* while she did the ironing—ironing even our underwear. I think she wanted to be Doris Day. Then when the truth was revealed, and Rock Hudson came out of the closet, she never mentioned either of those actors again. In a touch of poisonous irony, she died of a heart attack while watching the afternoon movie. It was *Pillow Talk*. She'd been grieving over stepfather Rod, who'd finally sundowned in his diapers in the raisin farm I'd help send him to. When the chest pain hit, she called her neighbor Mrs. Seymour from the bed, but it was too late by the time the ambulance arrived. Mrs. Seymour said that that when the paramedics gave up on the CPR, Tony Randall, who played Rock Hudson's neighbor in the movie, was just pouring himself another drink on screen—as if that was a detail I needed to know.

Move Over Darling starred James Garner in place of Rock. Doris, his wife, had been missing for years and he was trying to get her declared legally dead. What I'd forgotten was that Chuck Connors was in it too—and there he was on the TV. He played the guy who'd been stranded on the desert island with Doris. What in hell was this all about?

"You know . . ." Genevieve said, and when I turned to face her—she'd changed outfits and hairstyles completely. She looked like Marilyn Monroe in a spaghetti strap summer dress. "This movie has an intriguing history. It was originally going to be called *Something's Got to Give,* starring Marilyn Monroe and Dean Martin. This was at the time Marilyn was going to sing 'Happy Birthday, Mr. President' to JFK at Madison Square Garden. Then she mysteriously died less than a month later. Her last day on the set she shot a scene with Wally Cox. The film got canceled and then resuscitated as you see it—with such different stars in the roles."

My head swam. I didn't know any drug that worked so fast—and this didn't feel like any drug trip I'd ever heard about. And . . .

Wally F'in Cox! He'd supplied the voice for the cartoon character *Underdog*—whose girlfriend was Sweet Polly Purebred! I suddenly remembered he'd also played the preacher in *Spencer's Mountain*—it had been a family favorite. Mom liked it because of the romance between Henry Fonda and Maureen O'Hara. I think Dad liked it because of the shots of a young James MacArthur without his shirt on—and my sister Serena and I liked it because of the scene where the deaf grandpa gets crushed by the big pine tree. Memories roared through my brain. My mother. Marilyn. The scene in *On the Waterfront* when Brando does the "I could've been a contender" line. He'd probably been in a cab with Wally Cox at some stage. They might've been in bed together. Now their ashes were mingled together. I couldn't hold it together.

Sophia came in dressed just as my sister used to be. Pig tails, a camel brown jumper and saddle shoes. She carried a tray with a plate of cookies on it and a tall plastic glass of milk. The sugar sprinkled butter cookies took a certain well-known male shape or the silhouette of a woman. She left the room without saying a word.

How lonely it must've been for my mother—loving a man like Dad—always wanting to be something she couldn't be and yet still proud of who she was. She called my father Jefe. No wonder she was so hungry when Rod showed up. Those afternoons of ironing suddenly seemed heroic in a way I'd never seen before.

"Cookie, Sunny?" Norma Jean Genevieve goaded.

"What?" I kept trying to focus—but everything was too clear.

She passed me one of the penis-shaped cookies, which I declined. She bit the head off and handed me one of the female ones.

"Come," she laughed. "Think of it as Communion. Eating the Host."

Images and phrases stormed . . . *Chuck Connors* . . . *Wally Cox* . . . *Marlon Brando* . . . *Rock Hudson* . . . *Jim Nabors* . . . *Doris Day* . . . *Marilyn Monroe* . . . *rifles* . . . *lunchboxes* . . . *broken swords* . . . *apron strings* . . . *stays crunchy* . . . *doesn't get soggy* . . . *move over darling* . . . *something's got to give* . . .

"Are you all right, Sunny? You look a little pale."

The cookie made me thirsty so I took a sip of the milk. I couldn't remember when I'd last drunk milk. My mind flashed to Pico and the earlier scene in that room with the rats and the clock. When I glanced back at her I saw that her outfit and appearance had changed dramatically again. Marilyn had been replaced by a dominatrix in a black leather corset with thigh-high boots of black and red, a plumed magenta wig and vampire red lipstick. In one black-finger-nailed hand was a shot-weighted riding crop.

"So, tell me. What did you expect to find inside my house?" she asked.

I blinked, trying to find my voice. "I—th-thought you'd already know that," I stammered, realizing that I had to be drugged. How was she doing this???

"Oh, but I'd like to hear you say the words. Before you arrived today, try to describe exactly what you've been imagining."

I had to get a hold of myself. To remember this was all some kind of illusion. Theater. Hallucination. CIA-style hypnosis. I took a deep breath.

"I expected you . . . to have an exotic animal pet," I managed at last. "Maybe a monkey or an ocelot. There'd be a bunch of kooky paraphernalia. And Fantasy Rooms. You know, like big baby cribs—a jail cell."

"Or a tree fort. So, you think I provide dark adult entertainment. Tell me more," she directed, and ran the crop up the inside of my thigh very slowly. "I love to know what you have in your mind."

I didn't care for her mention of a tree fort one bit—but I gulped down my rush of fear and jabbered on. This broad left El Miedo for dead.

"There'd be people in costume. A dungeon—a man being stretched on a rack."

"Fascinating," she murmured, pausing the crop in my lap and tracing down the zipper line. "What's the *strangest* thing you thought you'd find?"

"Other than *you?*"

She let out a laugh. After her experiment with me the other day—and all that was happening then . . .

"I can't say," I said, afraid to say anything. "Maybe a naked girl in a cage . . . on a giant hamster wheel. I don't know. I . . ."

"Oh, Sunny," she beamed. "Isn't this fun? I knew you would repay my interest. Now, what would you be most afraid to find?"

That stopped me again. El Miedo . . . or . . .

"I wouldn't be too keen on finding a dead body—being a homicide detective and all. But honestly . . . ?" I mused, shutting my eyes. Why was I being honest with her? "I'm afraid right now. I'm afraid I'm going to find a room filled with pictures of me. Pictures taken of me over the years when I didn't know I was being watched."

"That's *extremely* interesting," she replied—and when I opened my eyes she had sandy brown hair cut short and a cement gray pant suit with a brooch on her right breast that looked like a piece of circuit board. How? I wanted to pass my hand through her to see if she was really there—wherever it was we really were. Whatever she was.

"I'll reward your honesty, Sunny. I'm going to take you on a tour, and you shall see for yourself if the reality of my residence lives up to the expectations of *your* fantasy. This, after all, has just been mine!"

If I'd been drugged it was too late to bail out . . . and I was way too damn curious and just straight up snuzzled. I couldn't for my soul understand the outfit changes . . . the room, the props. But she didn't give me time to mull it over.

We began upstairs on the top, third floor, taking the Sweetheart stair machine mounted in its frame of iron figures. There was a guy with winged sandals, a woman with snakes for hair, and a man playing a lute for a gathering of animals. As we hit the second floor landing and made the turn to ascend further, I could see the doors to all the rooms were closed, which added to the occultish atmosphere of the house. The layout contributed, with alcoves and skylights arranged in unexpected places, then a sudden narrowing of a hall to what looked like another staircase system—perhaps a servant's quarters in the old days, or maybe still. There was a discontinuous, dreamlike air about the house, as if it existed in different parts of history—as if we could step through one door and be in the conservatory of an English country estate. Choose another hallway and we'd end up on the balcony of a Storyville bordello.

At the first door we came to, which like all the others was painted an enameled white, she gave an exaggerated knock. After a moment of silence, she opened it with a large skeleton key. All of the doors we visited on that floor she opened with this same key and the contents were exactly the same. They were all empty. Except for a light fixture embedded in the ceiling rose, which was repeated in every room and resembled a woman encircled by a dragon, the chambers were bare of any furnishings, the walls painted a flat white, the floorboards polished hardwood.

"Disappointed?" she asked with a barracuda smile.

"Confused," I answered. Meaning stone blown spun out.

"There's more to a seemingly empty room than there appears," she replied. "An empty room can be filled by the mind of someone who enters. But this is only the top floor. Now it's time to descend. Into another world."

That got my heart beating.

We rounded yet another corner—the house was certainly much larger inside than it looked from the street—and came to either an oversized dumb waiter or a dwarf elevator. On the steel door she rapped again—and this time a metallic echo came in reply—which made me jump. The sliding surfaces clanged open on a pulley weight and there appeared a very small and very old man. He wasn't a midget—just unusually short and wrinkled with age. Each of his ears sported the largest hearing aids I'd ever seen—so large that it was fortunate that he was afflicted in both ears because his head would've been off-balance otherwise. He was dressed in a flamingo pink bellhop uniform and looked like he'd just woken from a nap on his feet.

"This is Mr. Dover," Genevieve announced and the little uniformed ancient snapped to attention when we stooped inside the steel enclosure.

"Down, Mr. Dover."

"We can't go up," I remarked.

"Mr. Dover likes to take instructions. Don't you, Mr. Dover?"

"Ye . . . ssss . . . ma'am."

With jerkingly anxious progress the wizened bellhop lowered us down through the house. We could've been in a diving bell.

"Isn't there a quicker way?" I inquired, feeling the walls narrow.

"Would you like to fall faster?" Genevieve queried, brushing my hand. "Indeed there are more efficient means. But I like seeing Mr. Dover at his post. He's had an association with this house going back nearly 70 years. Haven't you, Mr. Dover?"

"Ye . . . ssss . . . ma'am."

Mr. Dover looked like he'd been in the elevator for at least that long.

"This house has an interesting history—as you correctly

imagined. It was once a very exclusive brothel. That's why I keep all the rooms on the top floor empty. In honor of the ghosts. Some very tempting, beautiful ghosts. And very tragic ones too."

"Like Mr. Dover," I suggested, regaining a bit of composure.

"Sunny's being naughty, Mr. Dover. You know what we do to the naughty ones."

"Ye . . . ssss . . . ma'am."

"What?" I asked. "Keep them locked up in a little elevator without a stool to sit on?"

She waved her hand dismissively. "Mr. Dover's not a ghost. Next you'll be saying that I'm one too!"

The elevator at last thumped to a stop, and Genevieve ceremoniously allowed Mr. Dover to hoist open the sandwich doors for us—a feat that made the old codger's back crack audibly. We stepped out into what seemed like almost total blackness as the doors scrunched shut again. Genevieve took my hand and it was like the touch of a taser. Mr. Dover fled utterly out of mind.

"This space was built out of a cave network that runs deep into the bluff," she said—with girlish excitement. "During Prohibition there was a speakeasy down here . . . and . . . a casino!"

With that, she hit a switch and a remarkable sight flooded into my eyes as a bank of spotlights on the floor burst on. Two sights actually. The first was that she'd changed again. She stood before me now decked out in the guise of an old-time nightclub singer. Platinum blonde hair, her bosom accentuated in a velvet mulberry colored gown. Like the other changes, there was no accounting for it. Either I was having a breakdown or . . .

The second thing to throw me was the space the lights revealed. Imagine an underground gambling club from Tommy gun times. A large yet low ceiling room . . . green felt and tall

stools for blackjack, a roulette wheel—a cashier's cage, mirrored bar, several round cocktail tables, a baccarat lounge and
a private room for high rollers—the sort of off-limits place that
everyone's wise to and all those who are in the know frequent
regularly. Mobsters, showgirls, politicians. The joint's always
jumping into the wee hours. The cops don't raid it because
they're on the take or at the bar. Liquor flows. Deals go down.

Now imagine everyone suddenly evaporates. One night
they vanish in mid-dice roll, drink or poker hand—and the
place is left exactly as it was that night—collecting dust, slowly
disintegrating, so that it seems like only the fog of spider webs
is holding it together. That's what it was like. Even the old
cigar smoke seemed to hang in the air, and the grime on the
mirror behind the still-stocked bar was so cloudy, it was as if it
contained all the reflections of those who'd ever been in the
room.

"I know," Genevieve sighed, looking out at the compelling
decay. "I should clean the place up—restore it to its former
glory."

"No!" I said, being honest with her again. "You should
leave it just as you've done. Anyone can have a few gaming
tables and serve up some booze in their basement. Having a
haunted casino is something else."

"I'm very glad you appreciate that Sunny," she said.

"I've heard rumors about places like this," I muttered.
"But I didn't know any survived. Not the real ones from the
old days. Imagine the things that happened here."

"Yes!" Genevieve enthused, and took my arm in hers—as
if we'd just made the discovery together. As if we were a loving
couple who had bought the house and were exploring its hidden wonders. I wanted us to play a round of blackjack—she
could be the dealer. We could've ended up on the dust and
moth wing baccarat table. But instead she led me to the
roulette wheel, the only piece of equipment in the room that
wasn't coated in cobwebs. It was set into a corner that had an

oil painting of old Funland on the wall behind. The proximity made your eye connect the Ferris wheel on the wall with the gambling wheel on the table.

"Care to try your luck?" she asked with a fetching grin.

"I already have," I said, as the white ball plicked around— just as I felt I was doing in her presence, waiting to find a slot to settle in. Her eyes seemed to shine with a scandalous unbearable possibility. When the wheel at last ticked around to a total stop, there was another sound, like a latch popping and the harbor view painting of Funland eased away from the wall on two hinges to reveal a passageway.

"Another surprise," I coughed.

"Now the real tour begins," she replied.

Into the unknown—and for me—the unthinkable.

4

I SUSPECTED THE PASSAGE HADN'T BEEN REWIRED SINCE the War, but the light from the ceiling's bare bulbs was supplemented by a regiment of wall mounted candles. Some took the form of soldiers, others like temple priestesses, the soft suggestions of the faces congealing with the melting of the wax. She looked at me to gauge my reaction—and I saw that she'd changed again. Her head was completely bald now —with pendulous earrings that took the form of prismatic dragons. Her outfit was a pimento red Spandex bodysuit. I tried to ignore it. All my cop training had been about not ignoring anything—and it all went right out the window. Or through the mirror.

A gallery stretched out before us lined with black-glazed ceramic statues of naked men and women about shoulder height. Some of the bodies had the heads of animals. Others were like huge insects or imaginary creatures. Feet turned into jagged talons, tails sprouted. An iridescent beetle-shell glitter reflected off the surfaces, and several of the figures had objects embedded in them—coins, clockfaces, dolls' heads.

Beyond these statues was a sort of museum full of apothecary jars and specimen vials swimming with the preserved remains of glass eels and tuberous things—various deformities and marvels . . . Siamese twins, a duck-billed platypus . . . placental sorts of creatures . . . something that looked like a rhinoceros fetus and polliwogs with enormous eyes. Then I had to look away. The other malformed, disfigured creatures were far too hideous to look at.

She let me move forward into an area of tall windowed cases. One was crowded with historical weapons—from shining, sharpened throwing stars and ornamental daggers, to handheld crossbows and blowguns. Another displayed exquisite examples of lingerie. There were brassieres that looked like they'd been spun of black icing sugar—corsets and teddies embroidered with topaz and sapphires. Beside this was a case that housed sadistic masks and costumes that looked more like they belonged with the weapons—Dark Ages chastity belts and mesh helmets that seemed better suited to containing a rabid ferret than enclosing a human head. Another contained a collection of prosthetic devices and medical equipment—hands, arms, glass eyes, saws, trepanning dishes, hypodermics and vises. The largest case was devoted to a single object—a grisly abacus that appeared to have been assembled from pieces of human bone. The wires I guessed were dried sinews that had been coated with some glistening-thin layer of gold. The frame was substantial enough to be in proportion to the strung beads, which in this case were authentic looking human skulls, frosted with a shining porcelain finish.

"Enough kooky paraphernalia?" she asked dryly. "Would you like to see my favorite?"

"Yes . . . ma'am," I gurgled.

Goddamn it, when you lose all sense of humor, you really have lost your balls. I couldn't let her impress me to death. Somehow there was an explanation to all this.

She pointed to the last case, which before her gesture had been dark. It illuminated as she approached it. Inside was something like a glass sarcophagus, which housed a truncated human form. Male, with a serene death face and no limbs, just a body.

"You may have heard of Prince Randian, the Human Caterpillar. Like the Half-Man Johnny Eck, he was a famous sideshow attraction—and played a crucial role in Todd Brown's inimitable movie *Freaks*. This is Gilberto, the Silkworm. He was born with the same affliction, only smaller. I met him in Lima, Peru back in the 1940s."

"You weren't even born then," I pointed out blandly. Somehow I had to keep this madness on some coffee shop chit-chat level. I sensed it would peeve her. It was the way I'd always talked to heavies like Freddy Valdez. That tone of voice had saved my ass.

"In addition to an absence of all but one of the vital appendages, he had an epidermal condition that meant only the purest silk could ever touch his skin," she answered, taking no notice of my comment. "Despite these impediments, he was a wonderful and imaginative lover, a generous, provocative conversationalist—the most complete man I've ever met."

I let that one go by to the backstop.

"When he died of the inevitable complications that had beset his short, noble life, I had him embalmed. It's a rare privilege I am extending, to allow you, Sunny, to view him. These other trinkets are merely trinkets—but Gilberto I take with me when I travel . . . wherever I go."

He—or rather it—could've been fiberglass. And even if it was the mummy of some circus anomaly—I didn't like it that he was her idea of manhood. I could tell my reaction miffed her. But she perked up quick, as if to keep the roulette ball rolling.

"Now I'm going to show you something even more personal —things I have either made myself, or have had made to my exact specifications. I call it the Members' Lounge. A unique collection of art that I have devoted hundreds of years to."

She was trying to overload my mind. I tried to stay loose and cynical.

But it wasn't easy, because she led me into what I gathered had once been an old wine cellar. It was now lit like an art exhibit and pristinely clean, but it was still laid out like a wine cellar, with racks upon racks of objects. Only they weren't bottles. No siree bob.

"Each is derived from a mold taken from a man I have instructed or been intimate with," she said, fondling a nickel plated one with a decided hook, which reminded me a little of a .45 I used to own. "Each has become a distinct piece of sculpture, a talisman. Some are cast in bronze. Some are wood carvings. Some are inlaid with jewels or engraved.

"Just look at this example," she said, handing me a bulb of ivory that made me think of an in-grown whale's tooth. It had hundreds of tiny markings like on a cribbage board.

"The technique of scrimshaw. This man was from Nova Scotia and had a seafaring family history."

"What about his medical history?"

"He was the captain of an oil tanker," she said, ignoring me. "Feel the detail!"

I was flabbergasted I have to admit—not by the detail of that particular specimen but by the magnitude of the whole collection. Some were made of titanium—others jade, onyx or carbon fiber. A few were no bigger than a chess pawn. One she made me examine was the length and girth of a small torpedo made of finely dimpled zinc.

"Soon yours will be on display here," she said. "Sophia took a mold the other day while you were reading."

I was so flustered I dropped the pewter one I was holding. Her hand snaked out and snatched it before it hit the floor.

"Don't worry, Sunny!" she chortled. "It's not time to pass the baton yet."

"I wish you'd stop calling me that name," I said, getting honest again.

"I know, Sunny. But you'll identify with it soon. You'll feel like a new man, believe me. Now, what do you think about puppet shows?"

"Aren't they for kids?" I snorted. If she wanted to play grown-up games, then maybe we needed to grow up.

"Not mine!" she giggled. "Come."

The next constricted hallway we arrived in was lit by fluorescent tubes. She steered me to a steel door which had a design stenciled in day-glo pink on it. It was that optical illusion thing. Looked at one way, it showed an urn or vase. Seen another way, the handles of the vase were profiles of human faces.

"Welcome to the Situation Room."

When she'd said the words "puppet show," I'd conjured up either a curtained theater from a Swiss chateau or some wonky kid's cardboard box creation. Instead we entered what looked like a Las Vegas hotel security command center, with a computer console situated beneath a wall of monitors. She pressed a button on the control panel and all the screens came to life. There were several rows and one large monitor, onto which I gathered any of the smaller images could be projected at full size. This proved to be correct, and the first image she enlarged was a man sitting on a toilet.

"Christ," I groaned. This was obviously a closed circuit system. There were other people in the house and this was her way of spying on them. A wave of disappointment and embarrassment washed over me. So this was the big mystery.

"What's the matter, Sunny," she purred.

Stranded . . . stranded on the toilet bowl . . .

"The guy's taking a dump. I'm not into potty training!"

Her face assumed a hard, uncompromising expression.

"First of all, Sunny. *He* is an extremely senior executive of the Ford Motor Company. He has an annual salary that would take your breath away. He is at this minute in a mansion in Grosse Point, Michigan. He's astride one of ten toilets in that house—the one I told him to be on—which is actually the one

reserved for his gardener, who speaks poor English and com-
mutes 45 grueling, expensive miles one way to trim his hedges.
But he's not 'taking a dump' as you put it. He would never consider even breaking wind in my presence unless commanded.
He is simply in position, just like Mr. Dover. I told him to be
where he is between certain times and he's there.

"Secondly . . ." she flared. "What you are *into* is insignif-
icant! You're here because I invited you. Don't forget that
again."

Suddenly she was all smiles again. "These individuals
you'll observe are in a totally different category to you. You
might think of them as clients, because that's how you think of
things. But that would imply I work for them. I think of them
as devotees, subjects—or as mere objects. They're all involved
in some form of training and discipline that I have tailored to
their particular psychology. I'm a philosophical erotic consultant. I smooth creases in libido—or add new ones. I realign values.
Our involvement is on another level. An extremely special level,
Sunny. This is why I am sharing so much of my privacy with
you. I want you to appreciate that."

I swallowed hard and glanced back up at the screens. "So
. . . these people . . . ?"

"Mr. Tanaka is in Kyoto," she informed me casually, indi-
cating a Japanese fellow who was standing upright in a narrow
cylinder, immersed to his chin in some yellow fluid. "And
doing well with his program."

I couldn't imagine what Mr. Tanaka's "program" entailed,
but all the other faces and figures that appeared on the wall
were seemingly involved in equally dire situations. One screen
was filled with what appeared to be a giant ball of twine,
which I had the niggling feeling actually contained someone.
There were many others, men and women both, confined in
vats or boxes. Some were naked, others restricted more completely in suits made of netting or wire. Gas masks. Animal
mascot uniforms. One tall man I noticed was imprisoned (if

that's the right word) in a Plexiglas rectangle packed with insect larvae.

"These images are coming to us live. From Taiwan to Toronto, Brussels to Bloomington, Indiana," Genevieve said.

So, the walls of 4 Eyrie Street were every bit as permeable as I'd imagined—I just hadn't considered the technological angle. Maybe she was richer and smarter than I thought. I felt windows in my mind opening, as she began to toggle the scroll mechanism and new subjects fluttered up onto the screens.

Then I was startled to see a face I recognized. He was perspiring heavily. He had on his General's uniform with the rows of medals, but below the waist he was stripped and wired as I'd been with the rats and Sophia—but with a large tube inserted . . .

He was standing before a wall of artificial hands that emerged and then retreated within holes. He kept grabbing at them impulsively, as if it was some arcade game.

"That's—but it can't be! I've seen him on television!"

"He's on television now," Genevieve answered. "Just a more select channel. He's in The Hague—having his thinking revised about a remark he made recently that 'International politics is a matter of shaking the right hands at the right time and lighting fires under the right butts.' He's receiving radical colonic irrigation via an apparatus I've affectionately dubbed 'The Bazooka,' while what passes for his genitals are wired to receive an awakening burn at regular intervals. His only means of preventing this is to shake the right hands at the right time. Every time he guesses wrong, he experiences a blistering pain in his groin and more high pressure colonic cleansing. This serves to remind him that the responsibilities and privileges of political leadership, diplomacy and sensible foreign policy are not matters of guesswork, canapé receptioneering or Viagra sword waving."

"And . . . he's doing that by choice? You've haven't—?"

"Oh, what is choice, Sunny? It's the deepest human mystery of all. Light a cigarette—are you choosing to kill yourself? Aren't we all prisoners to some inner command? It's their own reflected faces the majority are ruled by. Some of these windows do indeed look into jail cells, as you may have imagined. But I'm not the jailer. I'm helping to organize a mass escape."

My eyes were drawn to a group scene—four men in blackout hoods stalking stealthily around with horse needle syringes raised like javelins. "What are those guys doing there?"

"They're remembering the importance of play," Genevieve answered. "They're commodity brokers in Chicago. They developed some imaginative ideas about playing with other people's money, including mine. The syringes contain a deadly neurotoxin. They're trying to Pin the Tail on the Donkey."

"But there's no donkey," I pointed out.

"No," Genevieve agreed with a malicious grin. "That's my play!"

I felt my mind cloud further. Cringe. Blur. Shear.

"This c-could all be . . . be rigged," I stuttered at last. "They're just shadows!"

"Shadow puppetry is my favorite form of theater," she answered coolly. "And shadows are my business. Nothing exists in the light without casting a shadow. And in the darkness, there is only shadow. Perhaps you need an example from closer to home to refresh your respect. Why don't you open that door across the hallway?"

"What is it? Another bathroom. Or a vomitorium?"

"One of my many mottos is 'See for yourself,'" she replied casually.

I didn't see any point in not doing it. Besides, I was still too curious about where all this was leading—what she had in mind for me. Before I lost my mind altogether. I opened the door expecting to find a guy's head poking out of an iron lung full of fire ants. Instead I gazed at an indoor swimming pool.

It was left over from the saltwater bath-house days of Cliffhaven. A grand faded frieze on the back wall showed a group of muscled naked athletes. Rusted art deco sconces in the shape of buxom winged ladies washed the other walls. Beside the water was a kid's toy pedal car—a black Cadillac convertible with dents in the side. The water was as murky as squid ink and many of the mosaic tiles were cracked. Two men were in the pool—I wouldn't say they were swimming. More like staying afloat. One had no legs and the other no arms. Both were dressed in women's one-piece bathing suits, one lemonade pink, the other aqua.

"That—can't be!" I squawked. "It's Falco Zagame and . . ."

"And Ernie 'The Ram' Brucato," Genevieve completed, easing into the room behind me.

The images, the people on the screens in the other room—that could've all been explained. She could've been sampling other web cams from around the world—she could've staged the scenes and then replayed them in an endless loop. The big shot I thought I recognized, he could've been a look-alike—an actor playing a part. But this . . . this was something else entirely.

I *knew* what Falco Zagame and The Ram looked like. I'd personally investigated no less than six gang killings they'd been implicated in over the years, not to mention witness tampering, from pay-offs to full traction hospitalizations. I'd had a hot putanesca thrown in my face by Falco's daughter and a rather frank chat with three of his knee breakers over some off-track betting. I'd pawed through the steel scrap in Ernie's wrecking yard looking for bloodstains and I'd sat across the table from him at his bistro, Dago Red (which many people thought should be renamed China White), his breath heavy with the smell of pork, garlic and fennel, when he made me a proposition I wasn't likely to forget.

These were made men with strong family connections to Kansas City, New Orleans and Brooklyn. They ran restaurants and owned city councilors—lived in big red houses with white lions out the front and had never once paid personal income tax. Men who'd spent their lives trying to rig juries, ballot boxes and trifectas, only to watch their empires eaten away by up-and-comers like Freddy Valdez. I knew these men. And I knew they were dead.

I'd been on the fringe of the crowds at both their boutonnière funerals. The backroom word at the Italian Social Club was that Falco's people took credit for Brucato's murder and vice versa. Their mutual assassinations had set the local families at each other's throats and ushered in a new era of underworld expansion and consolidation that rippled out from Wetworld to affect the whole city—if you traveled in my vicious circles. There was no way they could both be here.

"Zagame's lost his arms—and Ernie—his legs!" was all I could sputter. This couldn't be happening. This was an ace she'd played—and I couldn't beat it. Never once had I imagined I'd find in the basement of 4 Eyrie Street the two rival syndicate bosses of my generation—both of whom were supposedly dead and had been given Catholic burials—still alive but mutilated, floundering in the remains of a dark old spa pool. They'd lived lives of continuous excess. Banquets, box seats and bulletproof windows. Now they were hacked and wallowing in ridiculous women's bathing suits.

"They've formed an alliance," Genevieve informed me. "Falco needs Ernie's help to wipe his bottom and feed himself. Ernie needs Falco's legs to help him get around. See their toy car? A black Cadillac. Falco pedals, Ernie tries to steer. And they have a nice bedroom with posters of Italian sporting heroes on the wall. Ladies, do you recognize my guest?"

"A crooked cop!" Zagame blubbered, trying to find the cement edge.

"If you're here, it's too late," Ernie bubbled. He'd lost a lot of weight, even without losing his legs.

"Don't pay them any mind, Sunny! They're persnickety because they have to share the pool."

She knew just how much mind I'd pay them. I was one step away from head failure.

"You got a big alligator in there or something?" I managed finally.

"You know . . ." she chirped. "When I was living in Australia, I witnessed a rare confrontation between an estuarine crocodile and a shark."

I was still gaping at the pitiful spectacle of the maimed mob bosses, feeling like I was standing beside a more threatening predator than either a croc or a shark. "Who won?"

"There's been a lot of theoretical speculation about such a contest. The odds typically run 2 to 1 in favor of the shark. The problem is that it's rare to see a saltwater crocodile fighting in open water. In the actual contest I enjoyed, both creatures were mortally wounded."

"Hear that boys?" I said, and listened to my voice echo back off the walls. Then I said, "I don't think this pool is big enough." When in doubt with women, get logical, eh? And when you feel yourself drowning . . .

"You're quite right," Genevieve snapped, and snapped a switch on the wall.

The dark ink pit lit up instantly, turning into a luminous rectangle of water that made the shapes of the two gangsters seem even more grotesque.

"What concerns them, and why they don't appreciate the therapeutic benefits their swimming privileges afford, isn't a creature that's vicious or aggressive, but which is nonetheless the most venomous in the world."

I peered into the pool, at first thinking nothing was there. Then I saw it. It was like a discarded plastic bag full of fishing line—and then it seemed to breathe and the membranous bell inflated . . . the tendrils undulating . . . vaguely astral against the mosaic tiles.

"It's a sea wasp," Genevieve said. "*Chironex fleckeri*. A marine stinger. The most deadly jellyfish in the world. Look at the gelatin blossom of its body—its means of propulsion. And see the tentacles? How long they are? Wilhelm Reich believed the expressive movements of the orgasm reflex are functionally identical with those of a jellyfish."

The stricken gangsters had become more agitated since the light had come on. Perhaps the sight of their pool mate increased their anxiety—or they worried the light made them easier to see. The stinger's tendrils rippled out searchingly. Then again, I thought, their own nervousness could be stirring the water. The so-called creature might well have been made of polyethylene. That thought renewed a hint of confidence. I stepped over to the child's pedal car and booted it into the drink. The thing at the bottom billowed across the mosaic tiles. Shit, maybe it was alive after all.

"Well, Sunny," Genevieve sighed. "I understand you may feel you have a score to settle with these old dissociates. But you are never to act without my permission. That's what Falco and Ernie have learned so well. I forgive you, because all this is still new to you—and because the vision of a miniature Cadillac at the bottom of a lighted swimming pool is so lovely."

She entwined one of her arms with mine in an unwholesome yet deeply arousing way.

"Now, ladies," she called. "Retrieve your vehicle any way you can. Come, Sunny. The next stop on the tour has even more to do with your life. Oh, yes. From now on tonight, it's all about you, you big hunk of man."

5

WE LEFT THE GANGSTERS AND PROCEEDED DOWN the hall to another forking passage, toward a large mirror. Our reflections seemed to blur. We must've crossed the path of an electric eye for the looking glass was another door, and as it opened, there came a cool breath from the cliff face.

Yet another unexpected facet of this false-bottomed house. A junior sized railroad track, as in the depths of a mine. Only, I recognized the weathered cars. They were from the Scenic Railway in Funland. The horizontal shaft we entered was lit by some battery-powered emergency system, a faint light every hundred feet or so—the tunnel thick with the odors of damp rock, old metal and aging timbers.

"Yes," Genevieve acknowledged. "The Funland tracks used to run much farther than you may have thought. Old Leopold Mandel, the designer of the park, built this house and treated the grounds as his private fiefdom. Until he lost control of the property in a wager—with the Madame who established the house as a brothel."

"You seem to know a lot about local history for someone

new to the city," I said, checking my pulse.

"Get in the front car," she instructed. "Why do you think I'm new to the city?"

"I would've heard of you otherwise," I answered and climbed into the rusted lead car, all of them painted a scraped yellow, the color of fun.

"You *have* heard of me, Sunny," she said, sliding in beside me. "Only you weren't listening well."

How she activated the controls I don't know, but the cars chugged off down the tracks and jerked around a corner. It was a very trippy sensation to be riding so close to her, feeling the heat of her body—and it was heat not warmth I felt—the scent of her all the stronger in the stale still cave air.

"I was once the Madame who won this house all those years ago," she said. "I've been many things in my long life, however impossible it is for you to comprehend. Legal technicalities have had to be juggled in time, and my plans and aspirations have changed as well. What has renewed my interest of late is a desire to reintegrate the property as it was once. For that I needed the cooperation of señors Zagame and Brucato. The one had title to the restaurant block, as you know. The other has deeded to me the land that includes the Funland parking lot. Funland itself passed back into the City's hands when the company that owned it went bankrupt. With the land I now own, I'm confident of being able to negotiate with the City for the development of the entire site."

The cars eked around another bend and down, a switchback route I surmised was a way of coping with the incline leading to the water's edge. The idea that all the times I'd looked at the Scenic Railway there'd been a covert route entering the cliff flipped me. Almost as much as her claim of being a brothel Madame from more than half a century ago. The damn thing was—that kind of mumbo-jumbo would've explained a lot. All the madness would start to make some sense. But that didn't make any sense at all.

"So, the land deal is how you came into contact with Stoakes and Whitney," I tried. I had to stay on track too, winding though it may have been.

"They came into contact with me," she corrected. "They were searching for something. Just as you are."

The cars wormed through the excavated rock, the emergency light reflecting the way I felt.

"They didn't come to very happy ends," I noted.

"Are you saying that as a police officer or as an ordinary citizen?"

"I don't know if I'll ever feel like an ordinary citizen again," I confessed openly. "The police cases are closed. My investigation's still on-going."

And that was dead true. I wasn't at all interested in Stoakes and Whitney as cases anymore. I was—I don't know how to say it. I was curious about them as people. As men.

"You imagine I did something to them?" she asked, her voice rising slightly.

"Yeah, honestly, I do," I nodded. "I don't know what. I sure don't know how. But you seem to have knowledge—and a secret power over people—particularly men."

"A secret power . . ." she repeated. "Are you afraid of what I'm going to do to you?"

"I have been from the start. And I am now," I said, being honest with her again. Talk about being in the dark.

The close moist tunnel kept on opening up before us, as her voice continued in time with the clinking of the wheels, the cars shunting gradually downward.

"Do you want to stop seeing me then?"

"I'm not sure I can stop," I answered—because that was the midnight truth. "But no, I don't want to. However old you really are, you do things I thought couldn't be done."

"I thought you believed it was all just shadows and illusion."

"I'm still hoping most of it is," I said, thinking that in the darkness with her I felt free of El Miedo at least. "But you kidnapped the heads of the Zagame and Brucato families, and that's one trick I know from my own life—my old life—how hard would be to pull off."

"Kidnapped is apt," she answered, as the cars clacked beneath a low-slung brace of timbers. "They are, after all, children. But no, I don't need to abduct anyone. I invited them. They came. Perhaps they didn't realize how completely they were leaving their old lives. But resistance always has a cost and hospitality always has a price."

Her even, emotionless tone made me shiver, like some cold draft from inside the cliff. And yet, she seemed all the more appealing, alluring. Pure woman. Pure window. Pure terror— or a temptation beyond anything I'd ever encountered.

"What will happen to them?" I asked. Up ahead the air was getting fresher and there seemed to be more light.

"That depends on how they work together," she answered without any inflection. "As far as my objectives go, their purpose has been served."

"And what is your *objective*? Are you going to turn all this into some pleasure kingdom of adult entertainment?"

"Such entertainments are much better left to the shadows of privacy. They enrich in the imagination there, whereas they tend to wither and droop when brought into the open. You know that, Sunny. It was the call of the forbidden you answered. And that's what's brought you here," she said. "The end of our tour . . . and the edge of a new beginning for you."

The cars careened out of the cliffside, through a blackberry bramble beneath the peeling remains of an old billboard for Dilley's Chocolates, then through a mess of bolt cutter-opened wire into the waste of Funland. It was cemetery black and no stars shone, only a couple of dimming sodium security lights from beside the broken-back roller coaster and the abandoned dance hall. I stared down at my watch and was shocked to see that it was after midnight. I'd only arrived a short while before. The time my mother used to expect me...

"You're surprised at the time."

"I'm surprised every time. With you."

"Intimacy warps time, Sunny," she laughed softly. "It can make you age or make you stay young. We've spent some time exploring my secrets, however much you believe thcm. Now it's time, and you can see that it's late, to investigate yours. It's very late in fact—in your life. But not too late. Ready for another surprise?"

The air had become heavy, but with a different smell—a licorice and ozone scent, like the past. I could feel my head swim . . . the barium orange haloes of the lights fogging.

"Why don't I feel like I have any choice?" I asked, hearing my voice as if from outside myself . . . more like El Miedo than the rugged man I used to see shaving in the mirror.

"Because you're trying with all the fortitude of your being to forget. To hide something from yourself your whole life you need a very big labyrinth—an amusement park the size of a city. Even that will not suffice in the end. Sooner or later you begin to cross your own paths. You see your reflection in places that you've been. You hear your own words coming out of the mouths of strangers. The streets swarm with mouths and eyes. Your shadow moves both ahead and behind—the panic mounts. You know that panic, Sunny. You've been hunting yourself like a suspect over the years. And the trail of your pursuit and your evasion has finally led you here."

This couldn't be Funland. Gone was the tidewater and rust spray—the gull and garbage smell. There was something . . . different. Wrong. It was the sharp soft fragrance of Bermuda grass and alfalfa . . . like the valley to the east where I grew up. She was either more deeply inside my mind than anyone had ever been—or she'd taken me—outside. Somewhere—somehow else.

"Come with me," Genevieve called gently. "The rain is about to come. You can smell it in the air. We need to go inside."

I thought of my recent visit to the deteriorated park, the denizen with the fake walkie-talkie—and the strip of pictures from the Foto Booth. I took her hand. I wanted to believe that we really were just down the hill from her lighted mansion. But the smell in the air stayed wrong and grew more intense. A decidedly inland smell. Crop fields. Orchards. Irrigation canals. We picked our way past the familiar ruined attractions—the same things I'd seen before in daylight, only now washed with the shadow of a later hour, giving them a deeper sense of vandalization and decay. Then we came to the Haunted House. The front yard was a graveyard with bright red blood dripping down plywood tombstones.

"I don't remember a Haunted House in Funland," I said—and felt my stomach churn—a twinge in my neck, like a clotted artery.

"Remember, I said that the boundaries of the park aren't what you take them to be," she answered. "Intimacy warps time like guilt warps memory. Unless you embrace both the shadows and the light, you're never where you think you are, you're always where you imagined you were—in some dream past—the dismembered, misremembered, ever present nightmare of Yesterday. The dragnet is closing. Time for you to turn yourself in."

"Into . . . what?" I asked, trying to control my breathing.

"We can only become what we really are," she replied. "Lead the way."

I took one step onto the creaky planks of the porch . . . *but I was back home in the valley. I was 14. Heat lightning . . . a rare night of summer rain . . . smell of the Bermuda grass and alfalfa. A carnival was in town. I had a summer job, collecting tickets at the Ghost Train. I was on a break. My older sister Serena was trying to pal around with the majorette Lindy Bramlett and Oriole Tench, the spinach farmer's youngest daughter. The two popular girls were swanning about in boob tubes and tight jean cut-offs. I wandered down through the* garish lights of the Midway—voices and rubbish whipping by in the wind.

"Have a throw and win a cuddly lion!" a guy with a Rebel Flag cap hollered. That was when I spotted Grier. I spat into a trashcan that stank of fatty food and spun sugar. Grier ambled over to one of the shooting galleries thick with stuffed animals and pulled out some money. I got talking to this sophomore named Gwen, a friend of my cousin's. When I turned back, Grier had won a bubblegum blue bear. A mist of rain came down but he just stood there, calmly aiming at the targets, popping them off. I was starting to get wet by the time he'd shot his way up to a colossal pink pig. Made me sick to see it. Then I saw Lindy and Oriole under an awning. I guess they'd ditched Serena. They headed to the Haunted House.

A jet of air shot up between your legs when you went through the front door, and like the Ghost Train, there was a stupid greeting as you stepped inside and the door slammed shut behind you. "Maniacal Laughter" the sound effect was called. There were quite a few such noises to be heard: banging shutters, creaks and whispers, rattling chains—the occasional scream. A carny named Wing had shown me a handbook of suggestions for the Haunted House which even advised supplying actors with small coffee cans with beans or washers in them. As the customers walk by, the actor shakes the can, supposedly frightening them into the next room. I guess they couldn't find anyone dumb enough to stand there shaking a can all night.

Outside, the summer rain started to sluice down on the metal and the taut canvas, and I could feel more than hear the presence of the agitated crowd. I inched my way forward, imagining what it would be like to be with Lindy Bramlett in the dark. She wouldn't notice my pimples in the dark. Suddenly a shrill cry came from up ahead.

The Hanged Man. Usually they used a dummy, but every so often, just for a laugh, Wing would get one of the other half-

wit carnies to play the part, kicking and twitching when any-one came by. The gallows were made of two-by-fours and the viewing hallway had been constructed to let only one person through at a time. Most people assumed it was just a dummy hanging down, so if the noose was attached to a safety harness worn by a real person, and if the person was made up with a bit of blue around the lips and eyes, and maybe a rope burn around the neck, a sudden jerk could get a good reaction. I wondered who it was—Chow Hound, or maybe Donna Donna with the Big Set On Her. They were both the sort of mildly retarded people who were ideal for such an assignment. I hurried through the shreds of black velvet and the tacky paper skeletons to get a look. But when I got to the gallows, the noose was empty.

Outside, it sounded like the rain had slowed and the noises of the rides and the music seemed infinitely far away. Inside, everything felt close and tight. Lindy and Oriole appeared to have gotten lost in the Maze of Horrors. I could hear them clat-tering about, their voices raised to an excited pitch. I wondered what had happened to Serena. She was always being left behind by her friends. A painted bulb glimmered behind a piece of cardboard attached to a belt-driven rotating arm. As the cardboard spun around, it cut the light and made shadows move across the hall like phantoms.

I was supposed to be back at work at the Ghost Train but I didn't want to go. I could feel the presence of someone—just ahead. I had this feeling that maybe Lindy had lagged behind—waiting for something like this. After all, she'd winked at me. Hadn't she? My face would clear up. I stretched out my hand. There was a tremor of air just beyond my reach. Lindy's perfume lingered in the tight hallway, diffused by the sting of pinewood—and the odors of all the other bodies that had squeezed through.

I stroked the face of the air. Then a hand groped my leg. Another hand in the dark. It brushed my jeans, then paused. I stiffened—waiting.

I must've sighed because the darkness distinctly answered back . . . "Shhh." Then a hand moved to my belt buckle. I froze. There was a fumbling, then the sound of my zipper being lowered—a deafening, ripping sound. My own hands had stopped still in mid-air, afraid of what would happen if they reached out—afraid of what wouldn't happen. I was being fondled. What would I do if someone came? What had happened to Oriole? Had they arranged this?

Ideas started to pour through my head. The air in front of me rustled. I felt a brush of movement at belt level—and my arm shot out to stop her. I held on tight. But it wasn't Lindy I grabbed. I felt soft synthetic fuzz and a chill went through me. Even in the dark, the shape—the texture was unmistakable. My legs were trembling and a dry retch taste was in my mouth. I snatched the thing up—as much to get it out of my way as to drag it into the light—bouncing off the walls, rushing to get out. But even as I hurried, I knew what I was holding just as surely as if I could see it. I felt the ears—the snout—and knew—that I was holding the giant pink pig that Grier had won.

We'd moved inside—Genevieve and I. Whether it was the same building we'd been standing in front of before I couldn't say—the Haunted House I'd never seen in Funland. Heavy smell of sawdust and cheap fabric. She was holding a stuffed pink pig. But I didn't hear any rain outside. Just our voices—and somewhere out of sight—someone shaking washers in a can. A slow, disturbing, rhythmic sound.

"Take your prize, Sunny. You've suffered for it. And made others suffer for it."

"N-no," was all I could say. I wouldn't have it then and I wouldn't have it now. She'd gone too far with this. This wasn't possible. This wasn't natural.

"Very well then," she said and produced a wooden stake and impaled the stuffed animal on it. "We'll see what light it can throw on your life in another way." Her other hand came out with a cigarette lighter and she ignited the pig, which burst into flames—only they didn't consume the object. The form remained, seething with pink phosphorescence that revealed more details of the space we were in.

It was the interior of the old carnival Haunted House—exactly like the one all those lost summers ago. Synthetic spider webs hung from spars of blackened two-by-fours. Skulls and masks lined the walls. The gallows were gone but in a shaft of light from a red cellophane spot hung a noose, stark white in the bloodshot motes.

"We've reached the heart of your secret, Sunny," she said, hoisting the burning pig toward the noose. "The twisted little drama that has distorted your life. You used to believe you were a good detective. I'm paid the fees that I command because I'm the best at what I do. So, let me lay it out for you."

The clunking chains sound could be heard as she waved the acetate stinking torch backwards and forwards, making phosphene afterimages in the claustrophobic air and on the walls. The images seemed to come to life, like shadows and reflections of her words—but appearing too quickly and too abortedly to be seen properly.

"Your father came from hardened working stock. In his family, men had always been men. Back in Arkansas they raised crops, fixed machines and built houses. Growing up in California, he grew up heir to these skills and to the values connected with them. He wanted a wife and a family. He wanted a better social standing for himself and his children—but he had a longing for male bodies, didn't he? He had a desire which he tried to deny, which became ever more violent. You learned about violence from a real master."

She swung the pig torch faster and the images massing and dissolving around us became more hectic and impassioned—menacing. The rattling of the can grew more insistent.

"Despite his genuine love for your mother and for you and your sister, he couldn't suppress his inner secret, just as you haven't been able to suppress yours. The blood-stained Vaseline jar that you found in the glove compartment of his truck . . . that you presented to your mother just before he died . . . when did you first comprehend that it wasn't only the evidence or residue of his actions—but the goal?"

The licking flames revealed a huge rubber tarantula.

"Your father was a physically fit, vigorous man, Sunny. The sex he had with the young men who lugged lumber and tools for him was rough. You realized that long ago. At a level below where you've been willing to venture, you've always known that his death wasn't the accident your mother wanted to believe, or the suicide you said were so ashamed of—his sacrifice of himself—which of course you could then resent and hate him all the more for."

The phosphene shapes flurried across the masks and skulls. The sound of heavy breathing surrounded us. It might as well have been my own.

"Deep in your mind you've always tucked away the truth that he was murdered."

"You think my father was murdered?" I cried as everything went silent.

"You do too," Genevieve answered thrusting the hot bright pig at me. "You *know*. You saw that one special young man heave a hammer at your father with all the might of his heart. You traced the shape of the claw head in the ruptured sheetrock. You knew just what you'd witnessed but you later refused to testify, so to speak. The repulsion—the horror was too much for you. That's what authentic horror is Sunny. What you can't face. That's the only true horror there is in life. So you lie and you lie and you lie—but you still can't kill the truth. That's the real reason you became a homicide inspector— because of a murder you helped conceal. And who was the murderer? Confess that name to me now. Say it."

"It was . . . Jake . . . my friend Frank's older brother," I choked, jaw clenched.

"Jake didn't just work for your father, did he?"

"N-no."

"What did your father do with him?"

"He . . . he fucked him."

"He loved him, Sunny. And Jake loved your father. Too much. Young, unstable—both of them in hiding. Both of them addicted to a kind of pain. It had to end the way it did. But it absolutely didn't end there, did it? You made sure of that. You transferred all of that ambivalence—all the hatred, disgust, jealousy and adoration onto Frank. Nothing happened physically between the two of you on your little jaunt to Mexico. *That's* why the memory looms large in your mind. Because of what you privately wanted to happen. So badly. Because when he was asleep in the car in the hot sun, you were torn between touching him—and beating his head in with a half-empty bottle of tequila. Because of what his brother felt for your father. Because of what you were terrified you felt for him.

"You became an investigator of murders because you knew a murder was what made you the man of your house before you were ready—and what's prevented you from ever becoming a man in fact. Jake disappeared—never to be seen again in your life—except in nightmare after fantasy, after endless waking drunken dreams. But what else happened? What other crimes were you party to—in a more personal, responsible way? Hm? What can't you so easily blame on what you thought of as your father's shame?"

She slowed the motion of the torch and the afterlight changed in time and form with her words. I heard the sounds of kids' voices through the walls . . . where I was slipping. Out of myself. Out of everything known and even denied.

"Your father dead, his lover and killer escaped—you sentenced yourself to the anguish he'd been wrestling with his whole adult life. If anyone ever hinted at you being a fairy—and boys are always being called fairies—you rose to the bait and raised your fists or cringed in loneliness. Then another character appeared on stage."

There was a scream in the dark and I jumped. She began twirling—slowly at first—and then faster, the flames rippling off the stuffed pig as she picked up speed, the ghost images flashing and stretching.

"Before you met your car thief friend Frank, you had another buddy—who did confess his feelings about you. He worshipped you and longed to touch you. To give you what he knew of love. One night he did—and you found it repugnant beyond words. He was trying to please you. But all your frustrated rage, all your accumulated darkness rose up inside you!"

Her spinning had extinguished the pink burning—the room, if it really was a room we were in, went black. Her voice sunk to a whisper, syncopated like the rattling can.

"You went on to thrash that boy. You defiled him. You made him want to die. And die he did. Murder? You know how many ways there are to kill someone."

"No!" I yelled, my voice seeming both muffled and unbearably loud in the closed-in space. Then there came the sound of Maniacal Laughter.

Suddenly a white light blazed and a figure appeared, suspended from the noose, chin slumped on one shoulder, eyes bulging. The face bore an impossible resemblance to Grier Woodley. It couldn't be him and wasn't him—but I croaked audibly.

"Beware the Hanged Man, Sunny. Or should I say, the Hanged Boy. Grier Woodley. All men whose heads end up in nooses are boys. But this one is special—because *you* put him there. Not your father or Jake—or Frank, who was, as you know, as heterosexual and virile as they come. He didn't have any trouble getting it up at the Mexican whorehouse, did he?"

"I didn't!" I wailed. "I don't know what you're talking about—or how you're doing this—but it's all a fake. A lie! I never killed anyone—let alone . . . !"

"No?" she scoffed—and her sensual features became a mesh of contempt. Her clothing morphed into the black robes of an Inquisitor and her head seemed to sit upon the draped body with a planetary vastness, like an oversized mask of mealworms. I wanted to faint.

"Your due process is overdue," she announced. "Now, you have the right to remain silent. You may invoke your right to have an attorney present, in which case your best advocate is Truth. You have the right to face your accuser, in which case you should examine the face of the boy who strangled to death in a tow rope, kicking when it all became real and final for him."

The Inquisitor's mask shook its terrible, bulbous distortion. Another spotlight came on, sickly green. Fixed in its glare on the floor was a lawn mower.

"It was in his family's garage that Grier was found. The carnival had moved on, but the Haunted House had given him an idea. A way out—after what you'd done."

"Stop it!" I shouted.

"You gave him the motive. Didn't you? You tricked him into being alone with you and then you beat him. You demeaned him. You took his dignity and made him swallow it."

"I didn't do it! He killed himself!"

"The guilty always protest their innocence, Sunny. Isn't that the rule you lived by as a police officer? Well, perhaps it's time to seek some other opinions. You know about Juries of the Dead. You've seen them in school plays and on television. I summon now the Jury of *Your* Dead."

A row of spotlights came on—a roll of sheet tumbled down to the floor—and then a strange black blob like a smudged fingerprint began to form.

"You may have heard of the Rorschach test, Sunny. Patients are shown a set of cards with inkblots on them and asked to describe what they see. A foxlike face, two figures embracing—a sexual organ. But in your case, we already know what you see in every random pattern. You see your own Shadow. And this is the place where the shadows come to life."

As she said this, the blurred shape that had formed on the sheet lifted off and moved toward me, as if a figure had stepped through the white membrane, although the fabric remained flat and unbroken. It was someone dressed in a black silk bodysuit. It took up a position facing me, legs spread, hands on hips, its faceless head raised—like some lost letter of the alphabet or an unknown punctuation mark.

"Behold your father, said to have died falling from scaffolding."

"You're insane . . ." I choked.

Another blot formed and a smaller figure emerged the same way. "Your sister Serena, who died mysteriously, falling from a tree house. Or a tree fort as you called it—always defending your terrain. Isn't it suspicious that she died only a few days before you savaged Grier?"

"This is a . . . lie . . . these . . ."

"Silence!" the mask commanded. And another black silk shadow took form out of the sheet. "Your old buddy Frank. The one you wanted in the front seat of a hot car on a back road in Mexico three years after Grier died. To see if what you feared about yourself was true. But you didn't have the guts and so you stayed afraid, wondering about his death—whether he was really running from the police . . . or someone else."

Two more black inkblot phantoms took form and joined the line. One noticeably female with a full contoured figure.

"Raven, Freddy Valdez's favorite whore. And Lenny Bhat—the dealer known as the Mongoose. Did Raven know you shot her because you were jealous of her relationship with Jack McInnes? That you hated her wanting him—but that you wanted him more?"

"You're mad!" I cried. Who had she hired to put on this charade?

"And did Lenny know that you gunned him down because he knew you killed Raven? That it had nothing to do with your partner's drug money?"

"Where *is* Jack?" I demanded. "What have you done with him?"

"Oh, so concerned. About your partner. Remember those threesomes with you and Raven. An excuse to be with Jack? Three is a crowd in the end. And now, since you think I do things to men, rather than showing them what they've done to themselves and others . . . let's consider Mervyn Stoakes and Deems Whitney."

Two more figures osmosed through the blotted sheet, this time wearing black and red.

"Here are two men whose deaths you think I somehow caused. And maybe I indirectly did. Maybe they couldn't handle the instruction I provided. Maybe I *am* guilty in some way. Do you confront me? Do you officially investigate me? No. You bury your responsibilities. You think letting the matters pass as suicides will please me and will free you to be more open with me. Like every investigation, you hunt when it suits you. And when it doesn't, you manipulate the evidence and the reports."

"That's a complete lie! I've closed more cases—"

"Enough!" the misshapen mask spat. "There are three more shadows from your past to come forward."

The figures that stepped into the light now, one by one, were of different colors, and their suits seemed to change hue as they moved. Two had female outlines. One was missing a leg. I swallowed down a clump of bile and tears.

"First, your old friend Jimmie. You called him a friend. Did you ever call him a doctor—or offer to drive him to one? For at least a year you worried about his health, but did nothing to help him overcome his fear. To be with him when he needed someone. His business partner did what he could—but he's not as smart or forceful as you. The truth is he's slow. You don't think of yourself as slow. Just slow to help a friend."

I did cry then. I should've done more for Jimmie. I was the only one who could've, maybe even when Camille was alive.

"And the lovely, lost Briannon," the Inquisitor's mask announced. "The girl who shot you because she was in love with you, and who used the speedball you'd given her at the end—to make things end. She couldn't bring herself to kill you—but she wanted to hurt you—because of the way you'd hurt her. She knew it was never really her that you entered. Never really her when you held her. It was this other . . . shapely shadow."

The other female form stepped forward, the sheer suit shimmering.

"You don't think I killed Briannon and . . . St—?"

"Where is wayward Stacy now? Where did she go?"

"You're way off . . . I didn't . . . I couldn't . . ." I stammered. Then I noticed that there was something in Genevieve's black robed arms. A tiny figure in a pure white stocking suit. Like a perfect little snowman.

"And this is the son you threw away. Or what he might've been if born. He'd be ready to join the wrestling team soon."

"Stop this nightmare!" I pleaded. "Please, this isn't . . ."

"You know the cards they use to test ESP, Sunny?" she continued without remorse. "Can you read the minds of the dead?"

All of the standing figures produced from behind their backs a white card with a black square on it. The white shape she held at her bosom, she threw on the floor. It plopped with an all-too-human sound. And then the body in the noose spoke. The stage make-up was intense. The eyes opaque. The voice clear and actorly.

"I'm the twelfth in the jury, Birch. I get to cast the deciding vote."

I hadn't heard my real first name in a while. It shocked me back to alertness.

"I find you innocent. You didn't kill me. Because you didn't have the balls. After you'd beaten me—after you made me do what I'd wanted to do—tried to do before—you beat me some more. You had to get the violence out of you. You couldn't bring it off in my mouth, so you broke my jaw. If you could've killed me in that moment and gotten away with it, you would've. But no one gets away with anything, and there's no statute of limitations on disgrace. I did what I had to do after what you did to me. But I get to cast the deciding vote. You're acquitted."

The bodysuited figures turned to look at each other, as in some stylized dance.

"I forgive you, Birch," the performer in the noose said, as the rope lowered to the ground and the dangling legs found the floor. "I died in a hot September garage with the smell of blood meal and lawn mower gas in the air. It felt so thick at the end. But you—you've been dying every day since. Now all I ask is a kiss. And I forgive you. Just kiss my dead bloated face once."

The corpse made up to look like Grier removed the noose and pushed the lawn mower out of the spotlight . . . inching slowly toward me.

"Go back!" I shouted. "Or I'll beat you again!"

"Just as I thought," Genevieve sighed, appearing now as she had the first time I saw her. The ashes of rose lounge suit. Brunette-auburn hair.

"This is—you're—sick!" I rasped.

She gave me an armor-piercing stare.

"But I also heal," she said. "I've opened an old wound, and let you walk around inside. That odor? That's the smell of the cremation of your boyhood friend, Grier. His parents were too horrified by the effects of the hanging to consent to a burial. And that damp, cold, earthy hint of putrefaction you sense now? That's what your sister smelled like, the slow, inevitable rot in the decomposing wood of the coffin. Her bones can still be found. But her ghost and Grier's are alive and unwell inside you. I think you should thank me for sharing them with you, so that you might at last leave them behind."

"I'd rather put my head in that noose. This is all lies, except for Jimmie!"

"Sunny, you've had your head in a noose for years. It's time for you to go home and get some sleep. Come back Monday at exactly 2 PM and we will look to your future. But you must bring me something again. Something you've stolen. Now pick up your dead son at least."

I stooped to retrieve the white figure from the floor, more entranced by the question of what it actually felt like than because she'd instructed me. I squeezed it and a pink cloud of gas erupted—I felt my legs wobble. The spotlights and the face-less figures all blurred like one big inkblot and I fell over, just the way my sister Serena used to do.

When I woke up, I was naked and alone in my own bed with Pico. Looking out the window, I saw my car parked outside. There was a text message on my cell. It said, *"Monday, 2 PM. Bring me something you have stolen or never, ever return."* I straggled back to the sack, my head whirling, my heart caved in, like a hammer hurled at a sheetrock wall.

6

ENEVIEVE IN A STARFISH BLUE SUMMER DRESS AND A
*French girl's wide brimmed straw hat. We were
strolling hand in hand through Funland, a warm
slow purple dusk with the lights of the rides twinkling. Young
soldiers in uniform hugging their narrow-waisted girlfriends
. . . heaving baseballs at towers of iron milk bottles or flinging
darts at a wall of breast-like balloons. Swing music from the
dance hall . . . the scent of hot pretzels.*

*The couples and the peppermint ice-cream faced children
wavered like silver gelatin ghosts. Their voices and laughter
continued but it seemed to come from a distance. Gradually
they began to fade, receding like sweaty handprints on stainless
steel.*

*She led me behind the skating rink to what appeared to be
an old bath-house, built out over the rocks where the seawall
would later be. I heard the sad faint harmony of the Andrew
Sisters singing "I'll Be With You in Apple Blossom Time"
dwindling away with the ping and clank of the rides. Then we
were inside the dank smelling baths.*

The only illumination came from candles in hurricane

lanterns. There were long copper troughs of trickling water, and a maze of square stone pools with steps cut into the side. Around the edges and all across the slate floor, ancient naked men lounged like reptiles—and real reptiles skittered—frill-necked things and iguanas—while rusted ladders descended into saltwater smelling darkness and iron catwalks extended out of sight, their railings embellished with ultraviolet salamanders.

From hidden chambers and platforms, and from the depths of the cement pits, there came sighs as in an opium parlor. Genevieve's dress was gone. She was nude now except for black glass stiletto heels, and as she stepped between the withered reptile men, the more deformed the figures became. Skin scaled . . . limbs contracting . . . gills forming. Misshapen heads of bass and sea turtles.

Water flowed through bars in the wall into a series of pools. Chameleons dotted the stone floor. Faces hung like damp masks from hooks in the wall in the shape of hands— and in the center of the room was what looked like an operating table positioned beneath a skylight.

"Take off your clothes," she commanded, and I found myself doing as she directed.

"Now lie down on the table on your back."

I was seized with fear. The sheeted bench beside the operating table was laid out with glinting scalpels and surgical implements—and a single luxuriant peacock feather.

"What are you going to do to me?" I demanded.

"Trust me, it's part of the healing," she said cryptically. "It's the most intimate thing that's ever happened to you."

I couldn't help myself. Intimacy with her was all I wanted. I lay down and looked up. The skylight was shaped like a human figure, radiant, like the reverse of a silhouette. An angel. I felt myself drawn up toward it, as if it were my own outline suspended from the ceiling. My voice was lost in anxiousness as I saw her hands move across the bench of blades.

What was she going to do? The terror and the yearning to know was more than I could take. Instead of one of the scalpels, she picked up the peacock feather.

"Now lie very still," she whispered. "I don't want to hurt you. Yet."

I couldn't keep my eyes open. I had to withdraw into my mind. Then I smelled her flesh draw near. I thought maybe she'd exchanged the feather for one of the scalpels because I felt a ripping pain, deeper than anything I'd ever experienced—and yet somehow pleasurable. Beyond pleasure. Like some ecstasy massage. But when I snuck a peek, I saw that the sensation was achieved with the peacock feather alone. Where for a second I thought she was going to castrate me, suddenly I craved the touch of the soft vanes . . . the simulation of slicing, an incision more extreme for being imaginary. She teased me with the soft feather and I felt every millimeter of skin tingle and wrinkle with the gorgeous agony. She whispered something I didn't understand—I thought she said, "Now it's time to cut out the past."

The feather stroked the scar where Briannon had shot me, a livid weal. The ridges of plume triggered a fire of nerve ache and then release. I felt my body go into seizure—the tremor starting deep inside the bullet hole and spreading in vibration after vibration up my spine . . . into the dead wings of my shoulder blades . . . and down my legs . . . burning my toes. The sheet beneath me was soaked, sweat pouring—and something else—a viscous substance like ectoplasm . . . and out came things I'd had inside in a mess of crystal scales.

She opened up the old wound and removed a handful of plastic Apaches that I'd once buried in our back yard . . . and then an Illya Kuryakin Palm Pistol from The Man from U.N.C.L.E show. She pulled out Pabst Blue Ribbon beer bottle caps that used to have little rebus puzzles inside . . . condoms, cigarette butts and a half-pint of Vat 69. And then she said, "Hold very still, this is going to really hurt."

And it did. More than I could believe. It hurt so much I cried out like a baby slapped into breathing air, and then she held up a .25 caliber slug. From a Beretta Bobcat 21.

"That can't be!" I moaned. "They pulled it out!"

"They didn't remove your sorrow," she said as she took the slug in her mouth and swallowed it like a Communion wafer. "I have. The memory wound is clean now."

I was naked, soaked and limp. She helped me to rise from the table, psychoplasm and sweat shining like a film of respiring algae.

"Approach the water," she said, pointing to the pools.

I stepped . . . between the chameleons and the lost time trinkets she'd extracted . . . into the water, as she held my head under. Beneath the surface, I could hear the ticking of the antique French clock that had sat on the mantel in Eyrie Street . . . and I remembered back to days long ago in the valley . . . to times before my father died . . . when we were happy.

Late August nights, my friends and me, we'd scale the fence and dive in the public pool, the light beneath the springboard undulating like a submarine moon. We'd become shapes, gliding and frogging in the pale green water luminously pleated against the tiles. Tadpoles and torsos jack-knifed, hoarding air to tunnel toward the drain where potato bugs unwrinkled— clawing up through thick bubbles back into the warm air that smelled of chlorine and the trampled weeds in the field that bleed milk when you squeeze them.

Night after night we swam in each other's bodies. Then waded single-file out of the shallow end and lay on the cement, phosphorescent, panting—until the silhouette prints of our wet skin diminished to single drying points, satellites blinking overhead. Sirens sounded across town, but not for us, not yet. Frank and the others gone, the light extinguished—I'd float on my back in the black water listening to my heart, my breath, the breathing of distant swimmers.

Now, held under the water by Genevieve, my skin had been

stripped away like a costume I'd been wearing. My face. Organs, bones and all. I was just a bright reflection like the shape of the skylight. Liquid light . . . becoming bubbles . . . becoming mist . . . becoming . . .

7

WOKE UP ON SATURDAY MORNING FEELING LIKE I'D LEFT my body in the back seat of a cab and had just had it returned by the day shift. I couldn't distinguish between the dream I'd had about Genevieve and what had actually happened when I visited her—which I was certain was some kind of profoundly altered experience. Even a person of significant wealth with a real sense of theater couldn't have pulled off what she'd done. How she'd accumulated so much info about my private past, I couldn't even begin to imagine. But while her knowledge was devastatingly correct on several points, it was wildly off the mark on many others—with the obvious intention of riling me. She'd wanted to press my buttons and she had.

My father's death being a murder . . .

I'm certain my mother would've never dreamt someone else was involved. She claimed he'd left a note, but I never saw it and it might well have been a fairly general thing—or something written at another time. The deal was tricky because Mom had needed the insurance money, and so the focus had been on accidental death versus suicide. As far as I was aware there hadn't been a police investigation, which later did strike me as odd.

But it's hard enough unraveling recent events—something in the past when you weren't there and were too young to understand anyway—it's impossible to be sure. And Mom purposely tried to keep things from us, for understandable reasons. Still, I had to admit, once Genevieve had set it out, I knew that she was on the right twisted track. That was the real seed of my interest in investigating murders. And I had seen Jake throw a hammer at my father. And I had put that Vaseline jar on my mother's dresser.

She was right about Jimmie too. I hadn't been as good a friend to him as I should've been. I owed him more looking after. I let him down—but I think he really did forgive me.

And she was right in some ways about Grier. Nothing could excuse what I'd done to him. It made me physically ill at the time and the memory of it made me feel that way again. But believe me when I say that she got it wrong too. If I'd been a girl, what Grier had tried to do in the Haunted House would've been seen very differently. Worse things happen to girls and women every day, but it wouldn't have been viewed as an expression of "love."

But here's the real reason why, despite all her theatrics, I didn't blame myself for his death. He was a suicide waiting to happen—waiting for an accomplice. He half liked the beating I gave him. That's why I bashed him the way I did—I had to take him past the point of satisfaction. That's the honest gutsick truth. I don't know what she was talking about with Frank—she was just working every angle. And her bringing up Stoakes and Whitney was more than a little rich.

What she said about Raven and the Mongoose was pure fabrication. I'm almost certain Lenny shot Raven—and for the blood simple reason that he wanted her share of the scam. He got whacked in vato loco revenge by either Freddy or one of his cholos. No mystery there.

Briannon? She was a dealer. She didn't need to get drugs from me—and after I was shot I had no way to get in touch with her. She went into hiding. I didn't give her any speedball—ever. And she knew her own way around a needle. As to Stacy, I'd have killed myself long before her. For her. And in a way, I did. Many times over.

She was a Tiffany earring you find in the sink trap. As soft as fur handcuffs and yet as sharp as piano wire. She knew wrestling holds and rainy day games I'd never even thought of . . . and sometimes when I'd least expect it, she'd laugh like a little girl and tell me some obscure fact . . . like about the two mile-long sausage in the Guinness Book of Records. Then I'd know I was heading into serious whitewater. Some babes like her—and there was no woman like her really—but I mean with her stretch limo looks . . . they'd have talked the catwalk . . . all about shopping sprees in Milan and Dubai . . . made sure I knew about the Park Avenue plastic surgeon she kept in a drawer. She told me about her jobs in a pet store and at an agricultural inspection station. Who lies about that kind of thing? And yet she did lie. All the time. One time she said she came from Wisconsin—the Land of Dairy she called it. Then it was Philadelphia . . . or Baltimore. But she never mentioned any other men. It was like I was the first. Like she was made for me. Every minute with her was a moment when I didn't know what would happen next. She had a fire and forget temper—and yet she was ticklish as hell. And she had a dream. She wanted to be a singer. She certainly had some unusual ways of practicing. A real voice too. Two parts amaretto to one part diesel. Plus attitude. Like a white Millie Jackson.

Then one day she was gone. She could be in Aspen or West Palm Beach. For a long time I thought she was everywhere. One night after we'd been to the greyhounds, I asked her how long she'd been tricking, and she looked at me with Uzi eyes, and said, "I don't do tricks, I do magic." I figured something bad happened to her. Or something sad. It usually does.

That left Polly's miscarriage—the loss of a fetus, not the death of a toddler in white sleepers.

And my sister Serena's accident.

I didn't cause either. I'd always take the rap for them in my heart, and yet I couldn't say what I could've done differently that would've guaranteed they didn't happen. Would that baby really have lived if I hadn't been fooling around? Maybe Polly just miscarried. Maybe Serena just fell, epilepsy or no. Women lose babies. Kids fall out of trees. I honestly don't remember all that was going on in the tree fort that afternoon. We were kids, new to being drunk—and I was just so grateful to be part of anything to do with sex. I shouldn't have been cheating on Polly at any time, let alone at such a vulnerable time. I should've been more careful with Serena and the scene that was happening. But seeing it all from a new distance, I knew I'd be exonerated in everyone else's mind but my own. What I was guilty of in both cases, is what happened after. Polly and I stopped trying to have kids—I about put the wedding tackle away altogether. And my grief over Serena turned into guilt. I had to be responsible because I was the male—and because I felt responsible, I let my guilt turn into anger that I vented on Grier. My assault on him did come suspiciously soon after Serena's fall. In that sense, Genevieve and her troupe were right. On one shadow hinges many others. Not as many as she made out. But enough.

That still didn't explain how she'd put the whole thing together.

I headed to Cheezy's to mingle with the regulars. I thought maybe the short order morning would restore some normality. It didn't. I sat down at my favorite seat and ordered my usual. Barb Huggins, the waitress with the retainer, looked right at me and said, "The ususal what?" I was so startled I couldn't think what I usually ordered. I walked home and got in the car and drove to McDonald's. Two egg and bacon McMuffins later I decided it was time to get straight back at the apartment. I needed basic menial tasks after what I'd been through.

Whatever was happening to me was as serious as murder. Or birth. I needed to shift gears.

I stopped off and bought an armful of cleaning products and hefty garden-strength trash bags and started piling, packing, scrubbing, wiping and in some instances, scraping. As small as the apartment was, the filth had accumulated. What sort of woman could I have ever brought back to a mess like that? Even Pico had been put off.

I cleaned out the refrigerator, the oven and the garbage disposal. I emptied the closet, I got under the bed. Every ketchup slop, porn rag, silverfish, blister pack, and chow mein stain got dealt with. It took four hours of the most manic cleaning I'd ever done, but the place sparkled when I finished—from the tops of the doors to the toilet bowl. I even found my old Explorer's knife that had been missing for 35 years. I ended up with ten bags of trash and two heaps of clothes and shoes that didn't seem to fit anymore, all neatly piled up for the St. Vincent de Paul bin. And that's just where I took them—and I felt much better.

For a little bit. Then just empty and restless.

So, I headed over to Wetworld, cruising past the aging streetgirls, looking like dog-eared dollar bills needing to be taken out of circulation. They weren't shaking it at this hour—just out to score—in preparation for another midnight, the only time anyone would want to seem them in fishnets and high heels anymore.

I'd barely gotten out of the ride when the Sidewinder buttonholed me. He was a North Georgia clay-eater who'd heard a whispered legend about California when he was a teenager, although he still lived at street level 20 years later, fencing iPods and dealing stuff like oxycodone—whatever would make the nut. Back when he'd hit town, someone had clocked him with a car jimmy and he'd had trouble with his balance ever since. I liked him though, and he liked me, especially since I happened to intervene when this cooker named Bucket Head was trying to shiv him over some hot cell phone cards. Old BH looked like a t-boned Hyundai when I was through, and the Winder wormed a little easier on the streets from then on because I put the word out I'd rupture spleens if I heard of him getting hassled. I admired him because although he lived near the drains, he never seemed to get much of the sludge on him. I asked him about some sleep relief.

He screwed himself up and unraveled around a corner. Wound back ten minutes later and laid a fistful of tan canoe-shaped pills on me.

"They're clean but they're mean, Chief. Lights out for real. If you're doin' 'em yourself, keep the safety on. And if you're givin' 'em to her, be right careful. You wanna pull the sheet up to her chin affer—not up over her haid."

"Thanks SW," I told him. "You watch your hillbilly ass. This is still the Coast."

"I hear you. I miss you and Cracker Jack. You kept things square."

"I'll keep the safety on," I said. "Who's been on your case?"

"New dick. They call him DA Baby."

"Padgett."

"Gave me the third degree over that slant-eyed cap onna look-see yesterday. Tole him to catch a green rabbit."

"He's one of mine. I'll see to it. Just a kid still. He's good people really."

"If you say so, Chief."

"What's the word on who did the shoot? The Ghost Tigers?"

"Naw!" the Sidewinder scoffed. "Wife did him! She was workin' on the side—on her back. Pay the kid's way to college. Hub's chained to the register. He got wind and called an early mornin' argument."

"Thanks SW. Try to keep off the skyline."

I gave him two Ben Franklins, and then decided on a

third—he needed the dough and I was glad to have bumped shoulders. And sad to see him veering off. You could go to the bank on anything he said when he didn't have the ringing in his ears.

I walked over a block to the Laotian store where the shooting had happened. My old instincts had said to go straight to someone like him when we'd done the canvass, but he'd obviously gone hidey hole on the day, only to be hassled by a less circumspect Chris Padgett when I'd gone home sick on Friday. The Sidewinder reminded me of a fundamental truth. When the cops get out of the gutter, the gutters get clogged. I went inside and saw the wife trapped behind the counter, not a soul in the place. I gave her a full five minutes to get anxious as I wandered the aisles and left all the refrigerator doors open before I made a deposit on the magazines in front of the cash register.

She had an oily smelling Smith & Wesson revolver pointed at me before I'd even zipped up. I wondered if it was the same gatt that she'd used to shoot her old man. Maybe she was smarter than that. I smiled and kept my hands at my side.

"What you do! What you doing?" she cried.

"I've pissed on your dream," I answered. "Like you've pissed on the dreams of everyone who's come to this town and this country to make a better life. You shot your husband in cold blood. Not some gangbanger. You. Him. A father. Word's out."

The fear and anger in her eyes was something to behold. I tried to think how many times someone had pulled a gun on me over the years. Of course, it's the ones you don't see pointed at you that you really have to worry about.

"The shame of going to jail will probably be too much for you," I said. "My advice is to stage your own death—make it look like another murder while the gang press is on. You might—if you do it right—get some insurance money into your son's college fund. And he might not learn the truth. That is, if he doesn't know already. But any way it plays you're done. Do yourself in or give yourself up. It won't end here whether you pull that trigger or not."

I could see in her eyes how badly she wanted to pull it. Hints of all the past traumas in her homeland, the hard road coming here, the frustrations and prejudices once settled, long boring hours in a borderland neighborhood, the drudgery of stocking shelves, trying to make a buck and buy a better life for her son. People pull triggers for pretty good reasons in my experience. She'd had hers. Now she had another one. I walked out feeling empty and light.

Sitting behind the wheel of the Electra again, looking ahead to my meeting with the recently and unexpectedly retired Jack McInnes—wondering what he had to tell me and what I could bring myself to tell him, an image of the High Five Bar came to mind. The flytrap where Mervyn Stoakes had quietly poured down a couple of straight bourbons and then slashed himself in the alley behind. I may have buried any official interest in the matter, but my private concerns were keener than ever and it had been bothering me ever since Lance pulled back the sheet. Why there?

The raptor pit of Wetworld would've made some sense— a place a lot of different kinds of people ended up ending up. Some of the scabies old-timers even called it the End Zone. The High Five was in an unexpected area to find someone like Stoakes at any time, let alone the last time. It wasn't near his work or where he lived. He didn't have a train ticket on him and his car was parked in the lot without any luggage. It wasn't a district known for picking up girls, or boys for that matter, and not an easy place to score drugs or place bets. It was an anonymous district, where men who didn't have credit cards took comfort in cheap draft beer and a Slim Jim.

That got me thinking again about the vista point on La Playa where Deems Whitney had gone to great lengths to blow

up his expensive car with himself in it. Putting aside the sensible question of why someone would do that—what would
drive them to that point. Why in the world would he have
driven himself to that specific point?

I began obsessing on the faces of the two dead men.
Something in their lives—they way they ended them. It spoke
to me. They spoke to me. I was certain Genevieve knew more
about both of them than she'd acknowledged. Much more.
Both men had had some kind of psychotic break. Both had
come under her influence. But in Whitney's case there had been
far too much precision, too much plain effort, for the temporary insanity argument to hold. With Stoakes, the tox scans
had come back clear. That was a key dent in my theory that
Genevieve was using chemicals to achieve her effects—and
beyond my own residual drug worries, the reason I hadn't sub-
jected myself to a test. If she was using drugs, they were of a
sort that slipped through the screen, and that's not easy to do
these days. Something else had happened to those men and I
was afraid it was happening to me. Something that didn't fit
into any standard theories. I pondered that for quite some
time—and some very wild notions passed through my mind,
like boosted cars through a toll gate. And then some very creepy
ones, moving the way the more seriously suspicious vehicles
usually do. A little too cautiously. As if the windows are about
to roll down any minute—and weapons appear.

But old cop instincts die hard, even in the face of the seemingly unexplainable. I dragged out my city map and a pencil
and started drawing lines. Stoakes owned arguably the largest,
best-positioned home in Foam, but it was a fairly unpreten-
tious neighborhood, still on the price bounce from the heavy
industry days. I drew a line between his street and Cliffhaven.
Whitney's much grander residence near the Gardens I connected in the same way. I couldn't see a link to either the High
Five or the lookout on La Playa. But that gave me another
thought.

Whitney's office was in the Virginia Building—a tower shaped like a giant Remington .22 cartridge. I drew two more lines, joining up where both men worked and 4 Eyrie Street. The High Five was almost precisely halfway between Stoakes' office in City Hall and Genevieve's house. The same with La Playa and Whitney's office. Both men, consciously or not, had chosen to end their existence at a point dead-on half-way between the dark playground of Eyrie Street and the hub of their old, usual lives. Neither one may have realized why he selected the locale he did. Still it was interesting to see it on a map. Something concrete.

I was willing to accept that Genevieve hadn't in some way "willed" their deaths. It wasn't that I doubted her capacity for mind control—I was beginning to suspend all doubts about what she was able to do. It was the way the men died that got me. They'd acted under duress, but my instincts told me that both had acted on their own volition. They'd learned something, experienced something—and they couldn't cope. Whitney had sent up a true flare, but they both had left messages in their own ways. Both had tried to destroy the evidence of themselves—or at least a kind of evidence. I felt a sickening rush of dread and desire. Their ghosts were sending me some kind of warning—but it wasn't one I could heed. My need to know what was happening to me was greater than my need to learn what had happened to them. Some cases you can never close.

I applied my newfound theory to myself, first connecting up my apartment with Eyrie Street and then the Precinct. Neither produced any obvious results. I tried my old house. Same deal. Then, on a hunch, I plugged in the Long Room— that, after all, was where I'd spent most of my meaningful time in the last few years. That result was very different. The halfway mark turned out to be down to the number on the door, the bar where Briannon had shot me, the same bar where I'd first gone for a drink with Stacy. Danger, blonde ice. I got a cold clear tingle when I drew the pencil line through it. Then the icy feeling of a chilled knife at the neck.

With that success in hand, if that's what you want to call it, I punched in the other player in the drama that I was concerned about. McInnes. I didn't bother with his old house or the apartment where I was pretty sure he now lived. I didn't worry about the Precinct he just quit working from. I ground the pencil tip into where the Jaguar House was and brought it down to Eyrie Street and I saw straight up that the place he'd chosen to meet that night had a significance I hadn't understood before. I wondered if he knew. I wondered what he knew. I could only wonder. I drove home.

Hartley called on the way. Earnest young schmuck. Ringing me on a Saturday. Wanted me to know we had an FTA of a key witness in the Grimes case on Friday. I texted Chris. First rule of disappointment—share the love. Keeps you sane. At least it used to.

Back in the cat box of my apartment, the scanner had a four car pile-up on the old 95 and a man exposing himself in Peralta Park. Too bad he didn't wait until after dark. We'd have had a good old-fashioned lynching to look into.

I copped a bonus in the late afternoon movie on TV. Alfred Hitchcock's *Vertigo*. Kim Novak looked so hot—and that line where Jimmy Stewart says, "One final thing I have to do, and then I'll be free of the past." I heard that. Then I took a long walk. It helped a bit, but you can imagine the kinds of scenes I saw in every window. The mannequins and misread signs.

I came back and gave Pico a slow, full grooming. She sucked up all my stroking and gave it back to me. Her fur was soft and smooth. I fed her then and microwaved a Health Lite Malaysian Treat for myself that had been crusted with frost in my ice box since Day 1 in the apartment. It was OK. Especially since I ate real slow.

I took a long lukewarm shower after that, my skin couldn't take either hot or cold water. Then I tried to find something to wear from what was left of my clean-out. Maybe I'd gone over-board. Nothing fit. There was no underwear at all. The only thing I could find was a clump of Polly's old panties down at the bottom of a drawer. They were the color of my mother's nasturiums. I tried them on. Silky smooth like Pico's fur. It was fucking tragic, but it sort of turned me on too. What was the big deal? Polly had worn my shorts in the past.

Chris and I played telephone tag as I took a roundabout route over to Cliffhaven. He was probably getting horizontal with the "girl." The second floor windows at Eyrie Street were beaming, but there were no cars parked nearby. After a half-hour, I walked down to the seawall and back. Then I dug into the fever night traffic for my rendezvous with McInnes . . . afraid of what he had to tell me and what I might let slip, but knowing I had to see him. Face him.

The Cabaret du Neant was in a side street off Peralta Avenue, the old Harbor Highway. In the bad old days, the Harbor had been almost two miles of nookie-on-the-side motels, adult bookstores, gunshops, pawnshops, and the all-night commotion of Devil Doughnuts (now that was a place worth buying a doughnut from). A bit of the grit still remained closer into the city, but now the strip was mainly fast food chains, a bunch of self-serve car washes and superstores like Ikea and Wal-Mart.

The Peralta District retained some of the sawed-off-cash only character because on the water side, the closed up Grain Terminal collapsed down to the 32nd Street Pier and was home to a bunch of homeless folk. Across the disused tracks, however, gentrifica-tion had started kicking in big time. People called it Poodleville because it had been colonized by the gay community. There were several meat rack bars and all the usual boutiques, decorator shops and design studios—a couple of advertising agencies had moved into the old warehouses. The one exception to the yup-scale trend seemed to be the Cabaret. I arrived early and made a note to tip off one of the health inspectors I knew.

I was greeted at the castle-like door by a prissy ghoul who gave me a green-lipped grin and said the cover charge had been waived that night. I took up a position at the bar that gave me a view of the johns and the main entrance, ordered a club soda and tried to still my nerves.

After my experience with Genevieve and the Haunted House, a horror-themed nightclub for pansies or even fauxmosexuals was the last place I wanted to be on this earth. McInnes was my only hope of some inside track. For the first time in a long time, I really wanted to see him.

Jack was five years younger than me, but he acted a lot older and looked a lot younger. I don't know how, because he made a practice of drinking more expensive Scotch than he could afford—in industrial quantities. He liked a Thai stick and a Swedish massage and knew where to find blow in almost any part of town on short notice. Still, I hadn't once seen him even close to sloppy. Never slurred a word or ever let his guard down. Ever. A natural cardshark. Blackjack of course. He'd been known to slip off to Laughlin and work out on the riverheads—but not so hard as to draw heat. His game was always tight. The only hint of any lack of confidence was the heavy cologne. He was three-fifths my size at the outside, but he was hell on wheels in a bar brawl, with flinty psychopath eyes that had made even trigger happy ex-cons and gang-bangers go to jelly. Had a thing for hard anal sex and rough stuff generally— and yet he always had a lot of ladies looking after him—and out for him, with real devotion. They called him Pappa Man. I just thought of ice water, 40/40 oil and Manilla quick-knives.

He'd grown up in Biloxi, Mississippi, which he always proudly claimed was the most corrupt town in America. His father had died on top of a big booty working girl, just like Freddy Valdez, and his mother had moved them to Detroit in his teens, which went a long to explaining his eat-the-wounded ethics (or lack of them). But he had a wry sense of humor. "The one good thing about a flat-chested woman is that you know what you're not getting." I shudder to think what he'd really gotten up to over the years, but he distilled the wisdom of his experience down to three principles, The Rules of Jack: "Never take an underage girl to a hotel with a roller coaster, fat men should never drive small cars, and if you like watermelon, you better spring for a big fridge."

He was as cold-blooded as they come on either side of the law—and yet, if you had to have somebody in a very dark alley on your side, the smart money would've picked him every time. Jack always did what was good for Jack, but if that was good for you, then you had a goddamn army—which is why when I left him, I spread nothing but good gospel for good measure. "Make peace with your darkness, Rit," he told me once. "Porn stars need to make wood on command. Guys like us need to have a monster to let out at the right time. Make a deal with your monster. It'll save your ass."

I suddenly missed him more than I could say, even if he had set me up. I'd put my life in his hands on more than one occasion and lived to tell the tale. I wanted to believe in him now, Brut 33 or no. And a part of me wanted to warn him about what had happened to Stoakes and Whitney, in case he didn't know the connection. Whatever it was going down, we may very well have all been in it together.

But that stuff Genevieve had suggested about us two was way off the mark. In fact, it made me feel better because it proved she wasn't infallible. If Jack was bent when it came to money (and he was a lot less crooked than many), he was pipe straight in the sack. She was way off the beam on that one. Just like she was with my sister.

Serena had epilepsy. It manifested early and caused a lot of havoc in our family. OK, I should've been looking out for her better. But she'd been up in that tree house hundreds of times. I didn't make her have a seizure. And I didn't push her out. We were having some fun—I wanted her to have some fun too. Cherine Derry was there for me—she had acne too. Tommy,

Cherine's twin brother, was interested in Serena. We'd been drinking some of the booze I'd snuck out of Rod's liquor cabinet. Juan and Julio came by. Some girl named Caitlin. Serena had a seizure. She fell. I felt sick.

"Another drink, girlfriend?"

"How about a fat lip?" I replied.

"Just asking."

"It's the same when the glass is empty."

Man, was I in the wrong bar. Where was McInnes?

I checked my watch. The atmosphere was starting to come to life and the smell was putrid—a mix of Halloween party latex, fuck-me cologne and carbon dioxide haze rising from the floor around the stage. The tables in the place were "gravestones" made of plywood and the sight of them—the memory of the night before—started bringing on El Miedo. And that got me wondering about that old ghost—how it had receded into the deeper shadows when Genevieve had come into my life. Or I'd fallen into her web.

Meanwhile, the booths were designed to look like coffins, and there was one real coffin in the corner that led to a ladder that took you down to a private lounge area where you could probably arrange for a session with some young "goblin."

It was still early for a place like that, but the crowd was starting to thicken—and harden. Maybe the waived cover charge and the rumor of a new shipment of Liquid Crystal had influenced people's decisions for the night. A local fashion guru I recognized from the newspapers showed up with two anorexic Asian women in black Lycra, and a couple of very affected hairdressers batted eyelashes at a steroidal bodybuilder in chain-mail. I kept darting Long Island peeks and I noticed there were a few older homos dotted between the coffins or poised at the far end of the bar doing the same thing. They tried to peer surreptitiously over their drinks, but their eyes lit up whenever a chicken appeared. One of the more ghastly ones actually licked his Campari lips. Made me feel sick. I wished

McInnes would hurry up.

I sipped my fizz as the minutes bubbled, working through what I wanted to say. Then the Midori green magic lantern slides began. Spirit photography from the gaslight era . . . chintzy bats and Day of the Dead faces. They slithered off the walls as a drag queen that looked like Boris Karloff's sister did a breathy Blue Angel number and the line to the Men's bathroom lengthened.

I ordered another soda. Beings began arriving that I'd bet money drank blood as well as Cosmopolitans. Even if I was wearing my second ex-wife's panties, nothing would have made me feel at home amongst such specimens. I just wanted answers.

What did McInnes really know about Genevieve? Was he somehow in all this with her—or just as foxed as I was? How much could I reveal of what I'd been through to get him to spill to me? What would anyone else believe? I looked at my watch again and thought about ordering a real drink as two middle-aged pantywaists bickered over a young ginger with a rhinestone studded codpiece and nails through his nipples. They were working up to a real pillow fight.

The Boneyard Band, who were obviously already cranked, snuck out of the wings and launched into a funky take on that old song "Spooky." They followed it with a decent cover of "I Put a Spell On You," the lead singer hollering like he had fluid on the spine and a wolf spider down his pants. *I put a spell on you . . . because you're mine . . .* I took another peek at my watch and belched some soda gas.

The band finished up their set with a presumably original and unbearably campy metal number called "I've Got a Resurrection For You," as a mad scientist had simulated sex with a Frankenboy, and two backup singers dressed like Morticia Addams screeched in a purple spotlight. I think one of them was a woman. Hard to tell in the dry ice mist.

The phantasmagoria of the lantern slides dripped over

made-up gothic faces and I wondered if there were any cops in the joint, working undercover. Maybe one of the specters at the back tables doing jelly skull shooters. I was starting to think McInnes wasn't going to show.

"You look like you're waiting for someone," a husky voice next to me said, as the live musicians fumbled backstage through their papier mâché cemetery.

A shemale had slipped in beside me. Black widow evening wear, scarlet lips, and an unnatural blend of some heavy masculine scent and Poison, Briannon's fragrance.

"I'd want to be in a place like this," I answered, pulling back.

"Looking for answers?" the thing said.

"I'm just having a drink."

"Of course," she/he smiled. "Just admiring the flesh. The lights. The theater."

"I'm not into the flesh, the lights or the trashy theater," I replied, as an Igor-costumed DJ and the Skeleton Dancers took the stage, waggling their lightning bug bottoms to some slow building disco anthem.

"You want some drugs then?"

"No, I don't," I returned. "And I'd be careful who I said that to, if I were you."

"You want to be like me?" the thing breathed, bringing its mixed perfume face close. "You know it's Teabag Night at the Tab Hunter."

"Listen," I clipped. "I'm happy to buy you a drink if that's what it will take to get you back on the dance floor with your friends . . . but I really wouldn't mind being left alone."

"That's why you're in the Dead Zone. That's what this place is, you know. It's where the desperates go . . . the ones who can't get play in the bars down the street."

"Looks lively to me," I quipped watching a zombie down a tequila slammer. "And I'm not trying to get play. Do you want a drink or not?"

"Oh, thank you, yes. A girl like me should take what she can get. And I still give as well as I get," the hormone monster flirted.

"Very nice," I replied. "But I'm not into it." Made me nauseous.

"Ooh," it giggled. "You're waiting for a knight in shining armor. I can do that too."

"I'm not . . . waiting . . . for anyone like you think."

"I rather think you are, Detective."

"What did you call me?" I demanded, as a waiter in a g-string minced past with a piña collada in a shrunken head. The music started to soar and the Skeleton Men went spastic in the clouds from the smoke machine. Had I heard right?

"I think I called you a desperado," she breathed in my ear. "You don't know what fun we could have in one of those private booths. What secrets I could tell you."

"I don't want to know those kinds of secrets," I said, wondering if I was speaking too loudly. God, the last thing I wanted . . .

"Don't be too sure," the shemale kissed.

"Believe me, I'll wait," I insisted, and started to reach for my shield.

"Yes, you will. Thanks for the offer of a drink. But a lady wants more, especially on her last night."

The thing gave my ear a lick which made me slap my head like an idiot—then she slunk off into the swill and jiggle of the dance floor, a fine curve of black polyester tush consumed in a gaggle of eyeshadow boys. Whatever he was, she'd played with my head.

Then, speaking of heads, I glimpsed one I recognized. The unmistakable flounder-shaped cranium of Detective Ron Haslett. His face swam up out of a red gel from above the stage. He was with a doughy guy we called Wadcutter, who worked in Infernal Affairs—and lo and be sick, Bruce Wyburn who'd moved to a Precinct across town. Well, well, well. Three holes in the ground.

They all looked a little high. It was perfect. The most notorious queer-hater in our Precinct, a fink from the Commissioner's office, and a chavala I'd been dick enough to give my prize single action revolver to for his birthday. Who knew, huh? It all made sense though.

They were headed into the playrooms with a Frosty Boy and a black dude who was a foot too short to pull off the Baron Samedi costume he had on. I waited another five minutes. I had half a mind to bust into the nether regions and catch Haslett or Wyburn redfaced—twofaced. Explain to them about making a rod for their own backs. But I couldn't stomach it. I forked out for the tab. Wisps of nitrous vapor followed me out the door past the bouncer with the executioner's hood and the packed leather jockstrap. McInnes had stood me up. Played me again, as he had with Genevieve. As she had—and still was. I wanted out of Lavender Land.

I made it back to the methamphetamine tilt of Peralta as a platoon of oiled and chiseled night commandos converged on the Anaconda Room. I kept expecting El Miedo to sneak up, but maybe the fresh air or all my questions about Genevieve pushed it back. I stepped up to the curb trying to pick out the profile of a taxi. Then I remembered my old deuce and a quarter was parked around the corner. No hay pedo. I could drive home. I was, after all, uncomfortably sober.

8

JUST ON SUNRISE . . . AN ABALONE SHELL SKY—TWITCHING awake to find myself slumped in my car about half a block down from my apartment building.

I was naked—except for a woman's camisole. Sheer black lace. I'd been sleeping or sleeping it off with the seat shoved back under some overcoat I didn't recognize. I half expected to find someone else beside me. Given the size of the car, I expected to have found a few.

I had what looked like a trace of ballistic jelly on my thigh. I didn't seem to have any cuts or bruises but I felt tender all over. Plastic. I stank of perfume and had the sort of shakes you get when you've been on rum drinks all night. I couldn't remember anything—except for flashbacks of the Cabaret. I'd been doing club soda the whole time at the bar. Dim aquatic faces after that.

Until the boxing match. I had a watery recollection of a cab ride with other people—like people coming from a masquerade party. I hadn't been to that Auditorium in years . . . down in Mex Town . . . all the street murals and placas on the brick walls.

Rico Salazar scored a KO in the 6th round. Huge upset, big money moving around . . . excited totacho smell of the crowd. I didn't think it was possible. I'd stayed too late at that nightmare nightclub to have made the fight.

McInness had stood me up. Then the beastly queen thing hit on me. I remembered that. But I couldn't put it together with the Auditorium. If, somehow, I had made it to the fight, something else had gone down in between and that was lost in the fog. Maybe GHB or midazolam that the lizards use to spike drinks. I glanced at my cell. There was a text message from McInnes. TPTB. *The powers that be*. I didn't know what that meant. Maybe some shorthand explanation why he hadn't showed. My keys were down on the floor below the dash—and dash is what I did to my apartment, wrapped up in the overcoat, feeling like some Bacardi prom date trying to make it back to her bedroom. Except I was scared shitless. What in the Lord's name had happened?

My stomach felt too rough for black strap. My body was one big cramp and my head was a rage in a cage. I needed proper sleep in my own bed with Pico purring softly. I wasn't supposed to meet the Padgett group for lunch until 1 PM. I fed Pico some liver-smelling paste. Then I popped half of one of the Sidewinder's lights-out pills. At least I knew where I'd gotten it. I figured after whatever had occurred the night before, it would help me replenish my energy. And I didn't want to risk the chance of more harrowing dreams. I pulled down the blinds, took the phone off the hook and switched off my cell. Maybe McInnes would ring and leave a message. I didn't like it that Jack was in the wind. Maybe trouble. Maybe in trouble. Either way, I didn't like it at all. I dove into the sack, trying not to think about what lay ahead that day.

But sleeping pill or not, I ended up having a dream—and a very harrowing one at that. *I was with Genevieve—ravishing in a see-through white robe, while I was anxious and perspiring in a silly kid's Buster Brown suit. We were lunch-*

ing at the Country Club. Padgett was there with his wife and in-laws, lots of honchos from City Hall and various local celebrities.

In the center of the room was a long white table. At the ends were two ice sculptures. One was a big breasted woman's torso, like the masthead from a ship. The other was a translucent Roman garden god—with a long handle. I thought it seemed a bit racy for the Country Club set, but no one seemed to be fussed. They were paying more attention to the larger ice sculpture that dominated the center of the table. It was an elaborately detailed dragon with spread wings. Contained within it like little hearts were maraschino cherries and juniper berries, so that it was tinted red, cherry syrup flowing from its nostrils like flames.

Little men in white starched jackets with sailor's hats and blue satin eye masks were boiling miniature lobsters, while outside, a group of topless women in fly fisherman's waders hauled rainbow trout out of the water hazard at the 18th hole.

Everyone ate in silence, except for the sound of the shells breaking open. Every once in a while, someone would bing a fork against a crystal goblet to get attention and then stand to make a speech. People would turn their heads as though they were listening, but nothing that I could hear was said, and one by one the "speakers" sat down.

Then the dishes were removed by old people, dithery and crippled nursing home patients, some in wheelchairs, others inching about on walking frames, so that they kept dropping plates and glasses, which crashed on the floor. No one cared because the special entertainment was about to begin.

A woman appeared, hair up in a bun, wearing a plaid skirt and a crinoline blouse, with a silver whistle in her mouth. Two high school boys stepped from out of a storage closet dressed in graduation robes and mortarboards, one in black, the other white. When they took them off, they were naked underneath. Both of them very well hung. The woman blew the whistle and they crouched down in the taut ready position of wrestlers amidst all the broken glass and crockery.

A tribe of little girls in fairy princess costumes filed in next. To each of the luncheon guests, except Genevieve and me, the girls handed a silk scarf as a blindfold. When they were tied tight, the woman with the hair bun blew the whistle again. The naked boys came to life and began to wrestle. Their exertion was loud and violent—their bodies clashing against each other viciously—as the shards of glasses and plates pierced their skin, drawing blood. The grunting slam of meat and bone brought the dining room to life. Until one of the boys lost his balance and the other pounced. The blindfolded crowd began to chant—how they understood what was happening I don't know. Perhaps from the panic in the breath of the boy on the bottom. Or the tense alkaline smell of the bodies. Then the superior boy, who had a huge erection, bore down on his victim until there was a gasp of defeat and collapse. He plunged his pelvis forward— the crowd saluted with upraised arms. He proceeded to pump like an engine, pounding to the hilt with a sickening violence as the guests at table began singing that Queen song "We Are the Champions." The boy on the bottom squealed horribly. Their bodies began to lose skin tone. They became transparent. When the boy on top at last let loose with a groan that shook every chandelier, the barbarous centaur they made froze. They'd turned into an ice sculpture, the leakage from their cuts dripping like cherry syrup. The ice sculptures on the center table began to tremble and the see-through Roman fertility god toppled over, snapping off his exaggerated extension at the clawed feet of the ruby-tinged dragon.

I woke with a jolt, my pillow damp from sweat, my head all oily with it. For a moment I feared I'd wet bed too. Fuck.

I'd needed the rest so bad I'd put out of my mind the lunch date with Padgett and the wife's parents. It was already 11:45!

I fell in the shower. I couldn't find anything decent to wear. Nothing fit! I didn't have time to think. The last thing I wanted to do was sit around a table with Padgett and his stuffed-shirt parents-in-law at a swank restaurant. He meant well. But he didn't know what was happening to me. I didn't know! They were going to laugh at me. Just like in the dream.

I slipped into the tightest fitting track suit pants and t-shirt I could find, a floppy old pair of sandals and threw on the overcoat from the night before and drove straight down to Kettletons to do some emergency shopping. The store people looked at me like I'd hopped out of a boxcar. I didn't care. There was too much else to stress about. And yet, the physical evidence gave my old cop mind a bit of relief, perverse as it may seem.

I used to take a 44 long. I knew that. I was certain. Now I was a 40 regular. I wondered what Lance Harrigan would make of it. All in my head?

No time. I bought a suit, a couple of shirts, a new pair of shoes that fit (a narrow size 8 down from a wide 11) a new pair of sunglasses to hide my face—and some Jockeys. In this wilderness of price tags, there are so many hidden costs.

I got to the fish joint in a fluff, blood pressure rising like the aroma of mussels and lemongrass. I kept thinking about those white-jacketed men in my dream boiling up tiny lobsters. In the foyer was a marble pedestal with a carved wooden mermaid set into it. I knew the mermaid was set in place because I gave it a nudge anyway. How many people, particularly men had stroked the mermaid on the way to their table? I was completely off-balance. I whisked past the bar and got as far as the maitre d's podium. Padgett and party were being served drinks, his father-in-law looking like a hardboiled egg in an Armani suit.

I think I still maybe could've pulled it off—or would've tried—until . . .

Until I saw Genevieve. Everything inside my head had jumped parole.

Her hair was jet black now and richly braided, the way I

imagine Japanese pearl-diving women wear theirs. But I knew it was her. I was certain.

She was dressed to the nines in a trim turquoise suit with a simple diamond necklace. What was even harder—was that she was dining with the Mayor. They were sitting at a cozy table right beneath a Giant Grouper on the wall. The Mayor actually bore a resemblance to the Grouper. Maybe that's why Genevieve had picked that table. Was the Mayor one of her subjects? Or were they just business associates? Fuck, fuck, fuck.

I glanced back at the Padgett group. It was now or never. The maitre d' slid up behind his podium and ran his eyes over me with an expectant and demanding expression. I saw Chris peek at his watch. Genevieve peered over the Mayor's shoulder. I wondered if she'd seen me—or if she knew by some other means that I was there. She must've known that I was coming. That's why she was sitting there. She'd come to observe me— to distract me so I'd really put my foot in it. My insides turned to gelatin and I booked. I knocked someone down on the way out—and someone else shouted. It was only when I reached my car that I saw that I'd grabbed the mermaid from the pedestal. I'd broken it neatly off at the base and stuck it under my arm. Jesus H. Christ.

Genevieve had told me to bring her a gift that I'd stolen. Without even consciously thinking of it, I'd followed her instructions. Her order.

It took me a few minutes to get my breath back and to get the car out of the underground lot. I was very glad I hadn't done valet parking through the restaurant—that would've been a goddamned disaster. I drove two streets over where the phone reception was better and I could get my thoughts together. Then I texted Chris that I was sorry I couldn't make lunch, but I was feeling very sick—which was very true. He probably suspected I wasn't going to show.

When I got back to my apartment I took off my new

clothes and carefully hung everything up. Now that the place was clean, I wanted to keep it that way, and because nothing else fit, my new togs were my new uniform—and my fragile wrestling hold on reality.

I gave Pico a saucer of milk. Then I took the phone off the hook again, switched off my cell (no message back from Chris) and shook out two of the Sidewinder's knockout bombs. I couldn't face anything else. All I could think of was Genevieve. I wanted her so much. The thought that one day, somehow, I might be sitting down at a table for lunch with her—out in the open—in plain respected view of everyone . . .

What on earth was I thinking? Call it psychotic delusions. Call it love. Or an aging uncovered alcoholic's last chance at something worth living for. Worth dying to know the truth about. Call it whatever the hell you want, I couldn't shake it. I just shook.

I took the pills and rolled into bed. Two Sidewinders and lights out until the next morning. That was what I hoped anyway. A day lost to recovery and refuge . . . and for a few hours at least no chaos of nightmares. Or El Miedo.

I crashed out cold. But later, when the drugs started wearing off, I guess the dreams came back. One did anyway.

I was up on a stainless steel stage. High above, mounted against a wall, was a massive projection screen, designed so that it appeared to be looking into a stone courtyard. It reminded me of where the lions might've been kept in the Coliseum. In this case the creatures it contained were giant reptiles—beautifully stylized dragons. Six of them. One was white, with skin so clear you could see the veins and arteries pulsing. Another gold—so bright it was almost reflective. The third was as green as moss with a pale fungal radiance like those toadstools they say exist in the Amazon jungle that emit a light strong enough to read by. The rest were all a brilliant vermilion with fleshy blue filigree patterns—and long blue forked tongues the texture of suede.

The idea was for people to stand alone on the stainless steel platform. Their image was then projected onto the screen above so that they appeared to be amongst the dragons. As you moved on the platform, the dragons reacted, hissing and threatening—each ready to claw the others to shreds to be the one who devours you. Compared to an average person, the dragons looked about 20 feet high and 60 feet long. Depending on how you moved on the metal stage, you could play the monsters off against each other. That was the goal. When a player stepped off the stage the dragons would pause, then slink away into their separate shadows to await the next player.

Monday morning. Heavy rain at dawn slowing to a trickle and then fading away. Just like I felt. I was back awake in my bed—not the bath or my car. I sat with the windows open trying to suck in the fresh air with Pico on my lap. When the stores opened, I hauled myself to the Koreans in my new bonaroos and bought some supplies, went home and made breakfast. The Koreans didn't give any indication they'd ever seen me before. I didn't care. I made toast, coffee, a three-egg mess with four slices of bacon and mopped up the grease with a puffy blueberry muffin. It tasted wonderful. And I threw up every last bit a half-hour later.

I broke into a cold sweat thinking about the job. The smells of the squad cars. The ash tray tasting coffee in the station house. The sound of the phones ringing . . . the feel of the papers—my desk—like my old desk in school. The routine. Now it seemed like I could put my hand right through the wall. What was I going to do? I couldn't just unravel in front of them all. And I couldn't put them at risk out on the streets with me either.

Pros and cons. Backwards and forwards. I debated with myself like in some hostage negotiation. But no matter how I twisted the cap, I knew what I had to do.

I finally phoned into the Precinct and said I was sick for real—I had to get some tests. After that I called Lance Harrigan and told him I was going to follow his advice. He was right, I was having some trouble I couldn't ignore. Boy, was he right.

I was going to see the shrink and my doctor, too. He seemed pleased—you'd have thought I'd told him I'd won a cruise to Puerto Vallarta. Then I phoned the Captain and the union rep. I laid it all out. I never thought I'd be able to say "unfit for duty," even when I had been, but it turned out to be a load off my mind. For all of about two minutes. Then pure blind frenzy worse than El Miedo ever. What if I was never fit for duty anymore? I couldn't imagine what it would be like to never Mirandize anyone again. What would my life be like without Probable Cause?

I just had to suck it up. There was no other choice. I knew. The way you know.

I spent the next hour and a half making file notes for Chris, everything I could think of about everything that was on the go or still in progress. I poured it out in nice tight bullet point form, just like shooting off rounds at the range. It made me feel a little better. Then I sealed it all up in a creamy manila envelope and drove over to the Precinct, hoping it would be either frantic with activity or as vacant as it gets. Colby and Strothers were heading into an interview room with a young black hustler. Haslett was at his desk but didn't look up. Chris was out and I dropped the envelope on his desk. Our desk. Then I skedaddled.

It was a clutching-falling-into-space sort of feeling turning in my shield and weapons, which I did down at the front desk to a taciturn duty Sergeant I fortunately hadn't met before. Like losing an arm and going cold sober at all once. But it was the stand-up thing to do for the sake of guys like Padgett and Novak. Out of respect for the job. Some last hint of respect for myself.

The really hard thing was I knew a sigh of relief would be echoed around a lot of lockers. Even Padgett's. That was the one that hurt the most. I couldn't bring myself to call him straight. I had to send a wussy text message. He was off doing an honest morning's work trying to catch bad guys.

When I got back to the cat box I had another spew and took a long lukewarm shower. I didn't have to shave. All my body hair seemed to just wash down the drain and my face, despite how I felt, was smoother and younger looking than I could recall. When I was dressed again in the only clothes that fit me—including some real men's underwear—I stowed the money Jimmie had left me, minus some walking around cash, left food for Pico and picked up the thieved mermaid. At least I'd fulfilled my mission on that score. Now I had some time up my sleeve.

And suddenly, I didn't know what to do with myself. I didn't have a set of handcuffs on me anymore. I didn't have authority. I didn't . . . know who I was . . .

All I had was a fantasy that lay behind the door of 4 Eyrie Street. And more shadows than I could count behind.

So I went looking for McInnes. I scouted the apartment he'd been living in on Tolbert. He still had three months left on his lease, but the neighbors weren't talking and the manager had no idea. Jack hadn't been seen in the last few days. I didn't like that. Then I jawed with the ham-and-eggers at Rooster Booster. I visited the desk at the Coolidge. I hit a titty bar and a watering hole called The Sportsman's Paradise I knew he used to frequent. I even swung by this karate dojo he'd been connected with. He'd either flown the coop or was lying very low. I didn't want to think about the other possibility. He was, after all, the guy who'd gotten me into this predicament. The appointed time rolled around and I headed to Cliffhaven, feeling like someone had slipped me a nitroglycerine tab. The thought of seeing Genevieve again made my heart beat faster than El Miedo ever had.

DOWN
A
BLONDE
ALLEY

![1]

I DROVE OVER TO CLIFFHAVEN LISTENING TO JOHNNY CASH singing "A Boy Named Sue" on the radio. For the first time in a long while my cell phone wasn't bleeping at me constantly. It was as if I'd become telephone invisible.

The giant African met me at the door. I'd been wondering when I was going to confront him. Up close he reminded me of Def Lov, the MC at the Congo Club, only with ridges of scars down both cheeks. He was dressed in a butler's uniform, but it made him look like an ambassador. Without saying a word he took the pilfered mermaid from my hands and led me upstairs to the second floor, which I'd been excluded from earlier.

The room he escorted me to gave the impression of being the size of the whole house. There was a grandfather clock with the dimensions of a totem pole and I half expected to find a giraffe grazing amongst the chandeliers. I couldn't imagine how the effect was achieved.

Masks of all descriptions covered the walls, as well as library case after case sagging under the weight of books. Despite the seeming authenticity of the objects, I couldn't help wonder if someone else had entered that room, would they have seen a different room?

Genevieve was seated in a chair made of cattle horns and hide. She had cornrows in her black sheeny hair and a nutmeg tint to her skin. But I knew it was her. She was dressed in a corset of what looked like hyena fur, with wet leather caramel boots up to her thighs, with one of her Arabian Nights cigarettes in a long silver holder, writing with a quill pen in a vellum daybook. Beside her was another chair. Plastic. Form-molded in the shape of a naked woman. In between was an acrylic plinth with a round bowl on top. Inside the bowl skirted two goldfish.

"Thank you, Mutza," she murmured to the scar-faced African. "Put the mermaid in the rock garden. I have a rock garden behind the house, Sunny, composed of gallstones from my devoted admirers over the years. Your humble offering will fit in nicely."

It galled me to think she knew where the mermaid came from. Even trumped up the way she was, she was all truffles and caviar—tweezers and rubber tubing. I tried to relax. Then I noticed a table-sized guillotine.

"I think you're drinking again. Over near the parcheesi table."

"No thanks," I said.

"Then why don't you have a look at my gallery in the alcove. I'll be with you in a moment."

I felt like a beetle exploring the geometry of a firelog. The "gallery" contained a host of vanities—all featuring a suggestion of her face as I first saw it that blood sun evening what seemed like a lifetime ago. A section of tapestry showed a comet streaking over a group of peasants gathered outside a fortress. She stood at the edge of the moat. There was a water-color of her and some European fop in a lace collar with a brindle whippet—and an engraving of her standing with some British officer in what looked like the Zulu Wars. Then a daguerreotype of her and the Indian Chief Geronimo . . . the cagey old warrior neutered and domesticated in a black top hat at the wheel of a Model T. In other photos she was posed with men like Sigmund Freud, Einstein, Babe Ruth, John D. Rockefeller and President Warren G. Harding.

In still others, that had been made to look like society page shots, she was wearing a taffeta gown with a smashed and frail Judy Garland and a debonair James Mason at the Hollywood premiere of *A Star is Born* . . . drinking with Broadway Joe Namath in a tight cashmere sweater . . . clubbing with a heavily medicated Andy Warhol in a floor length mohair coat.

From Niagara Falls to Negril, her image appeared, in and out of time. World's Fairs, state funerals, tickertape parades and art happenings. There was even what purported to be a portrait of her signed by Picasso. It reminded me of the not so fun mirrors of Funland. But like everything she did, the illusions were well done. I ambled back into the main room to investigate her reading material.

Whole shelves were devoted to esoteric and erotic art—and the erotic arts. Love potions. Deviant practices. Bondage and fetishisms. Then there were rows of medical texts. Anatomies, physiology, clinical neurology, the effects of captivity on behavior—as well as two well-referred-to works called *Essential Psychopharmacology* and *The Combat Surgery Emergency Handbook*. And of course, bless her black heart, she had good old *DSM*. But by far and away, the largest portion was devoted to magic and the occult. From phrenology to astrology, the Cabala—and a vast subsection devoted to alchemy.

"Find anything interesting?" she queried, putting away her pen and ink, and blowing on the last page.

"What's all this alchemy stuff?"

"I've been involved with alchemy for several hundred years," she replied. "And I've achieved no little success. But the art is complex. Even for me."

"It looks like a lot of gibberish to me," I told her. Her

queen-throughout-the-ages act was starting to really irritate me—or scare me beyond all bounds.

She laughed. "One of the more believable explanations regarding the origin of the word 'gibberish' links it to Geber or Jabbir, an 8th-century Arabian alchemist, who disguised his teachings in an intricate terminology that only the initiated could understand. I found him very entertaining and wonderful in bed."

"You've got a lot of . . . uh . . . interests," I said, blowing her off.

"I do," she agreed. "Under various pseudonyms I've recently written a monograph on the Costa Rican poison dart frog and designed an ultrasonic pain field generator which has attracted the attention of both the CIA and NASA. Last year the Pittsburgh Symphony performed a symphony I composed and another piece is being presented in Hamburg."

I was about to fire something back when an object on the table between us caught my attention. It was only about eight inches high—an enameled and satin-covered egg-shaped ornament with a duck-like bill.

"Tap on it gently," Genevieve said.

When I did, a remarkable transformation occurred. The enamel and satin finished exterior shed itself to reveal an armored plating. Stage by stage, the armored panels broke away and folded in. The interior sections were all ingeniously hinged pieces that seemed to endlessly unfold to form finally, a winged dragon of great majesty and ferocity. There was no mechanical process at work that I could discern, and the creature which emerged was unaccountably large relative to the initial egg.

"A gift from the 18th century," she said without expression. "One of the master artisans of Bavaria. There's no metal at all used inside. Each of the internal pieces was derived from the artist's own fingernails, saved, carved and polished after being melded together in an arcane process he invented. It's the only one of its kind. It took him his whole life to make—and has the doubly unusual capability of retracting or re-enfolding itself, and will do so soon, of its own accord. Now come sit down with me."

I crossed over and sat down on the naked plastic woman—which squeaked beneath me. There was an oil painting on the wall opposite, filled with dark, sinuous shapes. I knew it was an erotic scene of sorts, but it was hard to tell exactly what the figures were doing, and I wasn't sure I wanted to know.

Genevieve blew a smoke ring, then plunged the cherry of the cigarette into the softness of her thigh. I squawked in spite of myself.

"Don't be alarmed," she smiled, as the smell of burnt flesh rose. "It's just my way of regaining clarity. Beethoven, it's said, would refresh his attention by thrusting his hands into ice cold water. Houdini, who could escape from almost anything except his own impotence, would swallow and regurgitate a tiny key."

"I usually just hit myself in the head with a big hammer," I said frowning.

"A big hammer? Like the one Jake hurled into the sheetrock? Well, you may need it. Because I want to discuss with you the issue of muliebrity."

"What's that? I've never heard that word." Jesus, she could play me.

"I'm not surprised," she answered, as the dragon began to close in on itself. "It's the female equivalent of virility—the measure of female sexual potency and allure."

Where in hell she was steering me this time? Just the mention of the sheetrock got me spinning. She knew that.

"Love is love and fun is fun. But it is always so quiet when the goldfish die," she said with dark eyes aglow. "Do you know who said that?"

"Not a clue," I confessed. "Hugh Hefner on a rough morning?"

"Ernest Hemingway. One of my favorite writers. A macho

man and closet homosexual." Then in one fluid motion, she reached over to the globe of water and plucked one of the gold-fish from its gentle swim and tossed it on the floor at our feet.

"Why are you always hectoring me?" I asked, noticing the dragon had folded itself all the way back into the egg.

"Would you prefer to be rogered?"

"What?"

"Oh, Sunny," she chuckled contemptuously. "I'm just breaking you down to build you up! We know what's drawn you to me, but that's what's drawn me to you. That you have so much to break down—and so much to build with once the last wall collapses. Now get down on your knees and lick that goldfish up off the floor."

"What?"

"You heard me," she said with deadly politeness.

"What if I said no?" I balked.

She brought her right boot heel smashing down. "I believe you just did."

I glanced at the smear of fish on the floor. "You didn't—I mean why . . . ?"

She looked up at me. Into me. With eyes full of beheadings and pageants.

"All the pharaohs, kings, queens, emperors and sultans of consequence have understood that the most satisfying enter-tainments are those that come at the expense of other people," she said. "Bread and circuses. You like them, Sunny. You go to a football game. You don't feel diminished—you feel the players are well rewarded for performing for *you*. Your ticket buys you the illusion of temporary, sanitized and beneficent ownership."

"Why can't they win for me then?" I grunted, trying to ignore the crushed fish. God, a little hint of ebony made her irresistible.

"That would spoil the suspense, which is the real pleasure you're leveraging. You would quickly lose interest. But you know from your police experience that sporting events are rigged all the time. Horse races, boxing matches. Falco and Ernie understood that very well. Money is the most obvious means of grading and therefore degrading other people. Sex is the most primal."

"What about violence?" I inquired, beginning to feel ready for some.

"Sex is a special kind of violence—and money is an abstraction of both," she answered. "Sex and money combined is the basis for almost all violence in the sense that you mean. Take the conflict between fundamentalist Islam and the West. You think religion's driving it? Hardly! Land and oil—in other words, money. But most importantly, how men and women behave. Radical Muslims fear a shift in the paradigm of dominance and submission in their culture."

"You're not saying women are in control—in the West?" Suddenly I could feel her fascinating me again. Fastening onto my mind. Changing and distorting everything.

"Control is the most misunderstood word in existence," she replied. "I don't say women are in control in American society. But neither are men. There are priorities, inhibitions, prohibitions, enticements and rewards. There is no control. What's at issue is dominance—and yes, I do say women are dominant."

"Then why aren't there more female executives or political leaders?" I inquired, more than a little surprised by the line she was taking. It kind of snapped me out of my own spin.

"Whether it's the CEO of the Frontier Bank or the President of the United States, these are merely titles. They're like boxes or containers."

She savored that last word and I flashed on Mr. Tanaka and his "program."

"You see the individuals occupying the containers and ignore the containers—the real nature of the power. You perceive positions of authority, forgetting that the authority isn't

inherent in the position—it's been *assigned* to it by an elaborately negotiated process. The positions themselves can be
divested of import."

"I'm not sure I follow you," I said, although she was certainly leading me.

"The alpha dog in a pack isn't *elected* like a team captain
or a candidate," she answered. "Humans don't like to think
too directly about the natural order of the wild—and yet can't
escape it. So they've developed ways to quarantine and euphe-
mize it. The Law of the Wild is modified through compromise,
cooperation and often corruption—which makes the positions
of authority you're thinking about actually ways of limiting
and managing power, rather than a license to deploy it."

"Put something in a box so you know where to find it?"

"Or a cage. I think of societal institutions in terms of game
reserves or zoos. True, there are more males on display. But
that is so they exert less influence in the wild. There is less wild.
Modern society overall is synonymous with the feminization of
the species. That's the whole point of society."

"Boy, my first wife Joan wouldn't have agreed with that
one bit," I shrugged, thinking back to the chingazos we used to
have. "She felt that women were completely oppressed."

For just a moment then it was like we were having some
adult discussion after a foreign film at some espresso joint. But
it wasn't.

"Many women believe that," Genevieve agreed. "Of
course, claiming oppression has always been a good way of
gaining more power. And even genuinely feeling oppressed still
isn't any proof of actually being oppressed, especially not by
some cohesive force in a systematic way. I'd never give males
so much credit."

"I get that," I nodded, coming back.

"I call a spade a shovel, Sunny," she shrugged. "And I'm
very democratic in my disdain. I said women exert more dominance than they like to admit. They just don't have the

courage to be open about it and take responsibility for it. Motherhood, for instance, is the most ubiquitous and unquestioned form of domination there is."

It was the first time I'd ever heard some hint of private emotion in her voice.

"So, now you have it in for mothers," I grumped, trying to picture what kind of mother and father—what kind of upbringing she might've had. I couldn't. Maybe the expression on my face betrayed my thoughts because she gave out a lilting laugh.

"Don't be so serious, my dear. Haven't you ever played a game or had a debate with a female? Or has it been just rote sex and arguments with a few drinks in between?"

"Mostly drinks and arguments . . . with some sex on the side," I answered, wondering how true that really was. Too true probably.

"Well, you need to have the sensuality of your mind awakened for what lies ahead, sweet Sunny," she continued. "So, we together are going to explore the matter of seduction versus violence . . . the seductive nature of violence . . . and the subtle but potent violence of seduction."

She pointed the remote at the oil painting. The murky erotic scene disappeared, as if the whole thing including the frame had been only a detailed projection from behind. That section of the wall was now blank and sketched onto it appeared stick figures in charcoal, red and ochre, surrounded by the outlines of hands and primitive silhouettes of beasts. Deer, antelope.

"Consider this scenario from the deep past," she said, as the central humanlike figures came alive to her words.

"Male and female mates are confronted by a larger, aggressive male. What do they do? The male alone cannot defeat the stranger. The female is physically weaker than both of the males, but working with her mate, the contest would at least be more equal. Do husband and wife take up arms together and try to defeat the intruder?"

"I guess that depends on if they have kids, or if the female's pregnant," I said.

"Let's say they don't. How do you imagine this ancestral scene playing out?"

"I think if the smaller guy can't talk or bluff his way out of it—and if they can't run away—he's in bad shape. He's either going to get killed or be driven off and the bigger, stronger guy is going to get the female," I answered.

"Get the female," she repeated. "Does the female join in and help her mate fight?"

The figures seemed to freeze as if awaiting direction.

"It's possible but I wouldn't bet on it," I replied. "I think the female makes the decision that the stranger might win whether she takes part or not, and she figures she might get better treatment from the victor if she doesn't attack him. Maybe even pretend to like him—let him have his way. If he's not a pig, then maybe she's better off than she was before. Less likely to be attacked again. If he's really bad news, she'd do better waiting until the dust settles and killing him when he's asleep. He can't be on guard all the time."

"So, the female who was to be gotten becomes the getter. Very interesting. The physically weakest, apparently most vulnerable figure in the scenario actually holds the balance of power."

The stick figures bowed and receded into the wall, taking the horned beasts with them.

"Now we'll play another game," she smiled.

2.

SHE KEPT SMILING. "SAY YOU'RE CONDUCTING AN investigation. Your search warrant—which you too often didn't worry about—allows you to examine one room of a single occupant apartment. Your goal is to conclude whether a woman or a man is living there at the moment. Which room do you choose?"

"The bathroom," I answered automatically, feeling a twinge of phantom limb pain about the job. The Precinct. I even missed the Captain for a moment.

"Why?"

"Because the place could be sublet. The stuff on the walls, the furnishings could belong to someone else. What's in the bathroom—at least the most visible stuff—will tell you who's living there right then."

"So, you'd inspect the toiletries?" she prodded.

"I'd check the kinds of products—the amount of products. I'd toss the waste basket. I'd look at the shower drain for hair. Prescription medicines. Birth control. Magazines. Powder. The look and feel of the room. The smell."

"Tell me. If someone wanted to be deceptive, which would

be easier—for a man to make it look like a woman was living in an apartment, or for a woman to make it look like a man?"

"Are we talking gay or straight? A butch woman or an effeminate man? Secondly, who's doing the inspection? A woman would see something different than a man. And are they gay or straight? A well-trained dog would be much harder to fool either way. A full-scale Forensics sweep would be definitive—and from experience would tell you what the dog already knew."

"Let's say it's you, on your own, with your own senses and prejudices," she answered.

"Is the apartment empty or full to start with?" I asked.

"That's another thing I like about you, Sunny. Your sense of detail. Let's say the place is empty to begin with—and that we're dealing with heterosexuals."

"Then I think it would be easier for a woman to make it look like a man lived there. If it was full, the other way around."

"Why is that?"

"If the place was empty, a woman could furnish it simply and sparsely and then plant some obviously masculine items. A few clothes and shoes. Cologne. Men's shaving cream. A girlie magazine. Maybe some sporting equipment. Leave the toilet seat up. A man would have more things to buy to create the illusion. A woman would have more clothes, more products in the bathroom and more personal items. In a pinch, a woman could get away with a fairly minimalist set with a few key things in position. I think a man would need more props—and that means it would be easier to go wrong."

"This is so illuminating, Sunny, to hear your thoughts. Tell me, would you agree that the more feminine a man is, the less masculine he is?"

"Y-yeah. I . . . guess." There was something so disorienting about her voice, her presence . . . like a vase of jonquils in a small room.

"Oh, I think you have," she said. "And just before, you put forward a more intriguing and subtle variation on this—namely that men can be understood in terms of their absence of femininity. They're defined by characteristics they lack—behavior they don't display. This has been the traditional way of thinking of females. Even with the crucial child bearing capability, women have often been viewed as incomplete or failed men—Eve born of Adam's rib. You've quietly turned this around and made femininity the standard by which men are defined. It's not in fact how full of masculinity, it's how empty of femininity that defines a 'man.' That's an intriguing alternative perspective. How empty are you, Sunny? That's a question society has been wrestling with for quite some time."

"They're wrestling with my masculinity?"

"What else is there to do with masculinity? I can think of only one thing. Hm, two things."

"All right," I said, confused. "Let me ask you a question. Go back to the figures on the wall. What would you do if you were the female in that situation?"

She summoned back the primitive figures with the remote.

"For starters, the arrival of an intruding male would come as no surprise. It would be something I'd been planning for—and counting on. I would've heightened the danger and drama of this in my male's mind. Wherever we were, we'd make it a habit to assume not just a defensive position, because unless you have great numbers, what makes a good defensive position is exactly what makes it as hard to launch an attack from as an attack against. Instead, we'd rely on the guerilla tactic of chicanes and booby traps. With skill, these can be hastily assembled and tailored to the immediate terrain and environment. Indeed they must be seamless with the environment to remain undetected."

As she spoke, the stick figures on the wall demonstrated the construction of various snares.

"These same skills would benefit our hunting activities,"

she continued. "And this is perhaps the real answer to your question. We'd always be hunting—just as I am now. We wouldn't just be anticipating an intruder, we'd be hoping for one."

"You'd want to be attacked?" I puzzled.

"Yes!" she said with a serrated edge to her voice, as the Cro-Magnon cartoon took a very insidious turn. "Think of it as inviting guests. My current male and I have fortified our position. We appear to be in the open and easy to attack. In reality, a natural pit has been disguised. Our interloper makes his advance. My male and I lure him toward the pit—he falls. Now we have the newcomer at a severe disadvantage. He may have been injured from his fall. He's psychologically jarred. He may be large and physically strong, but time in the pit will change him. Any food and water he carries will soon run out. Dehydration, hunger, exposure and the mental torment of fear and isolation will break him down. The taunts and jeers of a woman who has conquered him will be especially trying. What's more, I now have the advantage of being able to sound him out without physical reprisal. Does he have a deeper courage and mental discipline—or was his threat based on mere bulk? What are his softest spots? How can I possess him so as to reconfigure his will around mine?"

"What do you do when you've broken him down?" I asked at last, astonished again at what I was hearing, breaking through yet another barrier of disbelief.

"Oh, Sunny," she smiled, with a corrosion resistant expression. "Once he's broken, he's rebuilt. Healed—and made whole. His trapper and tormentor becomes his savior. What might've been the end of his life is the beginning of a new life—with a new purpose. To serve me and to be sustained in me. He becomes the basis of my army, a stud in my stable. Once I'm absolutely sure he's ready, I retrieve him from the pit and hitch him to my dogsled."

"You treat him—like a dog?" I huffed, and I suddenly

heard in my head the howl of timberwolves through subarctic pines.

"Of course," she nodded. "Aren't working dogs treated with fondness and care? Wild males long to chase and broken males love to pull in harness. Do you know the best way to run a sled dog team? You put the alpha dog in second position and run the beta as lead. The beta dog will drive harder with the true pack leader directly behind, and the alpha will push the beta dog relentlessly. Then, when the beta is spent, you still have the alpha dog, who will haul all the harder even though exhausted. That's because the alpha isn't elected captain. He *is* captain."

"You'd be a bust-hump football coach," I remarked.

"Yes, I was," she replied with a poker face. "I told you I've been many things in my life. Once a teacher in Ohio—a small, coal miners' high school. When the male coach was killed in a car accident—I had to take over or there wouldn't have been a season. There were eyebrows raised of course—but I delivered. Every player on that team practiced equally hard—and everyone played in every game. Win or lose, I made those boys feel like men—because that's what a real female can do."

"Behind every great man is a great woman?"

"*Inside* every great man is a great woman," she retorted. "And vice versa. When the prostitute or the lone female thinks like a soldier—and the soldier or the lone male recognizes himself as a prostitute and finds some of those skills within, that's when civilization begins."

"Geez, and I thought it was when someone laid down some laws," I quipped.

"What I've been talking about is a law—the deep law," she replied. "And now it's time to start the next level of your training, Sunny. I know you long for the fullness of intimacy with me, but that must wait until your next visit. Nevertheless, you're about to witness and engage in some very hot, wet sex."

I swallowed hard as Sophia entered the room dressed in a

spicy little suit that reminded me of an organ grinder's monkey. All I wanted was what Genevieve promised. If it couldn't be with her—this time—and that promise thrilled me—then Sophia would do nicely. I was itching for action. All the worries and wondering had been banished. Temporarily.

The young girl took my hand and led me two doors down the hall, although it seemed much farther. What a difference a door made in 4 Eyrie Street. I tried to keep my mind blank and open. Which was a good thing, because when the door swung in, we entered a room that was set out in a way I would never in a million years have predicted—and yet which was absolutely familiar.

It was a police station interview room. A large steel-legged table with a laminated top dominated the space—with but a single businesslike chair instead of the usual three or four. The chair faced a foil silver mirror, which I knew was really a window, and that Genevieve was almost assuredly watching from the other side. On the table was a heavy white telephone and in the corners of the room beneath the mirror were two black speakers. Other than these items, it was like so many rooms where I'd detained and deposed suspects over the years. There was a gray absence of sympathy and natural light to every square inch, and even the back of the white enamel door had been fitted with metal plating and a slotted window with the illusion of a view into a dead gray municipal hallway that wasn't there.

"I'll come back when you've seen what this room has to show you," Sophia whispered, handing me a folder and closing the door behind her with a steely click.

I was certain I was being observed. I pulled out the chair and sat down at the table.

The folder looked like the usual police case file, except that on the cover was a white cartoon goose wearing a sun bonnet, like something out of a children's story. Inside was a dossier of photos that contained anything but child-approved viewing.

They were glossy black and white 35 millimeter photographs of people having sex—the kind of shots a PI would take working a divorce or blackmail angle, someone trying to sabotage a politician, or the paparazzi sticking it up a celebrity. It took me a few seconds to get past the grain and texture. When I did, I couldn't believe it.

The first batch, paper-clipped together, were of my first wife Joan. In the one on top, she was on top—in the bedroom of our first apartment. I couldn't see who the man was. In the next one I could. It was Warwick Bunting, who'd lived just above us. The next photo showed her getting it from behind. Then we'd moved apartments and she was up on the counter with some repairman. I could almost make out the logo on his shirt. Another one looked like it was taken in the room where people lay their coats at a party. Steven Lumley was checking her oil. My hands shook. There was something impossible about the images—they all came from years ago for starters, and I recalled my earlier fear. Some had been taken with a telephoto lens, but the angles and the detail in other shots couldn't have been achieved unless the photographer had been right in the room beside them. They had to be fakes—and that helped me cope with what they showed. Still, I couldn't get past the fact that I recognized some of the men in them—and Joan in all. I knew this was just another mind game of Genevieve's, but the images got to me.

The second clip file contained shots of Polly, and those frankly floored me. There was a period when she'd gone back to church. I thought it was a good thing. One of the photographs showed her on a picnic blanket with this guy Stewart who sang in the choir with her. They were kissing like teenagers with a plate of fried chicken and potato salad beside them. Then . . .

No back door deliveries, huh, Polly?

Another showed her polishing the knob of Hagen Kelty, an earlier police partner of mine in the front seat of a car. But the pics that really got me were a group where the man's face was never clear. I have a feeling she didn't care much about his face though. I threw down the folder and watched all the black and white body parts spill across the table.

The phone rang. I answered it on the fourth ring—tempted to rip it out of the wall.

"An interesting new perspective, yes, Sunny? Interesting from several angles."

"They're forgeries!" I yelled into the phone.

"You've worked with a lot of evidence over the years. You'd have to say they look authentic, wouldn't you? What's more, now that you've gotten used to them—they feel true, don't they? To your intuition."

"I don't know how you did it, but these can't be real," I insisted.

"Real. Illusion. You're obsessed with that distinction, Sunny. Don't you know women are trained in illusion and camouflage almost from birth? Make up. Fashion. Diets. Beauty tips. Perfume. Douches. Lingerie. High heels. Mascara. Lipstick. Nail polish. Surgery. Lubricants. Birth control! It's war paint and the honey trap, love. The prostitute finding her inner soldier. You want a woman to be an actress—not an actor, of course! Yet, you cry for reality. Then you see the reality. How would you describe that nearest shot of Polly?"

"You're enjoying this," I said. "But it isn't her."

"Ah, so it's pride then. You can't believe that what's good for the gander is good for the goose—which comes from an earlier proverb—about what's sauce for the goose. There's a lot of sauce in those photos."

"What's your point?" I asked. "I'm a cuckold many times over? More humiliation?"

"No, Sunny," the warm voice at the other end of the phone replied—like a smooth consultant. "After the initial shock wears off you'll see there's a very different message in these photos. You've always believed that you were the one playing

up—your male pride. But you've also always felt guilty, like
you were doing your women wrong. Even if you can't accept
that some of the photos before you are real, you can't deny all
of them. It may be that your indiscretions sometimes inspired
your wives—but look at your first wife, Joan. Who didn't she
take to bed? Or on a table—or the deck of some neighbor's
house? If you concede the authenticity of even one of these
photos, you see your life in a new light."

"I'm not feeling better," I said.

"I understand that," her voice said. I worshipped her voice.
Even in torment.

"Look at the shots of your second wife Polly, and that one
particular partner. You know the one I mean."

I picked up one of the photos in that series, titillated and
repulsed all at once. Polly's belly was big—the other shots
hadn't been from the right angle to see it.

"Turn it over. You'll see the photos are dated."

My stomach turned.

"Say it out loud. Into the phone—so that you can hear
yourself."

"This is just about the time of the miscarriage," I mumbled
into the receiver, but it sounded so much louder in my head.

"Imagine the effect of vigorous sex with a man like that on
a pregnant woman. Have you ever considered that maybe Polly
may have played some role in her own miscarriage? She was
carrying the baby. She was supposedly the nurturing environment. She doesn't look too nurturing in those photos does she?
Or maybe she does—in a different way."

"No," I sighed. "She just looks . . . human. I'm still the one
who drove her . . . to that."

"Oh, Sunny," the voice bounced. "You don't even know if
it was your baby! You're the most loyal traitor I've met in
recent memory."

"Gee, thanks."

"Yesterday's innocence, like guilt, is tomorrow's despair,

Sunny. I grow more hopeful for you all the time. Which is why I must make you suffer more now."

"Great. A kick to the groin perhaps?"

"No doubt," the voice said softly. "Life is always a kick to the mind, the heart, the loins—these are just metaphors for our deeper being."

The lights went dim and the phone line went dead. I hung up the receiver and watched as curtains of organic patterns began to insinuate themselves across the walls like the silhouettes of vines and creepers. A jungle soundtrack rose, but not from the speakers. Raucous cries of distant birds . . . frogs . . . howler monkeys . . . and far away, but getting progressively louder, an infectious drum beat.

The mirrored rectangle before me changed aspect. The fog of my reflection cleared into a window or a television screen— it was hard to say which, because the image seemed to be both immediately on the other side of the glass and also very remote—as in another time and place.

It was a seedy hourly rate motel room, presented in such detail, I knew exactly what the bedspread smelled like. The linen would have a harsh industrial laundry odor, an attempt to reassure patrons of some attempt at cleanliness (which ironically would serve to remind them that other bodies had been in that same room but an hour or two before). The bedspread, however, would only get cleaned every so often, and so would've absorbed a flood of colognes and perfumes, sweat, mucous—all the evidence that we leave behind in illicit circumstances. Only when there's a kind of crime do we think of evidence.

Genevieve entered the room—but as a redhead, like my first wife Joan—dressed in a bargain rack pistachio green cocktail dress. She was followed by Mutza, laid and sprayed like a Wetworld pimp with plenty of bling. The pulse of the drum beat increased in intensity.

I knew the instant they appeared what would happen, but

the experience of actually seeing them together in that setting was something else entirely. She was going to make me watch her having sex with another man—and not just any man. It was cheap and stereotyped and yet it had the primal hypnotic quality of some essential conflict and release. They seemed to undress in syncopation with the rising urgency of the percussion—the heartbeat of the primeval jungle in an adulterous motel room.

I knew he would be large—the theater of the scene required it. But that doesn't begin to convey what I saw. He'd had it strapped to his leg with a leather thong and at first it appeared just to hang, reaching down to the floor. But with her caresses it came alive, thickening to match its extraordinary length— becoming a creature unto itself. The drum pressure rose as Genevieve stroked and cavorted with the organ, as much as with the man. And then the speakers in my room crackled.

Both she and Mutza wore electronic collars. But unlike the one I'd worn earlier, these were voice synthesizers and they distorted the input in very contradictory ways. Genevieve's voice had the deep, forbidding quality of something out of *The Exorcist*. While the obsessively endowed black sex lord spoke like a canary in some Warner Brothers' cartoon.

I'd never in my life seen anything as rough or mesmerizing. And then to hear the distorted voices . . . the layers and levels of meaning. I don't need to tell you all the details—how thoroughly he possessed her—although it seemed more like she was acquiring him.

Take the most extreme scenario of a black man and a white woman and magnify that in your mind . . . and you still wouldn't begin to understand what I saw.

The moment I had my pants pulled down, the light in the motel room flickered like the end of an old film reel. The drumming stopped and suddenly there was Genevieve looking like Ava Gardner in *Mogambo*. Mutza stood beside her wearing a zebra skin suit and a black derby. They took a deep bow and the viewing window went dark.

Sophia came back into the room dressed in only a black tri-cot chemise and g-string. There was another door in the inter-view room that I hadn't noticed before. She helped me out of my pants.

The room she brought me to was empty-white except for one distinctive piece of furniture—a giant version of a Dilley's Chocolate box in the Valentine shape of a heart. Standing beside it, to my abhorrence, was the kid with the Gandhi tat-too. He was dressed in an old-fashioned blue and white Navy suit like the Cracker Jacks sailor. He gave me a smile that made me want to flatten his face. Then he opened the lid of the huge box. Sophia took my hand.

Two carpeted stairs led down to a condensed honeymoon suite. Red satin everywhere—a black silk sheeted waterbed in the shape of a heart with puffed red pillows. I tore off what was left of my clothes and descended. This was at last some-thing I understood. After all my fears about the changes in my body. My shrinking size. My loss of weight and hair—the feel-ings I didn't understand. I didn't care. Having become aroused to the point of madness I wanted only one thing. And I got it. Sophia and I happily nuzzled and tussled in the dark, the splish and splash of the fluid beneath us, and the darkness and the warmth of the space created a sense of submersion. Immersion.

She slipped off the bed to sweep the pillows away, and then bounced back into the wave world, spooning up against me. She kept her g-string on, but that just got me more worked up. I slipped into the wave world inside her. She was light and fragile—young. I went slowly at first. I felt all my inhibitions and horrors stream out of me. We were entwined and united. Slick, slippery . . . swaying and bobbing in the dark. All of Genevieve's tests and tortures—all the questions and recrimi-nations seemed worth it. We went on, floating and flounder-ing—Sophia making the softest noises over the turmoil in the water beneath us and the uterine dark around.

Then I sensed a tightening urgency in her—a contraction around me—and a new intensity in her breathing. I began to thrust harder. Again and again I collided with her bottom, which seemed skinnier than what it had looked like up above in the light.

I knew I couldn't hold on much longer. She wailed—and I let go—when a seam in the waterbed burst, and we thumped to the floor in a spasm of climax—warmth and wet cascading over us in an amniotic flush.

The scene in the Jaguar House when Raven had been found in the skin of the punctured waterbed washed through my mind—but there was something else. Another one of those sinking feelings. A sunken feeling.

Suddenly, the lid opened and light flooded in. Genevieve was standing on the edge leering down. She had on a yellow wetsuit. Beside her was Sophia, wearing the Cracker Jacks sailor's outfit. I might've been lying in a pool of my own blood.

"A surprise in every box," Genevieve said, shaking her head.

I stared back up the stairs at her . . . and Sophia. Genevieve produced a long flashlight—and shone it down into the depths of the saturated honeymoon heart. The beam hit the body beside me and played across the flesh. First the black flimsy underwear—soaked and disheveled. Then that ungodly tattoo. And the face! It was the boy from the ferry—and in the hot violating light I saw to my further alarm that his neck still bore the painted marks of a noose-like impression. He'd been the one to play the part of Grier the other night.

I let out a sound I didn't recognize. The kid must've sensed I was about to reach out and strangle him because he slithered fast, flopping off the bed like a catfish.

"Be angry with me if you like," Genevieve nodded. "But not young Sal. There's more to the picture than meets the eye, Sunny. And I give you at least a little credit to recognize the textural nature of the depth you've been plumbing. Time for the full reveal, Sal."

The kid whisked off the g-string and gave me a good long look. He then exited with a splash via the same hidden door that Sophia must've used. I felt hoodwinked beyond bounds.

"Don't look so devastated, Sunny," Genevieve scolded. "You've had a rare and mystical privilege. You've experienced the Divine Pair—the Syzygy. The Original Man in almost all mythologies is hermaphroditic. This has been a crucial step forward in your training. Now, go through that same door. At the end of the hall you'll find a place to clean up. Your clothes are there. Tomorrow when you come at 7 PM sharp—you must bring me another offering. Not something that you've saved or stolen. Something that you've won—that you've earned through true effort or skill. Goodbye my lovely Sunny. Until next time. When you and I *will* mingle, at last. More deeply than you've ever known."

3

I WOKE UP ON THE FLOOR OF MY APARTMENT WEARING the wisteria colored lingerie I'd earlier bought for Briannon but had never given to her. It about made me piss myself.

I had no idea how I'd gotten into the things. It was Pico who'd roused me—she was licking my arm. Instead of the transparent stuff I'd found in the bathtub, I was covered with a sticky yellow film with the predigested odor of babyfood. That—particularly the smell—made me throw up.

The patching suggested some of the crap had been washed off—but not enough. It was a good thing I'd lost so much of the hair on my body, because what remained of the goo had dried to a crumbly paste. On the floor beside me was a pink and yellow plastic trophy—a sculpture of a nude woman clutching a giant corn cob. It said *The Rumpus Room— Midnight Cream Corn Wrestling Champion*. I knew it was only circumstantial evidence, but the smell of the residue was nauseating even after a shower and the scrubbing—and I did have a diabolic flashback about a bell ringing and sweaty men waving dollar bills. Then again, I had far more unsettling flashbacks about Eyrie Street. I lay there crying, letting whatever was left inside me leak out. Pico stayed with me. I couldn't have handled a person seeing me in that condition.

It took another hour of tactical scrubbing and spraying deodorant to get the situation in hand, but I couldn't get control of my mind so easily. I wanted a drink. A whole bottle. El Miedo had seemed to fade when I'd met Genevieve, but another kind of fog had rolled in. Deeper and more terrifying.

I found the suit I'd bought hanging neatly in the closet, which I hadn't expected. I put it on. It didn't fit as well. I reached in the pocket of the trousers and found a wad of Jimmie's money. He was looking out for me still. I decided to get some breakfast. Not at Cheezy's. I went to that Fresh Start place that had gone in where the dead man's barbershop used to be. It was clean, bright, bopping—and the Fruit Muesli Muffin deal was great. A double shot of espresso and I started to perk up a little. But I had the jitters bad. Not booze jitters. It felt like what I imagine would be the onset of Parkinson's.

Then I had a glance at *The Sentinel*. Another DB had been reported.

The dismembered remains of an unidentified transsexual had been found at the bottom of the old Grain Terminal. Both a John and a Jane Doe, the corpse had been mangled from the fall into the encrusted machinery in the chute and had been in the water for a couple of days.

I knew the cops who'd worked the scoop. I'd had beers with them in days gone by—probably salivated over a few pole dancers with them too, if I could remember.

I knew the painful jokes they would've made about a floater—the expressions on their faces as they'd try to keep the horror and dismay under wraps—and in what organ it would settle when they weren't looking.

I knew so well the cold, bland matter-of-factness that would be painted over everything like shellac—and that special lonely sound of bad news that few people outside the job ever take notice of—when the crime scene tape gets strung up and the wind hits it.

I could hear a promiscuous gust coming in off the bay and strumming the tape around the Grain Terminal entrance. That ominous throbbing whir is the real sound of trauma death. Not a gunshot or a scream—or squealing tires. Not the crunch of metal or shattered glass. In the end death sounds like a wind-whipped strip of taut striped tape—that finally snaps and flutters, and gets stuck back up. But only for as long as someone like me cares—until they find enough pieces of the misery that were left behind to think they know what happened.

Then the strands come down and there's just the wind again—or people trying to rent a room. A liquor store reopening. Sometimes a plastic flower cemented to a dented streetlight.

There's a reason why violence rhymes with silence. You come to understand that when you carry a shield.

Sitting there amidst the bright morning bustle, I realized just how much I knew about death.

Like the spirit blue glow of Luminol and the story it tells.

I'd once seen a bathroom where a young woman had been sodomized, bludgeoned and then slashed to ribbons—bagged, hauled away and set on fire in the State Forest. The whole room fluoresced, because every single inch of it had been bleached by the killer. Every square inch of white tile. Meticulous. Not one trace of blood. Only a chemical smear job that hair-raisingly suggested just how very much arterial spray there had been.

Watching the other normal denizens enjoying their breakfasts and magazines, I thought of stab victims. What color the blood is when the liver's been fully compromised and you know calling the paramedics is a waste of taxpayer's money. And with dead street people—how a nauseatingly sweet smell of rotting apples means that pus is coming from a region of gas gangrene—or how the bacteria in certain abscesses produces an odor like an overripe Camembert cheese. You have to be careful handling them. You have to treat the dead with care. I turned back to the newspaper, afraid the chirpy caffeine crowd would catch a whiff of my thoughts seeping out.

The DB report referred to an attempt to match the DNA with any known missing persons. My instincts gave me a strong suspicion that it wouldn't match anyone exactly, and I thought of the last text message I'd gotten from Jack.

I knew now in my gut who that body belonged to—or who it had once been. Only one person understood what it was becoming. What it had been becoming before it stopped like a knock-off watch.

And that was where my instincts stopped. That was where another kind of tape was strung.

Without realizing it at the time, I may have been the last person McInnes had talked to. He'd kept his appointment, whoever or whatever had happened.

Why he'd done himself in was a mystery I had yet to solve. Maybe because of what he'd become—and maybe something of that sort is what had pushed Stoakes and Whitney over the edge, whatever edge or defining limit they'd found.

My old cop habits were trying to help me cope with something outside my understanding—maybe outside all understanding. Which in a way . . . if I'm honest . . . when the drink was going down warm and friendly . . . was what El Miedo sometimes did.

It'd be wrong to say it was always the night vision green terror or the gasping for breath. Often it started with an inside tip or a buddy's good word.

That's another thing about violence—about brutality. It not only ends quietly, it often starts that way. In my experience, the most deadly kind always does. The rest is just knocked out teeth and loss of pride. I closed the paper and paid my bill.

I felt like hitting Shenanigans. But the bars, Wetworld, street girls, nothing would do anymore. I knew there was only one solution. I had to confront Genevieve. Only she could tell me what I needed to know. And the promise of being with her . . . or the threat . . . ? What was my life if not seeing in every threat a promise?

But I couldn't fool myself anymore. I was sodden armpit scared.

I decided to split the difference and blow some time at the Long Room. That had always been a safe haven in the past— a place to lick my wounds and get my bearings when things got crazy. Not anymore.

Wardell didn't know me. Literally.

I even tried Flip Wilson's Ugly Baby joke on him, but the Dell clammed up like I was some street freak. I left after five of the longest minutes I'd ever lived.

I was shaking so badly by the time I got back to my apartment, I couldn't piss straight. There was an ambulance parked down the street and a squad car with patrolmen I didn't know. That was the only thing that dragged me back.

I shuffled closer to get the skinny, knowing the moment I saw where they were parked that it had to do with the Duke. It didn't take long to get the run-down. He'd passed quietly in his sleep like an old dog—discovered by a real dog, lying amongst his yellowed newsclippings and his rotting sleeping bag, a plastic Slurpee cup beside his head, brimming with coins.

I slunk off before I started to lose it, and made it all the way to my kitchen table before the tears broke loose. I'm not sure what I was crying for—him or me. You wouldn't think a homicide detective, even one on sick leave—or maybe even permanently retired—would spill his eyes out over an old street person dying peacefully of a stroke. I'd spent years examining corpses. People with their intestines wrapped around their necks. Dental records. Feet and hair found in mulching machines. A femur in an incinerator. Floaters. Maybe I just hadn't cried enough in the past and now all those bottles of

Beam I'd poured in were gushing back out, distilled. Big thick stinging drops that smelled like Stacy's nail polish remover. I put on a Lou Rawls CD and let it flow until I was empty.

I boiled a can of minestrone soup but I couldn't eat. I turned on the TV. The only decent thing on was an old movie. *Nightmare Alley* with Tyrone Power, but it was way too dark for the mood I was in. I swallowed one of Sidewinder's barbiturates and tumbled into bed. A little more sleep under my belt might come in handy when I faced Genevieve. And maybe the dreams wouldn't be too clear. But fuck me, I was wrong again.

I was before a cylindrical-shaped thing like Mr. Tanaka's. A giant chimney glass. I was watching a human head alternately rising and sinking, as I had countless lemon seeds in years of ginatonics. The air bubbles adhered to the head at the bottom and then lifted it to the surface where the bubbles burst and the head descended back down to the bottom. Over and over again. Like a kind of clock.

Then I was inside the container—I could breathe underwater . . . I was swimming through the bubbles into a lighted pool. There was a drowned racehorse lying on the bottom— which when I swam closer I saw wasn't an animal body at all. There was a broken motor inside . . . and two little men dead at the controls, like the kind on a tractor. The champion stallion was actually a machine they'd been operating. Suddenly, from out of the dark, a school of women appeared. They were wearing old-fashioned bloomers and hoop skirts, but swimming fast and carrying spearguns. I turned and tried to swim back the way I'd come—trying to reenter the giant ginatonic glass where the head was rising and falling . . .

I woke up to an incendiary sunset, just like the first night I'd gone to Eyrie Street. I had a shower with my eyes closed. My new suit was way too big for me. I felt sick with fear and filled with light—younger than I had in years—brimming with rage, hope, sadness, yearning and dread. Before, I'd wrestled with myself about going back to see her. Now there was no question. The thought of true intimacy and maybe truth. What else was there left to hang onto? My shield? That was gone.

It was time for a full body cavity search. I grabbed my latest trophy and drove like an old lady over to Cliffhaven. Genevieve answered the door herself, knowing who it was who knocked—probably knowing better than I did.

She had a Della Street look happening. Tierra del Fuego eyes. I don't know how she did it. I wondered what one of the biometrics boys would make of her. She was different every time I'd seen her. And yet she was always the same. I blew off the reality distortion—I was in another world now. I knew now that I'd always been in another world every time I'd seen her. I gave her the new wrestling trophy—from The Rumpus Room.

"Congratulations," she smiled. "I can see you really won this one. I'm afraid I have sad news about Falco and Ernie."

I shook my head, not wanting to hear any more sad news. But new rules.

"The jellyfish?"

"No," she replied. "I think Ernie panicked and dragged Falco down. It was either heart failure or drowning that got them. Mutza kindly disposed of the bodies."

She produced a plate with what looked like a human hand on it. "Care for a bite?"

"Ugh," I wheezed. "You're not—!"

"Oh, Sunny!" she snickered. "It's just sponge cake! You didn't think it was Falco's or Ernie's, did you? I made it because it's Tuesday."

"What does a severed hand have to do with Tuesday?" I demanded, still feeling the bile leaking back down my throat. I didn't know how much more I could take.

"Tuesday comes from Tyr's day—the Norse god who volunteered to bind the great wolf Fenrir and did so at the price of a hand. You see, even on a quiet ordinary evening we're surrounded by mythological acts of violence and heroism."

"Yeah, right," I said, waving no.

"You haven't had a lot of formal schooling, have you?"

"I took a matchbook correspondence course once," I replied. "Learn About Refrigeration Systems in Your Spare Time. Sadly I lack discipline." Bitch.

She smiled thinly. Gracious. "What did you want to be when you were young?"

"A Human Cannonball."

"No, really. What did you dream of becoming when you were a real little boy?"

"As opposed to what? A wooden one?"

"As opposed to the little boy you've been all your adult life."

"I don't know," I sighed. I thought—why doesn't she stop fucking with me and fuck me? Or fuck me over forever if that's her plan. Instead I answered her truthfully.

"The usual stuff I guess. Fireman. Astronaut. Major Leaguer. Just as long as I could bust spy rings, battle sea monsters and explore lost mines while dressed like a cowboy."

She tittered. "Chuck Connors. Do you know what I wanted to be?"

"My first thought is Evil Mastermind—but I'll say a princess. Isn't that what most girls start out wanting to be— before they go ga-ga for horses? A princess who will be rescued from a terrible dragon. Unless, of course, you're one of those who wanted to be the prince, which sort of fractures the fairy-tale. Or maybe . . . *you* wanted to be the dragon."

She chuckled again, but not in the way I'd intended. Not at all. Her face clouded disturbingly. "Did you know that's what my last name means? A wyvern is a mythic creature from her-aldry. A fearsome winged dragon with a barbed tail. I have an intricately detailed picture of one tattooed on a very private part of my body. It took almost a thousand years to get the detail right. You're going to see the tattoo, Sunny. It's in a secret place underneath my wings."

"I don't see any wings," I said.

Best I could do.

"Oh, you will, Sunny," she whispered. "You will."

She rose and led me upstairs. The house was dead quiet now and seemed like an ordinary shorefront mansion. Whatever crackpot things she said, I could only think about her fragrance. I felt dizzy and torn loose from all my moorings. But seeing her wings—that's what I'd bought my ticket for— the real dark ride.

Beyond the haunting of Stacy and the leering haze of El Miedo—and trying to escape them both through Briannon, my whole life of late—too late—had been the disappointment of wives, the scent of second-hand snatch and the rings of truth along a bar—and all the sickness and insecurity that came with chucking that crutch in the fire.

I'd rolled over bodies. I'd put dickwads in handcuffs. I'd gobbled onion grease burgers behind the wheel of a fat old car, the machine equivalent of a living fossil. I was ready to see some damn wings. Who could've been more ready than me?

We reached a door in the second storey hall that I didn't remember.

"I'm going to take you into that bedroom with me," she said, and her voice seemed to come down a longer hallway than I'd ever investigated.

"It's a very special bedroom. Just for you, Sunny."

After all the longing and hoping to touch her that way— the fear and frustrations—the "training" she'd put me through—it had all been building up to this. To know her body. To be inside her. The shadow garden.

"Open the door," she invited, and when I turned, she'd changed. She wasn't only blonde now, her face was totally different.

I'd been with her the whole time—but what did time mean in Eyrie Street? In any case, I recognized too well who she looked like. My jaw dropped like a weight. Even her voice seemed to change so that she sounded just like Stacy . . . the air

conditioned funhouse I slipped into one summer night when El
Miedo was closing in. The woman who always called it "making love" and sang to me when me made it. A woman in a
dream I couldn't stop having and yet could never have. A voice
more like a fragrance that tortured me. *"Only memories
remain . . . the ghosts and the pain . . ."*

"The face you see is often a face you've saved," she said.
"A face you've tried to throw away. To forget. Or a face you've
folded with great care and hidden in a drawer. Does it appeal
to you now as much as it did then . . . once upon a time?"

I couldn't answer. The vividness almost made me keel over.

Genevieve pushed the door in the hallway open, and what
met my eyes couldn't have been real—and yet was there before
me in unrelenting detail—right down to the knick-knacks on
the nightstands.

It was our bedroom—the one I'd shared with Polly when
I'd been cheating on her with Stacy. Banging fresh pussy and
going out of my mind.

It was all there. The same dreary flocked wallpaper I never
got around to taking down. There was even the illusion of the
lemon tree that stood outside our window—while here we
were now on the second floor of a tall house on a cliff overlooking the harbor.

The only difference between the marital bedroom and the
chamber I faced was the chains bolted into the walls on either
side of the bed—with plush ermine grips to encase the whole
hands, not merely the wrists.

"Should I undress?" I asked, and I was surprised at the
meekness of my voice.

"You do not undress! In my presence, you strip—you peel!"

I was taken aback at the vehemence of her tone and nodded dumbly, too overwhelmed to say or do anything differently. Removing my clothes, my body felt more foreign than
it ever had—as if I was made of some kind of plasma, unable
to maintain shape.

She produced from under the bed a strawberry pink nightie, the exact kind Polly often wore.

"You recognize this?" she asked, stuffing it under my nose.

I gulped and nodded.

"Put it on."

"What?"

"Put on your wife's nightie!"

My eyesight misted, but when I'd laid down, naked but for the filmy nylon, and she'd secured the restraints to my hands and allowed me to feel how suspended I was, in a crucifixion pose on the bed, I clearly saw her take off her clothes, slowly, ritualistically—tempting and teasing me with each revealed inch of her flesh, her perfect fragrant, haunted flesh.

When she produced the harness I gasped.

"Oh, Sunny," she laughed, coy and girlish again—and then cruel and hard. "I hope you weren't so arrogant to think that you were going to enter me!"

The harness was made of some kind of antlers, but the actual attachment looked like it was made of living glass, jeweled with a hieroglyphic pattern that I seemed to recognize. The face I remembered from so many hungover mirrors and remorseful mornings.

"Spread your legs," Genevieve—in the body of Stacy—commanded . . . her full smooth breasts jutting forth, the jagged belt tight around her waist and pelvis, the jeweled projection, pointing accusingly at me.

"Are you going to . . . ?"

"Just some simple role reversal, Sunny? Is that what you think?"

She gave me a smile that chilled my blood.

"It's something you've fantasized about, isn't it? But no, Sunny. Bodies, like rooms, change with time and mood. Your body is changing. You've felt it, tried to deny it—begged for an explanation. But I think a demonstration is so much more instructive. What I'm about to do now will clarify things for you even as it mortifies and disorients you. Because you see, this apparatus is modeled on your own contribution. The member you remember provided the mold. And I'm going to use it to penetrate you . . . in a very new way."

I tried to leap from the bed, but the restraints wouldn't let me. Then when her words penetrated my understanding, the restraints were unnecessary, because I fell back onto the bed, limp and bedraggled, shrieking. My body had changed. It was no longer mine at all—it was some new form. Only it didn't feel like a form. It felt total and deep. I stared down and saw my breasts, small but firm. It felt like a damp chicken breast when I rubbed my thighs together—then a fleshier part—like sashimi.

I was a woman. I smelled like a woman.

She gently massaged the crystalline head against me, and my body trembled. I understood now. In the tissue and the organs. I could hear it in the pitch of the screams that came out of my mouth. Then she entered me.

At first it hurt—but then I began to lubricate around the implement. Only it seemed to warm and pulse with my heat and moisture. My head spun. My arms drew back, the nightie pulled open, my tits jiggling as she thrust, at first slowly, then more deeply.

Then from out of Stacy, I saw Genevieve's wings unfurl, like luminous shadows. Neither like an angel's nor a vulture's—but something fiercer—more regal and wretched all at once. Armored with pain and light. At last I spied the tattoo gleaming like molten metal. I had to close my eyes to keep them from burning. But I couldn't keep them closed.

The jagged bone points in the harness cut into her with each stroke—so that blood spurted. I was covered in blood and mare's milk—fish paste and zircon beads of sweat.

Shards of memory and ripped silk music of busted zippers and panting—scratch of distant tango music rising above a broken surf. Visions of naked men on giant microscope slides . . .

scent of lemon leaves coming in the window . . . exploding glass and soft animal parts . . . car going over an embankment . . . bladder bursting sobbing blood and Vaseline smell of bottle rocket cheerleader ozone . . . now . . . now is the time to die in colors.

The flocked wallpaper room returned in a mess of silver entrails and strewn petals.

I'd been murdered and reborn in one unnatural act.

When my heart, if my own heart it still was, started beating normally again, I saw that Genevieve had changed again. She was back to the woman I'd met that Molotov cocktail sunset when I first thought she was a high class hooker and that maybe McInnes was doing me a good turn. I, meanwhile, had changed further.

I knew without having to glance at the oval looking glass who I'd become.

I was beautiful, ruthlessly blonde and fifteen years younger. I was exactly what Stacy looked like that first night I saw her. The clothes Genevieve pulled out from the closet for me to wear were the same as what the temptress had on the summer night I fell for her, right down to the wristwatch and the earrings.

The next thing I knew I was fully and expertly dressed, looking just like my ghost lover . . . who could sing the past away . . . but at a price I could never afford . . . and was still repaying . . . all these nights later.

"Tomorrow, when you return, Sunny, the crisis of your transformative education will have passed. Soon you'll be seeing yourself and the world in a new light."

"I don't believe this!" I howled, my make-up that I'd never applied running like black tears.

"Of course you don't," she said, nodding. "How could you? That's as it must be. And you still have so much to learn. Now go home . . . *straight* home and have a hot bath. Don't try to run away from this, as your first instinct used to be. You can't. It's not like surgery. It's far deeper and more complete.

Or soon will be. That's why you must take care. You're in a transitional state and you must look after yourself to avoid harm."

"Harm?" I squalled. "You've done something to me—!"

"You're absolutely right, Sunny," she agreed. "I *have* done something to you. You've been infected with a gift. Cursed with what you wanted from the moment you glimpsed this house. Something beyond your imagination. Go home now and nurse yourself. A new life is beginning. Retreat back to your old life tonight and turn the lights down low. Come the morning, you'll feel refreshed and ready for the final stage."

My make-up kept running as she led me down the stairs and out the front door, the house still quiet, no one around. I probably looked like hell. I wanted to look good, to look sexy, desirable. They weren't some empty wishes—I suddenly *felt* them. I could sense a subtle but pervasive shift in my perceptions. My walk like my voice had changed. I didn't have to think how to act.

Another part of me wanted to slap her down right there. Stomp her to a pulp. But I couldn't. I clicked away on my heels. Like a girl.

My first thought was to drive as fast as I could back to the apartment—snuggle on the bed with Pico and eat the other box of Dilley's Chocolates that I'd stowed in the pantry. I wanted to cry my eyes out, to try to get straight. To think of a way out. A way ahead. But Genevieve had advised me to go home and I wasn't in the mood to follow her advice. Her words had led only to impossibility and mystification. Another world? Fuck, another form of life. I needed to strike out on my own.

When I got behind the wheel—and the old car seemed so wrong for me—I found myself driving down the street and around to the empty parking lot of Funland.

I was suddenly gripped with the notion that there had always been a Haunted House there. I'd just forgotten it. Or had wanted to forget it. It didn't take away from the razzle dazzle she'd been able to pull off, but it would've made it easier to explain. I had to see if the Foto Booth was there. I don't know why. What could it possibly matter now? Nothing made sense. Nothing! I slipped inside. But not before I glanced at my Lady's Rolex. It was much later than I thought—maybe in every way. 2 AM. I'd been in Eyrie Street far longer than I'd realized. I'd been way too long at the fair. And now I was part of the freak show.

A near full moon was riding high and the wind was coming off the water, not cold but noisy, clanking in the torn metal and the vacant buildings like a restless dream the park was having. Gulls and pigeons slanted through the faint fluorescent light in the parking area, disappearing and reappearing as they crossed over into the dark of the dead rides.

I had to know, in the only way I could think to find out, if what had happened on my last visit was an hallucination or something real and solid that I could touch. Maybe I was hallucinating now. God help me.

Frayed wires pinged against steel. This was a place to dump a body. A place to hide out—and wait for something to trip the web. Intruder. Fresh game. Woman on deck. But I had to see for myself. I had to verify.

When I made it to the other side of the Midway, I did. There was nothing there. Where the Haunted House had been the other night was like a hole in a mouth where a knocked-out tooth used to be. I wondered if I'd even been in Funland, or if I'd just been glazed out in Eyrie Street. For all I really knew, I might still be sitting on that sofa in the front room with a silk scarf over my eyes. Dreaming awake.

But if I was dreaming, than I dreamed I heard a bottle smash. It brought instantly to mind the makeshift hovels I'd seen during my day visit. Suddenly I realized I was no longer a big, meaty detective with a police shield and a registered handgun. That was the first dread rush of a new truth—and I'd say my balls sucked in—but I'd be lying. And crying.

It was too late too quickly. Some insect alertness in the hive mind of Liquid Crystal had tipped them off. Four of them, all lit up with the drug. Shadows converged, hands grabbed. Then I was flat on my back.

I felt them tear at me. Their faces loomed up before mine, more odious and misshapen than any masks in Eyrie Street. Primal. Bestial. Day blind things that lived by scent and vibration. One was an albino.

"Do her man, do her!" he gurgled.

"Give me that bottle! Yoo gonna bleed baby! Up your fuckin' ass!"

And I would've bled—all over the littered, abandoned Midway where they used to sell Sno-Cones. I'd have spat acid at them if I could've. But I didn't need to—because in one instant a meteoric light did to their eyes what they wanted to do to my private parts. I only caught a blinking hint because I was on the ground. For a heartbeat I thought Genevieve had set the park on fire—or the Special Tactical Unit from the old days had come to rescue me and set off a phosphorous grenade. Maybe I was just having a brain bubble.

But no, the explosion of light was real and directed. It sliced into the faces of my tormentors like a laser. Then came sounds I knew—the hiss and whoosh of a fire extinguisher and the thud of metal on skull. There was an alacrity to it—a kind of artistry. Measured. Restrained. I'd never learned that as a cop. It was always a partner who got squeamish that had pulled me off before I did too much permanent damage.

"S is for Security," I heard a voice out of the nova say—then a leather heel planted hard in a trachea. Suddenly, I was being raised up off the pavement and brushed off, like a princess who'd fallen off her steed.

It was the Blue Knight. Despite his diminished eyesight, he clearly knew exactly what he was up against, and as someone who'd had more than his share of parking lot brawls and streetfights, I have to say, he handled himself in a way that made me glad I'd never locked horns with him. Back when I had horns. They all lay before him blanketed by a layer of dry-chem foam.

"N is for Night. Night's not good. You OK?"

"OK," I replied. "Thanks to you."

"OK thanks to me," he repeated, as if this were a large new thought.

"Do you know them?" I asked, pointing to the four ferals he'd laid out.

"N is for Night. T is for trouble. They're T. But no more trouble tonight."

"No," I almost smiled. "Thanks to you. T is for Thanks."

"T is also for tea," and he made a childlike gesture of raising a cup. "You need some."

I was in tatters and ajar. My whole world had been turned on its head and I was still getting my heartbeat back down below the redline—but I knew what he meant. He was inviting me back to his ratty, lonely refuge. His home.

That place was appropriately the old infirmary, fortified now with accordioned metal and nailed slats. Inside, a large Coleman lantern was burning—and as many as fifty scavenged candles, lending the space a soft religious aura. I stared around as respectfully as I could.

He'd harvested the clown heads, the tin ducks and figurines from the Shooting Gallery, as well as several hundred stuffed animals. They were mounted on the walls or set up on cardboard boxes, plastic milk crates and rusted oil drums. Others hung down from a section of exposed pipe on strands of fishing line. They shared the space with more fire extinguishers than I'd ever seen. All four types in all sizes, arranged in squads, platoons, battalions, regiments, divisions and corps.

Once I got past this assemblage, my cop trained eyes took in a hotplate, a rotting futon, and a piece of art I think he'd made himself—a montage of faded tickets for the rides arranged around the face of a child he'd either been or had lost custody of.

He had a couple of fisherman's stools to sit on, one of the old booths from the Merry-Go-Round as a lounge chair—and a dented silver corn dog wagon as a shelf unit, upon which sat several boxes of Crispy Critters.

I sat down on one of the stools.

"You're authorized," he said, reaching for a big tartan thermos. "But your pass has expired. I told you D is for Day."

"You . . . remember me?" I blurted and almost fell off the rickety stool.

"Y is for Yes," he said curtly, unscrewing the cap. Then more gently, "And for You. I remember You."

Did he see through me? Maybe I was still myself! Whoever that was . . .

"You remember me—from when?" I asked, accepting a mug of steaming herbal tea.

"F is for Fun and for Flashlight—but sometimes for Foto," he said and took a seat in the cup of Naugahyde he'd pirated from the carousel.

"But I'm different!" I gasped.

"Everyone's different. Every time. I had to radio for instructions."

Jesus! Don't we all want to radio for instructions. I resisted the urge to ask him where he got his. I still couldn't believe what I was hearing. It was more magic—if that's what I was involved in. But of a very different kind. I hadn't allowed for any kind up to my first visit to Eyrie Street. Except El Miedo.

"You really . . . recognize me?"

"Y is for Yes and Y is for You. Yes, I recognize You."

"But—I was a man! The other day—I was a *man*! Look at me NOW!"

"I gave you a Day Pass," he said, and blinked his eyes behind his froggy glasses. "Not good for Night."

Maybe he was just nuts. Or I was. Or we both were.

"I was a big man—do you understand? Now I'm a woman."

"Everyone's different, every time," he repeated, and I decided that he was a simpleton. But a moment later he said in a lower voice, "And you were different once before . . . when you arrested me."

"What . . . do you mean?" I said . . . my new female voice drying out in the air.

"Before Fun," he answered, and stared down at the gouged linoleum floor, which I saw he kept remarkably clean.

I couldn't believe I'd ever crossed his path—let alone arrested him. I wanted to radio for instructions big time.

"Why . . . I mean—what did I arrest you for?"

"I was unauthorized," he said simply, and glanced up at his wall of ticket stubs as if for support. Or maybe not wanting to remember more.

I honestly didn't know what he was talking about, but it occurred to me it might have been back when I was in uniform. I took the term "beat cop" a bit too much to heart in those days. B was for billy club. Wouldn't it have been ironic if I'd administered the blow that started him radioing in for instructions—and here he'd just saved me from a gang of gargoyles.

"Do you want to tell me about it?" I asked. Maybe I was back in danger again.

He twisted his head at this and made a garbled sound—which I realized was a very good imitation of radio static.

"Everyone's different. Every time," he replied, the tea steam misting his glasses.

Those words seemed to satisfy him, to calm him—and they started to sink in with me. If only we could remember that everyone's different every time we meet them. What a difference that would make. And it's funny, because that's the way a cop always approaches things—only too often with suspicion and contempt masked as authority and control. For the first time I suddenly saw my old life as being a Black Knight. Not a protector of FUN, but a projector of FEAR. This ragged dignified loner was no coward when it came to getting tough, but he was a better guardian of the peace than I'd been. That was humbling. I'd always thought I was a halfway decent, halfway honest cop.

"I'm . . . sorry . . ." I said, and I meant it. I didn't care what he'd done. I wondered how he saw through me. But maybe he just did and couldn't say how or why. I knew what that was like. Just as we can fail or refuse to see what's so obvious to everyone else.

He made the radio static sound again and then said "Roger that," with his head turned away from me. I was curious where his walkie-talkie had gone. He must've been getting signals directly now.

"S is for Security. And Security Escort," he said, setting down his mug on the floor and standing up.

It was the weirdest goddamn thing. I got this feeling all through me—like different hormones at work. A deep cellular change.

As goony as he was, I'd have spent the night with him. I'd have gotten down there on that futon with him. I bet he hadn't had a woman in years. I could see—not just with my eyes—but down below—inside—that that's what I was now.

But I could also see that that wouldn't have made him comfortable. S is for Security. He was a gentleman, loony or not. And I felt unaccountably like a lady in his presence. My Blue Knight. A member of the same proud order as the Duke of Earl.

He selected one of the newer, compact fire extinguishers from his arsenal and eased down the Coleman flame. Then he led me back to the gate with his expensive headlight on, a bell out on the harbor gonging. There was no sign of the gargoyles. They must've skittered back to their holes with skin rashes and sore heads.

When we reached the trembling fence I kissed him on the stubble of his jowly cheek. Odors of dried sweat and Crispy Critters. Tea and kerosene. It actually felt natural and right.

"I'll remember you," I said.

"Roger that," he answered and gave me the little fire extinguisher. "Live and learn, control the burn. Extinguish the flames and you extinguish the fear."

I accepted his gift, realizing that it held more meaning to him than I could ever understand. Like so many things.

When I got to the car I turned to wave.

His headlamp shone back like a freelance moon, then the beam swung around and started retreating back into the ruins of Funland. His beat. The kingdom he protected. Where he rescued maidens and kept the peace.

4

I WOKE UP ON WEDNESDAY MORNING AND I HONESTLY hadn't thought I would. After I left the Blue Knight I had a breakdown in the car on the way home. The car didn't break down. I did. Weeping. Pounding on the windows. I ran inside when I got home.

A guy who looked like Ricardo Montalban was sneaking out of Mrs. Ramona's apartment—clutching a bunch of clothes. It didn't really surprise me. Old Lothario winked at me and dropped a pair of pants going out the hall door. He didn't notice and I didn't tell him. I picked them up. I didn't want anyone gossiping about Mrs. R.

God only knows what they'd say about me. Things could get complicated. I snuggled on the bed with Pico, trying to understand what had happened. I couldn't. I just cried, wondering when it would end. If it would end.

I'd taken on female form—and not just any female. I'd transformed into someone who looked just like Stacy. I wasn't sick in the head—something more pervasive and profound had happened. The thought of my appointment with the psychologist seemed absurd. I reached for the Sidewinder's sleep pills.

I'd meant to take them all, hoping not to wake up—just wanting to dissolve like a capsule in water. But I didn't. I hadn't been able to face down El Miedo or the nightmares before. For all those years. And so the ghosts just kept coming. Until I became one of them myself. And now I was finding human form again. Only a different one.

When I woke the second time I'd returned to outer male appearance but not my old self. Stacy had been about 5'8" and I figured I was an inch taller and still quite a bit heavier. My equipment had shrunk to the size of a chick embryo. Inside I could feel a distinct change though. A different kind of being. I didn't know if it was female—or something more alien. Suddenly all those tabloid stories about people being abducted by Martians didn't seem so laughable. Maybe that's what Genevieve was. Something from far away—only a woman outwardly, which it seemed she could modify at will. All the time before I'd tried to believe I was going insane and having hallucinations. How simple they seemed compared to the truth.

But I could feel my reversion wasn't complete. I realized I'd had a few of these episodes now. That's what the blackout escapades had been. They seemed to be getting more intense.

Then, when I was in the kitchen getting Pico some food I noticed that the images on the Foto Booth strip had materialized more fully. The woman's face had become clearer and more confident—and much more attractive. A heartbreaker.

The final frame was almost a spitting image of Stacy wearing my too-big sports coat. It was like a police Identikit. Morph my face into a beautiful frozen blonde. Mid-30s. Like an angel with a mood disorder. But you could still recognize my eyes.

Like the tracks of the Scenic Railway, Mistress Genevieve's powers extended far beyond normal expectation—and I wondered how much tape would be needed to cordon off the crime scene of her influence. What kind of tape I couldn't even imagine.

My cell phone rang. It seemed to go off like gelignite after all the silence. Her? No. Padgett. Shit. I couldn't take the call. I couldn't. It was like something from another time, another life.

I let it ring through to voicemail. A moment later the message signal beeped. Chris sounded concerned—but trying to be cheerful, which only made him sound more anxious. He was paired up with Monty short term, with Haslett floating. He made a joke about that. Monty wanted to set me up with this woman named Elena, a nice Hispanic babe he and his wife had met at their Latin Dance Class. Said she was shaped like an art deco lamp. I wasn't sure if that was a good thing or not. I was too wigged out to picture Head and Shoulders and his big mama learning to salsa. Jesus de Christophe. A nice Hispanic woman trawling dance classes for a Mambo King out on a date with yours drooly! And they say irony is something you study in high school. My mind was a mess and hearing the Cub's voice only made it muddier.

What was even worse, my old Birch thinking was still very much at work. Big ham-fisted dumb ideas—like whether taking it up the butt as a woman would be different than as a man. How's that for honesty, huh? I always did have a knack for scaring myself. Guess I hadn't lost my touch that way.

Which made me ask the question if it was at all possible to scare the Dark Mistress. She had to have some vulnerability, some side entrance. That's what a large part of my job and in fact my whole life had been—finding people's weaknesses and bearing down on them until they broke apart. Maybe something of those old skills could come into play now—now that I knew how serious and how fucking whacko things really were. I'd been playing too short a game against an opponent beyond my estimation. But everything was different now. Not only me.

I realized that knowing about Genevieve—and I didn't know nearly enough obviously—but now the scent of what appeared to be her body—the soft but viselike whisper of her mind in mine—the afterimages of her entering me with the vestige of my own stolen maleness—that changed the world. Not just my body. The whole damn rulebook went right out the window. Right through the mirror.

I looked at the clock. The appointment with the shrink Lance had arranged for me was coming up. As he'd never seen me before, he probably wouldn't notice anything. But the other people in my building would. Soon there'd be more questions than I could cope with. I was starting to understand what had happened to Stoakes and Whitney—and Cracker Jack. The 10-10 furlough. How would I end it, if it came to that?

While others on the job had bought into the Glock, I'd called in the marker on my seniority to select the SIG P-229. I liked the feel of it. But now I'd turned it in—and my .22 LR boot gun too. I'd re-registered my old personal Walther PPK in Polly's name for her protection. The modified Thunder Ranch carbine and the choke-bore Savage were locked up at our old place for their protection. And mine. Suddenly, I was short of stopping power. Just when I needed it most. You see, I really do have an honest streak when it comes to some things.

The sharpness of that thought got me focused. If nothing else talking with a stranger couldn't hurt. It was something to try. I put on the female underwear from the night before. Why not? Maybe I'd had a kink before and not admitted it. Now it was part of the training, like shooting off rounds at the course. There was enough support for my shriveled genitals, and I somehow felt comfortable in them. I rolled up the sleeves from the shirt I'd bought—and it sort of worked. It was warm out— the harsh heat of summer coming early. I didn't need a jacket. The one I'd bought the other day was too big now anyway. As were the pants. Then I remembered the trousers Mrs. Ramona's friend had dropped. They actually fit. I slipped the strip of Foto Booth pics in my chest pocket, snuck out of the building as quick as I could, and drove over to the shrink's

office at Republic and Cass. His name was Turcell and I tried
to picture what he'd look like as I missed every stoplight.

The guy who ushered me into his salmon-carpeted office
with a lead gray leatherette couch and teak-finish Formica
desk, turned out to be about 50, lean and springy like a fitness
maven, with thinning hair. He'd just given himself a spray of
a mid-range Yves St. Laurent fragrance and he wore a buff-
colored sports jacket over a pesto cotton shirt. I was certain he'd
never handled a handgun, let alone had one pointed at him.

My old cop sense was on full suction, silky panties or not.
The thought and feel of them actually gave me a little erection.
Little being the operative word.

He probably thought I was somehow trying to skate on
work. That's where people who aren't on the job can't understand it. He'd have no Yves St. Laurent way of knowing that I
missed hobnobbing with the abrasive caseworkers and the
hardbitten parole officers. I missed signing in and signing out.
I missed the clumpy white powder soap in the wash room. I
missed Chris' banter and Monty's dandruff. I missed them all.

He took his seat and motioned to a foam filled chair on the
other side of the desk. Then he stroked a hand over his head,
the way that guys with thinning hair do. He gave his wedding
ring a twist. There was a group of family photos behind him—
his kids holding out cards with their names on them, and a
foursome of adults holding up their racquets on a tennis court.
He had an Art Gallery calendar angled at the edge of his blotter. The featured artist was Jackson Pollock. I'd at least heard
of him. The sample work looked like a kid's painting.

"I'm glad you came in to see me," he began. "You look like
you want to talk."

"Yeah," I said, staring at the photos on his window ledge,
the degrees mounted on the wall and all the shelves lined with
books. Everything was so perfectly in order. I wondered what
Genevieve would say. Would he be more resistant to her, or
would he fall that much faster?

"So," he prompted, smoothing his thinning hair. "I know confidentially that you were involved in an on-the-job shooting a while back. Please tell me about it."

"I was shot at close range in the groin by a drug addict and informer that I'd been screwing," I responded. "I was obsessed with her."

"Hm. How were you obsessed?" he asked, perking up. Then he added, "Please remember that everything you say is confidential."

"I met her as part of a case I was working," I replied. "One thing led to another, as it often does—or has with me. She reminded me of someone else—from the past. Before I knew it I was sneaking out on my wife all the time and fucking this chick every chance I could get."

"So, it was like an addiction."

"It wasn't like an addiction," I corrected. "It *was* an addiction."

"How did being with her make you feel?"

"Good at the time. Bad later. Awful. But better than the dead feeling before I met her."

"How did the shooting come about?" he asked, his voice still as even as his books.

Christ, people wall themselves in with a lot of crap. As if anyone with any jimmy can't see right through them. But I was going to give his little ping-pong game a shot.

"I told her it was over. I made a pretense of a police matter on the day it happened. But it was personal. And to be honest, I knew what would happen. I think I wanted her to kill me."

"Really?" he frowned. "Why?"

"I don't have a bunch of smiling faces at my desk like you," I said. "And I couldn't face my wife anymore. I barely wanted to touch her and I couldn't get a hard-on for her without pharmacy help. We made each other sick and I knew she could smell what was going on."

"Smell is a very strong word," he remarked—and the way he said it made it look like he'd just caught a whiff of something festering.

"Neither of my two wives was stupid," I answered. "Only me."

He fingered his hair again, thinking what to say. "I very much appreciate your candor, Detective Ritter," he decided.

I couldn't recall the last time someone had called me that.

"Most of the people I talk to I can talk to for weeks—and even years, and they're not as open as you've just been."

"Maybe I'm finally growing up," I answered.

He nodded again and then started musing.

"So, you've been divorced twice. No children?"

"None that I know of."

"Tell me about your state of mind when you met this girl. You said she reminded you of someone. Was there an earlier incident?"

How could I explain to him that my life was only "incidents"? It was the marriages that had been the deviations.

"I fell for a hooker," I replied. "Wanted to be a lounge singer. She was the best sex I'd ever had. Very kinky—but innocent and teenage too sometimes. It happened when my second wife was pregnant. She lost the baby."

"And you blamed yourself?"

"Wouldn't you?"

I kept looking at those happy pictures staring at me. The color of the carpet. The messy masterpiece of Jackson Pollock.

"Well, let me ask you briefly about your childhood. I don't want to get bogged down in the past when there are problems in the present that worry you. But very often the key to problems in the moment lies in the past."

"I've heard that," I said and managed not to laugh. "My father was thought to have committed suicide, but he was really ly murdered. Pushed off a construction scaffold—he was a builder—when I was 10 years old. He was really gay . . . doing

young guys he hired to work for him. He couldn't cope with
other people knowing. One of his young friends gave him a
push because he wouldn't come out in the open with it. I saw
it happen—and I never told anyone. Just let the young guy
skip. He was the older brother of one of my best friends. I'm
pretty certain he's dead now—either of drugs and alcohol or
violence like the kind he was used to."

"I see," Turcell said—not seeing at all, only stroking the
remains of his hair. "And—and you never told anyone?"

"I made sure my mother confronted my old man's sex
thing, although I'm sure now she already knew."

"What did you do?"

"I found a jar of bloody Vaseline in his truck. I put it on
her dresser. I guess Dad didn't like the texture of lubricant. Or
maybe he was just old school."

"Hmm," he murmured, stroking and stroking. "Did you
understand what you were doing?"

"Sure. And no, not really. What kid could? I wouldn't have
understood at all—I mean what in hell is blood doing in a
Vaseline jar? But I saw him actually doing Jake. Had him bent
over a pile of roofing tiles, pumping him like a girl. Only real
hard. More like some kind of animal."

My earnest host took an openly deep breath at this,
crossing and uncrossing his legs.

"That must have been . . . a very difficult thing . . . to
witness."

Witness. Another name for spying. He wouldn't have
lasted one day on the job.

"Yeah," I agreed, stroking my hair in time with him. "It
was even more difficult because my Dad wore a hard hat to
work. He could sink a nail faster than you can log onto your
computer. I knew what I was doing—but I didn't know anything. I was a kid."

"Did he . . . ever . . ."

"No! He was a good dad. He never touched me that way ever.

He kept that all bottled up and ready to shoot out for others."

"But you carry the scars."

"You don't carry scars," I said. "You wear them—like clothes that always fit, whether you want them to or not. I'm sorry he died. I loved him, even though he lied and lived a lie. He tried his best to make it true. And I've seen a lot of dead bodies over the years. I don't like to think what his must've looked like. That I didn't look at. But I know that what happened would've happened whether I was there or not."

"And how did it affect you? Did other people know?"

"About him screwing younger guys up the rear? My mother knew, well before my little offering, I'm sure. My sister, sort of. I always thought other people did too."

"Did you worry what they would think of you?"

"I later beat a sissy from my school who'd come onto me. Soon after, he hanged himself in his parents' garage."

Shit, he wasn't sure how to take this, and I thought maybe I'd swamped him. But he recovered.

"Tell me about your sister."

"She was two years older than me. She died three days before my attack on the other kid. She was an epileptic. It made her shy and sort of immature."

"How did she die?"

"I invited her up to the tree fort. Dad had built it for us back when we were little. When Mom got remarried, we rediscovered it. My friends and I went up there to hang out and read *Playboys*. Then one day a girl came along—and her brother. A couple more kids."

"And you included your sister?"

"We had a complicated relationship. I was jealous of her because she got special treatment, and she didn't always treat me nice."

"So . . ." he struggled. "W-was there some kind of game? A sex game maybe—with others—your friends involved? And it went wrong?"

"That's one way to put it," I replied. Maybe he had some cop in him after all.

"Is it the right way to put it?"

"Don't know. Didn't know then. Less sure now. I was just trying to lose my cherry—to bust my nut like a guy should do. I'd like to think it was something innocent that happened to Serena—and she just had a seizure and fell. But we all want to be innocent, don't we?"

"No, Mr. Ritter," he said, shaking his head. "That's strangely not true. And I'd actually think you'd know that. Some people—in fact all of us at some point in our lives—want to be guilty. We want to be judged. And we want to be punished."

Damn me, I was starting to like him a bit. He was on a roll.

"Oh, there are lots of times—maybe most times—where we try to get away with things. But sooner or later a situation comes up where we judge ourselves, for whatever reason. We find ourselves guilty and we want the larger world to reach the same verdict. We're all quite capable of sentencing ourselves much more punitively than any court or parent—or even God, if your belief inclines that way."

"You may be right," I sighed. Then I paused, letting him savor that little speech before I started in on the real issues. What was the point of talking to him, if I didn't fuck him up?

"How much would you say I weigh?" I asked at last.

"Oh," he pondered. "Maybe 170 pounds."

"What would you say if I told you only a few days ago I weighed 230?"

"I'd be very much surprised," he snipped, looking quite a bit surprised. I could tell he felt the conversation slipping into new territory. "That's a dramatic and disturbing weight loss in such a short period—and for someone apparently reasonably healthy."

You're telling me, I thought. Then I stood up and asked, "How tall am I?"

"5' 9". Maybe a hair less." He smoothed his hair again.

"What if I said I was a good 6' 3"? Or I used to be—just a little while ago."

He hesitated at this, and then responded carefully, "I'd get out a tape measure and show you otherwise. But let me be clear, are you saying your body has changed size—that in a matter of days you believe you've lost more than 50 pounds? And that you also believe you were recently several inches taller?"

"Yeah," I said, sitting back down. "And it's continuing."

He wasn't so detached now. He was starting to think he had a live one. Maybe he'd get some sort of case study he could write up.

"You feel like . . . you're shrinking in size?"

"I don't feel like it, I *am*," I replied. "I'm changing. I'm becoming something else. *That's* what I wanted to talk to you about. Not that some drug slut tried to shoot my balls off or that my old man was a fag."

Suddenly all his grad school theories about childhood traumas and self-punishment didn't add up to so much. But he kept his superficial cool. I've always admired that.

"I see," he said. "That must be very concerning to you. What do your friends say?"

"I don't have any friends left," I answered, but I saw the tack he was taking.

"What about your co-workers?"

"A few comments got made a couple of days ago. Since then I haven't been in to work. The changes have accelerated hard."

"And now you're afraid of going back. Because you think they'll notice?"

"Believe me, they'd notice!"

He didn't smile at this. He swiveled around to examine the photos of his family and a funny, distant expression crossed his face.

The real trick is always to let people interrogate themselves. Beating the pulp out of them only works on some—and
I've actually never had much luck that way with women.

"You know . . ." he muttered. "This is a little odd, and I
don't mean to digress, but you've reminded me of something—
from my past.

"When I was in college, I worked part-time as a night janitor, cleaning office buildings. And sometimes for a laugh, the
guy who worked with me—I can't remember his name—we'd
rearrange the employees' personal photos. Once we did an
experiment—my first psychological experiment I realize. We
gathered up some of our old personal photos and put them in
this one fellow's office. He worked in accounts for a mutual
company. Jacob Betz. I don't know why we chose him, other
than that he didn't have any pictures up. But when we went
back on that floor a week later, I noticed he hadn't taken them
down. When we came back in that building a month later, the
photos were still there on his shelf. An unrelated group of complete strangers looking out at him every day."

"Some people go through their whole lives asleep," I said
blandly. Why is that strangers are always complete or total,
and the rest of us are only trying? What the hell.

"True," Turcell nodded, still lost in his memory. "But this
case was unusual. One night a few weeks after that we went
back again to clean and found that his office had been emptied.
Our photos were gone. I got curious and made a fake call the
next day. Mr. Betz no longer worked there. I pressed a bit harder
and learned that he'd just passed away. Sudden heart attack. I
found out a couple of his workmates were holding a service for
him. There were four other people there beside us. We made up
some story about how we knew him—the guy I worked with.
Poor Mr. Betz had no family, no friends really, other than a few
fellow employees. At the service, the photos we'd slipped into
his office were prominently displayed. The woman who
worked next door to him had wondered about their appear-

ance out of the blue—but she hadn't wanted to pry. She'd even tried reaching the people—my aunt and uncle from Muncie no less—to let them know about Mr. Betz."

"That's sad," I said.

You know if it's sad, it's probably true—or tells a truth.

"I think that might've been the defining incident that led me to pursue psychology," he acknowledged, as if I'd asked. "I'm sorry to have gone off on a tangent. But you got me thinking about photos—what's actually there versus what we want to see—and what conclusions we draw from what we end up seeing."

"I always like other people's stories more than my own," I answered.

"I guess I mean that we could examine some old photos of you. And we could take a photo of you right now to compare—to have as reference for your next visit. I think that would allay some of your anxieties."

My anxieties.

"You don't believe me?" I asked pointedly.

"I'm not saying that," he returned. "All I mean is that any physical changes you've undergone, or are undergoing, can be documented. Analyzed. We can look at old and recent photos. We can weigh you, stand you against a wall and mark your height with a pencil. Scans, X-rays and blood tests can be done."

I was sorely tempted to pull out my ace card right then. But then I thought, why do his job for him? I was still hoping he'd have something to tell me. Something I hadn't thought of. Something that might—save me. More fool me.

"So . . ." he continued, looking nothing like he had at the start of the interview. He was fully engaged now. Animated. Wracking his brain. "What other changes are you aware of? You said you were becoming someone else . . ."

"Some *thing* else," I corrected.

He started a bit at this. Then I let him have it.

"At first I thought I was changing—into a woman. Now
. . . I think I'm turning into . . . some kind of creature. A female
creature."

The office went dead still at that.

"I . . . see . . ." he said, and I could see him gripping the
edge of the desk. The Formica, the leatherette, the family photos, the textbook cases and the recollections of every deranged
thing people had said inside that office—it all was opening into
a hole before him. He had to grab on to something.

"I must tell you," he said softly, and with effort. "That you
don't look like some sort of creature—or female—to me."

"Not just now," I agreed. "But I can transform. The
episodes are like seizures."

"Trances?"

"Attacks. And they're happening more frequently. More
fully. When I change back, I'm not changing all the way back.
Look at my hands for instance. Each time I become less myself
and more . . . I don't know what."

I held out what used to be massive knuckledusters with dig-
its that had been broken repeatedly. They were slender and
shapely now. Smooth. Feminine. Like the hands a lot of men
imagine stroking them.

"You do have very delicate hands," he admitted. "But
some men do."

Case in point.

"I've lost body hair," I continued. "And my butt is rounder.
I'm developing breasts. My dick has shrunk. And when the
transformation takes place, it disappears entirely and a cavity
opens up. A . . . *vagina* . . ."

I let that last word really sink in.

"Mr. Ritter," he tried, finding his voice again. "I know that
what you're telling me is difficult and disturbing for you. It's
concerning for me to hear. But believe me, as—as frightening
as it may seem, these are not entirely uncommon delusions.
Men frequently have been known—"

"Delusions?"

"Distortion of perceptions. Unwanted fantasies."

"This isn't about some distortion in my head—it's about one in my crotch," I simmered. "I'm not talking about bad dreams I'm having. I'm talking about a nightmare I'm living."

He sprung up from his chair as if he was charging the net in tennis and reached for one of the many volumes on his fake teak shelves. I hoped to hell it wasn't going to be *DSM*.

It turned out to be a much thinner book with a blue spine. He fanned the pages and then found what he was looking for. I was afraid he was going to tell me something about male rats under stress. Instead he read aloud, *"He described seeing and hearing a voice from another head, that was set on his own shoulders, attached to his body and trying to dominate his own head. He believed the other head was that of his wife's gynecologist whom he believed to be having an affair with her."*

"Who's that?" I asked.

"It's an extreme case of autoscopy, the self-shooting of a phantom head reported by a clinician named Ames. The patient was suffering from schizophrenia."

"So," I almost yawned. "You think I'm nutso and you can't help me."

"I think you're suffering from a powerful delusion," he answered soberly. "And in looking at this book, I'm reminded that its author, Andrew Sims, defines delusions as 'abnormal knowledge,' which is how I should've characterized them. It's precisely because of this that I think I can help you. If you were to undergo some molecular or cellular transformation before my eyes, I'd be much less certain of being able to assist."

I half snickered. It's always when vaginas suddenly appear that men stop feeling so confident. Then the coin that had been in the slot since I sat down dropped with a ring.

"Let me tell you something else," I said, getting more comfortable in the foam-back chair. "You spoke about judging earlier. Well, I'll let you be the judge of whether this is abnormal knowledge or not. A part of the change that's happening to me is that I can read men better now. For instance, I know there's another woman who's caught your eye. Maybe where you play tennis. It hasn't gone anywhere yet—and it probably won't—because she's just a symptom of a deeper problem. A deeper problem you have."

"Really?" he said, not quite sneering, but close.

"You're frustrated with your wife. You wish she'd be both more assertive and submissive in bed. You feel like you should know how to talk to her because you're a shrink, but it's tough for a barber to cut his own hair."

He opened his hands. "Those sorts of generalizations apply to the majority of middle-aged married men."

"You'd like to engage in some light S&M," I replied, and his forehead wrinkled up beautifully.

"A bit of spanking and some role playing. You've never been involved in a threesome—you're worried about how you'd perform with another woman with your wife there. Although you'd like to try. But what you'd really like is to introduce another man."

His face had tightened up and I could hear his breathing. There was an alkaline sweat scent under his Yves St. Laurent cologne now.

"You're afraid of what your wife would think if you suggested this. But you think about it a lot. In fact, it's why you're attracted to this other woman. Something in her makes you think she'd be more open to that sort of thing. You haven't been aware that that's what appeals to you about her, but now you'll see it plain."

"How do you think—you know this?" he asked, and he sounded genuinely curious now.

"Call it feminine intuition," I said. "But here's the most important point. You've only lied to me and to yourself once since I've been here. And as you probably know, lies tell more truth than truth."

"What—have I lied about?" he coughed.

"The name of the guy you worked with cleaning offices," I told him. "You remember his name all right—and for the simple reason that you had sex with him. On more than one occasion. Probably during those late nights in other people's offices. It meant something to you, and you've never been able to deal with it. Now all these years later, bored and disappointed with the sex that you occasionally do have with your wife, you've been thinking of him again. You've thought of him at various points in your marriage. But in the last year he's come back strongly in your mind."

"Mr. Ritter, this is the most extraordinary thing you've said yet."

"Let me go one better. What would you say if I could tell you his name?"

He blanched openly at this.

"Are you afraid? I'm sorry," I said, getting to my feet. "I didn't mean to scare you. Really."

"No!" he gasped. "Tell . . . me . . . the name . . ."

"Andrew Pollock."

The effect this had on the good psychologist was even more than I'd reckoned. He exhaled so deeply, he had to burp back air to remain balanced in his chair. His face seemed to crack and reform, and I thought he'd either break into tears or go into cardiac arrest.

"How . . . in hell . . . do you know that!" he cried finally.

I let him hang. He'd forgotten that I'd probably conducted a lot more interviews, and a lot more serious ones than he had. Despite what was happening to me, I was still a cop somewhere inside, and a shrewd one if not always a respectable one. He could've stonewalled—but when the crunch came, he gave himself away. Just the way he'd wanted to, without even knowing.

When I was good and ready, I went on. "As I told you, something's happening to me. Something much weirder than what's just brought you unglued. But part of what's happening to me is that I've woken up. I'm more attentive than I've been—maybe more than is natural."

"But how . . . ?" he wheezed.

"Consider it a party trick," I answered. "You're an open book. Your clothes, your cologne, the décor of this office. Then there are the family photos, placed behind you so that you don't have to look at them—they look out. Notice the center one, the family shot. I can see from here that the kids are holding up name cards, only the cards are wrong. Andrew is holding up Cynthia's card—Cynthia has Sean's and young Sean can't seem to decide which of the three he is. It's a family joke about how much time you spend outside the home—remember us kids? The two pictures that include your wife flank the children, which says a lot. Yet the children are smiling. You're probably as good a dad as you know how to be given how busy you are—and who you are.

"On the surface you've got a happy family. But look a little deeper—or from a different angle. The two pics that show your wife are your wedding photo taken ages ago, and a group gathering at your tennis club, and from the looks of you and the budding trees in the background, I'd guess it was taken very recently. Your wife is part of the other doubles team—and is on the other side of the net. The sandy blonde woman right next to you is the one you've been thinking about."

"That's remarkable," Turcell blurted. "I swear to you nothing has happened."

"Oh, I believe you," I confessed. "But it gets better—and simpler. Look around this office. Everything has its place. It's excessively organized. Yet there is one thing obviously askew. I'll come back to it. I noticed it the moment I sat down. Let me go on.

"Someone comes to see you. A male. You freshen your cologne. You know he's a cop who was shot under tawdry circumstances—an appointment arranged by a concerned colleague of his. You find out, not surprisingly, that there's been a lot wrong in his life. Sadness. Violence. Rawness. Then he tells you something that really is surprising: he's changing shape. He's lost significant weight—and more improbably, height. What does that do? It triggers a memory in you. In this overly neat, professional office, you suddenly interject a very personal story. Why? Because you hear something in him that resonates with you, even without realizing it.

"So, what of the story you told? You acknowledge that it involved a crucial incident in your life—it influenced your career choice. Hadn't thought of it in years, huh? Then you claim you don't remember the name of your fellow janitor— but you talk of pranks and mischief—not merely on an isolated occasion—but a pattern of behavior. What's more, you went together to Betz's funeral—as a couple. You didn't see it then, but you may now—what you described is conspiratorial behavior. People remember who they engage in conspiracies with. Believe me. They choose those kinds of accomplices more carefully than marriage partners. That's why most marriages fail. They aren't conspiratorial enough. I knew the second you said you couldn't remember his name—a dismissal within an admission, the first rule of interrogation—that you were hiding something—and because of your occupation and training, I reasoned you were trying to hide it as much from yourself as from me."

The expression on his face was priceless.

"Our interview progresses—I relate to you even more outlandish things. So you go to open up a book. But which one? Look at how many you have to choose from. Literally hundreds—and many, many of them filled with more outrageous and more relevant anecdotes than the one you presented. If men, as you claimed, frequently have the kind of abnormal fantasies you attribute to me, then why didn't you cite one of those? No, you selected a case about a phantom head. I didn't see the connection to my problems, so I considered there must've been some other factor at work in your selection—an underlying struggle or debate you've been having with yourself. The first name of the author of that book is the same as your first son: Andrew. It's not an uncommon name, but its appearance twice in the midst of an uncommon discussion said something—and when I put it together with the other factor, and all the other sense data that had been coming in, I had my hunch."

"But what—what was the other factor?" he asked, almost pleading.

"Look at your desk calendar," I said. "The featured artist is Jackson Pollock."

"He's a famous artist. Or was."

"Everyone in that calendar is I'd bet," I countered. "The trouble is it's almost June now, and his month is February."

"Well, I probably went back to check some meeting date," he insisted.

"Of course," I nodded. "And you have a calf-hide datebook right beside your phone. Plus you have a computer, which I know has a spreadsheet calendar—and you have a new secretary, who looks just like a younger version of your tennis friend, to keep you up to date. That's exactly why the calendar is all the more revealing. Pollock isn't such a common name."

I didn't think he was going to stop shaking his head. I was glad I'd laid it out for him, because he'd have thought I'd been stalking him otherwise. I rose from the chair, listening to the subtle hiss of the foam regaining its usual shape and enjoying the silky panties' texture.

"Don't worry," I assured him. "Confidentiality runs both ways."

"He killed himself!" Turcell ejaculated. "Over the last Christmas holiday. I only found out in February. I'd seen him just once or twice in the last few years. Nothing ever happened. But I knew he was troubled. I didn't know what to say. Then he called and I—I ignored him."

"Maybe there wasn't anything to say," I said, feeling sorry I hadn't left faster.

"I'm a psychologist!" he warbled, and I could see he wanted to wipe every book off every shelf. "We'd had—a bit—of an affair—after I'd gotten married. I couldn't open all those old doors again. He was an illustrator. He'd moved to New York, and whenever he was in town, we'd catch up for a drink. Nothing—sexual—after the affair. It was all in the past."

"Almost everything is," I said, and let him weep, elbows planted on the Formica, the ghostly faces of his happy kids looking on. I didn't think it was square to leave until he'd gotten a hold of himself. When he finally did, he gazed up at me plaintively.

"I'm so sorry about this. I could—and would be happy to give you a referral, although I doubt you'd want that. If it's any consolation, I think I'll be much less certain I can help anyone in the future."

I tried to smile at him and I think I did. Jesus lord, the scams we try to run.

"Don't judge yourself too harshly," I said at last. "Maybe this is just the old detective in me talking . . . but you might want to do some more investigating into what kind of crime was actually committed. An obstruction or even an abetting charge is very different from pulling the trigger. People end their lives for lots of reasons. You owed him courtesy not salvation."

I turned toward the fake teak door.

"Mr. Ritter," he called gently. "Maybe . . . this is just the foolish tennis playing closet homosexual psychologist in me talking . . . but perhaps you shouldn't think of what's happening to you—whatever it is—as all bad."

"No," I conceded, with my hand on the door knob. "You're absolutely right. And that's the most worrisome part of all."

When I was alone in the elevator going down, I pulled out

the strip of photos I was going to show him. Up until but a few hours ago my world had been full of witness statements, ballistic reports, bulletin boards, mug shots, blood stains on sidewalks and fattening food in unmarked vans. Now, like Mr. Betz, I saw a stranger more complete than myself.

5

DEEP DOWN, I KNEW THE MOMENT I'D ENTERED Turcell's office that there was nothing he could do for me. It had helped to talk about it though—to release the secret into the light. I only hoped I hadn't broken him completely. The look on his face as I was leaving told me he'd be a long time thinking about that session.

The trouble was, I was back to where I'd started, but feeling worse. My skin was sore all over, like I'd been hit repeatedly with a paintball gun, and the pressure in my head felt like my skull was pressed in a diamond anvil. My voice and gait were changing. I felt distinctly smaller, younger, leaner but rounder. Badunkadunk. I always was an ass man and Stacy had an ass that drove me wild.

I couldn't bring myself to look into a mirror. I was still outwardly male, but I could feel another spell coming. I had to get home and safe, in privacy. Maybe if I could remain conscious, I could watch it happening. I felt a wave of dizziness as I got in the car. From what Genevieve had said, there was more to come. The only consolation in the whole warped thing was that I knew now I wasn't losing my mind.

The changes that were taking place were real.

Of course this meant that I was on my own. No medical treatment could save me. Mine was a relationship with some species of monster or alien being. And I was becoming a monster or alien being as a result. Doctors and psychiatrists offered no solutions. Something unnatural had befallen me, and the only answer I could think of lay with some kind of supernatural remedy. Or combat.

When that thought really hit home, the next thing I was going to do came clear. It was the only thing I could think of. There was just one person I was aware of who dealt in things supernatural. The only person like that I'd ever met. Zandra the Seer.

Her real name was Adele Bixley. I'd collared her years before when I was coming up. She was running some spirit bunco thing. Someone blew the whistle and I drew the straw to shut her down. The thing was though, when I was reading her the riot act, she said some X-File things. She said she "sensed" that there was a tree house that figured tragically in my life. And she knew some very detailed facts about a murder investigation that had stumped the department—which later proved to be right on target. Down to the shallow gravesite.

One rainy night about a year later, in my first rail 'n' bail phase, I went to try to find her. I don't know why. I needed some different kind of company.

She'd gone "legit" but was still pretty woo-woo—working out of her house doing tarot readings and telling fortunes—a cottage on Spritzer Street, over behind the freight yard on the other side of town. I found her all right. And I got my fortune told. Big things were in store for me. Happiness. Success. Of course I knew she was just trying to tell me what I wanted to hear—especially me being a cop who'd busted her balls earlier. But it was raining hard and I couldn't face driving over those railroad tracks alone and sitting in a bar watching *Matlock* or *NBA Highlights*. I knew if I got in the car El Miedo would come, so I brought out one of the bottles of Beam I carried. She dragged out a bottle of cognac and lit some candles. She was the first older woman I'd been with since Mazatlán—and I didn't have any trouble at all. Just the opposite. I pounded her like a racehorse the whole damn night long. Come early morning when the switching yard was grinding to life and I was rolling over to get dressed, she took my arm and said, "If I were you, I'd be very careful."

I remember yawning at the time and saying something like, "How can I be careful? I'm a cop." Or "I'm always careful, sweetheart." Some throw-away line. As a grown man, until I met Genevieve, there was only one thing I'd ever been afraid of.

Then she said, "I mean with women."

"You got some disease?" I jabbed. She seemed like such a wallflower I didn't think she'd had much action—although she lubed up like a damn waterfall.

She shook her head and said real serious, "I see shadows in your love life."

"Babe, everyone's got shadows in their love life," I told her. What did she know of shadows?

"I see them repeat like omens. Premonitions."

"Premonitions of what?" I wanted to know. "Death by heartache. Or heart attack? You're freaking me out here."

She said, "It's not death I see for you. But something stranger."

"What could be stranger than death?" I asked.

She didn't have an answer. I figured she was just tired or trying to give me the brush-off. But now when I think back on it, maybe I'd freaked her out. Maybe she *had* seen something in my future. I'd gotten my answer at last in any case. What's stranger than death? Feeling your loins and maybe your soul threaded through the needle of a love outside all bounds— becoming something you can't be—and yet perhaps have always been—in dreams and nightmares, and premonitions in the rain.

I drove home to find a package had arrived from Genevieve. It contained more female clothing, including a forget-me-not blue summer dress and a pair of white strap sandals. There was also a box of Dilley's Chocolates. Delectables. I threw it in the waste can—and then retrieved it. They were pretty good.

I took off all my clothes and tried to rest. About 15 minutes later it happened. I cradled Pico in my arms until the shaking started, when she leapt away in fright. I wet the bed—but not with urine. It was that phosphorescent gel-plasm again. Prisms of skin and a pheromone odor in the room like ozone and teenage period. Only it was me.

Images of Genevieve's body swept through my head. Earwigs and metal crutches. Men trapped in hourglasses in the shape of women, suffocating in red sand.

Then the visions passed and I was calm again. The form held steady. I could feel the new body relaxing into itself. My skin was so smooth. I had curves but no visible cellulite. I took the shaving mirror from the bathroom and inspected myself.

God, it was hypnotic. Revolting and beautiful. Me.

The sensation in the end was more intense and yet softer and more dissolving. More complete in body. For a moment I did feel blessed to have experienced that on my own.

Then I made the mistake of looking at my face in the mirror and the horror of what was happening hit me again. I'd become some kind of mutation. Not a female—but a living ghost in female form—with an unnatural hunger. I sensed it without being able to locate it. Nymphomania of the spirit. I wanted protein and lightning. Every nerve and secretion. Whole strangers. Their damp glistening minds and armored hearts. Every dream. Every indecency. Every innocence. I wanted them splayed open for me. To encompass bodies and beings like an amoeboid thing and absorb them into me. So I touched myself again.

Oh, the sugared almond. The little bald man in a boat.

I fondled and mashed myself again and again—until the bed was soaked and the room smelled of orchids and oysters. It was only exhaustion that brought me back to clarity. The form was holding.

Dressing myself as a woman—as Sunny—I understood the name Genevieve had given me in a new way. It seemed to suit my personality and body shape. My bearing. I was girlie in figure and snap, but sassy and brittle. Stacy. But not.

The black miracle kept hitting home. Yet I found I knew exactly what I was doing. Everything came naturally. Underwear, make-up, clothes, shoes, earrings. It was as if I'd done it every day for years. I had to keep going. I had to see the Seer. There was no one else left to consult. I only hoped she was still living in her house on Spritzer Street.

She wasn't. By the time I'd driven over to that side of town, I'd checked myself out in the rearview mirror about twenty times and had come close to committing gross vehicular manslaughter. The realization just kept arriving with new force.

Zandra's, or rather Adele's house, was still there but was now part of a game park of old charm amidst two square blocks of new apartments and townhouses, and a shopping plaza. No one answered the door when I knocked and I noticed an electric guitar in the hallway through the curtain. There was a pair of size 12 Nikes on the porch and a petite set of floral Birkenstocks, too small for what I remembered of Adele. When I peeked in the mailbox I found envelopes with other names on them, a male and a female.

Just like people, parts of a city change when you're not watching. I didn't know what to do, so I hit a Yellow Pages in the plaza. Maybe she was still working the fortune telling angle somewhere else. I realized how foolish I'd been. I'd moved three times in the intervening years, maybe she had too. But I still thought she might be doing the Ouija thing. Leopards don't change their spots—normally.

There were a lot of ads for fortune tellers. Psychics. Clairvoyants. Spiritual Advisers. No sign of Zandra. I figured it was a long shot that she'd change her moniker and still be in the game. And even if she had, I couldn't wade through the whole list trying to find her. I was filled with despair. I really was alone—not the kind of woman who would be alone for long—but on my own against Genevieve.

I loved her and wanted to kill her . . . with all my wayward heart.

Suddenly I craved the noise of the phones ringing at the Precinct. The bullshit of the job. Anything to get me out of my head.

Then I got the idea to drive back past Adele's old house one more time. I thought I'd seen the woman next door checking me out as I was leaving. She looked to be about Adele's age. Maybe she knew where the Seer had slipped off to. I didn't have any other ideas. I was all out. The woman was out in her flower garden when I pulled back around.

"Excuse me," I said, sounding like a babe who smokes menthol cigarettes. "I don't suppose you know an Adele Bixley. She used to own the house next door."

The woman looked me over good. I was glad I had a nice dress on.

"She still does," she answered finally. "Rents it to my son and his girlfriend. Why?"

"I'm trying to locate her, and this was the only address I know of."

"I have every Titus Logan book," the woman announced proudly.

I didn't know what she meant by that. Maybe she was a bit loopy.

"Do you know—do you have any idea where I could find Adele?"

"I'd try her store," came the reply.

"What—store?" I asked, taken aback.

The woman peered at me a little suspiciously then, but gave in when I smiled.

"Why The Third Eye. Over on Haveman. Do you live in the city?"

"I know where Haveman is," I said.

"I think 16th is the cross street. Tell her I have every Titus Logan book!"

I promised I would, wondering if maybe Adele had gotten lucky with some author. I've never been much of a reader so I hadn't kept up with things.

The Third Eye proved to be an old hostelry that had been refurbished and was now devoted to books about superstition, self-help and sexy women riding big lizards. A darkish looking woman in a bright orange sari worked the cash register while a queen-of-the-night type dusted shelves and Celtic music played in the background. You could get Viking runes and solar energy pyramids—but the principal stock was books and more books.

There was a selection dealing with all manner of New Age hoo-haw—from harmonic convergences to the Sacred Symbols of Mu. The primary emphasis, however, was on horror and fantasy, and a prominent display table was devoted to the works of none other than Titus Logan. *A Blood Moon Watches . . . My Name is Yesterday*.

I found a shelf dedicated to witchcraft and sorcery. Interesting stuff, particularly a volume entitled *The Powers of the Succubus*. I was skimming along through Chapter 2 with raised eyebrows (plucked I might add) when the woman in the sari fronted me.

"Would you like some help?"

"Actually I would," I said. "I was hoping . . . to be able to meet (I almost said "find") Adele." I was going to add that I was a friend, but I didn't think that would wash. "I'm a fan of the store," I said. "I've heard so much about it. I'm visiting from out of town."

The way the woman pursed up her face suggested she was rather protective of Ms. Bixley, and my cop sense told me that in a place like that they'd have a pretty good idea of people who'd been in before. I gave her a big flash of pearly whites. Gone were the yellow from all the booze and smokes.

"Adele is very busy," she said, but she took my arm and began whisking me toward the polished wooden stairs. "But since you're from out of town."

I gave her another shot of blinding white teeth when we topped the stairs. Plus I was going to make a purchase. *The Powers of the Succubus.*

"Adele," the woman called around a partition, "You . . . have a fan from out of town. Do you have a moment?"

We rounded the partition into a loft space where an older and considerably plumper Adele Bixley in a black dashiki and a quartz pendant sat rapping at a laptop beside another desktop computer at an old-fashioned roll-top desk overflowing with books and manuscript pages. A heavily papered bulletin board hung on the wall over her workspace and light poured in through high ceiling transoms. It was a space-lift feeling to see her again—this way.

She wore bifocals now and on top of the cubbyhole part of the desk was a skull and a Venus figurine. Books and CDs were stacked on the floor everywhere. There was a framed poster for some movie called *Suspiria*—along with a mounted stag head that looked straight out of a Scottish castle.

The sari woman swished off downstairs as Zandra waddled up from the roll-top.

"You'd like a book signed?" she asked, and seemed to expect me to hand her one.

Then the coin dropped and I realized the book in my hand was the wrong choice.

"You're . . . Titus Logan . . ." I said stupidly.

"A secret that is becoming ever more widely known," she grunted. "I'm off to Minneapolis for a writers' festival tomorrow. I'm very busy. I see you don't have a book for me to sign. How can I help you?"

"Why . . . Titus Logan . . ." I gawked, trying to take in the changes since I'd seen her last.

"Sometimes I like pretending to be a man," she sniffed. "But it's not something that isn't public knowledge. It helps me separate the tasks of running a bookstore and crafting fantastic fiction. Now, if you'll excuse me . . ."

"I need help," I said. I didn't know how else to put it—but the way I put it seemed to pique her interest.

"What kind of help?"

"I need to know . . . about creatures who can change shape and appearance," I said, my voice collapsing to a whisper.

"Shapeshifters?" she answered crisply. "What kind? Skinwalkers? Windigos? Werewolves?"

I glanced at the two Titus Logan paperbacks beside her desk. *She Speaks the Night* . . . *Horns and Haloes*. They were sensational and cheap looking, but I was proud of her. The bulletin board over her desk was thick with fan letters and news clippings.

"I . . . I didn't know there were so many . . . kinds," I gasped, feeling like an idiot. What the hell did I hope she could tell me?

"We have an excellent reference book in stock called *The Encyclopedia of Therianthropy*," she announced. "That's the proper name for a shapeshifter—a therian. It covers all the famous shapeshifters, from the Greek God Proteus to the Berserkers, the Norse warriors who were thought to be able to turn into bears. There's everything you need to know about werewolves and vampires—the Tengu—Japanese bird monsters who can become human . . . selkies or seal maidens . . . the white buffalo woman. There's a very good essay on the Frog Prince theme and Beauty and the Beast . . . in addition to some interesting speculation about genetic engineering and the possible influences of new biotechnology in an article called

'The Shape of Creatures Yet to Come.' It's very comprehensive with some brilliant illustrations."

"But—what about people—who think they're becoming something else?"

"There are a couple of good books in stock about Inner Animals and Spirit Guides—and one addressing the Neo-Pagan and Roleplaying Games communities. Let's see . . ." she said, waddling back to her desk and consulting the other computer screen.

She tapped away at the keys. "We've had a book called *Greymuzzle* and another called *The Feline Mystique,* but those are out of stock. There's also one called *Snake Clan* on the shelves right now, which has to do with tattoo enthusiasts, but I haven't personally read it. One of the problems of being a writer—so little time to read!"

"But . . . I mean . . . people who actually . . . who believe . . . that they're . . ."

"Oh, the psychiatric aspect. In the main reference book I mentioned there's a chapter on therianthropy and mental illness. Multiple personalities. BDD. And of course, there's quite a bit of information available online. Just Google on Therianthropy or Shapeshifters. You'll find tons of links. Now, if you'll excuse me . . ."

"No!" I cried. "I don't want information. I want advice!" And then I burst into tears, which is sometimes an excellent strategy. It certainly had the desired effect on Titus Logan. She offered me a chair and handed me a Kleenex.

"You know, my dear. I have the strangest feeling that I've met you before. But not in a way I can pin down."

"Maybe in a past life," I sobbed, trying to gather my wits.

"Perhaps," she said without inflection. "In any case, you're obviously distressed about something. I am, however, very busy. Please tell me how you think I can help. Briefly."

"Let me put it this way," I snuffled. "How do you kill an evil shapeshifter?"

"Oh!" she nodded, sitting back down herself. "I . . . understand now. You're a writer! I might've guessed. Just getting started? And you've hit a block? You should come along to one of our Newbies Workshops. They're every Thursday night at 7 PM."

"I'm not a writer," I answered firmly. "And I don't want to steal your ideas. I'm after professional advice—of a more personal kind."

The way I said that last bit must've made an impression on her because the tone of her voice changed.

"I'm not quite sure I understand the nature of your query then," she replied, putting her laptop to sleep.

"I'm not sure of the *nature* either," I said. "Because it's outside nature. As in supernatural. Do you just make up stories about that sort of stuff? Or do you actually believe in it? Seriously."

"Yes," she answered after a long silence. "I didn't use to—although I thought I did. But I only really started to believe when I started writing. Something happened to someone I knew."

"What was that?"

"The book? It was a ponderous apprentice novel. The title was taken from a line by Joseph Conrad. 'It was one of those experiences which throw a man out of the conformity with the established order of his kind and make him a creature of obscure suggestions,'" she recited.

It had clearly been a big deal for her. Still on her mind.

"No, I mean what happened—to your friend?" I interjected.

"Let's just say it heightened my sense of the possibilities—and the dangers in life."

"Something's happened to me," I offered.

Her eyes seemed to pass over every inch of me, scanning me like a metal detector.

"I've become a creature—of what did you say? Obscure suggestions."

"I see," she said, looking even more closely at me. I couldn't tell if she wanted to call the police or get out her notebook. "Tell me about it."

"So you can get more material for your books?"

"Touché," she said after a short pause, her face wrinkling into an expression of still deeper engagement. "Why don't you—cut to the chase?"

I tried to think of how to put it. "I need advice . . . on how to kill a monster."

The room went silent for an uncomfortably long time. Then she spoke.

"What form does this monster take—usually?"

"Female."

"So," she said after a long pause. "You're asking me about how to kill a woman?"

I could tell she was running it down in her mind, trying to work out how whacked I was. What could she say to get me out of there as fast and as safely as possible? Then all at once her expression changed.

"Or rather," she continued. "A creature who takes the form of a woman. And perhaps . . . can make others . . . change form too?"

"You've got it," I said under my breath. By god, she did have some powers.

"Well, let's be clear," she said after another pause—sitting upright, smoothing her robe and adjusting her quartz pendant. "I'm no expert. So, let's speak in hypothetical generalities."

"I'm with you," I nodded.

"Let's say we're collaborating on a book. You have this idea about a female shapeshifter. She's evil—or at least a malign force. Does she have a totem animal associated with her?"

"You mean like what a tribe likes to eat?" I asked.

"No, no," she shuffled back. "A totem animal is held in high regard not because it's good to eat, but because it's good to *think*. Is there an animal or creature associated with the Being?"

"A dragon," I said. "A wyvern—a dragon with wings and a barbed tail."

She paused again.

"Hm. All right. If we were contemplating how such a creature might be subdued—or ultimately exterminated . . . speaking hypothetically . . . we'd first consider fire. Mythologically, dragons have always been thought to breathe fire or to emanate from fire—and therefore, symbolically at least, turning the flames back on them has often been viewed as the best way to eradicate them. Dragons can also be stabbed—in the soft parts beneath the scales. And stabbing suits our female metaphor. The first problem is that the dragon's fire must be withstood to turn it back on itself—and stabbing requires the guile and the courage to get very close. But a more serious problem is that even if we overcome these obstacles, a shapeshifter can't be killed so easily. Only an attack via extremely personal means can undo a therian."

"How do you mean?" I asked, leaning forward.

"The age-old practice of sympathetic magic," she answered. "To eliminate a shapeshifter, we'd need a talismanic weapon that had been in the possession of the Being—but was now in our hero or heroine's control. For a female creature, it would be especially important to have something intimately associated with her. Something that had her scent. Something both symbolically associated with her and directly, physically connected with her."

"Supposing . . . we did?" I said. "What then?"

"This becomes a binding agent—a way of neutralizing her magic. Paralyzing her. She would then need to be stabbed and ritually set on fire—or to have her own fire quenched."

"So," I answered. "As . . . collaborators . . . that's how you think the story should end?"

"The tactics need to be fleshed out—but the strategy is right," she replied.

"What happens—if the strategy fails?" I asked.

"One of two things," she said after a moment. "Either we must find another hero to do the deed. Or the dragon's wings get wider and the barbed tail gets sharper."

"Thank you," I said. "You've been very generous. I wonder . . . would it be too much for one last request?"

"A *last* request?"

"It could be. I'd like . . . to have my fortune told," I said.

On the surface, she didn't seem to miss a beat, but her words gave her away.

"Yeah, I thought as much. What'll it be, a palm reading? Or the cards?"

There was the old carny grout in her voice again, softened with snake oil and weariness.

"Neither," I answered. "I want you to tell me what you see. Just you."

"Prosperity, health and romantic happiness," she sighed.

"No, I mean it," I said. "The truth."

"The truth?" she smiled wistfully. "That's what people say they want and then don't want to hear. That's why I started writing fiction. Besides, what makes you think I know the truth about anything? I write paperbacks under another name. I run a bookstore."

"I want to know what you see," I answered. "I may not like it, but I want to hear it."

"Very well," she said with a deep inhalation. "Believe what you will—and don't blame me."

She closed her eyes and slowly became like a figure in a wax museum. After at least a minute she spoke, but in a far-off, reluctant voice.

"I see health, prosperity . . . and a long life. An unusually long life. I see . . . things I don't recognize . . . I can't describe them. And something to do . . . with a dead policeman. I see both peace—and violence . . . I see . . . some kind . . . of happiness. And . . . some . . . some kind of evil. Or maybe . . ."

She seemed to collapse in her chair, with a look on her face that reminded me of Serena coming out of a seizure.

"Thank you," I said finally, getting up to leave. "Are you OK?"

"Yes," she answered mechanically. "What did I tell you?"

"I think—you spoke the truth," I said.

6

CREPT HOME IN THE CAR AS CAUTIOUSLY AS I COULD, my hands shaking on the wheel. What Zandra, Adele or Titus Logan had told me filled me with both terror and hope. I ran into Mrs. Ramona in the hall on the way in. She seemed very curious about me, but I wasn't forthcoming. I didn't ask her who was sneaking out her door in the night with an armful of laundry. Soon I knew the whole building would be buzzing about Ritter's new girlfriend. But that was the least of my troubles just then.

Another delivery from Eyrie Street had arrived. Black evening wear. Very expensive and stylish, with some undergarments that would've raised the flag if I still had a pole. In a bottle shaped like a female genii, a new perfume called *Misbehavin'*. Her instructions were to come for dinner. Eight o'clock. What undid me was the command to "bring the cat." The words of the Seer kept coming back to me.

But I wasn't ready for war. Such a gross collision of will—an irrevocable challenge—needed more planning and intel. Genevieve was the only one who knew what was really happening to me. This was my one chance to see if I could get her to tell me. If not, then the Devil or Midnight first, more dras-tic action would be required. I suited and scented up. Then I shut off my cell and left it on top of the scanner. One of the songs on the oldies station heading over to Cliffhaven was called "My Girl Bill."

When I arrived at Eyrie Street, Genevieve's appearance once more astonished me. She was all crepe and powder like a moth, elegantly dressed in white with an accent of lilac, like some Four Seasons matron—a patron of the fine arts, not a priestess of the Black Ones. Clutching Pico, who seemed none too happy to be back in that house, I would've said the woman before me was in her late 60's. Still, I knew it was Genevieve, and she grew progressively younger and more beautiful as the evening wore on.

For reasons she didn't explain, dinner was served in the lower depths, in one of the private gaming rooms off the dark-ened casino, a candlelit chamber of oak with an immaculate white linen and crystal table set for two. Mutza was not to be seen, but maybe he had already done his service, for everything was in place, and the Madame of Eyrie Street dished out the food for us herself, an aromatic Mediterranean concoction, with some superb wine.

The quiet was so deep, I thought I could make out the dis-tinctive ticking of that ornate clock I remembered from my first night. Or maybe it was the rhythmic revolutions of a rodent wheel. Pico heard it too. The Dark Mistress had made me stuff the miserable thing in a cage stowed at my feet below the table.

We ate in silence. Or rather, I ate in silence. She knew my questions were gnawing at me, but she refused to address them, saying firmly that there would be time for them after dinner. "We are, after all, civilized."

Instead, she told me about her travels, interrupting herself only to adjust my posture or correct my table etiquette. She'd been everywhere—Istanbul, Copenhagen, Montreal, Nairobi. She was on my last good nerve, but I had no choice but to listen, to bide my time—as her mesmerizing voice wandered, telling me about the guitars and cathedrals of Cebu where Magellan planted his cross . . . the Bund in Shanghai . . . or the sunlit apartment on the Reforma near Chapultepec Park in Mexico City where she'd brought more than a hundred men.

Then, after we'd finished the crème brulée with berries that she served for dessert with a sweeter wine, I got lost in her reminiscence about a hot summer night in Cairo, listening to the lute-like sound of the oud, a fat-bellied string instrument meandering up from the Nile. Suddenly, the story stopped cold, and with a foreboding change in her voice, like the snap of a doctor's glove, she said, "Now it's time for you to express further devotion. Bring the cat."

I didn't have a choice, so I gripped the handle on the cage as she led me back up through the labyrinth of hallways to a room in the back of the first floor. It had a glass roof and smelled like a hothouse, which in part it was. But in the center, on the white tiled floor, stood a large terrarium, inside of which was a long, thick and beautifully patterned snake—black predominantly with a white underbelly and gold diamonds along the top of its body and on its head.

"This is Caligula," she said. "A diamond python. Isn't he handsome? He's not venomous, although he has a lethally strong grip, and the capacity to open his jaws to accommodate extraordinarily large prey. But he hasn't been fed in a long, long time. So he's very hungry."

I couldn't help notice that the serpent, which before had seemed rather languorous, had tensed—its shape all spine and nerve now. A verb instead of a noun.

"Why don't you go ahead and do what you're going to do?" I asked, hating her.

"You don't ask why?" she questioned with a slightly raised eyebrow.

"Disappointed?" Maybe I could find my inner bitch.

"No," she replied, batting me down. "I take it as a sign of

ever more complete submission. You know the answer too well. This is the sacrifice you must make to learn the answer to your question."

I felt a nail strike deep in my heart, then the fit passed. I was cold and shiny again. Brighter than the python.

"Yes," I shrugged and handed her the cage. I was hungry for answers.

She opened the cage and took out the cat I'd saved and had cuddled at night, then she lifted the lid to the snake case and dropped it in. The doomed feline was stunned with betrayal and fright. But only for a moment. Then its animality took over. It tried to find a way out of the terrarium. It circled its adversary. The serpent moved with a totally different kind of agility. Pico hissed and raised her back. She snarled and lashed out with a claw. I was proud to see how she defended herself. But as Genevieve had said, the snake was very hungry. I turned away. I had to defend myself too.

"That's very good, Sunny," she said.

"Blame the teacher," I said between gritted teeth. God how I wanted to see her squirm.

"I'm flattered," Genevieve replied.

"So, what are you?" I asked. "Notice I didn't say *who*?"

"I noticed."

"A witch? A succubus?"

"Do you know much about succubi?" she asked, with a splinter in her eye.

"Just that they're to be avoided like the plague."

"Too bad they're so beguiling."

"Even a crack whore can be in the right mood."

"You're very sexy when you're cornered, Sunny."

"So, what are you?" I repeated. "Female, male, reptile, long distance traveler? I can't understand it, but I know you're not human. Are you from outer space—or out of time? You're not really a dragon, any more than I'm really a woman."

She nodded slowly at this and opened her jacket like a butterfly opening its wings. I was shocked to see not a body underneath, and certainly not her beautiful, pendulous breasts. Instead it was like looking at a series of silk screens that had been blasted by a shotgun or slashed by machetes. My eyes were drawn through the ruptured fabric into a chamber swarming with roaches and centipedes. Effigies covered in cobwebs appeared—and I fell forward . . . into catacombs full of acts and shadows—more autopsy than orgy.

There were naked men in a trance mindlessly trying to mate with elaborate torture machines like iron maidens. Priests and nuns groaned from crosses beside men in three-piece suits impaled like expensively dressed scarecrows. Screaming men contorted in hot metal cages in the shape of female torsos. Men with their eyes sewn shut thrashed in crab pits or sloshed in quicksand. Other men were forced to jig as ridiculous automatons in an enormous cuckoo clock—or were decapitated by valkyrie machines with battle axes shining like mirrors. There were men and women sealed in clamshells the size of grand pianos. Young girls and boys sacrificed to giant carnivorous plants, their bodies encased in a sticky dissolving membrane as the tendrils closed around them. Other figures were embedded alive in cement pillars that formed the braces for a hived cave system full of shrieking bats with eyes that burned like sulfur.

Then I saw it. Her. She had the multiple hunting eyes of a furry rainforest spider, only more alien still—with a squishy maw of body—mandibles and dark moist tentacles, each of them rich with sucking mouths. Beneath this was a swollen bladder of transparent tissue the color of a termite queen's abdomen. It pulsed with the heartbeats of nests of fetuses . . . slick pink tadpole things, becoming blind cave fish . . . amphibians, then at last fully formed humans, strangling in their bubbles—their rubber faces stretched against the film of the sacs before some kind of enzyme, like clouds of diatoms, attacked them, absorbing them back into the host as nutrients—their

entire brief lives lived in captivity within the Creature. For the
Creature.

But the hunger could never be sated. I realized at last what
I was up against. Some ungodly transformation, grand theft
body—a crime against nature had been committed—and I'd
been an unwitting or at least a witless accomplice. I'd changed
forever, I knew that now. But I was not really a woman. I was
only a nerve inside a Creature. A shape of perfumed meat within a shadow within an ancient blackness perhaps too dreadful
to comprehend itself.

"Well?" I heard her voice call, as the eyes and mouths and
membranes receded.

"No," I sobbed. "Why me for God sakes? Why me!"

"Stop your crying, pretty girl," she cooed, without malice
or irony. "It won't help you and it won't erase what's happened. Or what must happen. You ask why? Because you
answered the call. You matched the profile. You wanted to
change your life and you couldn't do it yourself. And you've
been able to withstand the process, where others have not.
That's all you need to think about now. I could tell you that it's
because I'm devoted to you, but you wouldn't believe me. Even
a Mistress needs an apprentice. And you know what it's like to
train an apprentice. I don't have children—and you know what
it's like to want a child. I've had centuries of lovers—yet I'm
still searching for love. You know that search. How desperate
it can be. It doesn't change a thing. Soon it will be time for you
to stop changing—at least so dramatically. You'll need to stabilize, to get used to your new form. Your new appetites."

"I won't," I said, trying to control myself, feeling my
breasts rise and fall with the exertion. "I know a way out."

"Like Violet?"

"Who?"

"McInnes. Your buddy. Or those other two? I think you
have a strength of character they lacked. And a weakness for
living. You're a survivor, Sunny. That's one of the important

things we have in common. It's one of the reasons you were chosen."

She uttered this last remark with a trace of a pathological smile, and some of the despicable images I'd just seen passed through my mind again.

"What in hell are you?"

"You think I'm a monster," she replied, and she looked luscious once more. Pure desire.

"A Gorgon of some kind. And you may be right. But don't forget—from Medusa's head sprang Pegasus. In any case, I don't really care. I am . . . what I've always been. I don't remember being different and I've never met anyone able to explain, so I haven't bothered to worry. Before you met me, you only thought you knew who you were. You believed what others who were equally lost told you. And you didn't like it anyway. You hated yourself. All those nights and years feeling in the dark for the doorknob of your own goodbye. I accept myself and I just grow stronger."

"Not if I can help it," I sniffed, pulling a Kleenex from my new purse.

"But you *can't* help it," she said. "Your transformation isn't complete. You have to hunt and consume to stay whole. Otherwise . . ."

"Otherwise—what?" I hiccupped. "What more can you do?"

"The scenes and images you saw—what you think I look like behind this shape? That wasn't me. Those are the waking nightmares that will overtake you if fail to hunt and nourish your new being—the private hells of all the prey who can't embrace the metamorphosis. Just as your body needs food and water to survive, your new being needs continuous nourishment too. Intimacies with strangers. The soft flesh of their fears and obsessions."

"So, you haven't just turned me into a woman, you've made me into a whore. Or worse. Some kind of life sucking . . . !"

She shrugged and produced from a hidden pocket in the wing coat her enameled box full of the beige cigarettes that smelled like an Arab market.

"You'll develop your own style. But creatures like us can't prey without also relieving and enlightening."

"How many . . . others . . . are there?" I whispered.

She laughed and lit up a cigarette.

"I won't," I said. "I won't do it."

"Then you've seen a glimpse of the torment that awaits you. Have you heard of Harpies—and the Furies? Those terrors of Greek mythology are nothing compared to what will pursue you, because you have your own private mythology—like your El Miedo. You can bring it to life in a way that gives you power and makes you more desirable, or you can be its principal casualty. It's your choice. Your own monsters or your own allies. If you can't maintain physical form, you can't live amongst other people openly. You'll wind up down in the sewer tunnels. The morphological trial will be unthinkable. Suicide will be a blessing. But it's harder to achieve now. Your transition is too advanced. You've become much tougher in body. You won't have the integrity of purpose to end your life unless you hunt, and the more you hunt, the more you'll hunger for prey. You won't believe how exhilarating that will be. How lucid you'll feel! Imagine being intoxicated with clarity. The juice and aroma of it will make you radiant. You won't be able to imagine turning your back on that supreme stimulation and rejuvenation. And why should you? For the sake of a lurid, violent death that will require all your will and then some? Or a skulking, vegetative existence with pariahs?

"You think of me now as some kind of evil, Sunny. But in time, whenever fragments of the life you suffered before flash through your mind, you may come to think of me as an angel. You asked me what I thought I was, and I answered honestly. I don't know. But for some I can definitely say I've been Salvation. Hope can't always look soft and pretty and bright.

It has to have some teeth and claws, or it won't be strong enough to be Hope."

"The only kind of angel you could possibly be is one that's fallen very far—straight into a lake of fire," I told her.

"Perhaps. But you started judging me before the door of this house opened. Imagine how old I must be. Yet, am I not beautiful and still youthful looking?"

She changed before my eyes—into a chocolate brunette with a bedroom muss to her waves of fragrant hair . . . packed into an indigo colored satin corset with eyelash lace trim . . . high heeled lounge slippers with a ribbon of teal. More woman than I'd ever seen.

"You're a crusted old demon behind a veil!" I cried.

"It's your veil too now, Sunny. You were once big and puffy, ugly, violent, repressed, angry—lonely. Look in the mirror now. You're gorgeous, desirable, powerful. Before, the only people who might've turned their heads when they saw you coming were junkie sluts and drunks itching for a fight. Now if you hunt and fulfill yourself, you'll be worshipped. It will take time and well-chosen prey. But you have the Presence, Sunny. You can become a devourer and inspirer. A goddess."

"An enchantress turning men into swine," I replied.

"More like turning sows' and boars' ears—or rather boors' ears—into silk purses," she grinned, with flechette eyes. "No one can become what they aren't already at some deeper level. Hunt the animal that comes to you, my dear."

It suddenly hit me with full force that I was never going back to the Precinct. No more vics, perps or sending evidence to Trace. My career as a police officer was over. I'd been gated out. My mind seized up.

"I have many other residences throughout the world," she sighed. "Seattle, New York, Berlin—Hong Kong. I'm going traveling soon—for some time. I need new air, new adventures. I'm going to leave you in charge of this house. You'll have Mutza at your disposal. He's immune to the Effect. He'll never disobey but he'll never transform. He'll do anything to please you—and you've seen for yourself how good he is at that. You may also have my sultry young playmate Marissa for when you desire a woman. They'll be your slaves, your pets."

"W-what happened to Sophia? Did she escape?"

"No one escapes me unless I want them to, Sunny. No, we consumed her tonight. She was the tender meat in the special dish I prepared for you."

I retched and tried to swallow—just like the python. Who knew if she was joking or not. She laughed at the expression on my face.

"Oh, you delightful vixen! As I was saying—you'll have a wardrobe of custom designed clothes, the limousine, and a generous allowance. All you need to do is hunt. Stabilize your form, learn how to use your new powers, master yourself so that you can master others. Grow your strength and refine your style. Once you do that, you're free to move and stalk as you see fit. Anywhere in the world you can manage. Your rate of aging will slow with each new capture. You'll become ever more attractive and lusted after. You'll never be sick. You'll only be hungry for the taste of fresh shadows. Oh, Sunny, if you could only see what you really looked like when you first met me, you'd kiss my feet in gratitude. What you mistook for masculinity was only height and bulk—fists and a temper and no faith in anything but your own swagger. Now, like it or not, you have faith in me. You've met a female you both lust after and would follow into battle. You may be a long time hating the truth about yourself—and me. But, as I said, you're a sur-vivor. Now stoop down like a good girl and clean my feet with your lovely tongue and lips."

I imagined breaking her leg and getting her down on the floor to batter with both hands—but I found myself instead easing her perfect feet out of the slippers. Without knowing how, I knew the way she liked it. My mouth just knew. I cov-ered every inch, licking and breathing across the moistened skin, nurturing it, kneading the in-steps. Needing to do it. Massaging and gumming her heels. Inhaling the scent of the wet, newly cleaned flesh. I wanted to extend my attentions up her smooth calves—higher—to her warm thighs, and higher still. But she wouldn't let me. She'd made her point.

"So, when do I move in?" I gibed, remembering back to Jimmie, the track and the bars I used to haunt—the extra tub of BBQ they'd always give me at the Chicken Shack.

"Your eagerness pleases Genevieve," she said. "But the rewards I spoke of must yet be earned. Something else is required. Simple. Definable. And very likely, deeply enjoyable. You must return to Ritter's apartment. For the last time."

"What will people think happened—to him," I asked, my voice breaking.

The turn of phrase was to her satisfaction. As was the tone.

"People have known he was unstable for a long time. And they *will* wonder. But fairly soon they'll posit suicide. Foul play will be considered—he did after all have enemies. He'd spent so much of his life making them. But there will be no body, so there will be no fanfare or police honor guard. He'd always feared he was just doing a job for a wage, and that's all it will amount to in the end. Every indiscretion, every infraction of the rules, every file note from what he called the 'Bureau of Infernal Affairs'—will all be scrutinized, and a unanimous verdict will be reached. He was a ticking timebomb, and if he took himself off to detonate, so much the better."

"Praise God," I said, stifling a tear.

"This is goodbye to all that—and that depressing apartment. But before you leave and embark on your new life—as a way of embarking on your new life—I'm sending a man to visit you there. Break him down so that his inner self comes forth. Dominate him through your submission. Let him have your high firm breasts. Let him tongue your voluptuous ass. Kiss him. Ride him. Let him take you from behind. Let him have you all the ways he can manage. But I want him when you're done. Deliver him to me when you've had your fill and this house and all the resources I've mentioned will be yours. Your new life will begin, with the incandescent meal that you cannibalize from him. I'll have my reward, you'll have your initiation. He'll know satisfaction and then recompense like he has never envisaged. Then we'll all grope on from there, each according to our destiny."

"So, I'm hunting—but on the leash."

"It's a long soft leash," she replied throatily. "As befits my belief in you. I would so much rather lick you than slap you. Don't make me scald you. You won't understand this yet, but it's extremely painful for you to think me grotesque."

"That doesn't even come close!" I snarled.

"Then we grow closer, in spite of your feelings. Imagine mine. The power I have over you and you still not loving me. Hating me. One day you'll know this scathing ambivalence. How wet it will make you. How angry. And how delectably sad.

"Here . . ." she said, and handed me the soft yellow scarf she'd used the first night. "This will give you strength and heighten your lust to be powerful in your new life. Because you will be powerful. I can feel it. There are new clothes and accessories laid out for you in the front room."

I killed her a hundred times in my mind on that endless journey through the halls of that endless house. But all that happened in fact was that I kept tasting her feet in my mouth, longing to have tasted more. As both a woman and a man. It didn't matter. She was as I said, pure desire. What could be more monstrous than that?

I got back to the old apartment and felt a twang of grief about Pico. Then I put on some Chet Baker. I stroked my fleshy clit and had an orgasm that wracked my whole body, curling under just a sheet, with the window open, listening to the night traffic, wondering about the man Genevieve would send to me in the morning. I hoped he'd be thick and vital so that I might

feed and grow strong. Perhaps strong enough to fight back—
or at least stick in the Mistress' throat like Pico in the long
gullet of that diamond snake.

And I remembered what Zandra had said about the only
way to kill a therian. You had to use some of its own magic.
Something she'd touched. Something intimate. Like the soft
yellow scarf. It was still heavily scented—redolent of
Genevieve's body. When I clicked off the bedside lamp, it
seemed to give off a breathing light. I slept without dreams for
the first time since opening the gate at Eyrie Street.

7

UT WHEN I WOKE UP IT WAS THERE. EL MIEDO. More real and physical seeming than I'd ever known it to be, except long ago.

It was standing by my kitchen table, as if it had been there for a while, peeking around the corner into the bedroom, watching me in my sleep. And watching over me too, I sensed.

I'd never thought of it before as anything but an insidious, malicious spirit before I met Genevieve. But now something—everything had changed—and I saw that while I'd resented it and had been petrified by it over all the stupid staggering years—arresting and detaining people, examining the ID tags on cold stiff toes—stalking nocturnal wildlife behind the obscene mask of the crime city—it had been something known and constant. Always there in the background. Someone on the inside. The ultimate informant.

A source of fear, yes, but also a way of dealing with Fear—the way a dealer comes to be both a figure that you hate and need.

Now that addiction had been cured. I'd moved on to some harder drug—I'd moved beyond drugs and all the human fears too. And so, I at last saw El Miedo as I first had back at the beginning of the black fairytale of my first wasted life.

No cloud of dust now. No footsteps echoing down a stairwell just below me or behind. No flicker in the eyes that stared at me from the bottom of a coffee cup or a snifter of cheap brandy. No halogen fog forming in the midnight of debauchery and crystal meth insects. It was just as it had been then.

Horrifying. Atrocious to look at. But mournful and downcast, isolated—impotent before me now. A ghost of my ghosts, but without a badge of authority over more me anymore.

It took the form of a man—a man the size of my father, or the way I first imagined him when it seemed he could, if he wanted to, reach up and touch the tops of the trees along the shack-lined orchard road. Only it was made entirely of crimson tinted Vaseline. Petroleum jelly coagulated with rectal bleed, which goes a sickly green under artificial light. It stood there, oozing, exuding and consuming itself to retain its shape. Tools would erupt out of the unguent flesh. Screwdrivers, claw hammers, saw blades and faucet handles. It had no head to speak of—only a corroded chef's hat ventilator, barely spinning. But it had an immense oily organ that hung down between the shining grease of its thick legs—with the squeezed stunted expression of a small boy—the mouth that spoke. That had whispered, shouted, threatened and cajoled.

It was a terrible and revolting specter from the past—but something protective too I understood at last. And now it had nothing more to say. Only a silent permanent goodbye.

It was as far removed from me as my forfeited job, the habits and misfortunes I'd so carefully cultivated, all the time pretending they were imposed—hands dealt me as I tried to stay on the lam. Always running out of time and faces.

Now I knew I would never see it again. Not in dreams or nightmares—or on crooked streets of perfume and fugitives from themselves.

Rock, paper, scissors . . . living darkness trumps even the longest, most flexible shadow.

Whoever or whatever I was, I was on my own now.

I did the respectful thing and turned away—not wanting to see how such a thing would disappear finally.

Besides, I had a battle to plan. A fight for the life of my miraculous entranced cancer. Maybe even a contest for my soul. I had to get right in my new head.

The past was gone in the time it took me to turn around.

I don't need to tell you who the man was Genevieve sent me.

It shouldn't have been a surprise—but it hit me like a ton of bricks. Chris Padgett in a Hugo Boss suit and glamor boy aviator sunglasses. He was puzzled to find me there—wondered who I was. He was worried about his *buddy*. He played the earnest investigator for a few minutes, and I could see that I'd been right about him being a smart, promising cop—just young and cocky. And I could see he really was a friend. He truly cared for Ritter and would've taken a bullet for him. Yet the moment I asked, "¿En qué puedo servirle?" I knew he'd take off his pants. Genevieve was right about the power women have over men. I hadn't seen it so cruelly simple before—how it actually played out. His cell phone kept going off, just as mine had, but it didn't matter. The more I let him have what he wanted, the more he showed me how stiff a price he was willing to pay. I learned just what his rich wife saw in him. His guilt afterward was like a delicious dessert for us both.

But I didn't send him along to Eyrie Street. I didn't give him Genevieve's card or raise any suspicions in his mind about her. I couldn't do it.

Part of the old Birch had been a kind of an older brother to him. The new me knew he couldn't handle the Mistress. I'd already given her Pico. I couldn't let her put Chris in the snake cage—because that's what it would've been like. Plus another part of me, and you know exactly which part, just wanted him all to myself. That white boy had no soul in him whatsoever—

except one bit—and it was a good big bit. Heaven on a stick.

I learned more about sex in the first 25 minutes with him than I had in a lifetime before. And it was exactly as Genevieve had said. The more I degraded myself, the more I mastered him. The more I gave it up, the more he lost control. Over the course of two hours, he took me—hard and long and in more positions than there are on a football team. And yet I owned him. Not just his fat cock that stayed so amazingly firm and full—I put a lien on his inner man. All the sparkle and the sprinkle fueled me. I sucked up his being and left him wanting more. And more. It was easy. So easy.

Did he respect me after?

What world do you live in? Of course he didn't. But he'd have committed a major felony to be with me again. His old self was doomed—and yet he was saved—because I knew he'd glimpsed the truth of himself. Straight lines don't exist in nature and he was no Cub Scout.

That gave me a little respect for him that I hadn't had as Birch Ritter, tough guy buddy partner.

I can't be sure if it was some old feeling for him or a new one, or if I wanted her to punish me—if the rush I extracted gave me more courage than sense. I only know that after he was gone I took the scarf and my old Explorer's knife—and my mini fire extinguisher, which just fit into my purse. And I braced myself for impact with yet another crisis of the unthinkable.

Still, I kept thinking. I had murder in mind.

No, not just murder. Liberation. Revenge and release.

But I knew my scheme had little chance of success. Not for lack of courage. I actually think as Sunny, I had more balls than Birch, who was really always afraid, even when his fists were swinging or his gun was drawn.

No, my plot failed for a more essential reason. Genevieve was once again one step ahead of me. She'd seen through my deception. I'd never towed the line in my other life. Maybe she knew there were parts of me I couldn't change—that even she couldn't change.

When I arrived, she was already gone. I'd been so worked up for an all-in brawl on some level I could scarcely conceive, the shock drained me. Infinite relief and absolute agony of disappointment. Betrayal. Swindle. Everything all at once. Torture and salvation both. It was like an orgasm of the spirit—and crapping in my expensive silk panties.

Before . . . before violence had always come so naturally to me. I'd never had to prepare for it. But now—now I could see a different kind of violence was in order. I'd have to learn the game from scratch. She'd really done me over. Made me over.

A large unmarked moving van was pulling out of the drive, followed by another long white vehicle that looked like a mobile hospital unit. Mutza was closing up the house. The wild spring was over and the Mistress had moved on to other hunting grounds. Cape Cod. Mustique. The Amalfi Coast. He didn't say and I got the impression he genuinely didn't know.

Without her now, he seemed to be operating on automatic pilot. But he gave me a letter from her. It was written in her own hand on thick cream-colored rag paper with a sumptuous yellow scarf frilled out around the top. Just like the one I carried with me. The sympathetic magic weapon I was going to use to assassinate the shapeshifter in her, and now pressed deeply to my face to catch her lingering fragrance—my last trace of the woman with a dragon in her heart who played with masks and puppets and led men through mirrors, enlightening and emasculating them in the same lightning flash of climax and revelation.

I sat down on the steps of 4 Eyrie Street listening to the cry of the gulls, the sun grating through the skeleton of the Funland Scenic Railway, and I read her letter to me.

Dear Sunny,

Don't be upset that I'm not here to greet you. And don't think that I was afraid of a showdown with you. My only concern in that regard would be that in my anger at your rebelliousness I might damage what I've tried so hard to nurture and protect. It will be a long time before you can do me harm, and when that midnight comes, I doubt you will want to. And if you do, I accept the consequences. I love violence, just as you always have.

For now my beauty, I have other devotees to look after, new conquests in sight, and more than a few investments around the country, and indeed the world, that require my attention. My intention had always been to leave you as I've left you. Padgett was my parting gift. Now you must fly and forage on your own.

I gave you the name Sunny, not only because it was a nickname from your childhood, but more because it reminded me of the name of a street hooker—which for a time at least is more or less what you'll be. But one of the things that I admire about you is your ability to improvise. Take your own new name when you're ready.

I knew that you would disobey me. You still have a streak of maverick, and I didn't, for all my care for you, feel you deserve the bounty I can offer. Not yet. There are some things—the most important things—we must learn for ourselves. Besides, Mr. or rather Ms. Padgett will no doubt look after you. His wife's family is loaded, so make sure she pays you well. There is nothing more scrumptious than stealing someone away from another person except stealing them away from themselves and giving them some-one new to be—someone they've always been, far back in the shadows.

I think you know now who Stacy really was—and what became of her. So, I must bid adieu. Who knows where we shall meet again. Tuscany? London? Rio? I will always be on your mind, and more than you think you will be on mine. I loved consuming you. I loved the taste of your infirmities—the aged-meat flavor of your manhood and all your little boy P.F. Flyer dreams and fears. So much fight and hope. Like all those ladybugs you used to catch in Skippy Peanut Butter jars with the lids you punctured with your father's Phillips head screwdriver. You have been given a new birth, Sunny.

But speaking of births . . . something I must warn you about, and I am sorry not to have passed on this instruction in person, concerns your reproductive power. I regret to inform you that this is the one way in which you are not fully a woman. You will not menstruate normally and you cannot conceive a child in the conventional manner. You can try, and knowing your character, you will. Perhaps repeatedly. Very likely nothing at all will happen until you grow much stronger. Later though, if the temptation still persists and your system seems obliging, be warned—only monsters and deformities will result. The creatures you saw in my specimen jars? I think you understand my meaning. I wish it were not so. But be cheered by what you can do through other means—the transformations you will trigger. The Darkness is gone—because you can see in the dark.

And now I pass on to you this last piece of unnatural wisdom. Those men in positions of authority we spoke of before? Who do you think some of the most authoritative have been—and how did they get there? I've taught many a whore to fight on his feet and in court instead of in bed and on her back. Those that remember the tricks of the harem become formidable indeed in their new flesh. And many women of power? Need I tell you?

We sort the men from the boys, my dear, and make them Mata Haris and Oprah Winfreys. We create both the Machiavellis and the Martin Luther Kings of the world. That is our penumbral calling. We come from beyond the Wild to maintain a secret balance. To do this, we must prey. But many might pray that we never stop.

Once you gain your full powers, only those rare few that you decide through profound devotion to infect with your innermost being will defy normal human mortality. But through those you merely contaminate with the wonder and inspiration of change, you can still have great influence. To do what I have done for you will cost you. Dearly. Remember that.

You see my love, I have actually submitted to you, weakening myself to bring forth your new life and make you stronger. That is my bright, enduring gift. That one day the shadow of your wings will stretch farther than you can imagine. If, at some moment in the future, you choose to use my gift to challenge me, so be it. I will always be waiting. Ready for a duel or deeper conspiracy. Until then . . . All my love . . . and violence (for passion, like hope, is always violent).

Sincerely, Genevieve.

After I read the letter I had a cry, but then the weakness of tears at such a time infuriated me and I wiped my pretty face and had sex with Mutza in the back of her Rolls Silver Shadow.

I knew my powers were increasing because Mutza gave in, coupling like a randy mandrill with me on the puckered leather seat. He refused to take me into the house, however—that was a sacred threshold I wasn't allowed to cross with the Mistress gone. So I had no idea which pets and playthings remained behind or how many masks and amulets had been removed. Had she taken Gilberto the Silkworm in his little glass coffin or some specially made suitcase? And Sal, the young hermaphrodite—another traveling companion? Was Mr. Dover still in position—or had he been relocated to some home for aged elevator boys? I knew I'd get no answers. So I asked no more questions.

I went back to the apartment and retrieved the rest of Jimmie's money—I hadn't even thought of my last paycheck. Then I drove Ritter's old Electra down to the parking lot of Funland and abandoned it. I could see in the rearview mirror that my face with its sensual heart-shaped mouth looked washed clean, like a bottle with the label peeled off. I was hot—and as cold as murder.

And so, I'd been sucked through the drain of her mystery. Like dirty floodwater in the floodlights off the seawall. Not just like an easy mark played by a pro. Like prey taken. And yet I was still alive, more alive than I'd ever been. Cursed. Saved. Damned. Freed. It was all the same and like nothing I'd ever known or imagined. Just as she'd promised that first night, when she no doubt saw the whole dark ritual opening its scaled wings as clearly as I thought I found my way back to my car, back to my life before her. Before I realized I was already gone, my shadows falling behind me as I became a brighter ghost. Luminous, hungry—but soon to be ready to hunt for myself.

I never went back to the old apartment. Straight up, I hit a dirty lawyer I knew from the past for a new name and solid ID. He had connections with the U.S. Marshals' office. I chose the name Serena Baker. Nice and honest sounding.

Soon I had a corpulent accountant helping me get the other things I had to have—a bank account, a credit card and a car loan. He was good with numbers and dodgy business—afflicted with a very small penis and absolutely committed to cheating on his wife. Plus he had a reasonable pain threshold.

Liked jalapeños traced around his nipples and a good sack massage with an Emory board. One step away from the Birthing Harness and some teppanyaki knives. Meanwhile I hooked up with Padgett again the day after we'd played in Ritter's place.

As soon as I had his total obsession I told him a tale to lay Ritter to rest. I said I'd been attacked in a jealous rage. I confessed I accidentally killed Ritter. Self-defense. Crying. Hysterical. By that point, he'd heard all about Ritter's mixed up history. He bought my story like he'd shoved the blade home himself. I said the body had been dumped in the harbor like countless ones before. It was never going to be found. Big Chris opened and closed the case as easily as he unzipped his pants—so he'd be free to play and cover me like a stallion, not understanding that he's really being slowly gelded, welded, melded into something new. Something better.

Thanks to him and my obedient accountant, I moved quickly from a weekly hotel in Wetworld to a roof garden flat overlooking BayFair, with a new living room suite, flatscreen TV, Jacuzzi and a king-sized bed with some "customized" equipment. Crass? Brutal? Like the Mistress said, I'm a survivor.

So, I've indulged in a lavish collection of temptation wear: virgin white corsets, starlight lace mesh and embroidered bead bustiers, sheer stockings and French maid garters—bras and panties in all colors—honeydew, cyan, papaya whip, viridian. And each week I treat myself to a new toy . . . like a soldering iron or a cat o' nine tails. Then of course, there's my assortment of Wartenberg Wheels. A girl can't make do with just one.

But all these are nothing—*nothing* to what can be done with the power of the wyvern mind. Genevieve was right about creatures like us. How naked all the others are. Wet and timid in their soft glass, hoping for the darkness to hide them, not knowing the Darkness sees all.

And when you begin to learn to paint with other people's shadows . . . reality itself changes. The question is what pictures you choose to make and bring to life. There she and I differ.

I actually miss police work more than being a man. The smell of shell casings and that feeling in the air coming out of a long interrogation to find the fog had rolled in. I have to remind myself about the hassles. No more forced entries or blunt force trauma. No more exsanguinations and red tape. But I still feel the pull of Wetworld. I think something inside me will always vibrate to the viper urgency of those streets. But the place is getting cleaned up. No sign now of the curbside girls from the old days . . . Pop Rock, Rodeo Drive and Lane Change. Like the lo-ball parlors and the Danish Blue bookstore, they've been taken with the tide.

Last week I was cruising the more respectable Chinatown end and I spotted Polly with a date coming out of the Dragon Garden. You never know who you'll meet. She was all over him like tactical nylon. Maybe she'd had one too many daiquiris before the plum duck. Or maybe she really cared. Either way I was sorry for her. He was a conceded powder blue leisure suit. He didn't even see me at first—he just sensed me. Then he gave me the look—and with her bazooms rubbed up against him too. She shot me one of her old tagalong penny smiles, because she knew how he stared at my ass. Don't worry, Pol, I thought. I'll remember him. I'll find him and fix his wagon. For good.

Now another unsolved summer night . . . vodka and cranberry juice neon of the Balboa Taxi sign seeping down into Frontera Street, the Liquid Crystal addicts emerging damp and urgent from their cocoons. I'm standing under a billboard for Dilley's new "Sweet Seductions" wearing as little as the law will allow. I thought I heard Stacy's song again, drifting out of a lounge bar. *"Wayward Heart . . . always leads me to you . . . Wayward Heart . . . not a thing I can do . . ."*

Padgett's meeting me on the corner. I call him Mitzie. He'll have told his wife he's working another case and she'll believe it, given the gang task force that was set up in the wake of the Laotian woman's death and the feud that's erupted between the Latino Brothers and the Ghost Tigers. Besides, she's putting in a lot of late nights herself since she's switched teams and joined the D.A.'s department. Now that her daddy's going to run for governor, she'll move up fast.

Mitzie wants me to apply to be the father-in-law's PA. He thinks I could have a lot of influence. That prospect appeals to me, especially if I could thwart the redevelopment of Funland forever. But I'd have to move to Sacramento. We'll see.

He isn't transforming anywhere near as quickly as I did, but I'll have to start showing him the chrysalis in the cadaver soon. Lance Harrigan will be next. They'll pull my sled. But in a very, very different direction than Genevieve imagined. I don't have her powers yet, of course. That will take some time. But I see now she had many blind spots about me. These will grow as I gain strength. Her weakness is her secret craving for devotion and the longing for a child.

I don't know about children just now, but I do know that I feel more love than I ever did in the past. Not simply the desire for possession or the reassurance of form and protocol that Mitzie's wife feels—that I used to feel. Something genuine that comes from the acceptance of responsibility and my immunity to jealousy.

All those old days spent trying to catch and handcuff men and women. Now they come to me to be handcuffed. For 25 years I thought I was brave and tough—and appeared to others to be. Yet I couldn't face my own shadows, my own violence, my own real fears. Real fears are the ones that have your scent. They hunt you down no matter where you hide— because they *are* you at your deepest level. Yes, I am a monster. But so was I before. Now I see I have a choice about what kind of monster I will be. Can be. It may seem strange to you that

I've at last learned something about nurturing and caring—but as the Mistress would say, maybe that's because you haven't looked closely enough at how you care. The true why of it, and what actually happens as a result. It takes a great fright to gain that perspective. To own those consequences. I intend to share that terror with as many as I can. Because I know in my loins the fruitlessness of seeking Hope in the light.

Real Hope lies beyond the shadows. You either make your way through them, or they come for you. And they always have a warrant.

Now I have plans instead of nightmares and empty dreams. For the first time ever. I'm doing a background course at the university to prepare me for entry at mid-year if I'm still in town. I'd like to study psychology—and I'm learning Japanese. Fast.

I'm taking singing lessons. And I've consumed every Titus Logan title. One day, some day, I'll be ready to face the Mistress. My powers will strengthen. Perhaps much faster than she anticipates.

Through Mitzie I managed to access more police data on similar types of incidents to the Stoakes and Whitney deaths—and Cracker Jack. They'd seemed unusual before. They weren't. Other cases had been reported in the last five years in Jacksonville, Memphis and Houston. In Europe, I identified more—in Stockholm, Zurich and Madrid. I'll continue to build up my intelligence file. I still have what old skills I possessed—but with a new imperative.

One point of vanity—I've vowed to have a limousine finer than hers. A midnight black Bentley. And of course, a limo needs a driver. You know my choice. Not an African giant but my own Blue Knight. I'm arranging laser surgery to fix his eyes. You'd be amazed to learn who he really is. S is for Security. His security. You can Roger that.

I don't know where Genevieve and her mutant entourage are now. St. Moritz, The Antilles, Vancouver. It doesn't matter.

I have time to gather my strength and grow my being. When I think of the MD 20-20 oblivion I might've fallen into, I do thank her. But I'm not one to lick her feet ever again. All my Benzedrine and malt liquor yesterdays are gone. This blonde alley leads to tomorrow. Because I know who and what I am. At last.

And so I can change form and yet remain intact. Who knows but that you're on your way to meet me even now. Male or female . . . an intimacy beyond your imagination. If you can survive the fear of yourself, you may find a window in the mirror.